ONE DEADLY EYE

ALSO BY RANDY WAYNE WHITE

DOC FORD SERIES

Sanibel Flats

The Heat Islands

The Man Who
Invented Florida

Captiva

North of Havana

The Mangrove Coast

Ten Thousand Islands

Shark River

Twelve Mile Limit

Everglades

Tampa Burn

Dead of Night

Dark Light

Hunter's Moon

Black Widow

Dead Silence

Deep Shadow

Night Vision

Chasing Midnight

Night Moves

Bone Deep

Cuba Straits

Deep Blue

Mangrove Lightning

Caribbean Rim

Salt River

HANNAH SMITH SERIES

Gone

Deceived

Haunted

Seduced

SHARKS, INC. SERIES

Fins

Stingers

Crocs

Megalops

NONFICTION

Randy Wayne White's
Ultimate Tarpon Book
(with Carlene Brennan)

Batfishing in the
Rainforest

The Sharks of Lake
Nicaragua

Last Flight Out

An American Traveler

Gulf Coast Cookery
(with Carlene Brennan)

Introduction to
Tarpon Fishing in
Mexico and Florida

Doc Ford Country
(available exclusively
as an ebook)

FICTION AS RANDY STRIKER

Key West Connection

The Deep Six

Cuban Death-Lift

The Deadlier Sex

Assassin's Shadow

Grand Cayman Slam

Everglades Assault

FICTION AS CARL RAMM

Florida Firefight

L.A. Wars

Chicago Assault

Deadly in New York

Houston Attack

Vegas Vengeance

Detroit Combat

Terror in D.C.

Atlanta Extreme

Denver Strike

Operation Norfolk

ONE DEADLY EYE

A DOC FORD NOVEL

RANDY WAYNE WHITE

HANOVER
SQUARE
PRESS

Recycling programs
for this product may
not exist in your area.

HANOVER
SQUARE
PRESS™

ISBN-13: 978-1-335-01360-6

One Deadly Eye

Hanover Square Press
22 Adelaide St. West, 41st Floor
Toronto, Ontario M5H 4E3, Canada
HanoverSqPress.com

Printed in U.S.A.

For Wendy, who knows why

"No one ever forgot the Great Hurricane of October 1910, not around here. Everything not torn away was salt soaked and rotted, trees down everywhere and marly muck. It seemed like our world would never come clean again, nor our souls either."

—Peter Matthiessen
Killing Mister Watson (a novel)

"During the storm [Mr. and Mrs. Joiner] left their fish house, built on pilings, trying to reach Sanibel Island in a boat with half dozen children.... After fighting the storm for hours, they last reached... McIntyre Creek and found that their infant [daughter] had been washed from the boat. The body has not been recovered."

—*Fort Myers Press*
September 18, 1926

ACKNOWLEDGMENTS

Before thanking those who contributed their expertise and good humor during the writing of *One Deadly Eye*, I want to make clear that all errors, exaggerations or misstatements of fact are my fault, not theirs.

Of invaluable assistance were Rev. Dr. Richard Schnieders (KR4PI), who is ARES Emergency Coordinator for Lee County, Florida; Bryan Stern and Brian Wheldon of Operation Dynamo; Lee W. White; Rogan White; Peter Boyd; Rory O'Connor; Dr. Justin White; Capt. Paul and Alec Primeaux; Capt. Randall Marsh; Danny Morgan and Dr. Richard Salisbury. I would also like to thank Brian Bauer, Tia Fijakowski, Brett Dubois, Dr. Richard Wilson, Dana Souza, Richard Johnson, and the staff of Shoeless Joe's at Crown Plaza for their post-hurricane kindness.

AUTHOR'S NOTE

The islands portrayed in this novel are real and faithfully described but used fictitiously. The same is true of certain businesses, marinas and other places frequented by Doc Ford, Tomlinson and pals. However, details regarding previous Florida hurricanes, particularly the killer storms of 1921, 1926, 1928, 1935, 1992, 2004 and 2022 were scrupulously researched and are factually accurate. Stories regarding the 1926 hurricane come from my interviews with survivors and families of survivors. Several of these accounts were confirmed by articles in Florida newspapers from the period. Details about the hurricanes of 1992, 2004, 2017 and 2022 reflect my personal observations and experiences.

In all other respects this novel is a work of fiction. Names (unless used by permission), characters, places and incidents are either the product of the author's imagination or are used fictitiously. Any resemblance to actual persons, living or dead, or to actual events or locales is unintentional and coincidental.

Find Mr. White at www.docford.com or email sanibelflats@yahoo.com. Ham radio operators might find him on HF bands, call sign KM4PON.

1

I returned an arcane Station Six pistol to the US Consulate in Cape Town, South Africa, unaware a storm that would forever change Florida had gathered to the north, fueled by a mirror that is the Sahara Desert.

In a world of electronic intrusions, I'm too often deafened to the silence of atmospheric tides, saltwater and sunlight—dynamics that can ignite a cataclysm six thousand miles away.

"Has this weapon been fired?" the consulate armorer asked.

The strange bolt action pistol lay on a table. Its bulbous barrel (an integrated sound suppressor) had the utilitarian aspect of a ball-peen hammer.

"At the range a few days ago. Five rounds," I said.

"But not in the field."

"Nope."

"A few practice rounds. That's all?" He sounded disappointed.

"With a bolt action single-shot, five rounds was four too many."

A Cold War assassin's tool was an ironic weapon to issue me, a marine biologist in Africa under the guise of tagging great white sharks.

He noticed the bandage on my knuckles. Blood had wicked through the gauze.

"Tough on your shooting hand. Too bad, Dr. Ford."

"Tougher to explain if I'd been stopped at the border," I said. "Shouldn't I get some sort of receipt?"

When I was at the door, the armorer spoke again. "Afrikaners call the stretch of water off Dyers Island 'Shark Alley.' I heard a Russian diplomat went missing there yesterday." There was a pause. "Or defected. Depends, I guess, on who you ask."

It was a question without a question mark.

Dyers Island, one hundred twenty kilometers southeast. It brought back the stench of thousands of fur seals and penguins fighting, breeding, dying, birthing pups on a rock the size of a parking lot. Blood, the ammonia stink of urine, verified that monster great whites cruised the island's rim.

I replied, "Can't say I've been there before. Maybe next visit."

"After your wedding, perhaps. An interesting honeymoon that would make. A few weeks away, isn't it?"

In state department/intel circles, there are no personal secrets, only classified obligations.

"Maybe," I said again. I tapped my wrist. "The COS wants a word before I take off."

He buzzed me out.

The US Consulate in Cape Town is a geometry of white concrete on acres of landscaped grounds. Tiers of bulletproof windows, three stories high, are dwarfed by the enormity of Table Mountain, a slower geologic cataclysm eight kilometers north.

Across the commons, Marines in BDUs were getting in a morning run. Kids with tattoos, jarhead buzz cuts, rocking to a navy cadence call.

Let 'em blow, let 'em blow,
Let those trade winds blow,
From the east, from the west...
Let those nukes, the new kids glow...

A foreboding message cheerfully voiced this spring morning in September, half a globe away from my lab and home at Dinkin's Bay Marina, west coast Florida.

Building A, through security, up three flights of granite steps. The Chief of Station slid an envelope across her desk, an encrypted IronKey memory drive inside.

After some distancing pleasantries, she said, "Don't download the files until you're over international waters. Are you familiar with Black Dolphin Prison on the Kazakhstan border?"

I might have smiled if I didn't know the place was real. Russia sends its twisted worst to Black Dolphin—terrorists, pedophiles, serial killers, the criminally insane. Cannibals.

"Named for a stone dolphin carved by inmates," I said. "No prisoner has ever left there alive from what I've heard."

Chief of Station indicated the envelope. "Until two years ago. There was an earthquake, the facility flooded. Guards evacuated and left seven hundred prisoners behind. We don't know how many drowned, but at least six escaped according to the few villagers they didn't murder." Again, a glance at the envelope. "It's all in there."

I started to explain, respectfully, that I was a poor choice to send to Russia.

Chief of Station surprised me by agreeing. "Of course. Not at your age, Dr. Ford." She was bemused. "And your skill set isn't up to...well. Let me ask you something. This morning, were you aware of the van shadowing you?"

I answered, "Until it missed the curve at Killig Bay. Was anyone hurt?"

Her flat gaze told me the subject was not to be discussed. "Our concern is, they know who you are. Don't worry, we'll look into the matter. Besides, you're getting married in a few weeks, aren't you?"

Not if a certain agency didn't stop leveraging me with extradition threats.

I responded, "That's the plan."

As I went out the door, she said something about the weather—
"Keep an eye on it," possibly, which I took as a reference to my
flight. Or marriage. Or both.

At Wingfield Airbase, a chill breeze was siphoning toward the
Sahara—another silent dynamic. At 36,000 feet, I opened the
IronKey while our pilots rode the North Equatorial Jetstream
across the Atlantic.

I read. I summarized. Six of Russia's most violent criminals
had left a blood trail crossing to the Caspian Sea and might have
entered the US via Venezuela or Mexico.

Might. But it made sense. Bratva, a Russian criminal brotherhood, and Wagner mercenaries had established crime syndi-
cates in major US cities, including Miami.

Thus the courtesy of briefing me, a biologist whose skill set
was doubted, but who could at least pick up a phone and dial
for help.

So why bother with the second, unopened folder on my laptop screen?

Why, indeed.

Sixteen hours in the air. I dozed, awoke when the pilot warned
of turbulence. Somewhere off Brazil, the plane pitched, banged
down hard into thermal clouds that mimicked tentacles. We
landed and took off again at sunset. Below revolved a familiar
green mosaic of seaward borders. South America. The coastline
tracked my past and the passage of time.

To port, a monoxide haze flagged Caracas. The largest tarpon
in the Americas had been landed there long before Lake Mara-
caibo became a swill of petroleum, plastics and industrial offal.

After that, there were only small pockets of light: jungle villages, fires burning, night islands of humanity linked by darkness, aglow like pearls, bright and solitary from four miles high.

We crossed the flight corridor of Western Cuba, Pinar Del
Rio. More solitary lights. Somewhere down there was a farm

town, Vinales, a baseball diamond, wooden bleachers, fields where oxen grazed.

I winced away fun memories of villagers and playing ball with barnstorming friends.

Nostalgia is a waste of time. The present is our only tenuous reality. It's all a rational person has. But there was something grating about the Chief of Station's smirk regarding my skills and age. And her reference to the impending wedding had the ring of sterile dismissal.

My betrothed—Hannah Summerlin Smith. Captain Hannah to fly-fishing aficionados from Ketchum to Key West. And the mother of our toddler son, Izaak.

In the Everglades, in the middle of nowhere, is a jet port that never got off the ground for environmental reasons. But its ten-thousand-foot runway is still used clandestinely and for commercial touch-and-goes.

Dade-Collier Training and Transition Airport is the official name.

They dropped me off in the wee hours of the morning, the air heat-laden, wet, ripe with sulfur. By 4:00 a.m. I was in my new truck, a gray Ford, crossing the Causeway bridges a few miles from the marina and home.

I reminded myself, *If you don't stop lying to Hannah, there won't be a wedding.*

Most of us have a nagging, destructive voice that second-guesses even the best of decisions.

Is that such a bad thing? mine argued.

2

An hour before sunrise is night's end, nautically speaking, on a barrier island that, from the air, resembles a gravid seahorse that is twelve miles long and just as fragile.

Dinkin's Bay forms the island's rotund belly. Our marina is among the last of the old Florida fish camps, which is to say it sits on a patch of mangrove waterfront, the docks are wobbly and buildings are not automated, galvanized barns.

A small marina is a village. Tribal in an easygoing way.

When I arrived, the chain-link gate should have been locked. It wasn't.

The handful of folks who call the place home should have been asleep.

Instead, I got out of my truck to see shadow people moving in a quiet, industrious way. A-Dock is where the deep water live-aboard vessels are moored. Cabin lights were on inside a couple, engines grumbling. The fishing guides, Jeth, Alex and Neville, are the rare early risers in our party-loving group, but they captain small boats. And 5:30 a.m. was too early even for them.

Why the activity?

I shouldered my Maxpedition bag and crossed the shell parking lot. The marina office door was propped open to catch the breeze.

Mack, who owns the place, was inside, screened by racks of T-shirts and tacky souvenirs, but I could smell fresh coffee.

On the glass counter at his elbow lay the marina's black cat, Crunch & Des.

The cat looked up.

Mack did not.

"I knew you'd come crawling back sooner or later, Doc. Suppose Hannah booted you out of the house for disappearing again? Don't blame her. A woman like that—strong, knows her own mind. Men would stand in line just to have a chance. We got a pool going about how long before you screwed this up."

The accent was Kiwi via Tasmania. His assessment was uncomfortably accurate.

"I was away at a conference."

"Always. What kind this time?"

"The boring kind. I learned a lot about pollution and vibrio pathogens. Food sucked."

"A shame. Bet it wasn't hard getting tickets to a piss-up like that." Mack was enjoying himself. "Vibrio as in vibrators? A lot of them are plastic. Or so I've heard."

I said, "Vibrio as in bacteria. They hitch rides on hydrocarbons, trash, stuff like that. Makes the little devils more deadly because they're mobile. Bad for people, bad for everything, including fish and sharks. You seen my dog around? I don't think that tracking chip on his collar is as waterproof as they claim."

"Marion Ford, the shark doctor," Mack mused. "Are you talking about germs that cause the, what-do-you-call-it, 'flesh-eating disease'? A couple times a year, someone cuts their foot at the beach and ends up buggered-all."

"They're a type of germ, I suppose."

"You suppose, huh? Pathogens and gobbledygook. No wonder people don't believe half of what scientists say." He placed a steaming Styrofoam cup on the counter. "You want sugar, help yourself. What happened to your hand?"

There are times when the best way to cloak the truth is to tell the truth.

"A great white banged into my cage—a shark-tagging deal. Like an idiot, I tried to push the thing away."

"Oh, sure you did. Just whacked a white pointer on the nose. It was the same with me when I hit fifty. Skin gets thin as an onion. Bump into a wall, bang my hand, I bleed like hell, so I'd make up some wild story. Well, wherever you were, you would've been better off staying."

Behind the counter, black windows framed waves freckled with arrhythmic stars and boat lights. He nodded toward A-Dock, where one of the gaudier floating homes, *Tiger Lily*, an old Chris-Craft cruiser, was pulling out. Aboard were two familiar shadows, JoAnn Smallwood and Rhonda Lister.

He waved a silent goodbye. "There they go, the two sweetest ballbusters in the slowest damn stinkpot around. The girls wanted to get a big head start just in case."

I put it together. "A hurricane warning, huh? How far out?"

He stared over heavy black glasses frames. "They didn't have TVs at the hotel where you stayed?" He smiled, grunted. "Sorry, forgot. You wouldn't watch the damn thing if they did. Good on you for it. Today's Friday and they're guessing Tuesday. Thursday, maybe, if it doesn't peter out. Which it probably will. Remember the last time this happened?"

Several years back, the deadliest of the big, a Cat-Five, was supposed to hit somewhere between Tampa and Naples. Two days before landfall, the governor caused panic by announcing, "If you don't leave now, it'll be too late."

"I remember," I said. "We all do."

The storm was memorable for unexpected reasons.

Mack is a big man, not tall but wide. Straw hat, Hawaiian shirts and Cuban cigars that are habitually chomped, seldom smoked. He came to Florida years ago with a knack for free enterprise and a need to escape criminal charges in Australia.

Something to do with running an illegal carnival show. If true, there were no better credentials for dealing with the quirky souls who believe that living aboard a boat, elbow-to-elbow with other boaters, represents a freedom suburbia can't offer.

"Never again," Mack responded, referring to the storm.

On the counter sat a bronze cash register, the old-fashioned kind. He punched the *No Sale* key. The tray clanged out. Arranging bills in orderly stacks was, to him, a morning ritual.

"I won't do it again, Doc. Leave this marina unattended with all the million-dollar houses around here? Not to mention the billionaires. That's like a welcome sign to every thieving bastard for miles." He finished a pile of tens and scooped up some twenties. "Last couple of nights, they've been casing the place."

My interest zeroed in. "By car?"

"One of those RHIB-hulled jobs the cops sometimes use," he said, meaning a rigid-hulled inflatable boat. "Big four-stroke engine. They took off when I zapped 'em with a Q-Beam."

"Did you get a look?"

"Too far away," he said.

"Maybe it was the cops. Coast Guard or FWC. The state sends outside help before a storm."

Mack didn't buy it. "Both times, it was after midnight, and they were running without lights. Those redneck bastards will never steal from me again."

I didn't associate rednecks with fast tactical boats. I made a mental note to do some night spooking of my own.

"What about Pete?" I asked. Pete, a cinnamon-haired retriever, was once owned by a geneticist-slash-dog-breeder. I'd found him lost, half-wild in the Everglades.

"Haven't seen that fish-eating dingo in days, I'm happy to report. Hannah called, said he swam across the bay to be with her and young Luke. Notice how much better the place smells when that dog of yours is gone?"

It was two miles on a rhumb line across the bay to the larger, more protected island of Gumbo Limbo.

"Not the first time he's made that swim," I replied. "I'll run the boat over later today."

Jeth, fishing guide and handyman, appeared in the doorway. He gave me a wave before saying, "Mack, I got that plywood stacked. Want me to start boarding windows? Or focus on getting rental boats out of the water?"

Mack gave up on the fifties. The question had ruined his profit-loving ritual. "Geezus, here we go again. The Hurricane Circus Drill. Three days it'll take to get ready, and three more days to open up. Not that it matters 'cause internet news will scare tourists away for a month."

The cash register door clanged shut. "Bloody pointless...but yeah, rental boats and canoes first. Leave the plywood until— you know. Turns the damn place into a dungeon, so hold off on that. Oh, and move the golf carts, anything with batteries, as far as you can get from the gift shop and my house. Bastards been catching on fire, they say."

I scratched the cat's ears and wandered out into the last blue hue of darkness. A nervous wind rattled the mangroves. About every twenty seconds, the wind gusted.

I timed the gusts and looked south. Chief of Station's directive—"Keep an eye on the weather"—was no longer a farewell pleasantry.

Something was out there.

To the north, beyond the docks, a hundred yards away, was a charcoal sketch of a sailboat, lights on in the cabin.

My pal, Tomlinson, the Zen Buddhist hipster with the big brain, was awake.

I told Mack and Jeth, "I heard it's only lithium batteries you need to worry about. But the news, you never know if it's political crap or legit."

I got in my boat.

3

Tomlinson said to me, "Marion, I'm not afraid of dying. It's the possibility I'll stay dead that really scares the piss out of me."

I had tied my boat, a twenty-five-foot Dorado, off the stern of his blue water sloop, *No Más*.

He said, "Leave this planet with all the screwheads in charge? Those ego starved politicos would whack off in a hanky if it got them a mention on Google news. Mother dogs and fart-huffers, the lot of them. On both sides of the latrine."

My pal sat in a half lotus position outside on the bow, staring at the last of the stars. A skinny, long-haired Buddha who's also a six-foot-something left-handed pitcher—with all the quirkiness this implies.

"Are you drunk or stoned?" I asked.

"Neither. But the day is young, amigo, so I'm optimistic. My galley is larded with enough food, beer and more beer for a month at sea." A bony finger pointed west. "See that?"

In the darkness, a pair of ice-white spheroids drifted above the mangrove rim.

"Jupiter and Saturn," I said. "What do they have to do with storm warnings? Or you dying? If you want to haul your boat, I'll help—after I see Hannah. How pissed off is she?"

He continued pointing. "Not Jupiter. To the right a few degrees, the brightest star. Vega. In the constellation Lyra. Shaped like a harp on star maps, but the ancients—Arabs, Egyptians, who the hell knows—saw a bird with folded wings. The Falling Vulture, they called it."

"Like a death symbol, you mean?" I said. "That's a long stretch even for you. If you're right, then everyone north of the twenty-sixth parallel is in for a bad week. Hey... Mack said he saw a tactical boat in here the last couple of nights. A big inflatable, hard bottomed. You know the type. Some bad guys casing the place, he thinks. You see anything?"

Tomlinson replied, "If you define a 'long stretch' as fifty-light years away, for sure. Doc—they found a planet out there. A perfect little earth, man, with its own sun. That's where I'm headed. Yep, and I'm leaving today."

He got up. Bent at the waist and touched his toes. Shook his arms, staying loosey-goosey.

I said, "Gad—put some clothes on. Pants at least."

"No siree, Bob. I'm sailing west just like I came into this beautiful, screwed-up world. Bare-ass naked and screaming. Entropy—are you familiar with the dynamic?"

I replied, "Antitropy? I think it has to do with vertebrates."

"No, *entropy*. Entropic. An invisible force, man, that governs chaos and the death of our universe. Mark my words, big fella, the kimchi is about to hit the F-ing fan."

"Uh-huh," I said. "How can I change your mind about leaving?"

"You can't. We'll stay in touch on forty-meters. I rigged an antenna from the mast stay. As you know, salt water is the best radio ground around." He slipped past me. Chuckled. "Hey, get it? That's like an oxymoron. Best ground around. Freakin' salt water. *Dude*."

Ham radio jargon. Tomlinson is a Morse code savant, and I'd recently gotten my FCC General Ham License. In this noisy computerized world, if the worst happened, satellites and cell towers couldn't compete with a coil of wire and a high-frequency radio transceiver.

I took a guess. "You dropped 'shrooms. Admit it. Is it starting to wear off? No way you're leaving here stoned, three or four days before a hurricane might hit. I'll throw a blanket over your head and tie you to a tree if I have to."

"Your fiancée is extremely pissed off," my friend responded.

Back on the subject of Hannah Summerlin Smith, finally.

"Who could blame a fine Christian like Captain Hannah for dumping a globe-trotting sinner like you? A dude who has stolen gold bars stashed under the house. And guns, all sorts of weird shit, hidden in the floors? Then runs off, doesn't tell her where he's going for the umpteenth time. Talk about an entropic boneheaded move. I'm *this* close to calling you a dumbass."

"Hey, not so loud," I said, because water also conducts sound. "You talked to her? She won't answer, but I left a bunch of messages. It's our kid I worry about most. This is my second chance at fatherhood, and I'm not going to screw it up this time."

"Dude, it's the guilt that kills us. Just because you don't believe in God doesn't necessarily make you a prick. Or an atheist. Just unattached. Sort of like walking on the field without a uniform so your balls are up for grabs. Not that I'm criticizing. Never forget, no matter what brand of twisted bullshit you pull, I'm always on your side." He grinned, tugged at his hair. "Come on. Who's your buddy?"

"She's that mad, huh?" I said.

Tomlinson replied, "Riddle me this: How many ancestors in her family named Hannah—we're talking Florida history—who didn't fall for a dangerous screw-up of a man? Can't blame the woman for being a tad jumpy."

He was referring to the first of four Hannah Smiths in the Smith lineage, a woman whose corpse, after the 1910 hurricane, had been found in the Glades, murdered through association with an outlaw known as Bloody Ed Watson.

Watson, it was rumored, had killed without remorse until confronted by islanders determined to avenge the young woman's death. His shotgun had misfired, though, and that was the end of Bloody Ed.

"Knock it off," I said. "That was more than a hundred years ago. Entirely different circum..." I paused. "Hey—please tell me didn't you put that nonsense in her head."

My pal pressed, "And it didn't end too well for your fiancée's great aunt, Hannah-number-three, either. Dude, and we both *knew* that fine lady." This was said with emphasis for a reason. "People shoot the messenger, don't they? So, ask her yourself. You know I'm not the type to pry."

I'd nailed it, apparently. Hannah, my Hannah Smith, among the most decent, devoted people I'd ever met, wasn't just PO'ed. She was scared of adding yet another bad man to her family's history. *Me.*

It was serious this time.

We went down into the cabin odors of oiled teak, diesel, sandalwood incense. My pal hadn't exaggerated. The space was a straitjacket crammed with supplies. Water, food crates, fuel, cases of beer, stalks of green bananas, an inflatable raft, EPIRB emergency beacon attached. It was all secured by rope or bungee cords.

Portside, the settee table was forward of a little navigation station that held ham radio gear. The galley was starboard side. A pair of non-pressurized alcohol burners for cooking—less of a fire hazard than kerosene, but still gave me the willies in this claustrophobic space.

I said yes to a Diet Coke. He opened an iced bottle of Hatuey beer—spoils from Havana—that caused me to change my mind.

"I flew over Cuba this morning," I said. "The western corridor. Pinar Del Rio and Vinales."

Tomlinson had donned a sarong and a T-shirt that showed his ribs. He smiled in a dreamy way. "Farm village with the wooden baseball stadium. Yeah, man. Sweetest people there—I hit a dinger as I recollect. In jetliners, I can't count how many times I've wished I had a parachute. You know, D. B. Cooper my ass down to a saner world."

The man was sober enough not to ask where I'd been.

His smile faded. "Storm trackers expect the storm to skirt South America, bounce off some islands and cross western Cuba. Damn, wish they licensed more of my ham radio comrades to operate down there. Hardly any—and most of those, they jam. I'm trying, though. Last night, I worked a station in Grenada. Guy said it wasn't bad at all. Fifty-knot winds and rain. The standard kimchi, but it was still a day south."

We were back on the subject of hurricanes.

I thought back to turbulence off a jungled coastline and realized the storm, after getting a head start off Africa, was following a flight path similar to my own.

"Tomlinson, do me a favor," I said. "Let's have *No Más* hauled out of the water. Or sail to Okeechobee. That's where most of the liveaboards are heading. I'll pick you up and we can stop in Clewiston for barbecue. They do vegetarian and there's a nice little museum, too. My cousin, Butch Wilson, runs the place."

Like Mack, he shook his head and asked a similar question.

"Remember that Cat-Five supposed to hit us a few years back? If the same thing happens, a hundred thousand people on this coast are gonna feel butt-dumb ugly and stupid again. The sky is falling, the sky is falling. What a freakin' shit show that was."

My response was the same.

I remembered.

We all did.

★ ★ ★

Eight years ago, when the governor announced, "If you don't leave now, it'll be too late," thousands of Gulf Coast residents fled north, a mass exodus on I-75, only to be trapped in traffic because there wasn't an empty hotel room between Naples and Atlanta.

The rains came. Cars hydroplaned, semis careened. An unknown number of pileups and crashes added to the chaos. Hundreds more ran out of gas and were left stranded on the side of the road.

Worse——or best of all——the hurricane missed its projected landfall and did very little damage to the west coast.

Later, angry evacuees would argue that they should've never left. It was safer to ride out a storm at home than risk death on the interstate.

A group of us, Mack, Tomlinson, Pulpo and Twiggy——dugout friends with nicknames——came up with a wiser plan. Or so we thought. Boats trailered, generators aboard, ice chests crammed, we caravanned our trucks east to a defunct hunting lodge in Central Florida. A thousand acres of cypress, pines and lakes loaded with bass, all leased annually and privately by an oddball friend of ours.

Talk about the safest of wise choices. The place was forty miles inland and far north of where the storm was projected to hit.

This was long before I'd asked Hannah to marry me. So our escape had a bachelor party feel to it. Not the sordid type that degrades all involved. No, we'd sit out the hurricane in comfort, do some fishing, grill steaks over a buttonwood fire, and have fun for a couple of days. By then we'd be at each other's throats, and presumably, a lot of storm damage would await us back at the marina.

That's not the way it happened.

The Cat-Five ricocheted off Cuba. It weakened to a Cat-Three and hammered the Keys before buzz-sawing up the middle of the peninsula, missing the west coast by—yep, forty-some miles.

By evacuating east, we'd driven right into the heart of the damn thing. It wasn't too bad. At first. Then around midnight, the eye of the storm went right over us, blowing in windows and ripping off part of the roof.

After a soggy, sleepless night, we cursed our "wisdom" when we walked out to inspect the damage.

In Tomlinson's words, "Shit-oh-dear. It looks like freakin' Nazis bombed the only road out. Where's Bogart when you need him?"

Hundred-foot-tall pine trees and power lines down everywhere.

It took a full day with chain saws and axes to clear a path. By then it was dark. Didn't matter. Mosquitoes and flotillas of fire ants made the decision. We packed up and wagon-trained west, only to be turned away at the Causeway bridge to the island we'd fled.

Closed for security reasons, we were told. And the bridge would stay closed "until further notice."

It was a smart call by authorities, in my opinion. Storm or not, an island that's been evacuated is a temptation to lawless types.

So we caravanned east, back to the leaky lodge. Days later, evacuees up and down the coast were finally allowed to return to their undamaged homes.

After the "deadly Cat-Five" debacle, Mack was not the first to vow, "Never again."

The sky is falling, indeed.

4

Hannah, from a dock on land her family had farmsteaded, said, "A man with an accent came 'round three nights ago asking for you. Asked if you were back yet. Or when were you expected. I didn't borrow on my youth, Marion, to deal with rough men—just me and Mama and the baby, alone in that old house. What was I supposed to say?"

"What kind of accent?" I asked.

"The foreign kind. Don't bother tying your boat until we've talked this matter through."

I had moved to throw a clove hitch around a piling.

"A Spanish accent? What time? Did you get a license number or a name?"

"You sure ask a lot of questions for a man who doesn't answer them." Hannah, tall, khaki shorts, white rubber boots, a loose blue shirt that couldn't hide her body, looked down into my eyes. Her eyes softened. "Sure is good to see you, Marion. Makes me want to cry. But I won't. Not again. What happened to your hand?"

I explained about the shark cage, then had to clear my throat. "Hannah… Darling, I hate hurting you more than anything in the world. It's just…complicated circumstances. Wish I could say more. But I…I'm pretty sure I can after we're married."

"A great white shark, huh? Don't 'darling' me. When it comes to honesty, that'll be two weeks too late."

"It's the truth."

"Uh-huh. I've fished these waters since Mama started hauling pot back in the day. What was I, about twelve? Never seen a great white, but lots of other sharks. And most of them wore pants. Doc, just tell me. Were you with another…? Someone else?"

"There is no one else. Now tell me about the guy with the accent. There's a reason I'm asking. It's not just you I'm worried about."

This was a reference to our toddler son, Izaak. I was eager to take the boy into my arms, confirm his warmth and heartbeat, the scented laughter that is kindred and unconditional. The kid, not even three, was already learning to throw a cast net, and he loved being out in my boat, just the two of us.

Hannah's eyes moved to the house where she'd grown up and where she stayed when not living with me. It was cracker style, more than a century old, with a metal roof atop a shell mound that had survived a thousand years of storms. Like my stilt house, it was built of turpentine pine still fragrant with sap. Malleable in a wind, yet dense. Hammering a nail required a borehole starter.

Her nephew, Lucas, was up there hammering now. A farm kid with shoulders. Plywood would turn the wraparound porch into a fortress. Her uncle, old Captain Arlis Futch, stood in the shade and offered animated instructions. Or he was describing killer storms the house had weathered since 1910 when it was built.

My dog appeared. He wind-tracked me, snatched a coconut off the ground and came galloping toward the dock.

"The guy wasn't Spanish," Hannah said. "Not French. I'd of

recognized that from high school class. It was dark, a little after nine. Pulled up to the mound in an SUV and got out. But first turned out his lights. I didn't like that one darn bit."

"What did he say?"

She turned, alerted by a dock vibrating with seventy pounds of retriever. "Asked if my dog bites, but that came later. 'Is Dr. Ford home yet?' just like I said. He knew you were gone, so why ask? And your friends don't call you Doctor."

"Did you phone the police?"

"Later, yeah, after he asked if the dog bites. I told the man no, but Dr. Ford's dog sure enough does, so he'd best get back in his vehicle. Pete's good for that, at least. Think he'd really bite?"

At full speed, the retriever acknowledged me with a glance, that's all, before vaulting over the cleaning table into the water. Pelicans, cormorants scrambled to flight, a flurry of squawks and excrement. The coconut surfaced. Pete surfaced. He jetted water from his nose, grabbed the coconut and pursued the birds.

"That's the strangest dog I've ever met," Hannah remarked. "Seldom barks, doesn't want to be petted. Doesn't care about people at all. Dumb as a bucket of rocks until he's not. Then seems almost as smart as a cat. Or am I wrong?"

I said, "On the positive side, he doesn't lick and he doesn't hump."

Hannah couldn't help smiling. "Well, Marion, until we get this matter settled, you and Pete got a couple of things in common."

On the boat ride back to the marina, I reminded the dog, *"Stay,"* every time we flushed a bird from the shallows. It probably wasn't necessary. Twice he'd pitchpoled overboard at forty knots. Twice was enough.

Pete's no Border Collie, but he isn't a bucket of rocks, either.

Which is why he ignored me, his wolfish eyes yellow, golden when the light was right. A dog of mixed lineage, I'd been told,

bred and raised by a geneticist until a car crash in the Everglades
had set them both free.

On my mind were other details gleaned from speaking with
Hannah. Accent-man had called her by name. Eastern European, she thought, based on movies, or possibly one of the Ara-
bic countries. He'd referenced our child. Didn't say, "your son,"
but the threat was implicit. If it was a threat. Her old house sits
on the highest elevation around. A shell mound twenty-some
feet above sea level, which was the man's excuse for stopping
late on a weekday night. He was new to the area, he'd claimed,
and needed a place to park if the roads flooded.

During storm season, this was a request so common that Hannah, being stubborn and independent, had rationalized it into
an excuse for not returning with me to the lab.

Boat trimmed, bow down with a following sea, I exited
Rocky Channel. To the southwest was Redfish Pass, the Gulf
of Mexico beyond. The deep-water cut had been cleaved by the
hurricane of 1921. One of the worst in history.

To starboard was a cluster of stilt houses similar to my own.
They'd been constructed around the same period by the Punta
Gorda Fish Company to shelter employees and ice. Yet there
they were. Board-and-batten, metal roofs, malleable pine stringers and joists all elevated on pilings.

I turned south.

On the mangrove plain were a series of tree-crowned peaks.
They marked pre-Colombian shell mounds, like the ones on
Hannah's property. Pyramids, some believed, constructed by
the Calusa people, contemporaries of the Maya. Islands such as
Josslyn. Useppa. Demery Key. Isolation had spared the mounds
from bulldozers. Their equanimity only hinted at cataclysms
in the past.

I nailed the Mailboat Channel and slowed as we neared the
mouth of Dinkin's Bay. On the northeastern rim, Causeway

side, estate homes lined the shore. Most multi-stories of stucco, roofs of red tile, set apart by hedges on sizable lots.

Millionaire's Row, some still called the area. The label is way out of date. Multiply one million dollars by seven, then divide by elite demographics.

Ahead, half-submerged, floated the trunk of a tree. But trees don't drift up-current on an outgoing tide.

I backed the throttle. The dog reared to his haunches. He sniffed the wind and grunted, then danced onto the forward casting deck.

Hold, I signaled him. "If it's not a manatee, that thing's got teeth."

An alligator, I thought at first. Occasionally the big ones stray into brackish water. As Tomlinson says, "They're tired of golf-ers taking selfies and shitting Titleists. A much-needed lifestyle change, you ask me."

I looked toward my home and lab, a mangrove outpost two miles south. The sailing vessel *No Más* was gone, somewhere in the Gulf, already underway and making way.

I shifted from dead slow to Neutral. It wasn't a gator snaking toward the marina. The pointed snout, the toothy lower jaw, were distinctive. This was a saltwater crocodile, six hundred pounds and half the length of my twenty-five-foot skiff. I knew because a croc expert pal and some local kids had tagged the same animal a few months back. A female. She'd been nesting in Ladyfinger Lakes, a thin water maze on the mangrove side of Millionaire's Row.

Unlike the man-eaters of Australia and Africa, the Ameri-can crocodile tends to be shy, seldom aggressive. But Pete will chase anything above, below or in the water. I tried to get his attention. A warning hand signal was to follow. The dog, though, had no interest in the croc. He was zeroed in on but-tonwood shadows behind the nearest house. There was movement there…a patch of fur, a canid tail—another dog or two. More likely coyotes.

Years ago, coyotes were a rarity on the island. Now it's common to see them alone or in packs, foraging like raccoons among bins of human excess. Blame relentless mainland construction. Florida's population boom has forced all sorts of creatures to the fringe-boundaries of survival.

From the nearest house, a voice called, "Hello… Dr. Ford?"

I spun the wheel and idled toward three stories of apricot-stained wood. Not the largest house, but the most stylish with pirate-ship-looking dormer rooms. Atop it all was a crow's nest deck fifty feet above the water. A HF high-gain antenna added a thread of pragmatic elevation.

The man who had called my name was there. Tall, lean, graying hair. He motioned and waited until I'd nudged onto beach and stern anchored, engine off.

We had met via ham radio. Never face-to-face aside from an occasional wave as I'd boated past. There are a handful of us on the barrier islands.

"Dr. Weatherby," I called up to him. "Call me Ford. Or Doc. Most people do. I'm not a real doctor."

He was a real doctor. Dr. Maximilian S. Weatherby from the UK. A stellar physician turned inventor. When the FCC issues an amateur operator call sign, it becomes public record. Open the right search engine, type in the call sign—internationally, doesn't matter—a tidy little bio is provided. Home address, occupation. Enough data to do a more thorough search.

"What the blazes is that damn thing—" he indicated the croc "—an alligator? Never saw a monster like that around here before."

The accent was Cambridge via public school and Oxford. Not stuffy. Easygoing. An openness to humor was in his tone.

"An American crocodile," I replied. "Good eye. From up there, you must have the best view for miles."

"Exceptional view. Come up for a drink if you like and explain how we can avoid being eaten. My sons took the red-eye back to London."

The hurricane was excuse enough for demurring, and that's what we talked about. The storm. Was he staying? What about his neighbors? The islands attract the quiet wealthy. Luminaries who seek anonymity, not glitz. His neighbors included a former VP who vacationed here often. There was also a foreign service diplomat, and in the next house down were the owners of an international chain of jewelry stores.

Names weren't referenced. Island etiquette. You know but pretend you don't. The same with boating etiquette. Good skippers don't peer into windows along the waterfront. Islanders leave the anonymous alone.

I cut it short. Hannah and our son, Izaak, dominated my thoughts on this hot afternoon in autumn. A cop friend of mine was supposed to call back. The Chief of Station in Cape Town might also have insights.

I'd been followed while in South Africa. *They* knew my identity.

Only when the dog and I were on plane, rooster-tailing toward the marina, did I remember what I should have asked Weatherby, a man who had the best view for miles.

Had Mack been right about a rigid-hulled tactical boat casing the area a few nights ago?

5

My cop friend, Ronnie Patrick, runs security for big utility companies prior to and after major weather events.

"Natural disasters" is a misused term. Hurricanes are a balancing dynamic, key to redistributing global heat, moisture. They uproot the old, they traumatize vegetation and spark fresh growth or destroy the weak. Hurricanes are disastrous only when humans are involved.

First, Ronnie gave me the good news as far as the marina was concerned.

He said, "Our trackers expect the eye to hit near Tallahassee in three to four days, so you should be okay. We've got the best in the world, but they're never sure until a day or so before. It could turn—hell, they usually do, right? Either way, if they tell you to bug out, bug out."

Tallahassee was three hundred miles north, ninety miles west. A sizable safety margin.

Ronnie and his team were bivouacked somewhere in central Florida, ready to run point for convoys of bucket trucks and FEMA workers. I was on the phone in my lab. A black epoxy workstation provided a place to sit. Along the wall were burbling, oxygenated aquaria. They housed anemones, octopi, bivalves and fish. Collecting, preserving and selling marine specimens to schools and research labs is what I do.

When I told Ronnie about Hannah's visitor, he guessed correctly. "Man, during a hurricane advisory? Cops can't drop everything because of one suspicious person. First responders are like chess pieces, you know, gotta deploy to wherever the storm hits. Wish I could break away, but hey... Can't you look after her?"

"Hannah can look after herself. Usually," I replied. "But the people who might be involved in this are on a whole different level." Without naming Black Dolphin Prison, I summarized what I'd read at 38,000 feet above the Atlantic. "You ever heard this story before? Think they could be a credible threat?"

"Escaped from Russia, you say?"

"Yeah."

"Where'd you get this intel, Doc?"

"From a good source. I was out of the country until this morning."

"Out of the...? Gotcha. Did you, uhh, make some new friends overseas?"

"Just the opposite. I might still have a couple of followers from that part of the world."

"Damn. I understand why you're concerned."

A few years back, Ronnie and I did a CQC refresher course at a facility in Moyock, North Carolina. He's the best pistol shot I'd ever trained with. A former sheriff from Indiana who'd had his book stamped in some very sketchy places.

There was a lot going on between the lines as we talked.

"If your intel is good, then you've gotta assume very credible— if they're in Florida. There's chatter about another gang, though. Or maybe the same gang."

"As in gangbangers?"

"More like mercenaries," my friend said. "After the last bad storm in New Orleans, some insurance executive type figured out looting could be big business with the right team. Not the smash-and-grab crap. Organized and mobile with dialed-in targets. The insurance guy did two years minimum security for fraud and stealing industry software. So he's got all the insurance models. All the data computerized. Where the rich ones live from Galveston to Key West."

I said, "His crew's operational? What's the guy's name?"

"A couple of years ago it was. They made their bones when that Category Four hit the Panhandle."

"Literally?"

"When rescue teams went in, they found I'm not sure how many shot execution-style. Three or four maybe. Like pros, you know? But there was nothing pro about the civilians they assaulted. Gang-style; torture, some they kept as hostages. But more like captives."

I said, "They took… You're talking about women."

"Mercenary trophy hunters," Ronnie said. "That part never made the news. The higher-ups figure the mercs got away with around twenty mil in cash, art. You know, big-ticket items— jewels, rare coins—stuff that's easy to carry."

"Geezus."

"Yeah. Not bad for twelve hours' work. That's the window, Doc. Twelve hours after a bad one. Law enforcement either can't get in, or it's too dangerous. Power lines down, snakes, sewage, all that crap. A year ago, when that earthquake hit Jamaica, they might have pulled the same thing there. MO was similar but the killings seemed to have more of a political feel. And they came up with a new gambit—set the target's house on fire."

I said, "Why? Why torch a place they plan to rob?"

"*After* they robbed it. If the target was in there hiding, analysts think it might have expedited matters. A turkey shoot. So who knows if they're still— Hang on a sec."

Ronnie muted the phone. When he returned, I said, "This insurance guy. What's his—"

"Andy Dimitry," Ronnie said. "Hey…and there's the possible tie with Russia. Andy is short for Anatoli, and Dimitry is, well, you know, which could mean something. Or nothing. His family is at least two generations Philadelphia. Construction, heavy equipment, then Andy started an insurance agency that took in millions but damn near never paid out a dime. But yeah, the last name sure sounds…"

He skipped ahead. "The family could've been involved with a certain organization from the start. The Brotherhood, they call it. Houston, Detroit, Miami, most of the cities have mob ties with that part of the world. You sure these guys are in the states?"

"At least six escapees," I told him. "They were headed our way, through Mexico or Venezuela according to the intel. The scary part is, like you said, their tactics. Execution-type killings, the physical assaults on—well, you know. Then I think about that guy, some stranger, pulling up to Hannah's house and setting it on fire."

"Or not," Ronnie said. "Ambushes her with questions about you. Either an obvious threat or the asshole's an idiot. The place these guys escaped from, is it named after a fish? The Flipper kind."

"Dolphin, that's the one," I said. "My source—overseas?— told me to keep an eye on the weather. I took it as, 'Good luck on your flight.'"

He made a growling sound. "Jesus Christ, Doc."

"Yeah, sort of pisses me off. My source knew about the storm before I did and gave me briefing material for the flight home."

"Home, sure, knowing Florida could be a target. Or was it because the escapees might have it in for you?"

I said, "Them personally? Unlikely. But someone in the food chain might."

"I need to pass this up the ladder right away," Ronnie said. "I read a white paper on…that prison place. Eyewitnesses. Former guards. When a guy's executed, they literally take him to the kitchen. Pieces, anyway, and make a stew or whatever the hell cooks do over there. Cannibalism. Torture, geezus. Yeah, I need to hop on this fast. You mind?"

Several minutes later I told my friend, "If the storm hits near Tallahassee, I can be there in a lot less than twelve hours. Boat, truck and trailer. Whatever you need. You interested?"

Ronnie said, "I'll put you on the backup security list and request a briefing update. If your intel is good, I guarantee Andy Dimitri and his Brotherhood guys have been busy somewhere in Florida during the last few days."

6

For Anatoli "Andy" Dimitry, the outlaw insurance exec, his last-minute storm prep began the same morning, a Friday, at a condo in Sunny Sands Beach, Florida, a few miles south of Lauderdale.

Moscow-by-the-Sea, people called the stretch of billionaire properties along A1A because it was a favorite sanctuary for Russia's wealthy expat elite. Many of them former power brokers, oligarchs who needed a safe place to invest their millions, and a refuge while they continued to run European assets they'd acquired during privatization.

At that meeting, Aleksandr "Sasha" Olegovich said to Dimitry, "Why is your Russian so shit? Such a famous proverb, yet you don't understand in the native tongue of your family?"

Growing up, at the prep school in Philly, the wise-assed kids, even a couple of teachers, had nicknamed Andy "Dim-bulb" as in dimwit Dimitry. Yet Andy, who despised being called dumb, smiled at Sasha, the aging oligarch and former MiG pilot who could have had him arrested by US cops, or killed, if he chose, with a phone call.

"Sorry, sir, yeah, my Russian, it sucks. If we're going to do business, I need to up my game."

"Up your…what is this expression, 'your game'?"

Andy responded, "Like out of respect for you and my grand-mother. I know that, back in the day, you and her were very—" this was a dangerous topic, so he changed course "—that you were members of the same Orthodox church in Belarus. I'll work on it. Promise. The proverb, it sounds familiar. What's it mean?"

Sasha, late sixties, the tail of a snake tattoo visible near his cuff links, repeated the proverb in Russian before translating, "'If you fear the wolf, do not stray into the forest.' So I now must ask, are you a coward as well as ignorant?"

You withered-up old prick, Andy thought, but he said, "You had wolves in the old country? That's cool. No, a coward—I mean, I've never seen a wolf. I'm just careful who I work with. Have you met those dudes? Especially the tall one, Grigori, Grigori Pavlo. The one who cuts his hair like a—what do you call them? Priests? He's got some seriously sick videos he likes to show off. On his phone, you know, claims he took them himself."

They'd been talking about the six escapees from some shit-hole prison in Russia. Andy was complaining that he'd already selected a new team, guys who'd worked security in New Orleans after that bad storm a few years back. True, they were fentanyl freaks and drunks, but they weren't butchers. They were goal-oriented bangers, which was key in the insurance biz. Profit was profit, no matter which side of the law you were on. Peddling policies or stolen goods required organizational skills plus a damn solid business plan.

Sasha, a military big shot, always had to get his way. He banged a fist against his chest. "Thugs, New Orleans ghetto filth. Not Russian. No heart, no loyalty. Why you argue? I finance, you do what I say. Friar Pavlo's videos are worth more than you will ever make in your life."

"Who?"

"Friar Pavlo—*Sergeant* Grigori Pavlo after only one year in war. Very intelligent—a corpsman in the army. You could learn something from this man. Too bad you do not speak the language—or understand the value of his art."

"His—you shitting me—his *art*?"

Andy tried to explain the freak was nothing more than a serial killer with a damn GoPro, but the oligarch cut him off. "What is old saying? 'Steal six coins, you are thief. Steal six thousand, you are executive.'" He spun his iPad around. "Here is list of names. Targets I have added along entire Florida coast. Important people. Wealthy. Powerful, not just the shit peasants from your insurance computer."

Andy couldn't protest again, not sitting on a penthouse patio, thirty-second floor, drinking gourmet vodka, where he could look down at people, bug-sized, on the beach, the purple-blue ledge of the Gulf Stream beyond. Something else nice was to gaze at Sasha's private helicopter, a Robinson R44, waxed shiny black on his own rooftop pad. It was Andy's way of ignoring a chiller of beluga caviar that sat next to an ashtray of Sobranie cigarette butts. Sasha lit another one, coughed into a monogramed hankie and said, "Eat. Eat the Russian way."

The man heaped a glob of beluga onto buttered white bread. With a spoon made of bone, he added a dab of sour cream, then motioned to the chiller.

"Try, is very best. But don't chew, use tongue. Eggs, they burst, you taste Caspian Sea. You taste mountain air of the Caucasus but with a hint of salt they say the dog runned across."

Andy had no idea which dog the man was referencing, but he wasn't going to eat that crap again. Back at his Philly prep school, they'd celebrated Ukraine Independence at a restaurant on Bustleton Avenue. Big table, lots of wealthy elders. He'd mistaken caviar for dessert, which is why he'd spit out a mouthful, saying, "Jesus Christ, this goddamn jelly tastes like rotten fish."

Dim-bulb Dimitry was born. Age thirteen.

"Not hungry right now," Andy said to Sasha. "Let's go over that list of targets you added."

Trackers had the hurricane heading for the Panhandle, so that's where they started. Barrier islands off Tallahassee. Addresses included a major art dealer and several rich rednecks who collected bullion and rare firearms.

"Yes, good place for storm to hit," Sasha remarked. "Guns, gold and diamonds. Always easy to sell."

They explored down the coast: Cedar Key, Clearwater, St. Pete, Anna Maria Island, Siesta Key, Venice, Boca Grande. Five to ten primary targets on each, or on adjacent barrier islands where the eye might come ashore.

"Is all about the eye," Sasha said for the twentieth time.

Andy balked when the list moved south, Punta Gorda to Naples. "They're at the edge of the cone, I get it. But odds are between Tampa and the Panhandle. That's why my guys are camped there now, Escambia County north of Pensacola. But Pavlo and his freaks, I can't trust them to—"

Sasha broke in, "Argue no more. The Russians operate on my orders. You operate on my orders. Understood? How far is drive?"

"From here to the Panhandle?" Andy had to think. "Eight, nine hours, so I can't stay for lunch. Too much to do. We need a couple of, you know, official-looking boats as cover." His wink-wink expression implied, *Steal a couple of boats from the local cops,* which the oligarch liked.

Andy bragged, "Yeah, and it was my idea. Let's hope to hell the storm doesn't hit in that armpit stretch of the Panhandle. The Big Bend area. A hundred miles of pit bulls and trailer parks. We wouldn't make enough to pay for fuel."

He gave the private chopper a wistful look.

Sasha ignored the request, saying, "More populated the better."

He poured himself another vodka, three fingers, and sprinkled in a few black pepper flakes. Something the old Soviet-types did to sponge up petroleum pollutants. Sasha, getting pissy again, continued, "Anatoli—you must stop using your American shit name. Is very disrespectful, as is doubting my judgment. South of Punta Gorda is very best place for hurricane and us. You ask why? Look at list."

There were two dozen names, all with insurance riders on valuables worth a bundle. Among them were the founders of an international jewelry chain, the Lászlos and a British inventor, a billionaire, who owned a work of art—a painting, Andy guessed—insured for thirty mil.

"Appraisals on that stuff are always crazy over-the-top," he said. "We could get five, ten mil in Europe, Israel, Dubai maybe. But, yeah, I see where you're coming from." He continued talking in a rapid-fire, Philly way, showing off his executive skills until he tripped over a couple of oddities on the list of targets.

Two were foreign politicos, Sasha explained. "Not worth so much in money, but their computers, you take, we trade for favors later." He touched a finger to his temple and smiled. "In my brain is a concert house. Smart, quite large—something you will never understand, I fear, Anatoli. Hah-hah!"

A coughing laugh.

There it was again, another Dim-bulb cut. Andy thought, *More like a whorehouse, you old perv.* He touched the iPad. "What about this guy, a marine biologist? The college professor types never have any money. Marion D. Ford. And he's got a kid. What, is his wife rich?"

Sasha responded, "A favor for friends in the motherland." He held up a warning finger. "No matter where storm hits, when there is time, it must be done."

"Time to do what?"

"A recent request," Sasha said. "A few days ago, five perhaps, a diplomat went missing in South Africa. My friends consider this a war crime. They want to know what happened to him."

"To the biologist? What was a biologist doing in Africa? Those people are all cheap, tight-assed nerds."

Sasha's contempt was visible. "I'm talking about the diplomat, you fool. What was biologist doing in…presumably making diplomats disappear."

"But why would a marine biologist…?" Andy was stumped. "Does this have something to do with caviar?"

The oligarch, done with his vodka, stood. "Enough. My ears are tired. There is bounty on biologist, his family, whatever it takes to do this favor. During storm or after, but soon. That's all you need to know for now. And you will work with Friar Pavlo, a monk—not a priest. A soldier as well! Biologists…you have no idea who biologist might be. Did your grandmother teach you nothing? Here is another proverb you should learn."

Translated into English, the proverb went: *In a quiet pool, devils are sometimes found.*

7

Traditionally, Friday is party night at the marina. PERBCOT, we locals call it, an acronym for Pig Roast and Beer Cotillion. The name's similarity to EPCOT has sent more than one tourist away disappointed.

It's usually burgers and oysters on the grill, not a piglet. And always kegs of beer, seldom fine wine.

On this late afternoon, though, the mood was dampened by what Mack had labeled the Hurricane Circus. Up and down the coast, motorists were waiting in lines for gas. Supermarkets were jammed. Building supply mega-chains, if not already sold out of plywood, drills, screws and generators, soon would be.

It's a slow-motion, sustained panic. We go into caveman mode, a primal response to predation. Grab all the food, fuel, water within reach, needed or not. To hell with everyone else until the danger has passed.

Jeth had just returned from Bailey's General Store, founded 1899. A big guy, cleft chin, he resembles the brawny actor in the old sitcom *The Beverly Hillbillies*.

"Doc. You can forget about taking a crap for the next two weeks. They sold outta toilet paper. Paper towels and Kleenex, too. I checked."

His stutter has lessened over the years, but he stumbled over the word "paper" a few times.

"Let's hope it doesn't come to that," I responded, then asked about the other fishing guides, Neville and Big Alex Payne.

Another *P* and an *N* that Jeth had trouble negotiating. It is our so-called frailties that I find most endearing in the good ones like Jeth. And reassuring.

I told him, "I'll help you guys secure your boats now or whenever you say. Then tomorrow or the next day, depending on how the storm tracks, maybe you can help with mine."

That's part of the circus. Trailer anything that floats. After that, opinions vary. Some fill boat hulls with water so the wind won't tumble them down the road. Others lash their boats to overhead trees so a flood won't carry them away, trailer and all.

Of the two schools, I preferred a variation of the latter.

Deepwater A-Dock was empty. The liveaboards had either fled or their vessels had been hauled. The exception was a houseboat owned by Maria Estéban and her school-age daughters, Maribel and Sabina. A few years back, I'd helped them make the crossing from Cuba. Now they were safely on the mainland, but their pretty little floating home needed tending to.

At sunset, the party mood brightened. NOAA's latest reported the storm was moving fast toward Grand Cayman Island at sixteen miles per hour. It was expected to strengthen, cross over Cuba, then spin toward the eastern edge of the Panhandle in five days or less.

Someone applauded in an I-told-you-so way.

This was the ringmaster component to the circus. If a rifle is fired into a crowded room, praying not to get hit, although without malice, is to pray someone else will.

The decision is up to God.

I returned to the lab, showered, dozed, and spent an hour on the phone with Hannah. Ten p.m. is tomorrow before dawn in Cape Town, so a call to Chief of Station had to wait.

The marina's black cat, Crunch & Des, batted at the screen door.

Pete's yellow eyes glared. His tail thumped the floor once, and he went back to sleep.

I let the cat in.

What hams would call my radio shack was in the next room across the breezeway. A bookcase, a reading chair, my telescope and a lamp formed a cozy little cave.

I tried Tomlinson on an agreed-upon frequency on forty meters, then twenty meters. Times of contact weren't mandatory, but we'd decided the top of each hour, noon to midnight, were the most practical.

No response.

"Negative contact, standing by," I said into the mic and gave my call sign as required.

The radio's spectrum scope provided cascading light. Across the dial, 14.000 to 14.350 MHz, conversations showed as a waterfall of colors, red on a sea-blue background. Oscillating voices, half a world away, resonated like fire, then flowed lavalike when I scanned the frequencies.

On 14.258, I monitored call sign OM3WM, which I typed into a search engine. Five thousand miles across the Atlantic, someone named Vazeky Stanislav was in conversation with K4CFG, a ham operator in Bloomington, Indiana. Listening in with an occasional comment was a local man, a friend of mine, his call sign, KR4PI.

When sound moves through the air, air molecules don't travel with the wave. They vibrate, one molecule colliding with the next molecule and the next, then on and on. It's a chain reaction that can ricochet off the ionosphere and travel across continents. When the vibration reaches the human ear, or an antenna of exacting length, the brain or software reconstitutes the vibrations as sound.

I had yet to do more than a cursory search on Max Weatherby, so I went to work on my laptop. Impressive man. Even more impressive was the sparseness of information available.

International overachievers have the juice to stay discreetly behind the curtain.

Dr. Maximilian S. Weatherby. Physician, inventor and CEO of something called ThermoRaker Ltd. Twice received the Royal Award for Innovation. Held more than fifty patents. Most had to do with thermal imaging optics. He'd invented a system that could scan a Walmart or a hospital and flag the sick ones with temps over 98.6.

This was prior to the most recent plague. When the plague hit, every government and corporation worldwide had, presumably, raced to buy the man's patented technology.

Dr. Weatherby's timing, as the Brits might say, was fortuitous.

In the *London Times* was a more revealing snippet. A decade ago, his company had provided "hardware" for a US Ballistic Missile Defense intercept test. It had necessitated lengthy stays in DC, Berlin and Moscow.

This implied contracts—and contacts—with military and state department agencies at the highest levels.

In the UK, MI6 is the equivalent of our CIA.

If there was a connection, it would not have surprised me.

Florida's Gulf Coast islands attract an international assortment. What had once been a staging area for the Bay of Pigs invasion long ago had, over the years, become a favorite vacation retreat for well-traveled intel types.

Another not surprising bit of information: Dr. Weatherby also owned a home, bayside, in St. Pete, Florida.

Atop my bookcase, next to a brass barometer, sits an antiquated globe. Visually, I connected three dots—London, St. Pete Beach and Dinkin's Bay. Meaningless until I traced a line to Moscow. The zodiac image thus formed resembled a global V-shaped glyph—a giant wing in descent.

This fanciful nonsense, to Tomlinson, would have been dire symbolism. It is a dangerous, complex world, however, with wizards competing from behind a multitude of curtains.

Dr. Weatherby, I decided, merited more research. Not by me. By pros who are friends of mine.

I went out the door. Took a long whiz off the porch. The opening into Dinkin's Bay was a Kodalith of half tones, a gray void that sparked with navigation markers, red and green.

Mangroves screened houses owned by the former VP and neighbors. But Weatherby's crow's nest, two miles away, was dotted by a single white bulb that was not the star Vega.

"Big-ticket items—jewels, rare coins—stuff that's easy to carry," Ronnie had told me. Then Jamaica, where the MO was similar but the murders had more of a political feel.

As he'd also said, tropical storms are tricky. You never know when the eye will turn and aim the rifle at you, friends and family. Or when thieving mercenaries will do the same.

Beneath the floor of my bedroom is a waterproof lockbox, another secret I've failed to share with Hannah. I scooched the bed aside. Found the lever. Used the key.

When the hidey-hole was closed, water-sealed and locked, a pair of Sig Sauer pistols, a night vision monocular, extra mags, surgical gloves and some other tools lay on the bed.

With thieving mercenaries in mind, I said to Pete, "If that storm gets close, we've got to convince Mack to leave. He had that prostate surgery, and he's not in great shape. Besides, I don't want him around as a witness. Jeth, either."

Aside from basic commands, talking to animals is contrary to good training habits. Also a waste of time.

The dog opened a wolfish eye. He went back to sleep.

Using encoded software, I pinged a couple of associates, Bernie Yeager and Donald Piao Cheng, both members of the US electronic warfare and intelligence communities.

My text read: Need 3rd Level flags, Dr. Maximilian S. Weatherby, London/Cambridge plus-ThermoRaker Ltd. plus-S-I-S. Cross Ref: Florida, Russia, Moscow plus-Black Dolphin. Expedite. MDF [North]

Ronnie Patrick was right. If mercenaries were planning a hit, they were busy somewhere in Florida on this Friday afternoon, a few days before the storm was supposed to make landfall.

I wanted to know if my unusual neighbor was on the island for professional reasons.

8

Over the weekend, NOAA's 5:00 p.m. updates were an excuse to gather by the marina bait tanks and drink an optimistic beer.

Optimism turned to denial as a group of us listened on Monday afternoon. The storm was a hundred miles south of Cuba. In a few hours, Cat-Four winds, tornadoes, would splinter the farm village I'd traversed by plane early Friday morning.

Tomlinson and I had played ball there. Our Cuban friends, the kids with homemade bats, the rickety wooden stadium, would they survive? In my head, I tried to picture the destruction. This led to the selfish inevitable. Was that baseball portion of my life over? Would Hannah and our son, Izaak, get a chance to share the fun I'd experienced?

Me. Me. There's more than one *I* in a hurricane.

The storm was moving like a greyhound. Twice as fast as average. Once it crossed Cuba, trackers predicted winds would strengthen and hit the Tampa area, ninety miles north of the marina.

"Baloney," Mack said again. "Remember that Cat-Five seven or eight years ago? The sky is falling, my ass."

The refrain reflected an argument going on up and down the coast.

Evacuate or stay?

Choose the former, then ask yourself, *Evacuate to where?* On a peninsula four hundred miles long and only a hundred-plus miles wide, to leave home was to risk driving directly into the rifle's crosshairs.

Marinas that tolerate liveaboards are nomad communities. Dinkin's Bay less so than most. The ladies from *Tiger Lily* and a few others had returned by car after finding safe moorings near Lake Okeechobee. Jeth's wife, Janet, was there, too, along with Neville and Alex, sitting at a picnic table between work breaks.

Mack had donated what was left in the fish market. On a portable grill, a slab of cobia was roasting in wood smoke. A bushel of oysters chilled in shaved ice. There was a bucket of beer, not a keg. Alcohol is a liability when clear heads are required.

Big Sammy Martínez, a native of Mexico, and his pal Cadmael, from Guatemala, joined the group. They and their families lived on the other side of the Causeway, but the guys had worked on the island for years.

Trusted friends. Familiar faces.

It was an impromptu reunion that, were it not for Captain Buffett's music, might have had a bittersweet note. Like a "Jamaica Farewell." Or a goodbye "Incommunicado."

Janet asked about Hannah, then about our forthcoming wedding at Chapel by the Sea on nearby Captiva Island.

I'd spent part of Saturday and all day yesterday at Hannah's family home, boarding up, moving boats, Izaak at my side the whole time, and also trying to make amends. I didn't go into that, though.

"She's decided to move the date to the Sunday before Halloween," I replied. "Too much going on with the storm and all. And it's...well, Halloween's her favorite holiday."

"A Southern Baptist? That's not what we learned at church," was Janet's response. After a quizzical look that pierced, she kindly switched the subject to shortwave radio and Tomlinson.

Janet and the *Tiger Lily* ladies remind me why I like women as people. They are also a private reminder that, for those not born with Hollywood looks, or who are past a certain age, the world, even now, is an unfair place. Like many, she and Rhonda had come to Florida to reinvent and recover after some failure, a divorce or personal tragedy.

Each woman had rallied. Each had said to hell with the ashes, and they'd forged a new home, a fresh life.

Tomlinson had hailed me at midnight, Saturday, on forty-meter band. I summarized for the group. He was one hundred fifty nautical miles offshore in seas four to six, no problem for an experienced salt like him. "Says he's headed for Panama City. So turns out he made a smart move." It got a laugh when I added, "And he sounded sober."

Rhonda, after a glance at Mack, said, "Normally, I can't stand the male screw-around womanizer types. And Lord knows, Tomlinson has bedded more wives than—" she turned to Janet for help "—who's the guy in the Bible?"

"Goliath?" Jeth guessed.

"Dumbass," Neville, his fellow captain, chided. "She's talking about a guy, not a type of fish. Those grouper bastards are taking over the wrecks. When's the FWC gonna open the season again?"

This begat two threads of conversation.

Janet spoke to Rhonda. "Solomon had, uh, I think six or seven hundred wives. Concubines, too. Not Goliath. It's in the book of...well, I'll have to look that up." She chuckled. "You might be right, though. If Tomlinson hasn't broken Solomon's record yet, he's damn sure closing in. Personally, I blame the wives."

JoAnn, with her deep Glades accent, said, "Blame 'em. Hell, I envy them. Tomlinson's idea of fidelity is no more than two women in bed at the same time. The guy's a lot of fun. And sexy as hell in a harmless way. Admit it."

Jeth said to Neville, "Dumbass? Goliath is a real person in the Ba-Bible. He's the one with the slingshot. Go to church. Some praying might do you some good."

Neville countered, "I still say the FWC needs to open a season on those grouper pigs-with-fins. Danny Kelly was diving the two-mile reef and damn near got swallowed whole."

"Tomlinson has incredible psychic gifts," JoAnn said to Rhonda, her longtime business and domestic partner. "We all know it's true…well, except for Doc. The guy's so sweet and thoughtful for a, you know—what he looks like is a Koochie Hound."

Rhonda's expression showed disgust. "That's terrible. Doc, don't let that mouth of hers put you off marriage." She dropped an unopened oyster onto the ice.

JoAnn turned to Mack, an unlikely ally because he, too, had romanced JoAnn's partner. "Tell her. Koochie Hound, it's a breed of dog. Remember the Westminster thing on TV we saw? They're not what you'd call beautiful. But tall, and sort of look like Tomlinson with his long…"

My dog, Pete, trotted into the circle. He'd been salvage diving beneath the docks judging from the barnacled chunk of something in his jaws. He dropped it at my feet and started toward the water.

A hand signal stopped him.

A six-hundred-pound croc was still out there somewhere.

Mack said, "At least he didn't drag a kayak back this time."

"Or a dinghy," Alex put in. "Remember that little Boston Whaler? Petey chewed the lines and was towing it back to the lab. Jeth thought it was a ghost boat. No driver, so how was the damn skiff making way?"

"Did not. And it was foggy," Jeth argued. He spoke to me. "That big croc was back in Ladyfinger Lakes this afternoon. Paul Boudreaux told me, so you don't gotta worry."

I released the dog. On my phone was a tracking app linked to the chip in his collar. This time it worked.

"What did Petey bring you, Doc? Looks heavy."

It was. I scraped some barnacles and dumped a pound of gunk from an old ship's bottle. Dense handblown glass, black, onion-shaped with a crooked hand-sculpted neck.

I passed the bottle to Big Sammy Martinez for inspection. "Think this is Spanish?"

Sammy held it up to the sky. "Like from Spain in the conquis-tador times? Could be. Around Tampico, the port, people find these sometimes. Not exact but, but you know. Those Spaniard *maricóns* were the first real gangsters. Hey—they kill most the Indios in Florida, too?"

Cadmael, from Guatemala, turned discreetly and spit on the ground.

"Eventually," I said.

Janet went silent while this was discussed. With another pierc-ing look she said to me, "Tomlinson told you he's sailing to Panama City?"

"Late Saturday night on shortwave. Yeah. He's probably al-most there by now. Don't worry, he's got enough food for a month."

"Did he actually say Panama City, *Florida*. Are you sure?"

"Of course. Well…no. But where else…" It took a sec to understand what she was getting at. "Geezus. There's no way he would sail all the way to… Central America is six hundred miles from here."

Janet filled in the blank. "Panama City, Panama. I know. I've been there."

Mack shook his head. "Naw, he's crazy but... What the hell am I saying? Of course he's crazy enough. If she's right, he's truly buggered-all. Tomlinson's sailing right into the teeth of that bloody storm."

I looked toward the narrowest opening into Dinkin's Bay. Fool's Cut, it's called, because of the shoals and oysters. The star Vega would soon appear above the mangroves there.

"Nope. Relax," I told the group. "He's sailing northwest. Definitely. That's what he said when he left on Friday. I'm sure of it."

But I wasn't sure.

JoAnn, who, like me, had grown up on the islands, sensed my uncertainty. "Lord almighty." Her eyes moved to Mack and the others. "Have y'all ever experienced what it's like? Been on an island during a really bad hurricane? A direct hit, not the kind that just glances by and gets the surfers excited." She gestured to me. "I have. So has he. A Category Five a long time ago. Go ahead, Doc. Tell 'em what it's like."

I said, "Ladies first."

Later, Big Sammy and Cadmael helped me do the last-minute heavy lifting. If the storm hit Tampa, we'd still get big winds and rain.

The first chore was cranking my bay shrimper onto a pair of rails that mariners call "ways." I'd bought the boat in Choko-loskee, a flat-bottomed workhorse with pterodactyl outriggers and creosoted nets. Built of heavy cedar planking, she was solid as a slab of concrete and just about as agile.

Securing the little houseboat owned by Maria and her daughters was next. A tri-axle trailer and hawser lines were required. Then we hiked machetes to a cavern of mangroves not far from the lab. "Mosquito ditches," they are called, dug decades ago to drain lowlands, and control the swarming hordes.

The three of us spoke, joked and cursed in Spanish. Cadmael, less so. His native language is K'iche' Mayan, not Spanish. A lot of Indios come to the states with no other language. It's tough on the kids. When they're funneled into Hispanic schools, their blank stares are interpreted as insolence. Or stupidity.

The mountain people of Guatemala are neither. I've spent enough time in the Central Highlands to know.

We discussed their readiness for the storm. Could I help? What did they need? They and their families lived just across the Causeway bridges. A lowland tenement area inhabited by workers essential to the tourist trade.

If the storm made a sharp right turn, they were in as much or more danger than those on Millionaire's Row.

When I pressed the point with Sammy, he only laughed. "Where we supposed to go, Poncho? Think about it. Those government shelters, they ask for IDs and shit." He turned to Cadmael. "Dude, which card you pull out first? One that says you're my brother? Or you're Mex-Tex with a grandkid? That *mierda* ain't gonna fly, man."

Cadmael understood enough Spanish to agree. "I did not enjoy walking through a desert to get the border. *Sí*, yes, we stay here. Water, a nice rain. At least we will have something to drink."

We settled up in cash. I dug out a pair of VHF marine handhelds as loners. Line of sight, it was five miles across the bay to where they lived. No guarantees but workable.

"Channel sixty-eight or seventy-two," I told them. "Channel sixteen if you're in real trouble and need the Coast Guard."

Sammy, five-ten, two hundred eighty pounds, or more. A gold tooth and sharp, wise eyes. Enough scars inside and out to know when to duck, when to fight. "Yeah, Coast Guard, uh-huh. Another smart idea, Poncho. They will maybe think Cadmael is Cuban, send him to Havana. How you like that, little *Abuelo*?"

"How much they pay per hour in Havana?" Cadmael wanted to know. "I saw a movie once. The cars are very old but at least there was no desert. Havana, *sí*. But wait. Not on a boat. My swimming is not so good and a sickness I get in my belly. No, I think better we stay here and enjoy the nice rain."

"Catch you later," Sammy said to me in English. He started toward the parking lot, then stopped. "Hey, what you and JoAnn said about that bad storm, you know, back when you were a kid?"

"When I was in high school," I said.

JoAnn and I had traded stories about a Cat-Five, a direct hit, while the group listened. She'd lived on Chokoloskee, south of Everglades City. Nearby, bayside, was the village of Mango. My uncle Tucker Gatrell had owned a piddly little truck farm and ranch there.

Sammy asked, "Was it as bad as she said?"

"I didn't think so at the time," I told him. "Looking back, though, yeah."

"This one. Maybe is worse, you think?"

I doubted if anything could be worse than the storm JoAnn and several hundred remote islanders had experienced. It was only the second Cat-Five to hit the Florida peninsula in more than a hundred years.

"The odds are against it," I said. "But just in case."

We found a duffel bag. Cadmael and Sammy left with the essentials—tape, candles, batteries, bug spray, the VHF handhelds, a bundle of PFDs—and some other emergency gear I hoped they wouldn't need.

9

Tomlinson still has a pretty good curveball. Not a knee-buckler but with enough left-handed spin to, in his words, "Drop it off the F-ing table."

Monday evening, a storm rotating similarly began to bight—a frictional reaction to vagaries of air that turned it sharply east.

On the phone, I told Hannah, "Now they're predicting Wednesday morning just south of Tampa. How about I fly you, the baby and your mom to a resort in North Carolina? A spa weekend. Lucas, too, if you want. You could all use a—"

"In your little plane? You told me you'd secured it in—"

"I did, Arcadia," I said. "No, a commercial flight. First class. I've already booked seats for tomorrow. It doesn't leave until early afternoon, so you have some time to think it over. The resort, it's supposed to be pretty darn nice."

"Did you book a seat for yourself?"

Before I could answer, she covered the phone. In the background, her gray-haired, hemp-smoking mother, Loretta, said something about Tampa and the "po-leese."

"That's terrible, Mama," Hannah replied, voice muffled. "Those poor folks up there. First they gotta worry about a storm, now this. Go put on the local news and find out if it's true. I'm speaking to Marion."

She shared a bulletin her mother had just heard. Two FWC officers had been shot, critically wounded while patrolling Tampa Bay. The day before, in the Florida Panhandle area, a third officer had gone missing, boat and all.

Unrelated events, the newscaster had reported.

An adrenal jolt warmed the back of my neck.

"All three were patrolling by boat?" I asked.

"Mama... *Loretta*. Were they on boats?"

Loretta, in her eighties, had fished and hauled pot, among other felonies. She cackled, "Where you expect marine patrol cops to be? On a camel? My advice is, tell your fish doctor to swing anchor." As she added, "Better yet, just tell him the truth about—" Hannah covered the phone again.

I waited.

The dog sat staring out a screened window. By noon tomorrow the windows, doors, would be boarded, double-anchored with screws. Aware of my silence, a pair of yellow eyes checked in.

Not something I didn't already suspect, I responded to the dog with a look.

Hannah returned. "Uhh...sorry, Marion. You know how she gets since that second stroke. Still thinks she's having a romance with the king of the Calusa Indians, and no other man is good enough."

It was a private joke that wasn't a joke. Loretta drifted in and out of reality—or pretended to, depending on her needs.

Nervous laughter was a rarity for Captain Hannah Summerlin Smith, the fourth Hannah in a family that had century-old Florida roots.

I let it go.

"What about those plane tickets?"

"Loretta won't behave in a Walmart let alone on an airplane. And we just got the patent approved on our citrus root stock. You know how hard it was to get state ag certification. Run off now and risk a hundred treelets dying if it floods?"

My nagging, irrational inner voice questioned her tone and motives. Hannah and her late business partner—a former lover, I suspected—had found a massive old orange tree in the Everglades. It was, perhaps, a direct descendant of seeds planted by Spaniards in the 1500s. Ancient root stock, she and others hoped, might be more resistant to a disease that had all but destroyed the modern citrus industry. A similar experiment had saved the grape vineyards of California.

I said, "Then I'll drive over tomorrow and help. I'm not leaving you there alone after what happened the other night."

"The stranger in the SUV? I can take care of myself," Hannah said. "So can Loretta. She might be off in the head a tad, but her eyesight's still pretty good—if you know what I'm suggesting."

I did. Behind their house in the citrus grove, Loretta and her elderly bingo friends knew where at least one body was buried. Back in the day, police had ignored an abusive man once too often. Loretta and friends were a tight-knit group of survivors, good at keeping secrets.

"Besides," Hannah continued, "what about the deal you cut with Mack? You know darn well he'll stay at the marina if you leave. And at his age, he's not up to—"

"I know, you're right, but I haven't convinced him yet. There's no need if the storm hits where they say."

"That's what I'm telling you," Hannah said. "We're fine. Birdy—she's a lieutenant now. Sheriff deputies cruise past our house every hour or so. And she already volunteered to sleep here in the spare room if the track slides south."

Sergeant—now Lieutenant—Birdy Tupplemeyer was a petite fireball with the mouth of a sailor and morals to match. My irrational inner voice went to work on that, too.

Reason won out. Birdy was tough and smart. She carried a gun and knew how to deal with the violent types. The same was true of Hannah. In the citrus grove was another unmarked grave as proof. That was our secret, Hannah and me; a secret we could never share.

Heaven help anyone who tangled with those three women.

"Could you have Birdy call me?" I said. "An FWC officer disappears in the Panhandle area, then two more shot in Tampa Bay? I have a friend—a reliable source—who thinks Florida's being targeted by a well-organized gang of mercs—mercenaries. Killers, thieves. Wherever the storm hits, they'll move in."

"A friend, huh?"

I said, "A well-connected friend. Honey, you need to listen. These are dangerous people. The very worst kind. Once I talk to Birdy, she's welcome to pass the information along."

Hannah asked a question she'd asked before. "How is it you know things before the police do? Marion, I get so frustrated sometimes, I could... I suppose you're gonna explain to Birdy what you've never explained to me? That hurts. Do you understand that?"

I said, "I didn't hear about the three FWC officers until just now. To me, it suggests a pattern. Two days ago, NOAA predicted the storm would hit near Tallahassee. An FWC cop disappears in the same area. As of last night, it was Tampa, and two more get shot. See what I'm getting at?"

"What I see is you're gonna piss Birdy off. A biologist telling a lieutenant deputy sheriff her business? Why, 'cause she's a woman?"

Before we hung up, Hannah softened a bit. "Stop worrying, please. How many hurricanes has this old house of ours been through? Doc... Marion, if it does turn, I want you here, safe with us. Not on that dang barrier island."

It was a nice thing to hear. But I felt even better when she finally agreed, for the sake of our son, to use the plane tickets if the morning NOAA update predicted disaster.

★ ★ ★

The encoded message from Chief of Station, South Africa, read, "Review files. Provide analysis per local knowledge. Under no circumstances attempt to intervene. Confirm receipt."

This was in response to information I'd provided about the three FWC officers, two shot, one missing.

From my laptop, I said to the dog, "What the hell's her problem? Limited skill set my rear end."

A desk assignment. An analyst's job is to discern ties between seemingly unrelated threads of information and/or events. I was good at it, yet her condescending tone rankled.

The dog got up, did a slow circle, plopped back down on the floor.

Crunch & Des, the marina's black cat, tracked the retriever as a lion might before pouncing on a water buffalo.

"Don't do it," I warned.

The eyes of the domestic feline can communicate a variety of profanities.

"Now, now, be nice," I said. "We might be in for a rough couple of days."

The Dinkin's Bay community prefers oddball literary names for pets. In the 1940s, Philip Wylie wrote about two Miami fishing guides, Crunch and Des. The gift shop macaw is Scarlett O'Hara. After Tomlinson and I had found the dog in the Glades, a veterinarian's paperwork required a name.

I'd written down "Peter," the first thing that popped into my head.

"You mean, 'Pete' like the funny-looking dog in the old *Little Rascals* TV series?" was the vet's response.

Nope. I'd recently reread *Far Tortuga*, a brilliant novel.

The Little Rascals was an okay explanation, though. It concealed my true intent, which the author, considering his background, might have found amusing.

I went to work connecting a timeline to a series of seemingly unrelated events.

Late Saturday afternoon, an FWC officer patrolling alone had gone missing, last seen in Choctawhatchee Bay, Florida's Panhandle. Also missing was the twenty-three-foot Guardian outboard she'd been assigned.

How could this be? A photo had been widely distributed. It was an open boat, twin Yamahas. The green-and-gold FWC badge emblem, port and starboard, made it easily recognized. And, presumably, somewhere in the boat's electronics suite was a tracking device.

Law enforcement vessels don't just vanish. Nor do vessels under twenty-six feet sink because, by code, the inner hulls must contain floatation enough to keep them afloat.

Pensacola is west of Tallahassee, but Saturday morning, authorities had urged residents on nearby barrier islands to anticipate evacuation.

There are many Millionaire Rows in Florida. Among the most exclusive were the Panhandle's Seaside Village and Santa Rosa Beach, not far from where the FWC vessel was last seen.

Late yesterday, a Sunday, NOAA had the storm tracking south of Tampa. I couldn't find much about the two officers who had been shot, only that it had happened near St. Pete Beach this morning before sunrise.

These events, in concert with NOAA's predictions, were no longer unrelated in my mind.

I sent my security pal, Ronnie Patrick, a text, **Call ASAP**, then got back to work.

The second folder provided by Chief of Station had been opened yesterday. It contained bios and mugshots of six prisoners who'd escaped Black Dolphin Prison and were thought to be in the States.

Monsters. Freakish gargoyles. That's what I'd expected. Instead, I saw gaunt, hollowed-eyed losers, skin tight on their skulls, casualties of something. Drugs, poverty, abuse. Themselves, more likely, and a self-loathing that prison had nurtured into rage.

"Kill them all," as Kurtz once said.

And here they were, pathogens on two legs. The walking dead in skin-shrouds of their own design. Tattoos. Serpents. Swastikas. Breastplate depictions of Christ dying on an Orthodox cross. Russian calligraphy. On eyebrows, fingers, were necklaces of death heads.

The bios of the six escapees truly were monstrous. Murder was the least inhuman outrage on a list of more than two hundred collective capital crimes. Nicknames assigned to the worst of them were grandiose, ill-fitting costumes when matched to the scrawny men in the photos. Direwolf. Chessboard Killer. The Vulture Monk.

It was as if the Russian media had attempted to mythologize their atrocities and thus pluck humanity out of the sewer.

I created a separate folder on Anatoli "Andy" Dimitry, the outlaw insurance exec. He was a prep school shyster who had tried to turn whistleblower on the multibillion-dollar industry that had revoked his agency's license.

Bad idea. It was safer to take on mobsters than legit bosses cloaked in legalese and thousand-dollar suits. The mistake had gotten Andy two years minimum security. But he had walked out after eighteen months and was still underground.

Maybe there was a connection. Maybe not. Someone, though, was chasing the hurricane and neutralizing anyone who got in their way.

The phone rang. Ronnie Patrick. Near the end of our conversation, I said, "Let's intercept these people before they get started. You've got the contacts in Tallahassee. Give FDLE a heads-up."

Ronnie said, "I like it. I just wish…damn, Doc. And you've got the contacts in Maryland. How about, hell, I'm swamped up here. Why not just call in the cavalry yourself? The intel comes from you."

I had switched to NOAA weather on my laptop. "Overseas, I'd give it a shot. But not in the States. The three-letter agencies are called Foreign Service for a reason. Hey—now they're predicting landfall between Bradenton and Sarasota. It's like the damn thing's following me."

"What do you mean by—" he started to ask but withdrew the question. "Yeah, it keeps turning. That's about fifty miles north of you, right?"

"Sixty plus," I said. "Ronnie, did you clear me on the security roster?"

"You're serious."

I was. And my nagging, irrational inner voice knew why. The Chief of Station's disdain had struck a nerve.

I said, "What I'm thinking is, hop in my truck after the 4:00 a.m. forecast. I can be in the Sarasota area before sunrise. The sheriff's department there needs to be briefed on what might be happening. It'll sound harebrained coming from me."

"Done," Ronnie said.

He then warned I'd be driving into a pre-storm logjam. Thousands of out-of-state utility pros, FEMA workers, and hundreds of bucket trucks, trailers hauling supplies and heavy equipment. All waiting to rush to the disaster if a disaster occurred.

"If Andy Dimitry's mercs are on the move, they'll blend in," Ronnie added. "Tattoos or not. He has software to pinpoint targets and already knows the drill. Even you, I'm not sure it's smart to come up here just to randomly eyeball... Well, the odds aren't good."

I said, "Maybe not so random. I'd be looking for an unmarked vehicle towing the FWC's twenty-three-foot Guardian. Unless they're idiots, they'll cover the boat with a tarp, engines and all."

The sheriff from Indiana was already a step ahead. "Uh-huh, what I was thinking. Use a boat with cop badges to hit the waterfront mansions. The mercs would avoid I-75, which is a hell of a mess already. So—hang on. I've got real-time traffic on my iPad. What do you think, from Pensacola, they'd take 19 south of Crystal River? Or US 41?"

I said, "Me, I'd want to stay near water in case I needed to splash the boat. The more local traffic the better. And I'd chart the boat ramps in advance. A private ramp would be my choice."

"Choke points," Ronnie said. "Exactly. Stick to the back roads. I know one of the FHP deputy directors. Doc, my advice is, let the state cops handle this. You're better off staying—"

"If the storm turns our way, I will," I said. "What I'm hoping is, the FWC officer who disappeared? Find her boat in time, she might still be alive. The mercs kill execution style, from what you said, but take some women hostage. Did any of their hostages live?"

"Depends on your definition," Ronnie said. "The only difference between murder and rape is, the dead only have to suffer once. Far as I'm concerned, guys who do that sort of shit should be given the hangman's cure for insomnia. But you might have a point, Doc. The missing FWC cop, they might keep her alive just for the…well, as leverage if nothing else."

I told my friend, "Light a fire under the state cops. And don't forget my security clearance. Those mercenaries are out there somewhere."

10

Andy Dimitry said to Grigori Pavlo, the monk with the GoPro on his forehead, "You've got to stop killing and raping cops. Filming that shit probably isn't such a great idea, either."

Pavlo, six-six, a skeletal one-ninety, got that burning look in his eyes. "Not dead is cop. I just come from her. Like cat with mouse. Why kill mouse when mouse is still lively?"

Geezus, Andy thought, another idiotic proverb. "Where is she? Can she ID you? If the cops get ahold of that camera, we're all screwed."

"ID? What is…"

"Identify you. Did she see your face? If she saw your face, goddamn it, we've got no choice but to…"

Pavlo, grinning, a black beard to his chest, reached for his zipper. "No. But she can identify this. Lead me to boat, I will prove is true."

The insurance exec walked away and didn't look back at the freak with the stringy hair, the nose, his skin a canvas of bizarre tats, the crown of his skull shaved bare.

A monk, not a priest, Sasha, the old oligarch, had insisted.

All his life, Philly included, Andy had heard rumors about sicko priests, but didn't know a soul who'd actually been groped by one. So in his mind, it was all just antireligious bullshit. Until now.

The difference between a monk and a priest was...?

Andy pinged his phone for an answer, changed his mind and said, "Screw it."

"Don't be rude," the phone's automated voice replied.

"Kiss my ass."

"I will not respond to that."

Christ, now even Siri was treating him like an imbecile.

Andy kept walking. A week ago, he'd made arrangements with a mom-and-pop campground on the bank of the Blackwater River, twenty miles north of the mansions on Pensacola Beach. A perfect spot to kick back safely until the storm trackers zeroed in. He was dressed for a leisurely company picnic, in contrast to Pavlo and his gang. Five fellow escapees and eight ratty *émigrés* in combat fatigues and boots. In Lauderdale, this rabble would have stood out. But not up here, where rednecks with hunting camps and fast bass boats dressed like Rambo wannabes.

In the rural Panhandle region, anything not camo was considered a daring fashion statement. This was cow country and farms. Narrow roads, trees bearded with Spanish moss. The campground, with its tiny outdoor pool, was vacant because of the approaching storm. Office windows were boarded, everything that couldn't be tied down had been removed.

The owners had believed Andy's story about utility workers on standby. He'd overpaid in cash. In return, he'd been given the keys to the gate. Security for their caravan of trucks loaded with empty crates that, Andy hoped, would soon be filled with big ticket swag.

The one exception was his personal vehicle. A Ford F-550 four-by-four that had been repossessed from a group of YouTube storm chasers. Huge mud tires with a deluxe camper built to withstand wind, rain, all the heavy shit associated with tornados. Pavlo, or his crazies, had used the truck to trailer the stolen FWC cruiser, which they'd covered with a tarp.

Sasha's orders. The old bastard, using his language skills as an excuse, was running everything by phone through Friar Pavlo, the Russian sergeant, which was scary as hell.

Andy approached the boat as if about to make a cold call pitch in the suburbs. He rapped on the side. "Hello? Anyone in there?"

From within came grunts and a kicking sound.

He lifted the tarp and saw the boat's green FWC markings. Even on tiptoe he wasn't tall enough, so he climbed onto the fender and peeked in.

There was movement in the darkness, then whack, something hit him on the jaw. Andy landed on his back in the grass and opened his eyes. Pavlo was standing there, looking down and laughing.

"What the hell?" The insurance exec rolled to his knees. "Get away from me... Why the hell did you do that?"

Pavlo shook his head at the mouthy little American. In Russian, he said, "Why are you all so weak and fat? One day, I will build a fire. A cooking fire. Ha-ha. As it says in the Book of John, 'Who eateth my flesh shall have eternal life.'"

Zero reaction from the American.

"You are such a stupid man," Grigori goaded in Russian. "You don't understand a word I'm saying. But *you know*. The fear, I see in your eyes. This makes me very happy. What a fun toy you will be."

Sensing an insult, Andy got up and used his phone as a threat. "I can't tolerate insubordination. Sasha will back me, goddamn it. I'll call him right now if you—"

Pavlo batted the phone away. "Was not me, fool." This was in English. "Here. I show." One-handed, towering over the FWC vessel, he stripped the tarp from the bow as if it were a bedsheet. "See? Is skinny little girl who knocks poor Anatoli on his ass. Are you crying?"

No. Andy's mind had gone blank. He was looking at an attractive woman, her mouth and eyes taped, wrists, too, but there was a blackjack in her hands. Furious, she swung blindly from her knees like a kid at a piñata party.

Pavlo, in a teasing way, tapped the FWC cop on the back... jumped away...then tapped her shoulder again when she lashed out.

"Goddamn, Grigori, she's...she's pretty damn hot. You know, good-looking. How bad is she hurt?"

The lady cop hadn't heard English since she'd been kidnapped late Saturday afternoon. Her head pivoted toward Andy while the Russian said, "Yes, a lively little mouse. You like? Speak to her. Maybe I share my toy when done."

Andy realized he was gawking. "Hello? Officer, I'm...I'm sorry this shit's happened." He walked closer. "I had nothing to do with...well, this unfortunate screwup. Illegals; dealing with immigrants, you know? Ignorant of our...anyway, I promise you'll be okay. Just relax. Are you hurt?"

The cop, her blond hair drenched with sweat, dropped the blackjack and pulled the tape away from her mouth. "Call...call the police. I'll tell them you had nothing to do...nothing to do with this, I swear. I'm so... Water. I haven't had water, I'm so thirsty. Please. Before I pass out again."

Her lips were parchment, cracked and bloody. Andy, motioning to the camper, told the Russian, "Get her some water, goddamn it. No, a Gatorade, one of those big bottles. And a shirt or something to wear; a robe, anything. Move it."

Pavlo responded with a look that warned of boundaries.

Andy whispered, "Don't let her take off that blindfold. Got it?" and went toward the camper. "One Gatorade coming up," he called from the steps, and went inside where it was cool, the AC on high in the clammy ninety-degree heat.

Even with the door closed, he heard the Russian's voice, then the woman battling, scratching, and her enraged threats. In that instant, Andy felt the panicky urge to get behind the wheel, crash the gate and escape toward Tampa and safety. According to weather updates, that's where the storm was headed, farther south. What stopped him, though, was the cop. Just the thought of being in the camper alone with a woman so fit and pretty was enough. Two or three days on the road, it would be nice to come home to something blonde and willing.

Question was, how to win the trust of a woman who's been assaulted by a freak wearing a GoPro? And who, under no circumstances, could be allowed to see his face?

Be kind, gentle, convincing, of course. Play the role of good citizen to the crazy monk's bad. It was no different than convincing a client that policy holders, no matter the claim, ever get paid the full etcetera, etcetera, etcetera. Blame lawyers, blame incompetent adjusters. Blame anyone but him and his agency.

If the woman didn't fall for his act? Well, if they were alone in the camper, she didn't have to be willing. Back in college, Andy and some frat buddies had been down that road several times. "Snatch shooting," they'd called those late-night outings.

Truth was, the former executive preferred using force.

Take Action. Take Power. Success Will Follow.

This wasn't a Russian proverb. It had been a plaque on his office wall.

Andy had pieced together a sort of welcome basket for the cop when the door banged open and in came Pavlo, the blonde folded over his shoulder as if he'd just bagged a deer. She appeared to be unconscious when he dumped her on the bed.

"Severe dehydration," Andy diagnosed. "Go on, I'll take it from here." He knelt at her side with a bottle of lime Gatorade. "Hello. Officer, can you hear me? Here's something to drink. I have a straw, I'll put between your lips. Don't be afraid." He fitted the straw. "Good. Now take a sip. You're safe with me."

The woman recoiled. She tasted the liquid and attacked the bottle, ravenous. Automatically, her hands moved to the tape on her eyes.

"Don't do that," Andy warned with a gentle squeeze of her wrist. "For now, anyway. It's for your own good."

Pavlo thought this was funny. "Anatoli, such a kind man. So important. Here, let my little plaything see how ugly you are." He reached, grabbed a fist full of blond hair and ripped the duct tape off her eyes.

Sunlight pierced the windows. The woman squinted, turned her head. Eyes blinked open, nose to nose with Andy, and saw his shocked expression.

Eyes slammed closed. "No...no. I didn't see you," she croaked. "I swear. Didn't see anything."

Pavlo was enjoying himself. "Is all yours," he said to the American with the noisy mouth. "How you say, 'You got no choice now.'"

11

Four a.m. Tuesday morning, a breathing darkness peppered the lab with rain. I made coffee, walked out on the upper deck and timed the gusts.

Sporadic. Fifteen to twenty knots of misting Sahara heat.

Two miles away, waves crashed the beach at ten-second intervals.

A disturbing omen.

Years ago, on the Mosquito Coast of Honduras, a local had told me his ancestors knew a *"huracán"* was coming by gauging the silences between waves. Eight seconds meant bad. Six seconds, worse.

I'd found no studies to confirm this. Indigenous people of the coastal Americas, however, had endured thirty centuries without the help of NOAA. When Rome was young, parts of the "New World" were already old and prospering.

Pete rammed the door open. His head weather vaned from me to the water ten feet below.

With a flashlight I scanned the surface for glowing reptilian eyes.

After a hand signal, the dog scrambled down a level, leaped
and landed in a spray of green. Water was alive with micro-
scopic fireflies that weren't fireflies. It was a soup of one-celled
aquatic organisms—dinoflagellates, part plant, part animal. Stir
with an oar or a dangling hand, and there would be meteorite
streaks, neon-bright.

In memory, a marina slideshow flashed. Night swims. Jumping from boats by the dark of the moon.

"Like jumping into the freakin' stars," was the typical drunken
comment.

The moon was dark now, one day before freshening its
monthly cycle. No matter the time of year, a new or full moon
signals a spring tide. Lower lows, higher highs when the bays
flooded.

This is shaping up to be nasty, I thought.

Overhead, a lone star measured the velocity of clouds. White
tendrils spun northward, displacing dry, warm air. The tendrils
mimicked an Arctic icepack that bulldozed good weather toward the mainland, thus creating a void.

Nature abhors a void.

Three hundred miles southwest, according to the 03:00 update, a Cuban farm village had been savaged. Clouds of glacial
proportions were now gathering Gulf Stream heat, strengthen-
ing, sailing toward Florida at speeds that varied between eight
and fifteen knots.

I summoned Pete from the water. Used two fresh hand drill
batteries and finished boarding up by sunrise. I test-started a
portable fifty-five-hundred-watt generator, then walked to the
marina.

"I know, I know, now they're predicting somewhere between
Siesta Key and Englewood," Mack said from behind the counter.
"Don't you ever have any good news? That's still, what, forty,

fifty miles of north of here. I'm not bloody leaving, so don't start on me, okay?"

"Good morning to you, too," I said. "Where's Jeth?"

"Bloody mandatory evacuation my ass," he muttered. "One of the local cops just stopped by. That's what she told me. The cops, firefighters, paramedics, they're all leaving the island if that damn thing tracks any closer. If I was a thief, know what I'd do?"

"Are your cottages all boarded?" I asked. Mack had invested his life savings in a beachside property, a cluster of midsixties, one-bedroom rentals. It had been a mom-and-pop operation that catered to nudists. Grin 'N Bare It was the cheesy name.

The New Zealander reached for his foul weather jacket. "If you've got the time, I've got the plywood."

On the way out the door, we watched Pete haul a tree limb toward a pile of trash recently salvaged. The limb was long, awkward to carry. When it snagged a piling, the dog banged head-first into the same piling and cartwheeled sideways off the dock.

"Smart like bull." Mack laughed. "You know what they should invent? A retriever that puts shit back in the water instead of junking up the landscape."

We took my blue antique GMC because I wanted to make sure it would start. Jeth put a tool chest in the bed and scooched in the front, a tight fit.

The island had a Third World ghost town feel. Windows boarded, roads empty save for a few stragglers fleeing toward the Causeway bridges. Some trailered boats overloaded with possessions too precious to risk. Blue tarps and bungee cords. Last-minute duct tape decisions that had the scent of fear.

I thought about Big Sammy and Cadmael. Two children between them plus ancestral families south of the border.

"Stupid me," I said aloud. "Should 'a stuck more tarps in there for them and some extra PFDs."

This took some explaining.

Mack replied, "Storm surge, right. All the hype about storm

surge. Every five to ten years, same thing." He looked over his shoulder. "When's the last time this island actually flooded? The whole island, not just the—"

Jeth answered, "More than a hundred years ago. That's what Tomlinson told us. Remember? He'd know, wouldn't he, Doc?"

"1920-something. Sounds about right," Mack said. He was prepping for another argument.

I said, "He's usually right about stuff like that." I'd already told them the skipper of *No Más* hadn't responded by radio since Saturday midnight. I left out another undertaking—I'd organized a list of ham radio operators, Gulf Coast to the Caribbean, who, like Tomlinson, were members of a fraternal secret brotherhood called the Freemasons.

They would CQ hourly, I'd been assured—ham speak for "attempt contact."

Jeth said, "Sure hope he's okay. But that's just like the dude, right? Takes off for weeks at a time, not a word. Then shows up out of the— Hey, let's stop for coffee. I'm gonna get a hot dog. You guys hungry?"

Thinking of Tomlinson, I said, "Of course he's okay. Probably at some Pensacola tiki bar right now eating oysters and telling lies."

Baseless optimism on my part. But with Tomlinson's Masonic brotherhood of hams on deck, I was hopeful.

The parking lot of Bailey's Hardware was deserted. We pulled into the 7-Eleven. Doors were boarded but, in red spray paint, Alan or Tom had scrawled, *OPEN COME IN!*

Rain, big summer-sized drops. It came in waves with a lawn sprinkler cadence, slung by a giant waterwheel a hundred fifty miles offshore.

On the way to Mack's cottages, we did a sightseeing detour down East Gulf that ended at a sandy expanse where the island's lighthouse, a navigational stalwart, had been a maritime beacon, Key West to Tampa Bay, since the late 1800s. It was a spire of skeletal iron, a hundred feet tall, crowned by a crystalline globe. Over decades, that globe had been fired by fuels that mirrored cultural change: whale oil, then lard, then kerosene before Edison and rivals had transformed the world.

"See?" Mack gloated. "The hurricane hasn't been born that can knock that stubborn bastard down. Don't know why folks are so damn worried. This island ain't going nowhere. Never will. Okay, enough wasting time. Let's get to work."

On the return trip to his cottage enclave, I slowed for a low spot in the road. Wind blew what looked like two lengths of garden hose across a puddled sheen. An iguana the size of a dachshund followed.

Mack leaned forward. "Geezus bloody oath...what the hell?"

Jeth was chewing his second hot dog. "Hey—look. A couple of snakes. Doc, do iguanas eat snakes? What kind are those, uh...bet they're water moccasins."

The snakes slid into the weeds. The iguana did an about-face and went up a tree.

Mack said, "Place is like a freakin' zoo. Shits-a-brick, and I thought I was done with poisonous brownies and the like. You should 'a run 'em over, Doc."

"Reptiles, they're looking for high ground," I said. "Anyplace that doesn't flood because of the rain. I didn't get a good look. Uh... I doubt they're venomous, though. And no, I don't think they do."

"Eat snakes you mean?"

Mack said, "Wish to hell they did. In Oz, I grew up scared shitless of brownies and taipans, the whole slimy lot. Poisonous as hell." He sniffed and looked at Jeth. "You buy three of those? That hot dog smells pretty good."

We pulled onto Mack's property. Munchkin-sized rentals, a common area in the middle. To the right at ground level was a small community center with card tables. Green roof tiles and a sixtyish Grin 'N Bare It sign were distinctive. Palms, lavender hibiscus screened the area from peepers. The beach was across West Gulf, a two-minute walk.

Jeth asked, "You really think animals know a big storm is coming? That's what Janet says. 'A course, she believes Tomlinson's a pah-para...has psychic powers, too."

Mack was in no mood for cynicism. "Don't badmouth that psychic crap. Not here, especially not now." He beheld the compound he'd converted into a tasteful, secluded retreat. "You'll jinx our asses."

"Snakes and animals. You know, birds and like that," Jeth said. "That's all I meant."

It gave us something to talk about while we off-loaded supplies and went to work in what had become a steaming drizzle.

12

I was in my old truck, on the phone arguing with Hannah, when I heard a profane howl. The community center door flew open and out came Mack, pants around his ankles. After two running steps, he tripped and splayed belly-first onto the sand.

Big men in their sixties do not fall gracefully. It was a painful indignity to witness.

"Sonuvabitch… Ouch!" he bellowed. "Call nine-one-one, quick. Get an ambulance. And stay away from that goddamn bathroom."

From one of the cabins, Jeth sprinted to the man's aide. There was a back-and-forth jumble—"What's wrong? What happened?" Mack saying, "Jesus Christ, I'm bit, I'm bleeding. Hurry up before I pass out."

I had the window down.

On the phone, Hannah said, "Oh, my Lordy, is that Mack?"

"Get on that plane," I told her again. "Please. This could be the worst storm in years, and you've got plenty of time to make it to the airport. Think of our son."

"Mack sounds hurt bad," she responded. "Run, help your friend. We can talk later about—"

"Not until I hear you say it. Promise me."

"Okay, yes! I promise to get on the plane. You want me to call nine-one-one, or just sit there gabbing?"

I made the call, grabbed a first-aid kit and knelt by Mack. He was trying to inspect two bloody pinpricks on the backside of his thigh.

"Sonuvabitching snake bit me. Big wanker," he groaned and glared at Jeth. "Told you you'd jinx us. Jesus Christ, is this really happening? Feels like a bad dream."

The man was hyperventilating, going into shock.

I squirted disinfectant on the pinpricks. A package of gauze came out of the bag. "Where did this happen?"

"Bit me right on the ass, goddamn it. You blind?"

"No, I mean where is the—" I gave up and charged into the office. The bathroom door was open. Coiled next to the toilet, partially hidden by a mop, was a big, healthy snake. The orange scales, speckled with a patchwork of yellow, were familiar.

"Found it—a corn snake," I called to them. "They're harmless. He's going to be fine."

"Huh?"

"A corn snake. Relax. Now I've got to catch the damn thing to show the—"

"Catch what?"

"Geezus, just tell him he's not going to die. Give me a sec."

"Hell I'm not," Mack wailed. "Get me to the goddamn ER. Jeth, find a knife. You gotta suck the poison out before it's too late."

"Suck the...huh? Hey Doc—he wants me to—"

I hollered to Jeth, "Don't do it. Understand? Do not do it!"

The warble of a siren told me EMS would arrive in a minute or two. They would want to see the snake before treating their patient.

Corn snakes aren't venomous, but they don't like to be messed with. The thing tail-mimicked a warning before I pinned its head. Then the snake curled five feet of scales around my arm while I guided it into a dented cooler.

The paramedic opened the lid and took photos. "I'll send these in for confirmation, but I don't think you're in any danger, Mr. MacKinley. Not as far as this snake's concerned. But you said something about pain in your arm and chest area? How bad is it?"

Mack tried to sit. "I fell on my goddamn face, what do you expect? At least let me pull my pants up. You sure that sonuvabitch isn't poison? It rattled like a rattlesnake and tried to bite me again."

The techs exchanged looks. They had noted their patient's ashen skin, the glazed eyes.

The second medic said, "Sir, I'm a little concerned about your blood pressure. And you seem to be hyperventilating. We need to do some more tests. How about we get you on the gurney and—"

"An EKG," the other said. "Any shortness of breath?"

Mack sputtered, "At my age and forty pounds overweight? Hell yes. But there's no reason for me to go to the— Hey, you aren't lying about that goddamn snake, are you? If it's deadly, I've got a right to know."

The paramedics explained that the shock of being bitten could have keyed a serious cardiac event. And this might be his last chance to get medical help for twenty-four hours or more because of the storm.

"A heart attack. Jesus Christ, what next? Now I'm having a damn heart attack." Mack moaned and touched his stomach. "Hell, maybe I am. I feel like shit. Like I'm going to bloody puke."

Then he did. Another humiliation.

They wheeled our friend toward the open doors of the EMS module.

I said to him, "Jeth will go to your place, pack a bag and meet you at the hospital. I'll look after the marina for the next couple of days. How's that sound?"

Mack lifted his head. Gazed at the neat little compound he'd created. "The Dinkin's Bay lifeboat," he muttered, a pet name for the place. It represented a last sanctuary for him and his marina family, immune to government meddling.

"Doc, you mind phoning Rhonda, mate? Don't care if it does piss off JoAnn. We had quite a thing going for a while, Rhonda and me, and I'd like to tell her—hell, a bunch of things I should've told her."

"I know, and I will," I said.

The man smiled a weary smile. "Bit on the ass by a fuckin' snake. Might as well have been my balls from Jeth's face when I told him to find a knife. God a'mighty, you hear his voice? Can't wait to tell that story when we're all back home again in a day or two."

The Kiwi via Tasmania was still chuckling when they fitted him with an oxygen mask.

"Call me Max," Dr. Maximilian Weatherby said on the phone. "No need for formalities if we're to ride out this little monsoon together."

For Brits, understatement conveys a playful confidence in the face of danger.

I was outside on the lab's lower deck, listening through a waterproof plastic case. Hannah, our son, Izaak, and her mother were at Southwest Regional, their 1:00 p.m. flight to Raleigh/Durham delayed by weather. Zero cell service inside a boarded room roofed with metal, so I'd found a dry little haven beneath a leeward overhang of my fish house.

No wonder their plane was delayed. Weatherby's "little monsoon" was well north of Cuba, a Cat-Four hurricane with Cat-Five potential that had narrowed its final approach. ETA was tomorrow before noon. The eye was huge, twenty miles wide, which put the marina and islands north in what shotgunners call the "ghost sites."

Weatherby added, "Are you certain you're set? Authorities don't close Causeway traffic until nineteen hundred hours, so you still have time to tidy up and get to the mainland. I'll keep an eye on things out here. What say you?"

Hams use military time in private conversation. Nothing odd about that.

We'd linked up earlier on VHF, monitoring the Amateur Radio Emergency Service on local two-meter and seventy-centimeter repeater towers.

Radio towers can be compromised, so we'd also made test contacts on high-frequency bands. Simplex. Antenna to antenna, no towers required. Emergency frequencies were preassigned. On twenty meters, 14.300 MHz allowed me to remind Weatherby and other operators along the coast that the sailing vessel *No Más* had been out of radio contact since Saturday night, so please be on the alert.

As always, I'd included Tomlinson's call sign.

Weatherby wanted more details, so he had phoned my cell to avoid FCC formalities. This made it easier to discuss my wayward pal. I didn't mind a little rain.

"Your friend's a Freemason?" the Brit asked. "I know people in the UK very high up in that fraternity. A distinguished family, you might say. Mind if I share this information? Might surprise you, the number of contacts they have worldwide."

The gusting wind, fifteen to twenty knots, made it hard to hear. When he mentioned something about his second vacation home, the one bayside in St. Pete, I stripped my phone of its case and said, "Could you repeat that, please?"

He said, "I spent Saturday night there. It's just a little cottage, but a lovely area called Jungle Terrace. You're welcome to use the place until this blows through. Be a sensible fellow, Ford. It's only a three-hour drive."

My request for background info on the Brit from intel pros had gone unanswered. Caution was necessary. Maybe there was a reason he wanted me off the island.

I said, "Me, sensible? I mean, come on. Three days ago, you drove to where the storm was expected to hit. Then yesterday, you drive back here knowing darn well we're going to get at least a chunk of it."

I waited, alert to the man's reaction.

He laughed. Self-effacing. Unconcerned with what I might be implying.

"Like they say, always run toward the gunfire. You've heard that old chestnut, I suppose."

I had. Many times.

Police in St. Pete wouldn't need to evacuate, he explained, unlike law enforcement here. So he'd returned in a rush to protect his property.

"Any particular reason you're concerned?" I asked.

There was. Last week, from the crow's nest deck atop his house, he, too, had seen a suspicious boat cruising the area after midnight.

"A crook's reconnaissance, I'd wager," he said. "If you're staying, Ford, I suggest you keep on your toes as well."

I mentioned the boat or boats Mack had seen, then baited him, saying, "Rigid-hull inflatables. The type cops and the military sometimes use. I wouldn't worry about it."

"But I am. It's a matter of economics and ego. Wherever I go, I collect bits of this and that. Art by local artists, books, some sculptures. Nothing hugely dear, but with ties to the area. In this case, Florida. A lot cheaper than hiring a decorator, don't you think? And, as I told my wife, our art collection might actually appreciate in value one day. Of course, I've yet to see that day. A dear, dear lady. She tolerates my dismal judgment with a grace that still makes me feel like an ass."

We both laughed.

"Art by local artists?"

"A few nice pieces, yes. You know the sort of thing. Sunsets and umbrellas, seagulls and the like. But nothing worth—"

I pressed, "There was a local artist—a genius, some say. Modern art, which is not exactly my...well, it's out of my league. He used stuff you might find in a junkyard—children's toys, cans, bicycle frames. Lots of old bicycles in the pieces I've seen."

The Brit went silent. He knew exactly who I was referencing.

I continued, "The artist was a friend of mine before he died. Had a studio on Captiva. Used to sell him fish. For years, I had no idea the guy was internationally famous. Ever heard the name Robert Rauschenberg?"

Weatherby, bemused or wary—hard to tell—replied, "Discussing an original Rauschenberg—at a million pounds for even a sketch—I think it would be unwise to...uh. You actually knew him?"

The physician/inventor had a valuable art collection. It was in his wariness.

I said, "It's a small island. A great guy. He insisted on being called Bob, but his real name—get this—his real name was Milton. That's what he told us, anyway. If you own a Rauschenberg, I could understand why you took the risk of—"

"No mystery there, Ford. I came back because I'm baching it. My adored wife and sons are safely home. No grandchildren yet, so why miss the fun?"

"Fun," I said.

"A unique encounter. At my age, when will I have another chance to experience a tropical cyclone? An interesting aspect, I think, is the effect solar flares, combined with a hurricane, might have on radio transmissions. There's data on the topic, but damn little, the combination is so rare."

"Solar flares? Max, that's out of my league, too. I'm just get-ting into the hobby. Data...data concerning what?"

"Check the literature, my friend. The *American Geophysical Journal* ran a piece on the topic. A more recent article was posted on the Amateur Radio Association web page. High-frequency propagation blackouts on the sun-facing side of the Earth dur-ing hurricanes. Ultraviolet radiation in the ionosphere. Fasci-nating stuff, what?"

I laughed. "Possibly—if I knew what you were talking about."

"All complicated space plasma physics. The fourth state of cosmic matter. I much look forward to running my own tests," the Brit said, then paused. "Apologies. A car just pulled into the drive."

"That's odd," I said. "Police? What kind of car?"

He replied, "Yes, very. Ring you back in a bit, Ford."

"Make sure you do," I told him.

He'd already hung up.

13

Less than twenty hours before a Cat-Five crashed ashore, I loaded a duffel with mooring tackle and tools. Donned heavy boots, gloves. Selected a pistol, checked the magazine and went out into a steam bath drizzle, Pete at my side.

The old blue pickup, which I'd driven for years, was a double-clutch anachronism parked next to my new gray Ford Raptor. The truck was a recent purchase. A concession to insane traffic in a state that has been overbuilt, overpopulated and crushed to its limestone bones by highways, stucco and lethally fertilized gated communities.

Until the new vehicle, I'd embraced the conceit that I didn't care what I drove, so no gaudy decals or Raptor badges for me. But I had added some emergency niceties. Mounted on the roof was a military LED Golight. Wireless controls could shoot the beam skyward or spin it three hundred sixty degrees. Forward, beneath a brush guard was an eight-ton winch that could snatch a tree off the road or me from a ditch.

In terms of electronic gadgets, it wasn't nearly as tricked out as my boat. Night or day, I prefer water travel to interstates.

My phone signaled a text from Hannah: On plane, Izaak asleep, Loretta's driving me nuts.

I took a chance and called. She answered, whispering, "Our phones're supposed to be off, but it's good to hear your voice. We've been sitting here thirty minutes. Whole world seems to go crazy whenever there's a storm."

From the next seat, her mother, a much louder voice, said, "Hey there missy, didn't they tell us to turn off our phones? You gonna get us all in trouble. No wonder that damn waitress hasn't brought me my Scotch-rocks."

I said, "Get some whiskey in her, maybe she'll fall asleep, too. Luke didn't want to go?"

I heard, "Stop swearing, Mama," before Hannah replied to my question. Her nephew, Luke, and her uncle Arlis would return from the mainland after the storm to protect the citrus tree-lets and clean up. Her cop pal, Lieutenant Tupplemeyer, would check on the pair and spend tonight and the next few days at Hannah's place when she wasn't on duty.

I asked, "Birdy knows which channels to monitor on VHF? I want to stay in touch if it's okay with you."

Like a lot of commercial fisherfolk, Hannah's home had a base station mounted inside, twenty-five watts, with an antenna strapped to the chimney. Sufficient power and elevation to easily reach my lab.

"I'd sure appreciate that," she answered. "I worry about Birdy as much as I'll worry about you. She said a friend of yours called. A man high up in FPL security."

"Ronnie Patrick, a good guy. I figured she'd pay more attention to a former sheriff than me."

"Who's that gang he talked about? Terrorists or just criminals? Think that's why the SUV pulled into our drive last week?"

"No difference between the two," I said. "Birdy's a trained

pro. But yeah, it's a possibility. A guy gets out, asks for me by name? I want her to know she can radio me when the cell towers go down. And they always do."

We talked a while longer before I heard a flight attendant say, "Phones off please, ma'am. The captain has an announcement to make."

Hannah, whispering, said, "Gotta run, Doc."

"Not yet. Wait for the announcement. I want to be sure they don't cancel your flight."

"If they do, I'll call first thing—if my dang phone doesn't run out of juice." There was a silence. "When this is over, we need to talk, you and me."

Loss, a distancing veil—it was in her tone.

I replied, "You didn't bring a charger?"

In the background, just before a click, I heard her mother, Loretta, wail, "That does it! I want off this goddamn plane if that waitress don't bring me my—"

Redial, when I tried, went straight to voicemail.

What would I do if Hannah's flight was canceled? Or if she'd been thrown off because of her mother?

Carrying the bag of ground tackle, I returned to the creek—a mosquito ditch—that Big Sammy and Cadmael had helped me prepare yesterday. An hour was spent debating with my conscience while I strung ropes and buried four unconventional anchors.

When I was done, the mangrove tunnel resembled a giant spiderweb. By sunset, my twenty-five-foot Dorado would be there, suspended from dozens of limbs. Spring lines would be lashed to a dozen more. Mangroves are rubbery, elastic survivors, their DNA perfected by storms since the Pleistocene.

There was a story behind this strategy.

As of 1922, long before the Causeway bridges, the only way to get a car onto the island was via ferryboat. The boat's first skipper, Captain Leon Crumpler, in his eighties when I was a kid, liked to talk about the early days in Florida. Smudge pots instead of window screens. Bat houses instead of insecticides. Swamp cabbage, smoked mullet with grits. And how to prepare for hurricanes.

Old Leon's favorite subject. He'd ridden out some of history's worst, including the storm of 1926 and a 1928 nightmare that had ruptured Lake Okeechobee's dike. The breach had flooded a hundred square miles, towns, farms, Seminole villages beneath fifteen feet of water.

With a snap of his fingers, he'd told me, "Jes' like that, young buddy ruff. Three thousand good people, men, women, kids, all dead. Probably more—and this back when only half a million folks lived here on Florida. Heck, we was finding bodies a year later, far south as Immokalee and Devil's Garden. Almost as bad as the Labor Day hurricane of 1935."

Because of the context, *Devil's Garden* had resonated when applied to the Sunshine State.

Another favorite topic was how to secure boats that couldn't be carted inland before a blow. Leon's advice didn't appear in books, but it had worked for me, my uncle Tuck and others during a couple of bad ones.

I was counting on it to work again. After the storm—if my boat survived—I wanted to be mobile in case the mercenaries came a-calling.

The dog and I hosed off. I left two messages for Hannah and checked the Delta web page. Her flight, ninety minutes late, was in the air, but were they still aboard?

Booting Loretta for bad behavior—or privileges demanded because she had bedded an ancient king—might have added to the delay.

Next, the weather. Wind was still east-southeast, fifteen to twenty knots, but gusts up to thirty-five were expected by midnight.

It was after five. Authorities wouldn't close the Causeway until sunset, which, officially, was 7:14 p.m. Beneath a turbulent, smoky sky, though, it would get dark fast.

"We still have two hours of wiggle room," I said aloud. "Let's check something first."

The dog followed me across the breezeway. Crunch & Des came, too. I knuckle-rapped a brass wall barometer. The needle dropped to 27.8 inches of mercury, only a few ticks above the lowest ever recorded on the west coast of Florida.

Oh…hell.

If I couldn't confirm Hannah and Izaak were on their way to Carolina, I would…do what? A single option flashed to mind. Run. Protect my family. I would trailer the boat, pack Pete and the cat into the truck, and drive to her Gumbo Limbo home on the elevated Calusa mounds.

Take a breath, I thought.

My panicky decision might have been prompted by a chemical reaction to the barometer. It's human physiology. Air has weight, density. An abrupt drop in pressure alerts the primal brain as if our spinal cords were mercury in a column of glass.

Animals feel it, too. Cats hide. Dogs pace, they slobber. It is an ancient dire wolf instinct that warns them to attack or flee but, by God, don't just lie there and be consumed.

Pete snorted. Crunch & Des swung a right hook and growled.

I motioned, *follow me*, and went out the door.

Something else affected by low barometric pressure might be the marine specimens in my lab. As pressure falls, air bladders in fish inflate. It would be a disorienting change. Research indicated that some littoral species, prior to a major storm, evacuate to deeper water. An electronic monitoring grid—a project conceived by the pros at Mote Marine—suggested this was true of at least some sharks and possibly stingrays, too.

This reminded me of Jeth's question. Did birds and other

wildlife anticipate hurricanes and flee? Long ago, as a teenager, I hadn't paid attention. This time I would.

But I couldn't just go off and leave the creatures, seahorses, fish and more trapped in tanks, so the next half hour was spent freeing specimens I'd spent months collecting.

Between trips I left a fruitless message for Hannah, and another for her deputy sheriff friend, Birdy. To linger inside the lab meant missing a return call, but no problem.

Once I was done, there was plenty to do outside.

An emergency backup antenna—one hundred thirty-five feet of wire, a Buckmaster dipole—had to be strung from the house, through the mangroves. I moved my antique GMC to an open gated area behind the mechanic's shed. A hydraulic boat lift and hawser lines provided stability and an extra four feet of elevation.

It was a needless precaution on an island that hadn't flooded in a century. Or so I recklessly believed.

My conversation with Ronnie came up for review. Check all private boat ramps, I'd told him, on the lesser traveled roads. There were no lesser traveled roads than those near the marina, yet I'd failed to heed my own damn advice. What if the gang of mercs had arrived a day early and were already looting houses?

I got in the new truck, locked the marina gate behind me and went for a drive. On Tarpon Bay Road, the phone vibrated with a secure portal. It was a text message from my intel friend, Donald Piao Cheng, that read,

Re: Dr. Maximilian Weatherby, Cambridge. Link with SIS (M-I-6) suspected but not confirmable. There is one red flag bisect Re: Russia-Black Dolphin. Subject's niece, a Red Cross volunteer, was criminally assaulted, same area, same timeline after a massive flood. Still working on details. More to come.

What the hell...?

"Not confirmable" as subtext had a very different meaning

than "not yet confirmed." I took this as a yes. Weatherby was connected with MI6, Britain's CIA. And his niece had possibly been assaulted by one or more of the six escapees.

Dead slow, I turned onto Periwinkle Drive. These threads began to connect, one by one, with what I already knew:

The physician/inventor had driven to St. Pete on Saturday, where the storm was projected to hit.

Yesterday, he'd returned here, directly into NOAA's updated cone of probability.

Didn't want to miss the fun, he'd told me.

A wealthy man creates his own opportunities. Weatherby's true motives, however, were suspect. Had his niece survived? Was his motive revenge?

Periwinkle, the main drag, was an asphalt vacancy, writhing palms, banyans, shuttered buildings on both sides of the bike paths, the island fantasy abandoned to fear and atmospheric tides.

The left turn to Millionaire's Row was a few miles ahead, not far from the Causeway. I pressed the accelerator in need of more information.

Didn't see another vehicle until a dual-axle camper truck from the opposite direction zoomed past. Black carbon wrapping, black tinted windows, oversized mud tires. The boat it towed was masked by a brown tarp. The trailer's yellow plate was Florida law enforcement.

Was it the missing FWC vessel?

I didn't brake. Didn't want to signal my suspicions. I gave the driver half a mile, then attempted a U-turn at Jerry's Grocery, a parking lot empty save for a sheriff's cruiser, green on white. Not local. From Palm Beach County, the other side of the state. Authorities had already summoned outside help.

I waved to get the officer's attention—a fit, ex-military-looking guy, red hair buzzed short. He was on the phone, so I pulled alongside, lowered the window and waited a minute before telling him what I'd just seen.

Cops are wary of eager, helpful civilians, and for good reason. But he had already gotten the word about the missing boat, possibly thanks to my pal Ronnie. Immediately the guy was on full alert.

"Don't know how I missed it," he said. "Anyone who tries to get on the island, we're turning them around. You're sure it was an FWC license plate?"

I described the camper truck again, adding, "Definitely a yellow plate. I didn't get the numbers. The boat, I'm just guessing, looked to be in the twenty-five-foot range. Completely covered by the tarp. I can show you where the local boat ramps are."

Now he was suspicious of me.

"What's your name again? You're heading to the mainland, right?"

"I'm staying on the island," I replied. "Most of the private ramps aren't listed on maps. You're gonna need a local to show you where they are."

"We'll handle it, Mr. Ford. You're aware there's a mandatory evacuation ordered? Your call if you choose to ignore it, but keep in mind there's a 7:00 p.m. deadline. All emergency responders will be gone, so you've got less than an hour. You're headed home, right?"

"Dixie Beach Road," I told him.

"You live there? You'll need a photo ID to prove it if you're stopped."

I countered, "Check the utility companies security list. My name's on there—or should be. Come on. How do you think I know about the missing boat? Give me a chance. I could help."

In folklore, redheads have a temper, especially those with buzz-cut sidewalls. The look the officer gave me warned, *Don't even think about it.*

Deputy Kahn, according to his name tag, touched the microphone on his shoulder and took off, no siren, but blue strobes echoed off low dusking clouds.

When the cruiser was out of sight, I spun my new Ford Raptor around and returned to the lab in a blinding rain. If cops were blocking access to Dixie Beach Road, why had Max Weatherby seen a vehicle on Millionaire's Row?

I found his cell number but called Hannah's North Carolina hotel first.

She hadn't checked in yet.

14

Andy Dimitry saw the nerdy-looking guy in the gray Ford Raptor snap to attention when they passed each other on the island's main road, Periwinkle Boulevard. Oversized camper mirrors showed the Raptor slowing, no brake lights. Then the truck turned left into a parking lot deserted save for a green-on-white squad car.

"Damn, a cop back there," he said to Pavlo. "Told you this was a bad idea. We should've waited on the mainland—that big island, what's the name?—until the storm passes tomorrow, tomorrow night. Same with our other four guys out here in the Jeep we stole. Bad business, man, to split your resources like this. Goddamn that Sasha, thinks he's so damn smart."

The freaky Russian inhaled the last of a doobie and dropped it out the window into a pelting rain. "Maybe 'cause he thinks you so damn not smart. 'Dumb,' Sasha says. Keep driving. Straight, five kilometers, then right turn." He tapped what looked like a lake on the GPS screen. "Here is Dinkin's Bay. We hide boat near ramp. Small ramp, Sasha says. Is man there—secondary

target—I must see privately." He swiped the screen eastward
to confirm the name of the larger protected island, three miles
inland, was Gumbo Limbo.

Andy's knuckles were white on the steering wheel, the road
slick now that it was raining again. "Privately? Bullshit. See,
that's how Sasha works. Pretends he's letting you in on a secret but tells everyone else the same damn thing. You're talking about the biologist, right? I don't get it. How much did he
say was the bounty?"

"Bounty? What is—"

"The reward for killing the guy," Andy said. "See, Sasha
doesn't know shit about—well, he's uneducated when it comes
to leadership, motivation, things like that. I've taken seminars
on that stuff—hell, I've *taught* them. What I tell students is treat
your employees like they're your most important clients—'cause
they are. Last few months, I've been working on a book. Motivational, you know? That'll be one of the quotes."

Pavlo responded in Russian because it was fun to speak hon-
estly and see only confusion. "Your tongue is not a teacher. Is a
cave for flies to breed because your mouth is always open. Put
that in the book you won't live to finish."

Andy looked over. "Huh? How much for the biologist? Who
is the guy?"

That got an indifferent shrug from the bony six-six killer
who, Sunday morning, while scouting Tampa Bay, had popped
two FWC cops just for the hell of it. Last night he had bragged
about how much his GoPro video "art" was worth.

"Freedom is reward," Pavlo said in English. "Is politics in
motherland. Diplomat games. The Brotherhood. You not smart
enough to—"

Andy balled his fist. "Kiss my butt. Try me. Freedom, you
mean like—what're you talking about? Freedom for both of us?
I don't get it."

You will, Friar Pavlo thought. *You all will.* His mind slipped back to Belarus, to his church, the Monastery of the Holy Spirit where he'd studied as a novitiate. He had unfinished business with a priest who'd schooled him on the Book of John. What fun it would be to cruise the Minsk spiderweb again as a free man.

That kind of freedom, this American fool would never understand.

"Oh, damn...now what?" In the side mirror, Andy saw flashing blue strobes, no siren yet, but coming fast from behind. "Goddamn cop car, he's gonna pull us over. What should we... No, I know what to do. Stay cool. But wait—" he remembered the blonde woman who lay bound, gagged beneath the tarp in the boat they were towing "—I told you we should've put her in the camper. Christ—in this heat? She's probably dead by now. Damn. We're screwed."

Pavlo said, "Go faster." The idiot American was slowing, steering off the road where there were boarded-up stores, a bank, a 7-Eleven.

"It's stupid to run, I mean, come on. What's the use? I'm in charge, remember." Andy gave the Russian a look. "I haven't killed anyone. The worst they can get me for is—"

"Faster," Pavlo ordered softly.

"Screw you. Use your brains for once. Christ, the way it's raining, the cop'll probably just ask for my license. Relax."

For three days and nights—in a parking lot near Homosassa, then Bullfrog Creek, Gibsonton, on Tampa Bay—Pavlo had tolerated this whining American's indecision. One way or the other, this would be the end of it. He swung his leg over the gearshift and tromped the accelerator to the floor. Boat and trailer fishtailed as the truck sped toward a three-way stop, no traffic on the road, but—

"Hey, *dumbass*. Get your foot off." Andy was wrestling the steering wheel.

Pavlo pulled his leg away. "Turn right, don't stop. Go, go, go."

They lurched through another intersection, straight ahead

onto a shell road framed by trees. Pavlo, his eyes on the GPS, navigated. To the left was a steel gate, *Dinkin's Bay Marina* on the signpost. A sharp right turn took them down what looked like a driveway but dead-ended at a narrow canal and a narrower boat ramp.

No sign, yet, of the cop behind them when they skidded to a stop in the blinding rain.

"Maybe we lost him. Or he was on another call that—"

"Shut up." Pavlo threw the door open, got out armed with an AK and a pistol on his belt. He motioned to a hedge of rubbery-looking trees. "Unhook trailer, turn truck around. I hide there and watch. Hurry."

Andy froze until the AK swung toward his face. He got out, popped the trailer's ball hitch and cranked the tongue higher, hoping the unconscious woman beneath the tarp wouldn't wake up.

"Don't make a sound, you bitchy little ice queen," he muttered. "Stay quiet or that freak will kill us both."

He was backing the camper truck clear when, at the entrance to the boat ramp, the green-on-white squad car appeared. It turned left and disappeared toward the Dinkin's Bay Marina sign. Seconds later, tires spun, and the cruiser charged in Reverse to block the camper's path.

"Step out of the vehicle. Let me see your hands." A cop's amplified voice over a loudspeaker.

Andy did it. Put a pleasant smile on his face—the obedient solid citizen—while the Russian moved catlike through the trees and pouring rain. No...more like a prehistoric bird on stilts. Stalking, no wasted effort.

The cop approached, gun drawn. He was a fit-looking redhead in a rain slicker, no hat and a brass nameplate that read *Deputy Kahn.*

"Afternoon, Officer Kahn. Geez... I saw your flashers back

there. Figured you were on a call, so I tried to get the hell out of the way. Was it me you wanted to stop?"

"Turn, face the vehicle."

Andy had been through this drill several times—DUIs, tax evasion, fraud, jumping bail. He knew what would happen if he didn't comply. He also knew it meant prison if he didn't lie his ass out of this nightmare.

"Officer, I've got ID. Mind if I reach into the glove box and get my—"

"Sir, I'm not going to tell you again. Face the vehicle, hands behind your head. Do you live on the island? Why'd you run?"

Christ, now the cop was snooping around the boat, which was no longer attached to the truck. Andy's legs began to tremble, worried the blonde would wake up. Or, worse, was dead because of what he'd done the last two nights to make the ice queen bitch doable if not willing.

He said to the cop, "I'm sorry. Like I told you, if you were on an important call, I thought the, uhh…the prudent thing, yeah, was to get the heck out of your way. I've never been in any kind of trouble in my life. Seriously, I'm a big supporter of law enforcement. You people do a heck of a job."

"Thank you. Is this your boat?"

On Andy's office wall was another motivational slogan: *Go Big or Go Broke!*

He took a breath.

"Sure wish it was, Officer Khan. No, it belongs to Florida Fish and Wildlife. Call them, they'll tell you. The head people in Tallahassee. My agency—I'm in insurance—they told me to drop the boat here. Sorry I was in such a hurry, but there's a heck of a hurricane coming. That's what I was told to do. Deliver the boat and get back to the mainland fast as possible."

The cop seemed to buy that. He holstered his weapon. "Was it stolen?"

"The boat? Yep, that's my understanding. I don't know, somehow it ended up in our repo lot. Like I said, any chance to help law enforcement. Why else would I be standing out here getting soaked?" Andy laughed as he said it, hoping the cop would take the damn hint.

"What's your name, sir?"

Andy had provided his team with a dozen fake IDs, all from FP&L Utilities, and all with the same fake name. Which was stupid according to the oligarch genius but, damn it, he'd been in a hurry, and just try spelling all those complicated Russian names.

"Donald. Donny Orlando," Andy said. "Officer, I'm 'bout to damn near drown in this rain. Think we can wrap this up?"

"Give me a minute."

"Can I at least sit in my truck?"

"Sorry, sir. This won't take long."

When the cop turned away, Andy's eyes found Pavlo, who had slipped into the trees near the squad car. His AK rifle tracked the cop. The cop glanced back...he stopped with one hand on his driver's-side door as if he'd heard something.

Andy heard it, too. A mewing, kicking sound from inside the stolen FWC vessel.

Shit. He waved to the Russian and mouthed the words, *Do it now!*

Everything slowed down after that. Vivid images...freeze-frames. Pavlo stepping out... BAM... The look of surprise on the cop's face, blood splattered, as he jolted backward into the driver's seat. The cop scrambling to close the door. Scrambling to draw his weapon. BANG. A second shot shattered the driver's-side window. Tires spun, hurled a spray of mud and shells. The squad car peeled out, the door flapping like a broken wing. It skidded left, right, then straightened itself, the cop at the wheel but hunched over, maybe dying in a silver waterfall haze.

That's what Andy hoped.

He hollered to Pavlo, "Yeah, that's what I'm talking about, dude! Now let's get the hell out of here."

Still in slow motion, the Russian, grinning, stork-walked toward the camper, rifle raised.

"Hey man, Grigori... Don't point that... What are you—"

Andy told himself, *Run*, but his legs wouldn't move. Like in a nightmare, the stork-walking monk, skull shaved bare on top, the GoPro blinking on his forehead, kept coming.

"Dude, we're on the same team, man. I bet that cop's on the radio calling for backup right now. We don't have time to—"

In the distance, a car collided with something, a tree or a metal gate. The engine revved, a screaming noise, tires struggling for purchase, then went silent.

Pavlo looked down the barrel at the trembling American. "Get down...move. Down on knees, you silly little peasant."

Andy, hands raised, still couldn't make his legs move. "Sure, anything. We can work this out. You know, come to a consensus. Consensus, that's always best. Just don't kill me. *Please?*"

The stork-monk laughed at that. "Storm will do that for me, yes? Or I kill later. No matter. Now is time for fun."

He was unwrapping something—a medical transfusion bag, it looked like. Like in movies. Plastic with tubes.

"On your knees like girl, little man," said the Russian. Then asked, "What is blood type you are?"

15

Outside beneath the lab's leeward overhang, on my cell phone, I told Max Weatherby, "Hang on...did you hear that?"

We listened in the silence of sporadic rain, him in his house at the mouth of Dinkin's Bay.

"Sounded like... Could be a transformer exploded," he guessed.

A gunshot is what I'd heard. Even a distant report has an edge, like a steel pipe hammering steel.

I was about to say this when the lights in the lab flickered.

"Power just failed here," Weatherby said. "A transformer... yes, must have been. How about your place?"

A second report, muffled by wind, didn't convince me. Then the lab went dark. Below deck, the generator's auto-start strained to full RPMs. Porch lights flared on brighter than before.

"Guess you're right," I replied. We'd been talking about the car he'd seen more than an hour ago. A Jeep four-door had pulled into his neighbor's drive, sat there for a few minutes, then did a slow retreat. Max hadn't seen it since.

"You didn't recognize the Jeep?"

"One of those big-tire deals," he said. "The kind you Americans seem to love. Can't tell one from another, personally. My concern, of course, was they were scouting the area. Especially my neighbors—a delightful couple, the Lászlos. They live alone."

"The jewelry store people," I said.

"Ben, Rebecca and their prize poodle. They're elderly. He's in a wheelchair. Family tried to convince them to evacuate, but Eastern Europeans can be quite a stubborn lot."

Maybe it was lucky, I remarked, they had a physician next door.

"Well, let's hope that isn't necessary. All the other neighbors are gone. This morning, what I assume were Secret Service checked out the VP's place. Then went to a house three properties down. I haven't been here long enough to know all the owners' surnames—diplomatic service, or so it's rumored. They left last week."

I said, "From Singapore, I think. The family must have some political juice to rate that kind of attention. The S–S guys didn't check on you?"

"Raffles Hotel," the physician/inventor replied fondly. "Best breakfast in Singapore. I must meet them after this damn monsoon business. What? Secret Service bother with me? Hah. Not bloody likely."

This was a potential opening. Raffles Hotel, Singapore, where I'd stayed many times, was only a few miles from the Russian Embassy. But I didn't want to risk a clumsy segue to the subjects of foreign service and Moscow. Not until I knew more about the man's niece. This required some probing.

"With the island evacuated," I said, "houses along your stretch of beach will look like easy targets. I bet your family's worried. Did you call the police?"

"About the Jeep? Immediately. No response, and I don't expect one. Not now. Not for twenty-four hours or so. Ford, my friend, have you noticed the time? I'm afraid it's just you, me and the Lászlos—unless you get in that truck of yours right now. Unlikely authorities will bar you from the mainland if you hurry."

My truck? I hadn't mentioned owning a truck. From my pocket I removed a palm-sized night vision monocular but didn't activate the switch. Fourth-generation.

It was a few minutes after the evacuation deadline. To the west, sunset was a boiling leaden smear. Clouds leached light but left no shadows. A triad of wading birds—egrets, ibis— soared past, white feathers dung-stained by dusk. They banked low toward a leeward ledge of mangroves already claimed by several pelicans.

I said, "Maybe it won't be as bad as predicted. The local bird population doesn't seem to be too worried. You have any birders in the family?"

His niece, I hoped, was the Audubon type. Brits often were. No luck.

A more direct approach was to ask why he expected to be robbed and if he had a firearm ready in case it happened.

This got a chuckle. "A gun? Me? I'm from the UK, remember? And certainly not the type that hunts people rather than grouse."

I put the NVM to my eye and flipped the switch. "I'd be happy to drop off a loaner if you're interested. Shotgun or pistol, whatever you want, plus ammunition. My boat's been secured but, tell you what, the wind's not too bad yet. I'm leaving now. Maybe have that whiskey you mentioned."

The man went silent. Two miles away, from high on a crow's nest deck, a smoky green laser pierced the twilight and found the deck where I stood. Thermal technology. A red beam found me, too. Infrared. Invisible to the human eye. But not to a night optic device.

I put a smile in my voice. "Dr. Weatherby, are you checking to make sure my heart's beating? Or is that laser attached to a target acquisition scope?"

The lights vanished.

He started to deny it, then gave up. "Apologies, my friend. Just curious—and cautious. I have no firearms, that much I can assure you."

"Too bad. You should. I can be there in ten minutes."

"Generous, but entirely out of the—" Weatherby muted the phone, distracted by something. A noise in the background. Static and a woman's voice, it sounded like, perhaps from a radio. He returned, saying, "Must say, I'm a tad taken aback by your technology. Rather sheepish, like a schoolboy caught peeping. What NODs system are you using?"

A MUM-14, gen-four, I told him, a type of Night Optics Device.

"Ah yes, the Arizona company. Guess I shouldn't be surprised. Cards on the table time, wouldn't you say? You've obviously searched my name. I did the same."

"I'm not a particularly interesting guy," I said. "Not compared to ThermoRaker Ltd. Very impressive. Passive temperature screening. Thermal cameras and lasers and something—I read this—something called 'augmented reality' weapons systems. Does that have something to do with drones?"

He responded, "And the internet has next to nothing at all on you, Dr. Ford. Which I find interesting, indeed. Now please, a gun. Why do you think I might need a gun? I can't help but wonder if you have sources who…well, it would be bad form to ask."

"I'm not a stickler for form. Ask away," I said.

It was an offer and a trap that the physician/inventor nimbly dodged.

"I've read too many novels, I suppose. But this gun business. There must be a reason you're convinced we'll be targeted. By whom?"

"Anyone with a boat and the balls to risk a few miles of nasty water in the dark," I said.

"I was hoping for an answer less vague. You're talking about tomorrow afternoon. Wait—or tonight?"

"Could be—unless they're already here. I'm thinking about that Jeep. It could've been some locals who hadn't evacuated yet. But maybe not."

This surprised him. He hadn't considered the possibility...or was he surprised because I had?

I said, "The wind's only twenty to twenty-five, which is do-able in the bay. A fast boat could get in and out before—but I don't know. That would be cutting it way too close for thieves. By midnight, wind'll be forty knots and a hundred-plus by noon. So, my guess is late tomorrow, after the eye passes, the first looters will show up."

Once again, the Brit was distracted by a garbled voice in the background. I said, "Okay, look... Come on, Max, is someone with you? Cards on the table, you said. Tell the truth about why you're staying. Just between us."

His response was a veiled admission.

"What an odd thing to say. My radios are on scan, so of course you hear traffic. But yes, quite right. If we're to ride out this blow together, perhaps we should both be more forthcoming. And more mindful of security. How's your C-W?"

This was a ham abbreviation for Morse code.

"Nonexistent. But I have software that translates and sends C-W. Does the hard part for me. In terms of security, though... well, face it, the bad guys, if they're serious, have it, too."

"But much harder to jam," the physician/inventor countered. "The bad guys, as you call them, do you have any idea who we might be dealing with?"

"You suspect a jamming device?"

"It's a tech-savvy world, my friend. So, satellite phones are a poor choice as well. Never mind solar flares during a hurricane."

"Then I think you already know who the bad guys are, Max.

Name the C-W frequency and we'll trade information. Say in thirty?"

"Well done, you," he said and hung up.

I had just crossed the breezeway and opened the door to the lab when my cell rang. "You've got company." It was the Brit again. "A vehicle moving toward the marina gate. Just the driver, looks like, but I can't be certain."

As he spoke, headlights, coming fast, panned the tree line that led to the parking lot. Pete awoke, trotted to my side, his growl a series of fart-like grunts.

"Geezus, Max. A heat signature ping from two miles away?" I didn't add, *Including through a wall of trees.* "Why are you really here?"

"Steady on, Ford. A little invention of mine—thermal imaging radar. Portable. Easy to calibrate. The car's most likely law enforcement. VHF radio signature, too. Don't do anything rash—not without including me in the fun."

"Fun. Right." I started to add, "I'm carrying a handheld—" when the vehicle crashed through the parking lot gate. I didn't see. I heard it. Mangroves blocked my view. Several seconds later a second vehicle roared closer, a heavy diesel engine. "Stand by, channel twenty-two," I told the Brit and started down the steps.

"Marine VHF? That's a Coast Guard emergency channel, yes. I can dial that in on single sideband—but there might be eavesdroppers, as you know."

"Give me a few, Max. I'll check it out and get back. No more cell contact for now, okay?"

I unholstered a Sig Sauer P-365, a palm-sized 9mm semi, and took my time crossing the boardwalk to shore. Headlights glazed treetops in a misting silver rain. The vehicle's engine was off. Or it had stalled. And the heavier diesel vehicle was gone.

Stay—a hand command to the dog. Rather than exit the path, I used mangroves as a screen before peeking out.

A familiar squad car, green on white, was there, driver's-side door open. Mud on the shattered windshield wasn't mud. In a sandy puddle, on his side, lay a man in uniform, his red buzz cut distinctive. Deputy Kahn of Palm Beach County had been shot one or more times in the face or head.

How the hell had he managed to drive blind with those wounds? He couldn't have come far. I knelt, found a faint pulse and radioed a VHF distress call for help.

The physician/inventor, from his base unit, came back saying, "Are you alright? Talk to me, Ford. Just in case, I repeated your mayday to Coast Guard Fort Myers Beach. What happened?"

We went back and forth. The physician/inventor took charge.

"Is he breathing? Roll him over. Direct pressure if you can, then CPR."

More light was needed. A pocket LED helped. Deputy Kahn's sidearm was gone. The squad car's interior had been ransacked in haste, radio wires cut. Somehow, though, they'd missed the body cam. It lay on the floor near the accelerator. They'd also left a first-aid kit, which I opened.

Weatherby didn't need to remind me that emergency responders had left the island more than an hour ago.

"Someone has to be looking for this guy," I said. "He would've radioed his location before making a—" I did another set of chest compressions. A bloody bubble exited the deputy's lips. I noticed his right hand—two missing fingers. A defensive wound. Or had they been snipped?

"Geezus, an evac chopper is what we need. Try nine-one-one. He's still alive. Not much else I can do, man." To the deputy I urged, "Stay with me, pal. Damn it, you have to live or they'll suspect I did this."

My handheld squawked. A woman's voice entered the conversation.

"Doc, you copy? It's me, uh…Lieutenant Tupplemeyer. We already have a chopper out there searching. Where are you? Deputy Kahn's transponder went dead about—"

I interrupted, "Birdy? Are you at Hannah's place?"

"Damn it, Doc, she's fine. Your kid's fine. Now pay attention. If the wind hits forty, our people can't land, so we're running out of time. What's the closest LZ?"

Ten minutes later, they loaded Deputy Kahn onto an evac Bell. Wind had dropped to an eerie calm, unnoticed because of the chopper's tornadic blades.

A plainclothes cop of some type had to shout for me to hear. "Last chance, Dr. Ford. No offense, but you're a fool if you stay. Grab your gear and let's go."

Again, I asked, "Who was the shooter?"

"Huh?"

I had to raise my voice. "The shooter. Kahn's dashcam, your telemetry system, your people have checked video by now I hope. He's missing fingers." I thrust out a hand as if to block a gunshot. "He saw it coming."

The cop acknowledged an EMT's "leaving-in-five" warning. "Look, sir, if I wanted, I could handcuff you and take you in for questioning. The weather window's closing—an hour at most, we'll all be gone. I'd be doing you a favor."

I didn't bother saying that, were I a suspect, I'd already be in cuffs.

"And the shooter will still be here. I'd like to know what I'm dealing with."

"That's what I'm trying to get through your head." Now we were talking guy to guy. "There's some bad shit going down on this island. Okay? So either get aboard or go home right now. Then lock the doors and stay there, or I'll come back after the storm and arrest you myself."

Six miles to the west, a second chopper, low altitude, panned the Blind Pass area with a spotlight.

"You're searching the wrong area."

"Say again?"

I pointed. "They're way the hell off. With a head wound,

Kahn couldn't have made it this far. But there's a private boat ramp a quarter mile from here. You want to find the shooter? Maybe that missing FWC officer, too? Contact that pilot, I'll guide him in."

The cop noticed my handheld radio. He took out his phone. "What's your cell number? We gotta go, but I'll pass the information along. Our crime scene people might be in touch, too. They've got to be in and out fast."

A midsized Bell kicks up sixty-, seventy-knot winds during liftoff. Crushed shell, sand, parking lot debris spun a stinging reminder of what was to come.

In the distance, the search chopper levitated and turned. A blazing white funnel glided toward Dinkin's Bay and the LED strobe I'd activated. My VHF had no access to aircraft channels, so the navigator and I, via text, settled on a two-meter frequency.

A quarter mile east of the marina, the chopper hovered, descended, lights blinking, into an illuminated cone of white. A homemade boat ramp was there with enough room to land. Nearby was the tarp-covered boat I'd seen earlier. I stood, I watched them load an unconscious female onto a gurney. My offer to help was refused.

By eight thirty, soaked, muddy, but not tired, I was back at the lab. I stripped, used the outdoor shower, water hot compared to bands of sideways rain.

The dog and cat were fed, and I had started the propane stove when my cell buzzed. Prying off a sheet of plywood had improved reception—a temporary fix that allowed me to stay inside and dry. On the counter, a Coleman lantern served as backup to the fickle Briggs & Stratton downstairs.

Hannah's voice said, "Thank God you were still on the island, Marion. You saved her, you saved that poor FWC officer. You didn't get hurt, did you?"

"No, I'm— Who've you been talking to?"

"Birdy. She didn't tell me everything. She can't. She didn't call you?"

"On the VHF, yeah. On the phone, you mean? How's the lady FWC officer doing? I know they found her."

"After what some guy did to her—or guys, I'm not sure—she's in bad shape, but still alive, thanks to you. That's what Birdy said—to thank you. Odd she didn't call. Now I'm worried about Birdy."

"Not much you can do from there. How is it? How's North Carolina?"

"The mountains smell like acorns, and folks serve tea on a tray," Hannah said. "Fancy. Our suite's got a hot tub and a great big shower with sprinkler heads from…let's say unusual directions." Her laughter was husky. "Too bad you're not here to enjoy it."

It had been a while since I'd heard warm, suggestive talk from my fiancée.

"Sounds inviting. You'd be okay with that?"

"Marion, I've got a courtesy bar and a Jacuzzi in a hotel full of strangers. All alone, just me, and Izaak's due for a nap. You helped save that woman's life, so what do you think?"

"I didn't save anyone, but I'm an idiot for staying here—that's what I think. Loretta's not with you?"

She explained that her cantankerous mother had caused a last-minute fuss by demanding to get off the plane. By then, flight attendants were all too happy to expedite matters. Loretta had been assisted into an Uber and sent to Fort Myers to stay with Captain Arlis, her nephew, Luke, and friends. Hannah and our baby son, Izaak, had taken the next flight, which was to Charlotte, not Durham.

"That's why I was so late checking in," Hannah continued. "I called Birdy right away to warn her Mama might show up at the house the day after tomorrow—you know, depending on the storm. But Birdy had to hang up real sudden like because someone was at the door. I heard the knocking."

"When was this?"

"Twenty minutes ago. Why would a person go to my place the night before a hurricane hits? Last thing I told her was, call you."

Hannah, the boat captain, was thinking about the SUV and the stranger with an accent.

"Doc, what's the weather like?"

At the counter I squeezed fresh lime onto snapper fillets frying in a pan. Wind and rain were cycling again, blustery, then calm, followed by gusts that shook the house.

"Bad and getting worse. Yeah, I could make it to your place by boat and check on her, but I'd never make it back."

"I wasn't asking, Marion."

"Don't blame you if you were. Look, Birdy's a deputy sheriff. It was probably another cop in the driveway. Or a local wanting to park on the highest ground around."

"That's what worries me."

"Understandable. So, what I'll do is hail her on VHF, and the two of us will stay in touch during the storm. How's that sound? Cell service won't last much longer. Keep that in mind if I don't answer."

"My Lord...don't know when I became such a fretter. I've been checking flights, thinking maybe I'll fly home after the storm early if it's possible. Sarasota if not Fort Myers. Hey—you didn't answer my question. Are you okay?"

In the breezeway, shielded from the weather, a second lantern provided a beacon if Deputy Khan's shooter hadn't fled the island. It was my version of a tethered goat. Holstered on my side was a Sig P-226 loaded with twenty-one rounds of Hornady Critical Duty. A Mossberg tactical twelve-gauge was secured by magnets beneath the table.

I replied, "Never better now that you and Izaak are safe.

Relax, stay there, enjoy the Jacuzzi and the fancy shower. Stop worrying, lady—but thanks for the invitation."

Dinnertime. I moved the Coleman to the table, sat alone and ate fried snapper, and wondered about the heavy diesel vehicle I'd heard drive away after Deputy Khan had been ambushed.

Russian mercenaries were to blame, I had no doubt. But had the mercs escaped to the mainland? Or were they still somewhere nearby?

16

After he'd shot the cop and left that fool, Andy Dimitry, to die in tomorrow's storm, Pavlo drove the tricked-out diesel camper across the Causeway to the mainland just before a deadline that forbade traffic on or off the island.

Deputies stationed at the toll booth gave him a cheerful wave and ignored his middle finger salute.

Americans were so damn soft. Floridians, worse. Good roads, too much food and no snow—or so he'd been told. This was hard to imagine after a life spent freezing his balls off in church housing and prisons, or trenches on the Crimean Peninsula. He wondered how Floridians would fare if they'd had to follow the Ural River, on foot, mostly, through five hundred kilometers of ice and mountains to the Caspian Sea. Then, thanks to a freighter owned by the Brotherhood, halfway around the world to Venezuela, which also had palm trees but was a shithole of peasants and amateur criminals.

Bratva—the Brotherhood. Pavlo had survived the group's initiation because, as a novitiate who'd been charged with murder, he'd had no choice but to join. Key members—black marketeers, porn traffickers, a judge, others—had kept him out of jail until even they were horrified by what he'd done to a nun... Well, the memory of that was so satisfying, Pavlo decided to save the details for later when he was in the camper alone with whatever new toy he could find.

And he would. Already, he had a target in mind, a woman who lived in an old house so high on a hill there was no risk of flooding when the storm hit. Hills were rare in this swampy, flatland state, but Sasha's men had scouted the area earlier.

Aleksandr "Sasha" Olegovich—one of the early members of the Brotherhood—had provided military-looking rubber boats stolen from somewhere in the Florida Keys. No numbers, no tags and poorly equipped. But that was okay. The boats were throw-aways—another kind of freedom. The boats were waiting near the woman's house now on an island, Gumbo Limbo, a village called Sulphur Wells, an hour's drive by road. By water, though, only a few miles from the millionaires' island he'd just left.

Pavlo took this as a divine blessing. In the motherland, there was a saying about fate and the will of God: *With mystic guidance, events meant to happen cannot be stopped by mortal man.*

The failed novitiate didn't think of himself as mortal. Angels lived inside his brain, soft voices that provided guidance. His hands could heal or kill with a touch. What doctors called "self-mutilation" was approved by his angels and the church, too, as "corporal mortification." To Pavlo, it was a purifying proof of devotion. He had used fire, razors, a meat saw once, to chastise his own body, then sutures and a blood transfusion kit to bring his mortal soul back from the abyss.

In military terms, the world was a walking blood bank. The army had supplied empty drip bags that contained an anticoagulant. Ready to be filled from the blood of the dying.

Pavlo's ultimate fantasy—as demonstrated by the Orthodox Skoptsy—was ceremonial castration. This he had done to other men in a testing, experimental way that had hinted a dizzying euphoria awaited. Earlier, back where he'd shot the cop, Andy Dimitry had provided a different sort of euphoria. Because of the Causeway closing, though, there had been only time enough to enjoy an oral gift and to drain the little fool of a liter of blood.

Type O. *Perfect.*

Ahead was a roadblock on this fast, four-lane road. Several police cars, flashing lights and barriers. The camper's GPS wanted to go straight, but he hit the blinker and, at a stoplight, took the turn lane to avoid trouble.

It was because of Dimitry. The fool had provided their team with fake identification cards that looked pretty good except they all bore the same stupid name, *Donald Orlando.* The American was no genius, but my God, why choose Florida's Disney World city? That was just dumb.

The light changed. Pavlo turned left onto Davidson Road, which took him off course through acres of tin can housing. Rows of trailers boarded up, deserted because of the storm. Easy targets if there'd been anything worth stealing, which there wasn't, and now...damn...he was lost.

Right side of the road were one-story tenements, adobe brown built low to the ground. Kids' toys, trash, a couple of rusty trucks. Working on one of the trucks was a huge Mexican-looking guy while a teenage mother, who was nursing a baby, watched from the apartment's open door.

Pavlo *loved* young mothers. They tasted so sweet; so milky. He stopped, lowered the window. His Spanish was better than his English after six months in Venezuela.

"Excuse me, friend. Which is faster? To get back to the main highway, should I go straight or turn around?"

The Mexican-looking guy approached. A wary, tough-guy expression on his face that was not bullshit. Pavlo had been around enough to tell.

"Where you headed, amigo?" the Mexican asked in English. A tat on his forearm read *Big Sammy*.

Pavlo made eye contact with the young, milk swollen Indio-looking girl in the doorway. "My Spanish is not so…it is shit, I am sorry. Anywhere north to get away from that *puta* of a storm. The interstate, I guess." He reached beneath the seat and found Dimitry's fancy Glock nine, seventeen rounds in the mag, while adding, "Do you and your wife need a ride? Or your daughter, possibly—no offense. I can drop you anywhere you want. Plenty of room. And lots of cold beer. My name is Donald. What is your name, friend?"

The Mexican had been ready to smile, but his eyes transitioned into feral reassessment. Pavlo realized he'd pushed too hard, too fast. *Damn.* But the guy's chest, his belly, were right there, an easy target through the open window.

Shoot the guy and drag the young mother into the camper for later. That's what the voices, his angels were telling him, and he would have obeyed if his cell hadn't chimed.

It was Sasha, the East Coast oligarch, calling on their private burners.

"You are very lucky," Pavlo said to the Mexican in Russian. "I would've used your wife as a sacrament. Perhaps tomorrow, after the storm?"

Big Sammy, not smiling in the rearview mirror, was noting the license number when Pavlo drove away.

Sasha wanted to go over last-minute details and changes in their plans.

"You are alone?"

"Of course, Lord Comrade. That's, you know, what we agreed when I use this phone. What is the latest update?"

They discussed the hurricane. It was expected to hit north of the island he had just left, but the eye was gigantic, almost fifty kilometers wide.

"The best possible news. A direct hit—the equivalent," the oligarch said. "This could be more profitable than we dreamed. Which is why I have streamlined our plans. Confidential, of course."

Pavlo said, "Not to be shared with the men. Understood."

"No one. Especially that buffoon. Where is he?"

"Dimitry? I left him on the island like you, well, like you ordered; left him with the policewoman who—"

The oligarch cut in, "I don't want to know who he's with. Does he have a vehicle?"

"That's what I was about to say. No. Just a...boat on the trailer that's parked where you ordered. He can't get across the bridge in time, if that's your concern. There is a marina near the spot. And one of the names on your list—a biologist. I told Dimitry if he dealt with that issue personally, he might be rewarded—"

"Don't worry about Anatoli," Sasha said. "He means nothing. But you, your talent for...your artistry for recording certain events. The dark money. We are very pleased with the recent product you've sent." The old man paused. Ice tinkled in a crystal glass. "You did not explain any of this to—"

Pavlo cut in, "To no one. Especially not to him. I hope my little hobby is profitable." He was referring to the dark market film industry based in Cyprus, another Brotherhood stronghold.

Sasha said, "Thus far, a nice addition, but don't rest on your laurels. And you're right, I doubt Anatoli's brains and courage even if he does manage to survive what tomorrow brings. This I share only with you. The mysteries of blood and genetics are God's little joke. Anatoli's grandmother, my God, in her day, I tell you, the woman had the most beautiful—" Sasha had a smoky, jailhouse laugh "—impossible, though, that a fool like Anatoli could be our—"

Grandson, the old man decided not to say.

He finally got back to how plans had changed.

"After the storm, you must get in and out quickly, and I've

thought of a better way. For instance, it is a four-hour drive from where you are to my location. Across the state, traffic will be backed up, some roads impassable. Do you know what I'm thinking? I'm looking at the answer right now. You are the man who deserves a reward. Within two days, we'll both be out of the country."

Pavlo could picture the former MiG pilot on his patio, smoking, drinking vodka, the penthouse view with a helicopter landing pad, an old man who wasn't too old to enjoy the joystick and pulling puppeteer strings.

"I think you are looking at a shiny black bird with propellers. Very smart, Lord Comrade." Pavlo knew his role—for now, anyway. Deference to this elder. Let Sasha be the genius. Let him embrace the pretense that they shared devotion to the old ways of the Brotherhood.

"Exactly. But there will be room only for you, the pilot—me, of course—and the most select items that you and your men recover. Travel light and fast like cavalry during the time of your great ancestor."

"I'm honored," Pavlo said and added several more kiss-ass compliments. He turned left and crossed a bridge on his way to a second, smaller bridge that led to Gumbo Limbo, the island where his men and the boats awaited. "Comrade Sasha," he said—a risky familiarity—"that name on the list I mentioned. The biologist. Are you aware that his wife and son live near our deployment area?"

"I know. Of course I know. There are no coincidences," the oligarch said, taking credit for it all. But he shared a hint of credit by repeating a familiar Russian maxim: *With mystic guidance, events meant to happen cannot be stopped by mortal man.*

"Does this surprise you?" The old man gave this a dramatic pause. "It does not surprise me considering your ancestor. Your genetics—Grigori Pavlo *Raspitin.*"

In Russia, patronymic family names were always spoken last.

The Latinized version was still revered in the secret orthodox-
ies of the Brotherhood. Even a century later, the mystic priest,
advisor to the czar, was whispered to be a dark angel. Immor-
tal, some believed.

Grigori Rasputin.

After dark, Pavlo snuck through trees to the back of the house
where the biologist's wife and kid supposedly lived when not
staying on the barrier island. Tall as he was, he still had to stand
on tiptoes to peek into a bedroom window because the place sat
braced on short, old-time concrete pilings, a one-story structure
with a screened wraparound porch.

A ceiling fan, bed made, polished wood floors. An expensive crib, an excess of toys suspended above. On the wall hung
an ornate plaque:

IGFA World Record
Capt. Hannah Smith
Megalops Atlanticus
Fly Rod Category
Four-Pound Tippet

Captain? Ha! A woman with an ego. Wealthy. How else could
a mother afford to waste her time with such games? Certainly
not a real naval captain.

Pavlo grinned his contempt and moved to the side of the
house. He wore a holster and carried a bag containing duct tape,
rope and a stainless butcher's saw. The wind canceled fears of
being heard. And if the woman confronted him, so what? He
would have fun now instead of waiting for the storm.

This wild, rainy night belonged to him, alone in the camper.
His men had retreated to an empty Publix parking lot. Most
residents in this little fishing village on the bay had evacuated. A
few lights were on at a commercial marina a hundred yards down

the road, but that place was deserted, too. Tomorrow afternoon, when the wind lessened, they would use the boat ramp there.

Get in and out fast, the old oligarch had said. *Travel light.* Pavlo was not clear exactly what that meant, but in his head, he already knew how it would go. When the worst of the storm was past, he would cross the bay with three boats and three mercenary teams. On the return, he'd be alone, just him, in the largest rubber transport. After his land-based flunkies had off-loaded items into the camper, he would lighten up some more.

The second bedroom he peered into was also empty. On the nightstand, open, lay a large old-fashioned Bible. He had a fetish for religious people, especially attractive females. The Bible caused a hopeful stirring in his thighs. What he saw in the closet, though, didn't mesh with a young, outdoorsy mother. The clothes were frumpy, out-of-date dresses, a couple of cheap wigs, too.

An old person lived here. But he'd seen the framed award on the wall. This had to be the right house.

He moved along a porch that was screened and boarded—then stopped. Above his head, inches away, a woman was talking to someone, or was on the phone. He ducked, held his breath and peeked through a crack.

Christ…it was a woman in a sheriff's uniform. Small, short ginger hair, her service belt on a table, a walkie-talkie and a pistol with extra mags. To the right sat a dark-haired woman, and next to her another cop, a guy with shoulders. At his feet lay a police dog in a vest, a *K-9 Unit* badge embroidered in gold on the side.

A curtain of rain sharpened odors. Pointed ears twitched. Black eyes blinked open. The dog sat, back straight, and growled.

The male cop noticed. "Guys, quiet a sec," he said and gave some kind of hand signal.

The dog bounced to its feet and trotted to the crack in the

plywood, nose-to-nose for a moment with the Russian, the male cop saying, "Something's out there."

Pavlo thought, *Damn brute*. In the Crimea, he'd been taken down by a military Malinois before and never wanted to go through that shit again. He spun—finally noticed the squad car parked close to the other side of the house—and didn't stop until he was a quarter mile away, safe in the camper. And the camper *was* safe—another donation from the oligarch. The vehicle had been built by some YouTube tornado chasers who'd gone broke equipping the thing. Kevlar coating, windows probably bulletproof, a frame that could be anchored to the ground with six corkscrew spikes.

That's the first thing Pavlo did—anchored the camper before bolting the door, rolling a joint and opening a bottle of wine.

Nice. Cool with the AC on high, listening to Agata Kristi, freaky bong-smoking rockers from Moscow. Electronics inside had been gutted except for a VHF radio, a wind speed gauge and a viewing camera mounted atop the cab. A three-hundred-sixty-degree monitor that, by dawn, might confirm the squad car was gone—hopefully the cops and that damn dog with it.

Simple math: three minus two equaled one woman alone in the old house high on the nearby hill.

By midnight, rain was constant, wind gusts near fifty miles per hour. The failed novitiate smoked, he drank, he listened to his angel's voice promise there would be a lull tomorrow. That's when he would go to the house armed with rope and tape and a butcher's saw and abduct a new toy to use while he rode out the storm.

Before passing out, Pavlo reminded himself: *Put fresh batteries in the GoPro.*

17

Distress calls on channel sixteen became panicky after midnight when gusts exceeded fifty knots. Boaters who hadn't found shelter were desperate to retract their decisions.

I sat, listened and read an old leather-bound journal, the propane hiss of a lantern to my right. Often, I could hear only one side of the radio exchanges. The Coasties at Fort Myers Beach had evacuated, but Coast Guard St. Pete's megawattage came in loud and clear.

A fishing vessel, bayside, Siesta Key, had swamped, no people aboard. At Burnt Store Marina, twenty miles north, two or more yachts had snapped their lines and were crushing boats downwind.

The US Coast Guard is as good as it gets. But now? Not much even they could do.

Every few minutes, on forty meters, I keyed the mic and called repeatedly, "CQ, CQ, hailing the sailing vessel *No Más*. QSL? Tomlinson, do you copy?"

Negative contact.

Before the internet went down—and it would—I decided
to research Weatherby's reference to the combination of hurricanes and solar flares. Maybe the reason Tomlinson didn't respond was atmospheric.

In one source mentioned by the Brit, I read:

An unlucky coincidence of space and Earth weather in early Sep-
tember 2017 caused radio blackouts for hours during critical hurri-
cane emergency response efforts, according to a new study in Space
Weather, *a journal of the American Geophysical Union…*

I skipped to another source:

…NOAA's [Prediction Center] had warned of a strong radio
blackout over most of the sunlit side of Earth, including the Ca-
ribbean. [Days later] NOAA reported that high frequency radio,
used by aviation, maritime, ham radio, and other emergency bands,
was unavailable for up to eight hours.

The Brit inventor was right. And I felt a little better about
Tomlinson's silence.

My research continued until the Wi-Fi died. Then it was back
to my reading chair and listening to weather updates.

At 2:00 a.m. on VHF, channel three, an automated voice
warned: "Catastrophic winds and life-threatening storm surge
expected to flood the Florida peninsula, Naples to Englewood."

Crunch & Des heard me comment, "That storm's starting to
piss me off. Darn thing turned again. It's headed right for us."

I was making tea. The scarred-up old tomcat flicked an accusatory tail as if giving me the finger.

Around 5:00 a.m., there was an eerie change. A lightning
squall doused the island and sailed north, bolts of electric blue
visible through plywood cracks. Its passing muted the gale, a
stillness so abrupt I felt as if I might be sucked into a vacuum.

To the retriever, I said, "Move. Hit the deck. Now might be your last chance to pee for a while."

Outside was the darkness of a thousand years, a Florida that no longer existed. Trilling frogs, crickets, masked waves that crashed eight seconds apart. A lone exception was the historic lighthouse, a distant rotating beacon that ricocheted off low clouds.

The storm was out there, four hours from landfall. A bad one, my Mayan friend had taught me in Honduras.

On the other side of the Causeway, my Guatemalan friend, Cadmael, might be listening. Big Sammy, too, on a coast where most adults lay awake, bracing for impact at dawn.

By porch light I signaled Pete toward land. At the end of the walkway, he sniffed, he wind-scented, he froze on stiff legs and growled. I used the little LED flood. Mangroves came alive with reflective canine eyes. A pack of coyotes fanned out in attack formation.

"Pete, whoa," I hollered.

Too late. Pete—no bucket of rocks but single-minded—was already ashore, trotting toward the largest alpha male.

"Whoa. Come!" I unholstered the pistol and leveled it atop my flashlight hand.

No need.

The retriever hiked a regal leg and took a piss that arched toward the largest coyote's paws. The alpha male went scampering. The pack followed.

"Dumbass," I said to the retriever. "Here it comes again. Back inside."

The wind, I meant. A sudden gust bowled through the trees, a shotgun blast that nearly knocked me off my feet. After a six-second pause, another blast followed.

Pete, with great pomp, continued to piss and mark his territory. Then he did it again. Froze, ears alert, and growled.

I grabbed a rope safety line I'd rigged, deck to mangroves, and used the flashlight. Glowing eyes is what I expected. Instead, the path to the marina framed a man running, full strides. Running to safety or running to escape. Scared. If it was the cop shooter, he'd somehow been jettisoned from the heavy diesel vehicle I'd heard pull away.

I yelled, "Hey—hey you. Stop right there."

The man vanished, then reappeared from the darkness, fighting his way into the gale. He called something. "I need help," it sounded like, hand to the side of his head as if he had an earache.

With the light, I waved him closer. Pete, at a trot, intercepted the guy. Didn't bark or growl but with a spooky indifference. It was as if he might piss on this interloper, too.

"Hi! Goddamn, a real person," the man hollered. He was almost to the bell post at the walkway entrance. "Does your dog bite? Buddy, grab his collar or something."

A week ago, a stranger had asked Hannah the same question. I held the pistol behind my back. "They all bite. Mind showing me your hands?"

"Show you my— Jesus Christ," he answered, but complied. "Get that damn light out of my eyes. My car broke down, so I've gotta find a hotel." He removed a hand from his ear long enough to gesture toward the marina office. "Is that place down the road open? I'll pay cash."

The accent was East Coast tough guy, but monied, not redneck. He was short, balding, but with hair to his ears. The foul-weather jacket was L.L.Bean-quality, slacks, a muddy mess as if he'd hiked through a swamp. So, sure, he might have been a tourist with bad judgment. But he wasn't.

I lowered the LED while lightning pulsed above the trees. Either way, my next move was to invite the stranger inside. Take a closer look at the guy's face and go from there. I would have done it but was silenced by a low rumble that became thunderous, as if a diesel locomotive were speeding toward us. I'd heard the same sound as a teen before a Cat-Five had obliterated the Everglades villages of Mango and Chokoloskee.

The man spun around. "What the hell's that?"

I cupped my hands. "Tornado. Come on, let's get in the house."

"What?"

Air temp dropped. A roaring blast of icy wind caused the walkway to vibrate.

"Hurry up, a tornado!"

The man started toward me, then decided it was safer to sprint toward the marina when he remembered the dog.

I hollered for him to stop. He didn't, so I called, "Pete, come!"

The dog passed me going up the steps, the locomotive roar louder but to the west. I bolted the door. In the bedroom, a space in the plywood shutter became a view port. Lightning, multiple bursts, revealed an ascending vaporous funnel a mile away. It vented trash skyward and pushed the nitrous scent of ozone through the stilt house walls.

Later, on VHF, I told Weatherby, "We're not going anywhere until this is over." The tornado had given way to rain and gale winds, east-southeasterly. Radio volume was at max because of the deluge. "The guy I saw—the shooter, possibly—is stuck somewhere around here, too."

I'd already contacted an Amateur Radio Response volunteer stationed on the mainland about the tornado. She would do her best to alert residents of Gumbo Limbo, Punta Gorda and areas in the tornado's path.

Weatherby hadn't seen the funnel cloud. There were no cracks in his walls of automated shutters. But he had heard it and tracked the vortex to Charlotte Harbor before his rooftop weather station, along with cell service, had failed.

"Ford, describe the fellow you saw. Russian, you think? What about tattoos?"

Last night, via Morse encryption, the Brit hadn't referenced Black Dolphin Prison, nor had he confirmed his ties to MI6. These two questions did.

I scratched the cat's ears and pressed the mic key. "Negative. American. East Coast, Jersey or Philadelphia, possibly." I gave that time to sink in. "If he hasn't blown away by now, he either broke into my truck or the marina office. Is your thermal gadget operational?"

"Copy that, stand by. I'll take a quick peek, and you tell me."

Rain pelted the metal roof. Wind tested the soffits experimentally, seeking entrance and leverage to rip the rafters away.

Weatherby returned. "CQ, Ford. Confirm, please, that you're in the main room of your home."

I did.

"Good. Rain doesn't help, but early morning hours, particularly before dawn, provide excellent thermal contrast. Yet, rather curious. It appears someone is with you. Another heat source. Body temp high. Hundred-and-one-plus Fahrenheit. Is your stove on?"

I had to think for a moment. "I'll be damned, that's my dog. There's a cat, too. Remarkable, Max. Really. What about the guy?"

"Negative thus far. Your vehicle, I suspect, is shielded by your home. The marina, the main building, is it cement block or wood? Never mind. I'll scan the windows again. Back in a tick."

The stranger was in the office, ground floor, the physician/inventor reported. Pacing and smoking a cigar or cigarette that burned at five hundred degrees centigrade. Shortwave infrared had been required to collect this data.

Weatherby added, "He's trapped, so all's hunky-dory for now. I'll keep an eye on him and check back. Think he was the one who, uhh, confronted the policeman you helped?"

I noted his careful wording.

"If not, he was either involved or he's running from the people who did," I said, then took a chance. "I'm curious. Why ask if the stranger is Russian? And the thing about tattoos. On the level. You're expecting someone. Who?"

"Ah, another rather odd question, Dr. Ford," was the response.

"Come on, Max. Send the info C-W if you don't want to talk about it here. I'll record and run it through translation software."

"I think not. Tattoos, though, well…put it this way. Have you ever heard of a bird called the Eurasian monk vulture?"

"Say again."

"A type of giant vulture, the monk vulture. Bloody thing has a nine-foot wingspan and weighs close to forty pounds. A veritable monster."

Yes, I had. It was in the IronKey files. An inglorious nickname for a psychopath, one of six who'd escaped and, I was now convinced, were either on the island or nearby.

"A monster," I agreed. "Yeah, I think I understand. You're going to need some help."

"Quite possibly we both will. The storm, my friend. I registered gusts at sixty knots, and that's nothing compared to… let's see, they're predicting one-fifty, a hundred and sixty in the afternoon. Probably lose my antenna. And what if that gentleman bangs at your door?"

On the table was a pack of double-lock zip-tie restraints. I said, "Can't turn away a stranger during a hurricane, Max. We'll switch to handhelds if our antennas go."

"Quite right, HTs, simplex. Now let's enjoy ourselves. This should be quite a show. And I'm still having fun monitoring solar flares and radio propagation."

Weatherby gave his call sign, adding, "Clear, standing by and seventy-threes to you."

18

Florida code requires that residential buildings be able to with-stand wind of one hundred thirty-six miles per hour. On the Saffir-Simpson Scale, that's a low Cat-Four, a number indif-ferent to the screams of an island being dismembered by a storm.

Around noon, there was a lull that fired a fresh assault. Deci-bel extremes became predacious. Hail and debris hammered the walls. Trees, uprooted, tumbled with the resonance of rockslides. I stuffed tissue into Pete's ears—couldn't find the cat. When I wasn't at the radios or mopping leaks, I donned shooter's elec-tronic earbuds.

The stranger I'd confronted earlier, according to Weatherby, had made a failed attempt to get to the lab. That was an hour ago. If flooding started, he would probably try again. Beneath a baggy shirt, I wore two holsters, one a concealed, small-of-the-back Galco. Zip ties and some other surprises were ready, yet I wasn't sure what my first move should be.

If the guy was on foot, running scared, maybe it was better to play the cheery good Samaritan. But what if he was armed? And what if the driver of the heavy diesel vehicle was still in the area?

Didn't matter. If he had information, I wanted it.

Below deck, the generator's clunking was muted by sonic forces outside. Time passed. The stilt house became a ship at sea. Pilings swayed, walls shuddered, stringers of pliant heart pine thrummed a sustained banshee wail.

I looked down from my laptop. Pete was shredding his tissue-paper earplugs.

"Bonehead. You wanna go deaf? I shouldn't even be talking to you, pal. Give me that—stop—open your mouth. You'll be crapping Kleenex."

A sleeve from an old shirt became a scarf. When I knotted it over the dog's ears, toothache-style, he thumped his tail and swiped my hand with a slobbery tongue.

This was a mad display of emotion for an animal who didn't like to be petted. Or didn't much care.

Only one other time had he licked me. Four years ago, in the Everglades, Tomlinson and I had found him lost, tick-ridden, dragging the remains of a Burmese python still attached to his neck. The snake's recurved fangs made first aid difficult. Pain had caused the dog to slap his thanks on my cheek.

Sound, in nature, is elemental. Sound is also a potent weapon. Whales use low-frequency waves to explode air bladders in fish. A toddler's shriek is painful enough to spook predators.

This time, Pete's response suggested relief and, perhaps, even mild affection.

"Don't go soft on me," I said. "Where's Crunch & Des?"

The cat was wedged behind the bookcase. As an acoustic shield, I provided a pillow, then did the rounds. The roof had sprung another leak. More pans were needed. Bolted to the wall was a base station marine radio. I reduced squelch before returning to my laptop, where I'd downloaded IronKey files from South Africa.

On the screen were the six gaunt-eyed prison escapees. I'd already scanned their bios but took a closer look at a file labeled *Pavlo, [Raspitin] Grigori. [AKA: Friar Pavlo; The Vulture Monk.]*

This gaunt-eyed loser, as I read, became a more credible threat.

> *Grigori Pavlo: Age 42. Height 195 cm, Weight 86 kg.*
>
> *Summary: A Siberian court convicted the failed Orthodox novitiate and mercenary of raping and murdering between 70-100 women, which makes him Russia's most prolific serial killer in the last century.*
>
> *Before completing his first degree at Monastery of the Holy Spirit in Belarus, Pavlo, then 16, was accused of assaulting a senior abbot and forcing the man to shave the teen's head tonsure-style. The same night two Orthodox nuns went missing and were never found. His nickname, the Vulture Monk, is associated with a chest tattoo, but probably dates back to an incident that occurred as a teen when Pavlo was accused of...*

My reading was interrupted by voices on the VHF. I pushed the laptop aside and upped the volume. Two fishing guide friends were exchanging updates. They were Tootsie Joiner of Boca Grande, twenty miles north, and Harney Hamilton of Bokeelia, ten miles northeast. Both from old Florida families with generational knowledge.

The storm had already sucked most of the water out of Gasparilla Sound, according to Tootsie.

Harney said, "Same thing here. Bay's like a dang golf course. Never seen her so low but heard it happened before. The 1960 storm drained the rivers dry but, man, when she come back in, she come back hard."

Tootsie agreed. "That tide's gotta go somewhere. If she drains from the north, she's gonna flood south. Happened in the storms of 1921 and '26. Kin of mine lost their baby overboard in that one. Surge caught 'em off the Mailboat Channel, didn't even know the baby was gone till they got to McIntyre Creek. One of the grandmas kept a scrapbook and I still got the clippings. Little four-year-old girl. Never found her, neither."

God a'mighty, I thought.

The men continued to talk while I considered the parallels. A couple of days ago, I'd run the Mailboat Channel on my way home from Hannah's place. And McIntyre Creek was only a mile west of the marina.

I peeped out into the chaos, hoping the bay had been sumped empty. Just the opposite. It looked like max tide when water should have been low and still ebbing. To the east, a wedge of my boat bucked wildly on mangrove puppet strings. I had removed any equipment that might blow away, so it appeared to be doing okay.

According to Tomlinson, the island had not flooded since 1926. A hundred years ago and a mile away, that same storm had taken a baby from the Joiner family, yet here was Tootsie chatting on the radio, riding out another bad one.

Hannah's family had done the same. Harney's ancestors, too, most likely. But Florida had changed since the days of fisherfolk and cow hunters like my uncle Tucker Gatrell. Add twenty million more people to the mix and a billion more tons of potential construction wreckage.

A NOAA nautical chart came out of the drawer, Englewood to Marco Island. I touched a finger to Gasparilla Sound, twenty miles north, and spun a counterclockwise circle as if dragging water into the Gulf of Mexico. The surge path rotated southeast and threatened every inhabitant between Bonita Springs, our marina, and Captiva Island.

As Tootsie had said, if bays to the north were sucked empty, flooding to the south was inevitable. A hurricane is a massive waterwheel. It redistributes heat and moisture and threshes the landscape clean, indifferent to building codes and human contrivance.

My finger spun the flood inland toward the Causeway bridges. Big Sammy, Cadmael and their families lived there in clusters of tenement ground-floor housing.

"Oh, damn...this is not good," I said aloud. "Those people have no idea what's coming."

I switched radios and frequencies. An Amateur Radio Emergency Service member wasn't optimistic about warning my immigrant friends on the mainland. Several cell towers were already down, and landlines were nonexistent among the partitioned souls from south of the border.

The next hour I alternately hailed Big Sammy and Tomlinson, then Hannah's home across the bay. Negative contact, all. I stayed busy. I'd done the same during the Cat-Five storm as a kid. A phalanx of tornadoes—I could still picture them snaking across the bay. That locomotive roar; docks, mullet skiffs, trash, one of my uncle's scrawny cows, all tumbling skyward. It was a *Wizard of Oz* horror, yet I'd felt no fear.

Odd, nor did I now. Emotion had been displaced by the immediacy of what might happen next.

I returned to the file on Grigori Pavlo, who, as a teen, had been accused of—I had to wince—necrophilia.

The bio continued:

> For more than a decade, Pavlo terrorized the region. Clothed as a novitiate, he lured women into his car, or a church, and assaulted them with tools such as axes and surgical saws. At age 36, Grigori was sentenced to life at Black Dolphin Prison but was released under a clause in Russian law that pardons criminals if they fight in a war and stay alive for more than six months.
>
> At age 39, he returned from the Crimean Revolt, was arrested for another murder and resentenced to life in prison, but escaped during a disastrous flood.

I studied Pavlo's photo. My assessment of him as a threat was downgraded. He was just another walking scar, very tall and emaciated, dark, dead eyes staring out from a skull that was shaved monastic-style. Shirtless, pigeon-chested. A massive black tattoo, a vulture in descent, reduced the man's heart to carrion. The image was more obscene for the bird's phallic, featherless neck. Russian script, a phrase, was tatted above and below.

Washing my hands put a sanitary end to the file.

"Doc... Doc, hey, Ford, you there, Poncho? Hey man... *Mierda*. Come in, Doc."

Big Sammy's voice brought me scurrying to the marine VHF, channel sixty-eight. He wasn't scared. Not yet, and he was dubious when I described the storm surge that was headed his way. Sammy, Cadmael, two wives, their children and an eighty-year-old grandfather were crammed into a one-bedroom, ground-floor rental only a mile from the Causeway.

I pressed the mic key. "Sammy, you've got to move, get to high ground. Are there any two-story buildings nearby?" His apartment was on Davidson Road next to acres of immobile aluminum homes. I didn't know the area well.

"Dude, it's blowing like hell out there. You crazy? Cadmael's son is still nursing, and we got the old man. What makes you think it's gonna flood? We safer here, Poncho. I just called to, you know, hear a voice. Make sure you're okay."

I was about to urge him to pack everyone in a vehicle and drive east but reconsidered. In seventy-knot winds? It was reckless advice. "There's got to be a higher building around there. If you're gonna go, *go now* and take those life jackets. Storm's just going to get worse, so break into a house. Any house that has a second floor. You don't have to know the owner. Use a crowbar. Whatever you need to do."

Sammy replied, "Yeah, right, man. We get arrested later for B and E or stealin' or some shit. Then what? Back across the border we go. Doc, hey, man, I like this little radio. Gets the weather and everything, and it's nice to just know you're there. When this storm's done, tomorrow maybe, we come to the marina and clean up. No charge. You helped us, Poncho. We the first to help you, man."

"Tomorrow, sure," I said as if I believed it. "We'll talk."

A child was sobbing in the background when we signed off.

I felt powerless, untethered, a jumped-off-the-bridge awakening. There was no going back. There was only free fall and the suspense that preceded impact.

I remembered the same numb resignation from that long-ago storm. When a tornado had peeled off the roof of my uncle's shack, we'd rushed around gathering valuables. Strange how, in a pinch, money has no relationship to the word *valuable*. First on Tucker's list: a jug of whiskey, a Winchester, of course, a bull-riding trophy and his journal, leather-bound.

The same book now lay next to the hissing Coleman lantern and my reading chair. Pages in pencil, stained with sweat and snuff, chronicled my uncle's fifty years of living rough in Florida. This included the Ten Thousand Island area—outlaw country, in those days—where a man called "Bloody Ed" had thrived and propagated and, through association, had contributed to the murder my fiancée's namesake after the hurricane of 1910.

Between bouts of plugging leaks, I'd skipped through the journal to Tucker's notes about the storm, which, in the instant of its occurrence, had crystalized who my eccentric uncle was as a man.

Outside, wind velocity climbed, gusts of one twenty-five by 2:00 p.m. Once again, Tuck's journal became a diversion. Cannon shots of jetsam battered the clapboard outside. Each thud and bang was a random assault, anonymous until a massive impact drew me stumbling into the galley.

It took one look to understand. Something had pierced the stilt house shield. Wind screamed through a hole when I pried the object free.

The dog, even with a scarf around his ears, heard me say, "Oh, geezus... Poor Mack. If he hasn't had a heart attack, he might when he sees this."

The missile was part of a sign that had once read, *Grin 'N Bare It Cottages.* Mack's treasured lifeboat property, two miles away, was being shredded.

A hand drill and screws patched the hole, so later, I didn't have to holler when Weatherby made radio contact.

"Finally, Ford. I've been trying since noon. Have you confronted him yet?"

"Confronted... Who are you talking about? The guy who broke into the marina office?"

The physician/inventor said, "Damn all. Lower your volume. Better yet, use earphones."

"You're worried someone will hear? I already am, yeah, earbuds, Max. What's this about?"

"I tracked the gentleman to your house more than an hour ago. The wind's so bloody loud, though...never mind that. He's there, Ford. He's there in the next room. The room where you do your work. There must be a reason he didn't make himself known. QSL? Understand my meaning?"

I faced the door that led to the breezeway. The lab entrance was outside, several unprotected and very windy paces beyond. Walls in the lab were thick, heavily insulated for storing ice and fish back in the 1920s.

Pete had also turned to face the door. I said, "You're sure?"

"Roger that. A human heat signature. Different room but same building."

"He's hiding," I said. "Hiding because the guy's afraid of my dog. I know who we're dealing with, Max. I'm pretty sure, anyway. Do you?"

Weatherby answered the question by dodging it. "Your signal on forty and twenty meters is damnably weak. Suggest you check antennas and grounding gear. The same with UHF. Around noon, several times, your fiancée hailed you on one of the police frequencies. Hannah's her name, correct?"

"Huh?" This made zero sense. "No… I mean, yes. But she's in North Carolina, so it had to be a friend of hers. A deputy sheriff, a woman, Birdy Tupplemeyer. Did you respond?"

"Roger, as a courtesy. But I'm pretty sure she said the name Hannah. She was concerned about a camper parked near her house. Strangers, one or two men. Said you'd understand and to make contact ASAP. But not on a marine channel. Her VHF antenna was knocked down. In fact, my friend, all of our antennas will be gone if this gets any worse."

Now I was spooked. If Weatherby was right, Hannah had lied about being in Carolina with our son. No…no way. This was way out of character—unless it was to spare me from worrying.

"Got stuff to do, Max. When the eye's overhead, we should get a ten, fifteen-minute break from the wind. Calm enough to check our antennas. What do you think, the eye's maybe an hour away?"

"Good hunting," was Weatherby's response. "Oh—when you confront the fellow in the next room, please pass along regards from my… No, just say, Hilary. Hilary sends her regards. Something like that. Pay attention to how he reacts and let me know."

Hilary, the Brit's niece, I suspected.

I asked, "Is she with you?"

"In a way. I'll explain later over that whiskey. Clear, standing by. Seventy-threes to you."

19

From inside my home, the only antenna I could confirm standing was a white fiberglass Shakespeare, eight feet long, mounted outside the south window and connected to the radio on the galley wall.

No wonder recent contacts had all been on marine channels. Normally, marine VHF was a dependable way to contact Hannah's old house—until now. The antenna at her place was gone, Birdy had reported. Or had it been Hannah?

Maddening. And during the worst of the storm… I hoped. A sixty-knot wind can knock a man off his feet. Gusts were double that now, one-thirty-plus. Lethal if I risked stepping outside.

Before the storm, I'd removed the multiband roof antenna in favor of the heavy-duty Buckmaster dipole. Forty-five yards of wire strung through mangroves should have been bulletproof. So what was the problem?

SWR meters on my high frequency radios verified Weatherby's analysis. I was transmitting, but feedline voltage and range were badly compromised. This meant my dipole antenna had been ripped away, which was unlikely. Unless…it had been cut intentionally by the man who'd broken into my lab.

"That sonuvabitch," I said. The dog, at my feet, opened a yellow eye and sniffed an odor new to the maelstrom.

Cigar smoke.

The fool was smoking in a building constructed of turpentine pine.

"We've got to get him secured before he kills us all," I told Pete. "This wind can't last much longer."

Wrong. The Cat-Five my uncle and I had experienced was a high-speed laser, gone in four hours. Not this storm. Tentacle clouds slowed overhead as if to suffocate all that could not be uprooted. A little before 3:00 p.m., a slab of my metal roof ripped free. Then a second panel went. They hammered the house like a fan battering its own cage. Wind noise, though, dominated until a waterfall roar added to the tumult. A crack in the plywood explained it.

Outside, waves off the Gulf of Mexico had breached the island, a gray torrent of trash and synthetics as if a dam had burst. The storm surge from a century ago had returned and was already starting to drown modern inhabitants to the south. All day there had been sporadic distress calls on channel sixteen. Now anguished dozens battled for attention. Transmissions collided; voices fragmented into shards, male and female.

"I'm sinking…dear God. Anybody, please." This from a lone sailor anchored in Estero Bay.

On Fort Myers Beach, a man's wife had been swept out the door into the Gulf of Mexico. "She's still alive… Coast Guard, do you read? I can see her…oh shit…where'd she go? Goddamn it, we need… *Please.*"

The radio became a chorus of the doomed who yesterday, secure in their condos and homes, were unaware of the avalanche to come. Help. They all needed help. Instead, there was only a vacancy of time and space in which yesterday's delusions were crushed.

The sky had fallen. And there was no escape.

"Pete, ol' buddy," I said to the dog. "If that water rises another six feet, we'll turn this house into a raft. See where it takes us. Or—" I checked the time "—wait until the eye's overhead. What do you think? Another thirty minutes, maybe, it'll get calm for a while, then water should flow out. Yeah, opposite direction—hey, come here. Your scarf's crooked."

I reknotted the retriever's ear protection and switched the radio from scan to channel sixty-eight. Eavesdropping on those about to die seemed a perverse intrusion.

Tomlinson came into my mind. If he hadn't made the Panhandle by now, his would be just one more distress call. No... my pal wasn't the type to raise a white flag and put others at risk.

Pointless to hail him on a ham frequency—not if my visitor had cut the antenna wire. I tried, anyway, using his call sign—KM4PON—and repeating, "Hailing the sailing vessel *No Más*. Do you copy. Does anyone copy? QSL?"

The radio's waterfall spectrum suggested I not only couldn't transmit, I couldn't receive HF signals from more than a short distance away.

I banged my fist on the table. "You dope, Tomlinson. Why pull a stunt like this now?"

Friendship begins with a random first meeting and ends with an unexpected departure. A job transfer, a new spouse, death. But some friends, a very few, always remain at our elbows no matter the distance. One of us would die first. Inevitable, and true for us all. But I wasn't ready to concede the loss of my sometimes vexing pal.

Big Sammy raised me again on channel six-eight. "Poncho... Poncho, it's me. Answer, man! We need help."

This time he was terrified.

"We in some serious shit, Doc. Water, like the floor started leaking. Now the whole damn room is—Cadmael! Hey, Cadmael, you putting that thing on backward, man."

I said, "Sammy, Sammy. Release the microphone key."

He didn't, which wasn't unusual for people in a panic. Background noises—a child's wail, a female screaming orders in K'iche' Mayan. Sammy was trying to explain to Cadmael how to put on a life jacket, but in Spanish. Glass shattered, an explosive report. It moved up my spine like a Taser.

Finally, Sammy heard me say, "You've got to take your thumb off the button so I can talk. What's happening there?"

Water had flooded in waist-deep and was getting deeper fast. One of the babies was floating in an ice chest. The old man had climbed atop the refrigerator, and someone had broken a window in case they had to swim for it. That's the noise I had just heard.

I tried to sound calm but wasn't. "How many PFDs—life jackets, I mean—how many did I…I gave you at least six, right? You got any more? Find anything that floats and hang on."

Sammy yelled, "Doc, call the Coast Guard, the cops, anybody. I tried but they don't… Oh, *mierda*! Cadmael, amigo, don't… don't go out that window. Cadmael, damn it. You gotta strap that thing around your belly. You gonna drown, man."

Powerless. The belief that help is always a phone call away is a modern delusion. Five adults and two children, trapped in a flooding room. Six life jackets between them.

I pressed the mic key. "You can't go outside, Sammy. The wind will… Don't do it, man. In that bag I packed, there's a coil of rope. Find milk jugs, cushions, anything that floats, tie it all together. Like a raft and stay inside. Do you copy?"

Sammy's response was cut short by a percussive boom, then more wild screams. The torrent had burst through their front door.

The last thing I heard my friend say was, "Poncho, tell the

police. Promise me! We gotta swim…get up on the roof. Yeah, and I'll tie us all together."

Fear in the voice of a friend strikes a tribal chord. In me, it produced an anger that teetered on rage. There was no one to fight, nothing to flee or blame. Instead, I glared at the door and cursed the stranger who'd broken into my lab. Then I got busy again.

Channel 22 Alpha is the Coast Guard's secondary frequency. I waited for a break in traffic to report Sammy's situation. When authorities were able—tomorrow, most likely—they would check on my friends across the Causeway.

The chances that all seven people would live weren't good, but another story the old captain, Leon Crumpler, had told me provided a thread of hope. Leon claimed that during the worst of the 1926 hurricane, he had survived by climbing up a Calusa shell mound and tying himself to a tree. For decades I had dismissed this as just another one of his tall tales. Not now.

The minutes slowed. A southeast wind wrenched more metal from the rafters. Another projectile pierced the wall. What appeared to be a spear turned out to be two feet of rebar. A steel rod. It would've killed me if not for the clapboard shield.

Loose objects, roof tiles, splinters of wood, even catfish spines had become missiles. Random, deadly. Years ago, when we'd fled my uncle's shack, he'd made me strap on a football helmet—a rare bit of foresight for Tucker, yet a caring gesture that lingered. The next day, among the destruction, he'd found a common school pencil embedded dart-like in the trunk of an oak tree.

"See this, boy? A Winchester ain't got this sortta power. God does, so it's best not to piss off the Lord Almighty. If you do screw up—and who doesn't?—pretend you're innocent and keep moving. Like you're dodging lightning bolts. That's my advice. The Big Guy's got plenty other targets who just sit around with their thumbs up their butts."

It had taken only two hours for the eye of that previous Cat-

Five to arrive. Now, almost 4:00 p.m., I recognized the subtle differences that were a prelude to change. There would be a gradual de-escalation that might last for twenty or thirty minutes. Not calm but calm enough for some poor bastards to think it was over. Along the coast these same people would add to the death toll.

The worst was yet to come.

Tarps now covered my books and electronics save for the marine VHF. I freed my laptop long enough to open a file tagged with the name of the outlaw insurance exec. I studied his photo to reconfirm my suspicions. Facial biometrics can be disguised. They change with age. Characteristics of the human earlobe do not. Next door, in my lab, hiding, indifferent to it all, was the man I believed to be Andy Dimitry, the insurance salesman turned outlaw.

Wind weakened incrementally as minutes ticked by. Flooding continued, the depth and velocity amplified by manmade strictures. Below deck, the generator swamped and died. Radios were now powered by twelve-volt batteries, thirteen amps. I lit another gas lantern and laid out weaponry on the bed. Gloves, safety goggles, heavy boots, LED flashlights. Wire cutters, a tactical listening device and backup handheld radios went into my cargo pockets.

A last touch: on a cushion in the front room, I placed a Colt Mustang .380, magazine filled with snap-cap dummy rounds.

The calm before the storm is an apparition, transient as a flash of green during the rarest of sunsets.

I signaled the dog, *Back*, stepped out onto the deck and bolted the door behind me. To the north in bilious, crepuscular light, Sammy and Cadmael were fighting for their lives and the lives of their families.

20

The last thing Big Sammy Martinez told the biologist before the radio tumbled from his hand was, "Poncho, call the police. We gotta swim for it...climb, get up on the roof. Yeah, and I'll tie us all together."

That's what he did while water flooded the kitchen. Used a coil of rope, tied it to Cadmael's life jacket and tried to do the same with the others. As a kid, Sammy had paddled around beneath a waterfall, Cascada de Tamul, ten kilometers south of El Sauz, the Mexican village where his mother had worked as a maid. But he'd never experienced a more frightening force than the volcanic sludge flowing through the door.

"Cadmael," he hollered, "hang on to something!"

Too late. The torrent hammered the little Guatemalan into the wall. Glass shattered and Cadmael was sucked out the kitchen window, pulling a child with him.

Big Sammy grabbed the end of the rope, braced his feet against the stove and was winning the battle until Cadmael's infant son, bawling in an Igloo cooler, floated past. He lunged and grabbed

the thing as both wives screamed. The old man, the patron, was
in a fetal position atop the refrigerator.

"Get on the counter. Climb, get as high as you can," Sammy
told them. He was struggling with the rope in one hand, the
makeshift crib in the other. "I have to tie you all in first, and
then we'll—"

That's as far as he got. His footing gave way, and he was blown
through a window too small for a man his size. A searing pain
in his stomach was ignored while he focused on keeping the
Igloo cooler afloat. Outside, the patio had become a whirlpool
of debris. Cadmael clung to a stucco archway attached to the
roof, which, along with the rope, was all that had spared him
and Sammy's stepdaughter from drowning.

Cadmael called something to his wife in K'iche', eyes wide
as he watched Sammy loop an arm, then his legs around a tall
stucco pillar. Still grasping the cooler, the big man inched his
way above the swirl. He got a hand on the top of the arch, let
the rising water help boost him and managed to heave his body
onto the crossbeam at roof level after the squalling infant inside
the cooler was safe.

The whole time he'd been repeating an Our Father in Latin,
memorized as a kid.

Cadmael, in Spanish, said to him, "Brother! I can't hang on
much longer. Take the rope, save the women, I'll cut myself
free and—"

"No!" Sammy leaned and extended his arm. "Grab my wrist.
I'll pull you up."

"But what about—"

Sammy shook his head. "One at a time. We can do this,
brother. First you, then the others. But stay low. This wind—
my God—it'll blow us off the roof if you don't stay down."

Hurricane wind was a sustained wail pierced by gunshot
sounds of flying shingles, aluminum from the trailer park. The
patio archway saved them. It was built of concrete and rebar.

When Cadmael was on his stomach, straddling the crossbeam, Sammy nudged the Igloo cooler closer to his friend. "Both hands," he hollered. "The wind is trying to blow your baby son away. I'll be back with the others. Our wives first, then the old man. And that bag Doc gave us."

Cadmael started to protest. Then his eyes refocused. "Blood... why is there so much blood? Are...you— Brother, look at your shirt."

Sammy did and realized broken glass had slashed his belly open, a six-inch wound. *Strange*...it had hurt like hell at first but now felt numb.

"Is nothing," he said. "Watch my stepdaughter. I'll pass the others up to you."

He did. In late afternoon when the wind began to slow and shift, there were six of them, face down on the leeward pitch of the roof. The infant, still bedded in the cooler, lay wedged between Cadmael and the mother. Sammy and his wife huddled as if warming their daughter on a nest. Floodwaters had peaked a foot below the patio roof and seemed to be receding.

"We must continue to pray," the patron, an old man, insisted. Now, looking up, seeing a disc of blue sky, he added, "There— observe. It is the Eye of God looking down. We must give thanks before He tries to kill us again."

Sammy knew that was inevitable. He'd experienced a minor hurricane a few years back and feared they weren't in the clear yet. Rather than frighten the others, he used the gradual calm to pour alcohol on his stomach. Next, he made butterflies with strips of duct tape, which required several wraps to close the wound.

Cadmael, now tied directly to the larger man, got to his knees while staring at the road. Among a streaming flow of wreckage was the upside-down roof from a house. Several animals— a couple of pigs, it looked like, a raccoon, pelicans, and a stork of some type—had climbed aboard to escape the flood. They roosted as calmly as sightseers on a river excursion.

"What is that?" Cadmael pointed and got to his feet. "Not the animals. That large orange thing? It looks like a...like a circus toy. Or a child's tent."

Sammy told him, "Stay down, brother. It's still blowing, and that *puta* wind isn't done."

"But see, the water is below the windows now." The Guatemalan, cradling the Igloo bassinet, stepped to the roofline. "The toy...it's floating this way. Yes, almost like a sign the storm is over."

"It's not...it's not over—and you can't swim, *pendejo*." Sammy squinted at the strange orange object. It bobbed and spun like a cork among wreckage from expensive homes, riverfront, two miles away. The wreckage included a canvas sun canopy, mooring bumpers off millionaire yachts, a swirl of plastic holiday decorations freed from storage by the surge plus the large orange oddity.

A giant blow-up Halloween pumpkin? he wondered and almost smiled. Ha! And gringos claimed that Mexicans were gaudy.

"Get down, at least sit," Sammy ordered. He was getting pissed. "Cadmael, if you fall, I fall. You are becoming a pain in the butt, my brother."

His friend squatted for a moment but couldn't resist the colorful carousel spinning toward them. He inched over the roof flashing onto the downward pitch. "A tent," he said. "Yes, a floating tent. But why would a tent float? Well...what a nice gift this would make for the little ones if—"

A bumblebee sound diverted Sammy's attention. He looked back in time to see a blur that was an aluminum panel knock the Guatemalan off his feet. The infant, inside the Igloo, flew from his hands. The cooler skidded down the roof, hit the lip of a gutter, teetered for a moment, then went over into the outbound flood surge.

Cadmael made a horrified mewing sound. He yanked at the rope and tried to go after his baby son. Sammy would have followed anyway but unknotted himself from the others first, calling to them, "Stay there, don't move."

It was a six-foot drop from the roof to the water. Cadmael, wearing an inflated vest, had already been carried downstream when Sammy paused, spotted the Igloo bassinet and jumped. He came up. His feet found the bottom, and he snatched the infant from the cooler, which was half-submerged.

The old man had also left the rope behind. "How is the child? Is he alive?"

Sammy yelled, "Stay with the women—no, wait! Patron, keep your eye on Cadmael. Where is he? I can't see Cadmael from here. Direct me."

"The child, how is my godson?" the old man demanded.

An archway wall provided a shield from the current. The baby was bawling, snot-nosed, tiny fists hammering in protest when Sammy answered, "Patron, come to the patio, I'll pass the baby up. Use the rope. Where is Cadmael?"

The women and his stepdaughter, on their knees, connected by a nylon line, helped secure the infant on what was now the leeward side of the roof. The wind had changed and accelerated during thunderclap explosions overhead. A pitchfork of lightning zapped a nearby tree. Smoldering palm fronds rained down. A power line attached to the archway burst into flames.

"Patron! Keep looking, find Cadmael. Where is he? The storm's coming back. I've got to climb up there, but I can't until we find him."

The only response was his wife wailing, "Mother of God, now our apartment...the building is on fire."

"What?"

"Is burning, Samuel! Can you put it out?"

Sammy had been in tough spots before, but this cascading nightmare seemed an intentional assault on his family.

Oh…shit. The power line had ignited the building's roof, flames orange, already feeding on wood. Above, the sky was a gaseous cauldron of gray. He looked heavenward and thought, *Damn you, God. Why? You can't stop long enough even to help innocent children? I've had enough of your shitty games.*

Sammy stepped out into the current, chest-deep, and searched for his friend and a structure—a car, floating trees, anything— that might spare them from the storm and flames. His eyes found the giant pumpkin-looking toy that had spun close to the patio before snagging a fallen power line.

A tent. The thing did resemble a colorful tent. It took the big man a second to link the object with the riverfront marina where he sometimes worked as a line chef.

Million-dollar yachts there carried expensive emergency equipment. Once, a plastic locker had tumbled off the dock, and the thing had burst open and inflated automatically. It had been a round rubber dinghy the size of a small car with a pumpkin-colored roof for people lost at sea.

Sammy tilted his head and apologized. *I'm an asshole. Forgive me. I swear that I will never again—*

He stopped himself. Foolish promises about drinking, gambling, infidelity and other such shit had been made before, and none had lasted more than two or three Sundays.

Help me find Cadmael, he added, which was honest at least.

"Patron, I need the rope. Hurry!"

Big Sammy Martinez yelled this as he battled his way upstream toward the oceangoing life raft.

21

My uninvited visitor had futzed my dipole antenna by scavenging wire to secure the lab's door from the inside. I had to bang and pry, then use cutters before finding him huddled beneath the steel dissection table.

"Who are you?" I said to the man I believed to be Andy Dimitry.

The boarded room was all half tones and shadows. Part of the roof was gone, lots of broken windows and aquarium glass. He sat up. "Is it done? Jesus Christ, please tell me that goddamn thing is done. I thought for sure I was going to die."

"The day's not over yet," I answered.

On shore, through the battered mangroves, my new truck was flooded, taillights on because the battery had shorted. Mack's home and office were in water up to the windows.

The man said, "Not over yet? Are you trying to be…is that like a threat? I had to take cover somewhere after hiding in a goddamn boat. That's not a hotel down there. It's a marina or something. I would've drowned if I hadn't waited for the eye to pass over— Hey, get that damn light out of my face. What is it with you and flashlights, mister?"

He appeared groggy, in shock, when he got to his feet. Bald on the top; stringy hair over his left ear appeared to be caked with mud. Or blood. For support, he used a four-foot fish gaff with a stainless hook at the end.

I looked up at a circle of blue sky that wouldn't last for long. "You waited for the eye to do what? Cut my antenna? Or to break into my house?"

"The wire contraption, you mean? That's because this shack, your cabin, I guess, was blowing apart. No, the eye passed over a couple hours ago. The other place—" he motioned to the marina "—started to flood, so I, you know, ran for it while I had the chance. Most people wouldn't mind a person trying to save his own ass."

The guy had mistaken the brief noon calm for the hurricane's eye.

I said, "You're a regular genius, aren't you? Thing is, why didn't you answer when I knocked on my own door?"

"Seriously...are you screwin' with me?" He touched a hand to the mud or blood on the side of his head. "I got hit by something. A board, maybe. And I'm damn near deaf anyway after six hours of that goddamn wind. Who could tell a knock from... Hey, pal, give me a break. I'll pay you, whatever. Just help me get off this island. You got a car, a boat maybe?"

By then he had a view of the wreckage. His voice softened. "Sonuvabitch. Looks like terrorists nuked the place. How long, you think, before that water goes down? I don't want to be stuck here. Man, seriously, I *can't* be stuck here."

"Sounds like poor planning to me," I said. "What's the problem—someone after you?" I was thinking about the diesel vehicle that had roared away and trying to get a look at his ears.

"Someone...huh? Hell no." He came toward the door. "Name's uh, Donald. Donny Orlando. I have business meetings

in Miami. Lot of money at stake, you know? Tell you what—
a thousand bucks cash if you get me across the bridge to the
mainland. That was one hell of a storm. Unbelievable. What I
need is a shower and a drink."

I played along. Stepped aside to allow him onto the deck,
where rain spattered but the wind wasn't too bad. "Say, Don...
Donny, how about you leave that fish gaff here? No shower until
the power's on, but you can towel off before you go."

He didn't drop the gaff. "Where's that big-ass dog of yours?
Dogs and I don't get along."

"He feels the same about people. Tell you what, I've got a
truck and a boat. Truck's over there." I pointed. "You can see
the taillights through the trees."

"No shit? Hey, yeah, the lights...so you remote-started the
engine? Good, let's get out of here. Or... I don't suppose you'd
let me borrow it. I'll bring it back tomorrow and pay you a
thousand in cash. A business deal. Sound good? We both win."

He went toward the steps, then reconsidered. Below flowed
a torrent of brown, shoulder-deep, that might have been the
headwaters of Angel Falls, Venezuela. "How the hell—that looks
dangerous. Wait...you sell fish for a living, right? So you must
be good with boats. I think we're gonna have to take a boat.
Where is it?"

I hadn't told him my occupation. His face confirmed my
suspicions when I said, "Drop that gaff and the bullshit, Andy.
We'll talk."

"The hell—Andy? Where you come up with that?"

My hand moved to the small of my back. "Same way you
know who I am. That's why you came here, Andy—Anatoli
Dimitry, correct? What really happened to your head? Did your
Russian buddies go off and leave you?"

The accuracy of that got a trapped-rat reaction. He was a
small-time suit used to being in charge. Tidy clothes mud-
ravaged, far from the boardroom, stranded and scared. He sized

me up—no weapons he could see. Next he considered a ruined truck he believed was operational. *Kill the biologist, steal the truck.* It was going through his mind.

"The keys," he said. "I need the keys. Hurry up. Where—are they—inside your place?" He raised the gaff like a club and side-stepped toward the house.

My attention swerved to a chorus of yipping and yapping. Coyotes—a drowning pack of them—caught by the surge. They came tumbling toward us through the mangroves.

Stupidly, I didn't think about how Pete might react. Then I did.

Pistol drawn, I ordered Dimitri, "Don't go inside that house. Damn you, don't open that door," but my visitor did it, anyway. Shrewd—like a rodeo clown, he popped the dead bolt, then hid behind the door until the bull came charging out.

A retriever, in this case. Seventy pounds of waterdog that had wind-scented coyotes before. He galloped out, dodged my hands. For an instant, training overruled instinct.

"Whoa. Stay."

Trembling, Pete danced to a stop. I'd almost grabbed his collar when the coyotes went howling past. Then he was gone, my dog. Lunged and leaped over the railing. When I looked down, he'd already been swept north toward the mouth of the bay. The scarf I'd tied was askew, and he was swimming hard, determined to join the pack.

Behind me, a door slammed. A dead bolt ratcheted like the bolt of a rifle.

The outlaw insurance exec was inside my house. And I was locked out.

22

The storm stalled overhead, so it was a blustery twenty minutes before patches of blue vortex signaled a reversal in wind direction. The time lag suggested the eye was humongous. It also reinforced my visitor's belief the worst was over and it was now safe to charm me, or kill me, and escape in a truck that had already floated away.

It was an error I was eager to promote. Time I'd spent scanning the bay, whistling for Pete, had sharpened my anger into an ice pick clarity. I knocked politely at the door and eavesdropped through the wall while removing hinges.

Weatherby's was the first voice I recognized, a call on VHF. When I heard a female voice, I crashed into my own home, pistol raised.

Dimitry threw his hands up. "Geezus, take it easy. I was about to let you in, anyway. You don't need a gun."

I replied, "That's right. I don't."

He misread my meaning and looked past me. "Where's the

dog? I told you I don't like dogs, so keep the damn thing away from me."

"You asshole, you saw what happened—the dog went over the railing." I looked around after confirming that Crunch & Des was safe, still tucked behind the stove. "You didn't find the keys to my truck, obviously. But you sure as hell tried."

The guy had ransacked the place. A table, chairs overturned, drawers open. Both HF radios ripped out by the wires. The pistol I'd left in plain sight was gone.

He saw my eyes. "Hey now, mister, take it easy. I didn't do this. Not all of it, anyway. The place was a mess when I came in. Sure, I searched, so where are they?"

I looked at my watch. "You've got exactly five minutes to answer a few questions. The truth, and you get the keys to my truck."

"You're lying. If you weren't lying, you wouldn't be holding a gun on me."

I holstered the pistol. "Now you've got four. Make it quick. Your name's not Don or Donald. You're Andy Dimitry, right? Tell me about the Russians. And their targets. There's a reason I'm willing to trade my truck for the truth."

"What reasons? What makes you think—" He saw my hand move to the holster. "Okay, so what? How'd you know my name? Hey, man, we can work something out. It's called consensus. You know what that means?"

I said, "A noun as in con man. Someone's been reading the dictionary. You have three minutes before I put you through a window. Talk."

It took ten. A rapid-fire summary interlaced with lies. He was the victim, of course. The mercenaries would kill him unless he escaped to the mainland. Most infuriating was his denial about targeting Hannah's home or targeting me.

"You can't control killers," he said. "That's something I should've learned dealing with the Russian mob."

I'd made him take a chair. "They turned on you and now you're scared. Know why, Andy? Because you're the weakest link. I get it. Where are they? I need details."

"You're gonna let me go, right?"

"I can't wait."

It was another few minutes before he pulled back a clump of blood-caked hair. "See this? Their leader, a psycho, he bit my damn ear off. You believe that shit? Chewed it, made me watch, and—get this—made me watch him *fucking swallow it*. Damn right I'm scared. You should be scared, too."

I said, "Their team leader, but not the real boss. And the real boss certainly isn't you. The head guy, who is he?"

He told me. I locked the name of an oligarch, *Sasha Olegovich of Sunny Sands Beach*, in my memory before Dimitry got up, saying, "Now, where are those keys?"

They were in my pocket.

Wind was gathering traction in the trees, sharp gusts, gradually accelerating from the northwest. Panels of rain sailed past as I followed him out the door.

I handed him the keys. The little pistol he'd found came out. He aimed at my chest, six yards away, his back to the same rail where Pete had leaped into an abyss.

"Know why I'm smiling?" he said. "'Cause you guessed right. The Russian bastard left me here to die in the storm. Told me if I didn't, my only chance of him not doing it was to kill a guy named Marion Ford. A revenge deal, I guess. Not that I care. What are you, some sort of spy? Living in this dump, you sure as hell aren't rich."

He thumbed back the hammer of the little Colt .380, not smiling but with a shell-shocked leer.

I displayed open hands. "This doesn't need to happen, Andy. Give me another name—the team leader. A guy with a big tattoo on his chest? That's him, isn't it? Take my truck, he'll never know. At least give me a chance to protect my son."

With his free hand, he was trying to open a knife he'd stolen from my drawer. "They call him Pavlo. Grigori–something Pavlo. That's him. Too late, man, you're way too late if Pavlo got his hands on your kid and wife."

I stepped closer.

He waved the gun. "Some call that lunatic the Vulture Monk, can you imagine? Slapped me, stuck me with a needle, took a pint of my... Insane, you know? Made me get down on my knees and pretend I was a...a... Then, Christ, like he was trying to eat my face off. But I...but I turned my head. Shit. Yeah, he...he *assaulted* me—so what? But guess who's gonna outsmart that freak?"

The tough guy from Philly couldn't figure out the knife. Frustrated, he made a moaning sound. Or was it disgust for the secret he'd just shared?

I said, "Press the button."

Dimitry did. A four-inch blade, Benchmark, deployed with a metallic thunk. Puzzled, his eyes floated a question: *Why did you help me?*

I said, "You don't have a camera, so the Sunny Sands Beach guy will want one of my fingers—or whoever Pavlo works for. I'd do the same. In fact, I have. That's procedure. DNA or a fingerprint."

The leer vanished. "You're saying you've actually cut...taken off a... Jesus Christ, who are you?"

"I'm the only person on this island who can help you, Andy. A few minutes ago, when you were alone in here, I heard a woman's voice on the radio. My...well, maybe my girlfriend, but I'm not sure. Why target her and my kid? I'm not gonna ask again."

"Shut up!" The little man's hands were shaking, the pistol at his side. "I know what you're doing, using my name over and over. Stop acting like we're buddies or you're a shrink or something because—"

I cut him off, "What did you mean, it's too late? Tell me."

"Hey—" he had looked toward the parking lot "—I don't see your truck. Never mind. I'll find it. And if that damn dog gets in the way—that's another thing, your dog. I let him outside on purpose, dumbass, just to piss you off." That shell-shocked leer again. "Where is he?"

I said, "Same place you're going if you don't answer my question."

He brought the pistol up, closed an eye, took aim. "Okay, mister biologist or whatever you are. I know zilch about a kid, but your girlfriend, Pavlo's guys probably have her by now. Which means she's better off dead. So, tell her hello when you get to hell—and thanks for the truck."

The little single-action Colt went *click*.

Twice more the hammer smacked a blank chamber. *Click-click*.

Before he could use the knife, I was on him—a double-leg, then a fireman's carry. Screaming, Andy Dimitry went over the railing.

Weatherby referred to Hannah, saying, "I'm not sure it was her, but a woman, the same woman, I think hailed you on simplex, two meters. I responded but she didn't acknowledge. That was more than an hour ago. I'm sure it'll all get sorted out, Ford. Nothing we can do about it now. Certainly not using HTs."

Handheld radios, he meant. The Brit had also lost his primary antennas.

"Negative. We've got to do something," I responded. "They're coming after you. I spoke to my visitor, a guy named Dimitry. Andy Dimitry. He was with them until...until he wasn't. You and your neighbors are at the top of their hit list. In this area, anyway. If this damn storm ever moves on, my boat might still be operational. I'll get out there as soon as I can after I check on Hannah and our son."

Might work was optimistic. After dealing with the insurance suit, I'd risked escalating gusts long enough to get a look at my boat. The surge had floated it high above the mangroves to which it was tied. A scarred-up fiberglass trophy, that's what it resembled. Grab rails were gone, and a fence post had harpooned the console, portside, forward of the helm. No telling if it was seaworthy.

I said to Weatherby, "Your sat-phone. I've got to get a message to police about Hannah. Even with part of my roof gone, I can't link up. Thing's dead, almost like I'm being jammed. Or it's because of solar flares—whatever you said. You mind trying?"

The Brit seemed to ignore my urgency. "Yes, yes, of course. Later. Did Dimitry—I'm familiar with the name—did he give you any more information? Like mention an East Coast crime boss? A Russian oligarch named—"

I said, "He did, but stick with me here. My advice is, hide. Lock yourself in a room and let them steal whatever they want. I wish I would've dropped off a weapon earlier because these people are killers. Copy? As in they won't hesitate. You know exactly who they are...don't you, Max?"

"I do. All too well, so rest easy. You asked if I had any firearms, which I don't. Remember? But you didn't ask if I had weapons. There's a difference. Let's leave it at that."

What the hell did that mean?

He said, "Very public, these marine frequencies—even at a miserly five watts." He chuckled, an odd, icy sound. "Ford, your visitor. Dimitry. Is he still there?"

I answered, "Last time I saw him, he was headed your way."

"Say again? My way...but not in a vehicle. That would be— oh wait, you mean—"

I said, "That's right. The surge is flowing toward the mouth of the bay, so keep your eyes open. I have a dog... I had a dog. Watch for him, too. Coast Guard is unaware of any this. Copy?"

A few seconds passed before the Brit responded, "Good. Wise choice. Let's keep it that way. I think it's better not to involve authorities with what happens during the next twelve hours."

"Except for Hannah," I said. "If you can get a sat-link, you'll do it for me, right? Contact police about her and our son? I'm also worried about a friend of hers, Birdy Tupplemeyer. She's been staying at Hannah's house."

"As soon as I can, of course. Until then, responders will have enough to do without wasting assets on me." Three times he clicked the mic key before adding, "An agreement between us. Understood?"

For the first time, I did. Or suspected, at least. If my sat-phone was being jammed, Weatherby was the cause.

23

Wind velocity can be gauged visually. At fifteen knots, foam lines appear on surface water. Bushes begin to move. At thirty knots, palm fronds mimic the wild streamers of a woman's hair. Offshore, waves crest, they kick spray—white horses, sailors call them. At forty knots, forests become animated. Limbs snap. The tactile swaying of skyscrapers can be felt on the upper floors. And the sea—wherever the sea may be—becomes a wilderness of collapsing vistas without horizon.

One nautical mile equals 1.15 statute miles. Knots and miles per hour are proportional. At 5:00 p.m., an assault from the northwest peaked at one hundred thirty knots according to Coast Guard weather, a signal strong enough to find my handheld.

The dark side of the storm had arrived—a cyclonic force. Mountainous winds, rain, a landslide of waves pushed tumbling boats, whole sections of rooftops, refrigerators, awnings, beach chairs past my home.

On a legal pad I converted knots to miles per hour.

"This is one for the history books," I said to Crunch & Des.

"One hundred and forty-nine miles per hour. I don't think the floor or the pilings can hold together much longer." My attention returned to making notes, a succinct record of this rare climatic event.

The cat's response was to hiss and raise his hackles. This caused me to write, *Some mammals seem to revert to ancient coding free of human dependencies—until feeding time. I hope.*

"Don't worry," I said to the cat. "I've got a plan B. There's always a plan B."

It wasn't much of a plan. I had emptied the refrigerator. It lay backside down on the galley floor and was filled with valuables that needed to stay dry. Heavily insulated, there was a possibility the thing would float. I'd also punched breathing holes in a bucket and made a bed for the cat—if he ever ventured out from behind the stove.

This brought Big Sammy and Cadmael into my mind. An infant, a toddler and five adults in a room that had started flooding two hours ago. If they weren't dead, they were probably dying now. As were untold others along the coastline, fools like me who had ignored Florida history.

I didn't feel foolish, just resigned. I've done day swims, night swims, long-distance entries and escapes from dangerous waters worldwide—South Africa, the most recent. Self-confidence had nothing to do with it. There are rip currents and seas that no human can survive. So you leap into the void, trust your training and transit into the unknown.

Plywood had been ripped from a front window. The room was sodden, but it was leeward of the northwest wind. At 17:45, a look outside suggested the worst was over. The surge had peaked within inches of floating my home into the bay.

"We're not in the clear yet," I said to the cat. "Maybe you won't have to learn to swim—or get a chance to bite me again. The water's turned. It's flowing out. Great news, huh?"

For a rational man, this was an odd thing to say under the

circumstances, especially to a cat. Yet my relief bordered on euphoria. After seven hours of jailed anger, I would finally be free. I had no idea what damage had been done to the island. That was something else I remembered from a long-ago storm. Those who had fled knew far more about the outcome than those of us who had stayed.

Catastrophe narrows the vision. Human nature being what it is, to survive is to dismiss the danger and immensity of destruction.

Sunset was an hour away. I had to cut the boat free before dark, so I ventured out when the wind was iffy but manageable. What I saw transformed euphoria into reality. The marina, maybe the entire coastline, would never be the same. Not in my lifetime.

The south deck provided a vista of ruin. Boats piled in junkyard heaps, fences uprooted, hectares of denuded trees, their skeletal limbs savaged by wind. Roof joists, honor bar fridges, beachfront hotel marquees had traversed the island and lay scattered like bomb shrapnel.

I realized, *This will take freakin' years—if ever.*

The surge had gutted Mack's home and the marina office. Fuel pumps, liveaboard dockage had been jettisoned ashore amid an acre of tourist T-shirts, hats and the roof off the mechanic's shed. Knifed into the trunk of a tree was a historic marker:

Bailey's General Store
(Founded 1899)

I moved toward the porch steps. My boardwalk to shore was gone, all but for the safety lines I'd rigged. Below, flotsam was animated with mud creatures of some type, caked in a slime of human incontinence. Petroleum, sewage, pesticides—a century of leakage, exhumed by the flood, had bonded with sand. The result was a K-Y Jelly mire that was suffocating animals that had managed to survive until now.

I stared down at the mud creatures. Removed my glasses, cleaned them and stared some more.

Birds, I realized. The shoreline was alive with the dying. Pelicans, terns, gulls, dozens, hundreds of them, cloaked in gray, disoriented, still struggling. Mangroves, stripped bare, had been ornamented with the body parts of white wading birds.

A dust devil vacuumed odors upward. Death. Chemicals. Excarnated flesh. And something else…smoke. Burning tires, it smelled like.

I carried my tactical bag to the windward deck, kicking debris as I went, and took out binoculars that weren't needed at first. Mack's golf cart was ablaze. It had set the mechanic's shed on fire.

Lithium batteries? My friends had fretted about that.

In the parking lot was a slow-motion collision of cars. Audis, Toyotas and Detroit's best, some on their sides, others deep in the mangroves, frozen, all, in a pinwheel pattern that mimicked the schematics of a hurricane.

Among them was my old blue GMC pickup truck.

Oh… Goddamn it.

I'm not sentimental but, years ago, after a clandestine flight from Central America, that truck had navigated another circle by returning me home to this island. Now that home and my truck seemed to be ghosts from a previous life.

The lab's eastern deck provided a better view. Maria Estéban's houseboat had floated off and crashed onto an oyster bar in the middle of the bay. The marina's fence and gate were gone, as was foliage that had been sheared for miles. I used the binocs. Bayside, black smoke boiled somewhere near Millionaire's Row.

To the west, a second plume shot sparks into a sunless sky. Structures worth millions were in flames. Ronnie Patrick's warning came to mind: *The mercenaries torch houses and kill targets as they flee.*

I hailed Weatherby on the handheld. "I think they're already here, Max. There's a fire near you. It's not your place, is it? Don't poke your head out, they might shoot."

The Brit had to crack a shutter to transmit. "Negative, but I can smell smoke. Ford, listen—two boats, about a mile out, are headed my way from the... I'd say northeast. Big rubber tactical boats, like the SAS use. Stay where you are. My dock's bayside. Don't come out here. They'll spot you."

I scanned the entrance to Dinkin's Bay. "How many people? I don't see anything and I'm using binoculars."

Weatherby wasn't. Didn't need them, apparently. "I count four...no, five men judging from their heat signatures, possibly carrying weapons. And something else—troubling news, I'm afraid. In fact, let me confirm and I'll get back to you."

I cut in, "Hold on. Hannah's place is a few miles northeast of here. Tell me now."

He said, "Don't leap to conclusions. What concerns me is, part of the Causeway bridge is gone. Copy? The bridges are out."

That wasn't unexpected. "You mean closed to traffic? Of course the bridge is closed, but it'll reopen tomorrow."

"No, no—gone as in *gone*. Part of it collapsed," he insisted. "A wave, must've been a hell of a wave, took out the whole mainland span. I can see it from here. Hell of a mess. I doubt if Coast Guard will scramble helos before first light. It will be days, maybe weeks, before law enforcement can get vehicles on the island. You understand the unusual position that puts us in, correct?"

I didn't respond immediately. The landward Causeway span was only a mile or so from Big Sammy's apartment complex.

"Ford, do you copy?"

I replied, "Yeah, our position, definitely unusual. But, considering what we're up against, I see this more as an opportunity. Know what I mean?"

"Precisely," the Brit agreed.

I said, "Try your sat-phone again. If the police don't confirm Hannah and my son are in North Carolina, we're not going to have that whiskey. And have them check on people in the Davidson Road area. That's near the bridge. Understood?"

There was no response.

I said it again. "Goddamn it, Max, phone the cops. QSL?"

Weatherby squelched his mic key several times, more like in surprise than a code. I heard him say, "Ford...they're here. Someone's coming toward the steps. Gotta prepare a special welcome, my friend."

Seconds later, muted gunshots reached me from two miles away.

24

Grigori Pavlo and his former cellmate, Yenin, were in a boat, idling away from the deserted fishing village on Gumbo Limbo, separated by four miles of wind and ragged water from Millionaire's Row. They had to yell to be heard because of the waves, but the wind was beginning to calm.

It would be dark soon.

Pavlo told Yenin, "Get your hands away from that bucket, fool. Don't let anyone touch it or open the lid. Same with the garbage bag. Not until I've spoken the necessary—as if you'd understand—the final words of consecration."

Yenin knew his giant friend was territorial when it came to his victims—toys, he called them until they were no longer toys. After that, their bodies were sacred. In some cases, each artifact was a godly offering, or so Pavlo claimed.

Secretly, Yenin suspected that punishing sinners was an excuse for kinky sex and making profitable videos. All part of an act. The crazier a convict was, the less likely he'd be gang butt-checked in prison. Which was okay because Pavlo, the Vulture

Monk, was real. He was a true mystic who had accurately predicted their escape months before a flood had freed them from Black Dolphin Prison almost three years ago.

"By the almighty power of You-Know-Who," Yenin responded playfully by rote. His hand was on the throttle. "Ready to go faster?"

Pavlo was hunched over, a fresh joint protruding from his beard. "You irreverent ass—no, not until I get this lit. Goddamn rain... Okay, yes, but I'll take the wheel once I learn how. If you can do it, driving a boat can't be that hard."

He grinned a wolfish grin.

Yenin pretended to agree, saying, "That's why I created these markers. Breadcrumb markers like in the fairy tale. They will lead us home like happy children when it's dark."

The boat was the largest of their rubber transport vessels, a nine-meter outboard that had been owned by a company called Towboat US, but the markings had been painted out. Trailing them was another boat, three Russian immigrant recruits aboard. Two smaller boats, five armed men, had left earlier despite the size of the waves.

The "breadcrumbs" were a dozen reflective buoys roped to heavy weights. They lay on a deck that was empty save for tools, weapons, the bucket and a garbage bag. This was a trick Yenin had learned over years spent poaching sturgeon. Even after a hurricane, Florida's weather seemed mild compared to running blind on a winter night in the Caspian Sea. No need for a GPS, which, on this boat, didn't work, anyway. Yenin had a plastic chart open on the console.

"Start dropping the breadcrumbs now," he ordered. They had reached the end of the channel into the fishing village where they'd launched. The wind was volatile, the sky a gray, an acidic mist already bleeding light.

Pavlo exhaled smoke and shook his head. "Piss off, you start dropping them. I'm not throwing those heavy bastards."

He took the wheel. Every quarter mile or so, Yenin dumped a buoy on a course that followed the Intracoastal Waterway where many of the navigational towers had been toppled. They were near the mansions at the mouth of Dinkin's Bay when Pavlo noticed something large, bright orange, floating near what the chart said was York Island. He made a sharp turn that showered the deck with spray.

"What the hell are you doing?" Yenin reached for a towel. "You're going the wrong way."

"Shut up. I want to see what that is." Pavlo had a heavy hand on the gas, no feeling at all for how to slide a vessel through quartering seas. "My angels tell me it's something unusual to see out here after a storm. A warning, perhaps—or something fun. Let's take a look."

The Vulture Monk and his voices. The topic could not be argued—not without violence, anyway.

They slammed through waves, heading toward intracoastal marker 13-A, which is why Yenin insisted, "Slow down. That's shallow water. Too shallow. See the chart?"

Pavlo ignored him. Several hundred yards away, the orange object became a tent with a flapping nylon door zipped open. There were people inside; people waving, one of them a huge man, shirtless. Behind him, two women. One appeared to be nursing a baby.

Pavlo began laughing. "Oh, you doubt the crazy wisdom of this shit? My voices—you see, my angels never lie."

Yenin braced himself for running aground, then made a bold move. He reached and pulled the throttle into Neutral seconds before the propeller nicked bottom. The motor's skeg banged a couple of times and the boat drifted free.

"Bastard fool. Why did you interfere?"

The Vulture Monk had the craziest eyes Yenin had ever seen. That much wasn't an act.

"So you can be rich, Grigori. So we can both be rich. See?"

He nodded to cresting waves that outlined a sandbar. "Hit that, we would've spent all night out here. What do we care about those people? It is a life raft. I've seen life rafts many times. Their yacht must've sunk. To hell with them, let's go."

Pavlo used binoculars.

"That big man...praise my angels, I know him. I saw him today. A Mexican and his teenage wife."

"Huh?"

"A Mexican—or from one of those peasant shitholes. He doesn't even own a truck that works let alone a goddamn yacht, you fool."

Yenin was sick of his own nervous laughter. And he was sick of the abusive Monk. "All the more reason to leave them behind, Grigori. Here...let me trim the engine and steer us away from that bar. Move over...please?"

Pavlo slammed the binoculars and grabbed his rifle, an AK with a full mag. "Go, drive. *Do it.* If I can't have the Mexican's wife, then he can't—"

"What are you doing?" Yenin ducked when the barrel spun near his face.

"The mother's nursing a... I want her. Goddamn it...can't you hold this boat steady?" Without aiming, Pavlo opened fire, full automatic, a rainbow of brass clattering at their feet.

Yenin didn't care about the Mexicans, but he'd seen the Monk's insane rages before. "Tonight, it'll be calmer," he said in a soothing way. "You want the girl? No problem. We'll stop on the way back, or you can shoot them all now. I don't give a shit. Come on, let's get rich and take the girl later. What do you say?"

Pavlo fired another burst and nearly went overboard in the heavy swells. "Look—did I hit him? I think I hit him." He was switching magazines. "Drop one of those buoys here. Nursing mothers are hard to find, and I don't want to forget where she is."

Yenin pretended to drop a buoy but didn't—no way was he

going to risk these shoals after dark. Then he powered toward a row of three-story homes that looked vacant among trees that were leafless or lay in shattered toothpick piles along the beach. Several hundred meters to the left, one of their smaller boats was visible among the rubble. Straight ahead was the second boat, three team members on shore. They'd been there for a while.

Pavlo consulted notes on his phone. "The tall house with the tower—a primary target. A British billionaire doctor. An inventor, too. Sasha warned he might design weapon systems for the military. A powerful asset. Get this—" the monk was laughing "—Maximilian Weatherby. How's that for the name of a rich ass-sniffing capitalist?"

"Who?"

"Weatherby. A billionaire with an art collection."

"No, Sasha. Who's Sasha?"

"Never mind. Just a shrunken oligarch prune. A member of the Brotherhood who thinks he's a genius. This is what we're after. A painting that looks worthless to me but—"

On the phone was a photo. Yenin pushed the phone away. "Don't. I have to concentrate, there's so much junk in the water." He tapped the console. "This boat is— See? Doesn't even have a kill switch. It did but, shit, that's dangerous in a rough sea, man. I fall over, the engine's supposed to stop automatically."

"Oh, there's a kill switch and he's standing beside you, Comrade." The crazy Monk, his beard a black flag in the wind, grinned at his own joke while, on the third floor of the tall house, a shutter slid open. "Wait. Slow down. I want to see what's happening. He's home, the Brit, there are lights. Sasha was right. He must have a generator."

It was calmer inside the bay where denuded trees blocked the wind. Their rubber boat slowed, pulled in close to the trees, Yenin at the wheel. The Brit's home had sailing-ship dormers, wood siding, amber-colored in the late afternoon light, four stories high. The third-floor window shutter had stopped moving. It left only a narrow space four hundred meters away across the water.

Pavlo retrieved the binoculars. The profile of a man appeared.

"Get your rifle," he ordered Yenin. "Go ahead—shoot."

The man inside the house disappeared, replaced by what looked like the lens of a camera. Or a sniper-sized telescopic sight.

"Shoot who?" Yenin was busy maneuvering the boat.

"You fool. What the hell's that British ass doing? Taking photographs? Shit, he could have a rifle."

The Brit's retractable shutter closed.

Down the beach was a larger house, a mansion, white stone and marble. According to Sasha's notes, inside was an old couple, the Lászlos, who owned an international chain of jewelry stores. On the second floor was their hidden commercial walk-in safe. Explosives might be needed. The couple also owned a dog or two, which would have to be dealt with first.

Pavlo swung the binocs. Two of his mercenaries were approaching the mansion from the north. One of them was a smart-ass kid, three tear tats beneath his eye. Maybe earned but probably not. Attacking the weakest targets first, though, was smart. And safer if the Brit had a sniper rifle.

"Drop me off there." Pavlo pointed, a radio to his ear, and hailed the smart-ass kid on two-meter military frequency while the boat idled shoreward. In the shallows, he hefted a bag filled with extra ammo, breaching tools, a block of C-4 explosive and thirty meters of det cord.

Yenin asked, "And do what after you're on the beach?"

Pavlo motioned, *Hurry up.* "I want a few rounds of covering fire. Shoot at Weatherby's house, third floor, on my signal. Then wait offshore."

"Weatherby?"

"The British billionaire. Jesus Christ, you Latvian idiot. Monitor the radio and learn to pay attention. I'll call when I'm ready."

Yenin opened his mouth to respond, then grimaced as if he'd been stabbed in the head with an ice pick. Pavlo clapped his hands to his ears to muffle a searing high-pitched agony that vibrated his skull.

"Jesus Christ…what the hell…"

He spun around. From the third floor of the Brit's house streamed beads of iridescent light, bubble-sized, that hosed one of their mule boats beached a hundred meters away.

The bubble stream vanished. The sound—if it was a sound—stopped and left a deafening, pressurized silence.

Yenin braced for another assault before saying, "My God, and it wasn't even aimed at us. What do you think that shit was? Hey—see the guy on the beach? He's one of ours, rolling around like he's been shot. Let's go get him."

"No, you fool. Stay away from the goddamn Brit. Now I understand why Sasha warned me. Bastard invents weapon systems."

"Who?" Yenin, still in pain, was massaging his ears.

"Weapon systems, dumbass. Stay away from his goddamn house—for now, anyway. Get your rifle ready. The moment my feet hit the water, start shooting, then get the hell offshore, around that point where he can't see you."

Pavlo, before he went over the side, touched the garbage bag for luck.

The female torso it contained was still warm.

25

heard more gunfire after I'd lugged tools through the mangroves to my boat and had to return to the lab for a chain saw.

"Max," I said into the handheld radio, "are you okay? CQ,
Max, do you read?"

No response from the Brit or when I tried Big Sammy again.

Carrying the saw, I hurried back to the mangrove tunnel. Mud
creatures were too exhausted to scatter. Dozens of pelicans—I had
to step over them, around them. The mud, ankle-deep, wasn't
mud. It was a slick coagulate that clung to my boots like cement.

I fell once, landed on my ass. With a machete, I hacked a
walking stick and made a third trip in pre-darkness, water sometimes up to my waist.

There were shadows. Glowing red eyes appeared when I used
an LED. Alligators, several over six feet, had tracked a greasy
exodus of dead birds, fish and a multitude of palm rats that had
been jettisoned from their nests. The rats, still alive, clung to
logs, a flotilla of plastics, solar panels and backyard propane

tanks. Squealing, teeth bared, the rats, squirrel-sized, battled for dominance and real estate.

A couple of gators pivoted and followed. Reptiles were hungry now that the barometer was rising.

My boat was in rough shape, but the three-hundred-horse outboard started. By then it was nearly dark. I made a final stop at my stilt house. All bones and wreckage, yet a solid scaffolding against lightning tracers of ionic blue. My Blackwater shotgun, barrel down, went into a rod holder. On a headband, I fitted the MUMs night vision monocular over my left eye. Darkness became lucent green daylight.

Mangroves took shape. Beyond Woodring Point, rooftops along Millionaire's Row formed a ledge. A single white light marked the Brit's upper deck. I'd run this channel a thousand times, but the bay was now a minefield of sunken junk. I didn't press the throttle until I heard an explosion to the north. It was a familiar C-4 report that might have been used to open the safe of two elderly jewelry store owners.

The boat levered onto plane. I hailed Weatherby, who this time responded in a whisper.

"These people know what they're doing, and they're trigger-happy. Suggest you stay where you are. They'll open fire if they see a boat pull up to what's left of my dock."

"Don't need your dock," I told him. "There's a mangrove area behind that stretch of beach. Water's thin, but I can get within a hundred yards of your place. Plenty of cover."

Weatherby replied, "Can't hear, sorry. Say again?"

The wind was less than thirty, but still a lot of noise. I dropped the boat off plane and repeated the transmission.

Weatherby replied, "No…no. Stay there, it's too bloody dangerous. I'll manage on my own and check back. If things get dodgy, I still have a trick or two up my sleeve."

That's what I was worried about. "Hang on. I'm thinking of my own safety. If you don't have a gun, then exactly what are you using to…" I didn't finish. It was possible the bad guys were monitoring channel six-eight.

The Brit understood. "You would need eye and ear protection. Industrial-grade, which you certainly don't have. Copy what I'm saying?"

I responded, "Laser?"

He repeated, "Eye and ear protection."

This was confusing. Lasers are as silent as sunlight.

"You're talking a sonic device?" It was an unlikely combination of high-tech weaponry.

"Both," Weatherby confirmed. "Ford…give me a sec. *Right*. More visitors, I'm afraid. Another pair of tactical boats, but larger. Transport vessels, I fancy. Yes…now they're slowing. Uh-oh, I don't like this."

I shoved the throttle ahead. "What's wrong?"

"In the lead transport there are two males and possibly a female lying on the deck. Breasts radiate a distinctive signature that…no, it's probably a male, but his body temp is abnormally low. So repeat, stay where you are until I ferret things out."

"Are you sure there's not a woman aboard?"

He replied, "Flat-chested, that's all I can say for certain. My God…next door, somehow three of them got into my neighbor's home, but now… Damn all, I can't take action because the Lászlos are in there somewhere. Stand by, Ford."

I reduced speed. "Flat-chested" did not apply to Captain Hannah Smith, but that wasn't the reason. To starboard, a few hundred yards away, a small yellow light had appeared. I shifted to Neutral until I understood. Maria Estéban's houseboat had been grounded there by the storm. The light was either a sparking battery or someone was aboard.

For a moment, Maria's headstrong daughter, Sabina, ten years old, popped into my mind. Could she have snuck back to the island and…?

Impossible. I'd cleared the place myself before doing a piss-

poor job of rigging mooring lines. Which left only one probability.

I told Weatherby, "Expect me in about ten. I've got ear protection, that's all. Understood? No special glasses. Don't do anything until I get there."

The NV monocular brought the houseboat into focus. It lay
at an angle atop an oyster bar. No obvious movement inside,
just the flickering light of what had to be a candle. Or a lighter.
I sped past as if I hadn't noticed, then swung upwind, killed the
engine and drifted close enough to tie a line to a cleat.

Inside was another mud creature, man-sized, huddled and
weeping on a soggy mattress. When Andy Dimitry sat up, he
resembled a Pompeii victim, caught by an ancient lava flow. All
but his face was cloaked in gray.

His eyes opened. "It's you. Thank God you came back. I
nearly died climbing onto this thing. Heard your engine and
thought you'd gone past and left me."

I stood in the doorway. "Stop crying or I will."

Maria's houseboat had come through with less damage than
expected. It was strange. The random vectors of wind and water
could flatten a landscape yet leave some structures relatively
unscarred.

"Dr. Ford—can I call you that? I shouldn't have pretended I
wanted to shoot you. I was wrong, but I was so damn scared—
not that I'm making excuses. I owe you, man. And I'll pay.
You're not gonna hurt me, are you? My God, that was a hell of
a dirty trick you pulled giving me an empty gun."

"Yeah, I'm such a thoughtless jerk sometimes."

"It was cruel, man. I wouldn't have shot you, just wanted to
give you a scare. I damn near drowned."

I tilted a chair up. "Sit. If you move, I'll zip-tie your hands
behind your back and tape your mouth."

He did as he was told. "Anything, man, anything you say.
Hey…how would you like to be a multimillionaire? I'm talk-

ing as of tonight. Seriously. Just don't go off and leave me, okay? That's the deal. Give me a minute. I'll explain how it works. *Please*."

I moved through Maria's houseboat room to room while he launched into a nervous talking jag. Post-storm theft, he said, wasn't actually theft. Financially speaking, theft was a good thing. It allowed policy holders to recoup money they deserved but probably wouldn't be paid for structural damages.

"That shack of yours," Dimitry said, "think your carrier is good for repairs? Bullshit. They'll pay a fraction of what they owe, and it'll be eight months before you see a cent. They'll drag it out, come up with every excuse, but always through a middleman. See? That's the game plan. How do I know? Because *I did it* man—until I got sick of screwing people over. I'm not such a bad guy, Dr. Ford. Honest. Give me a chance, I'll prove it."

In ten-year-old Sabina's room, I rescued a strand of blue-and-yellow beads. In her sister Mirabella's room was an iPad still dry in its waterproof case. Maria and her daughters had fled in a rush, as had thousands of others. Now what they'd left behind was fair game for the jackals who, inevitably, flooded in after a storm.

Dimitry, one of the jackals, was chattering away because he was afraid of me. And more afraid of the Russians.

"Say your policy is five hundred grand. If the carrier hangs onto your money and invests it right, the check they finally cut—a year later, if you're lucky—it won't be much more than the interest they made off the principal. Then they'll double your rates next year. Sick, huh? You've lived in this area for a while? How many properties you think got damaged?"

The houseboat wasn't built for cruising, but there was a base station VHF in the galley. I gave it a try, anyway. The battery was dead. On the portside floor, because of the tilting angle, personal items had collected in heaps. I knelt and searched.

My silence made Dimitry nervous. "Seriously, take a guess— no don't bother. Close to a quarter million damaged homes.

That's the industry's projection. Statistics, all computerized. Of those quarter million claims, carriers will flat reject about half. A fact. Look it up. Another hundred thousand claims, they'll lowball by eighty percent because they know, statistically, that middle-income, poor people, will take the first damn check they see without a fight. They're that desperate. And they say I was a thief."

Three passports—Maria and her daughters—went into a waterproof bag. A sodden checkbook and a book of Sabina's handwritten poetry went into a separate bag. I walked toward Dimitry. "On your feet. Do you speak Russian?"

"Do I... No. Well, yeah. A little. But you haven't heard the important part yet. See, what carriers *will* pay for are big-ticket collectibles. Specific items individually insured. They can't argue the value, and the appraisals are always sky-high. So—you know, the steal-from-the-rich thing. Policy-holders actually make a profit, so nobody gets hurt."

I said, "Never thought of it like that, Andy. Doing your victims a favor. You're one hell of a guy."

"Exactly. No...not victims. Not my victims, anyway. The carriers are going to screw them on flood and structural, so this is the perfect workaround. That's where you come in."

"Me? Sounds exciting." I downed a second bottle of water. An hour after dark, the temp was mideighties. Even the rain outside had a visceral heat.

"Damn right it's exciting. Helping people, even though they don't know it." He pointed vaguely toward Millionaire's Row. "There's twenty mil in jewels, rare art out there, all with itemized, full-value riders. Paintings by this guy, Washen... Washenberg-something, and a walk-in safe loaded with gems, diamonds, all heavy money shit. Ever hear of the Kashmir Sapphire? A jeweler, an old crippled guy, wears the damn thing as a ring supposedly. Like taking candy from a, you know... Stick with me, Ford, you're gonna be rich. Just do what I say and—hey, I can't see!"

I had extinguished the candle. "Rauschenberg was the artist's name, not Washenberg. And it doesn't matter as long as I can see. Come on, you're going to introduce me to your Russian friends."

His reaction—terrified. I had to use duct tape and zip ties before forcing the guy onto my boat.

When I radioed Weatherby about finding my visitor, he replied, "Anatoli Dimitry. That's what I figured."

I said, "Max, how about an update on the unidentified passenger. Are you sure it's not a female?"

"Still not certain. One of the larger boats—a transport—turned around for some reason. But they'll be back. Clear, standing by."

26

What I hoped was a saltwater crocodile turned out to be a drifting tree when I jumped the bar into Ladyfinger Lakes, backside of Millionaire's Row.

A croc would have spooked clear of my skeg. The tree did not. Thin water requires planing speed—about twenty miles per hour. The impact kicked the boat's stern in the air and threw me into the throttle. For a sickening few seconds the propeller tried to buzz-saw through wood. Then the engine died.

The insurance exec made whooping noises because his mouth was taped. I tilted the lower unit high, drifted clear and tried again. The engine revved. There was torque. I hadn't spun the hub—a huge relief.

"You don't have to whisper, but keep your voice down," I said, and ripped off the tape. Wind noise, the crash of distant waves blotted everything else. Dimitry was on his side, dazed, forward of the console. It had been a rough crossing.

"What did we hit? Geezus, cut my hands loose. Feel like I'm gonna vomit. Where are we?"

I lifted him by the elbow. "Take a seat and don't move until I tell you."

"I'm dying of thirst, man. So goddamn dark, how can you see? You can't see—this is crazy."

Without NV optics, he would've been right. We were tunneling into the darkness. No sky, no horizon, only the boiling sparks of a house fire ahead and the sulfuric odor of mangroves.

The prop was kicking mud.

I killed the engine. "Quiet. Just listen. We're going to drift closer, then I'll get out and wade us ashore. Tell me what to expect from those guys. How are they armed?"

"What to expect…armed—are you kidding? Not until you get me on the other side of the bridge. That was our deal. I've got to have something to drink, man."

"The only deal you have, pal, is me. Either do what I say or get out of the boat. Find your own way home." When he didn't respond immediately, I did it—clipped his cuffs and rolled him overboard.

After that, Dimitry was eager to cooperate.

I made him slog alongside the boat while he answered questions. He clung to the gunnel but still had a tough time keeping up. The bottom was muck to the knees. Three times he lost his grip and had to catch up in a splashing panic.

"Hey—wait, help me," he pleaded. "There's something out there. Huge, geezus. Something moving like a shark. Hurry, I told you everything I know. Goddamn it, help me in the boat."

Dimitry motioned aft. I turned long enough to believe he'd seen the tree we'd just hit. "Yeah, a hell of a big shark—but not until you convince those Russians they need your big brain."

"Shittin' me—how?"

"Won't be easy," I agreed. "Try using your big mouth."

The man lost his grip on the gunnel again. He trailed farther behind when I slipped overboard and towed us toward the light on Weatherby's fourth-floor deck. Mangroves stretched along the backside of Millionaire's Row. Isolated to the right were more mangroves. They rimmed a shell mound where larger trees grew. Buttonwoods, gumbo limbos. Centuries ago, there might have been a Calusa signal fire there.

I clicked the mic key several times, used my hand as a windshield and spoke softly into the radio. "I'm three, maybe four minutes out. Approaching from the back of the property. I'll make sure your neighbors aren't trapped first. Acknowledge?"

Weatherby's response was flat, almost robotic. "The mercenaries, they know, and they're headed your way. Nothing I could do. Get out of here. Run."

"How many, Max?" He talked over me while I scanned the shoreline. I had to ask again, "How many?"

"At least two. I repeat, two. Conventional kit, tactical lights and weapons. Laser sights but no IR. Ford, listen. The unidentified person in their boat, I don't think he's alive. Or she's alive. The body temp keeps falling."

I said, "Could be one of theirs."

"Maybe, but listen. They must have put a tracking chip on your visitor. Understand?"

"What? But there's no cell service."

"I can't explain it, but get rid of him. The insurance guy. He needs to be on the bottom. *The bottom.* Acknowledge—and put your ears on. I can't wait much longer."

GPS chips can't transmit from underwater, is what the Brit meant. Pete's GPS collar came into my mind and then was gone when, behind me, Dimitry bellowed, "Shoot...shoot the damn thing! Look, look, from the direction of that fire. Goddamn you, help me into the boat."

He had fallen, still terrified of the tree we'd hit. Or so I believed until I turned. Flames streaked a region of black water that was furrowed by a massive wake. In neon green, I saw details. The dinosaur head and bulk of a six-hundred-pound crocodile was gliding toward us. I slogged and lunged, grabbed Dimitry by the arm, then froze. On the mangrove shoreline was a man, a rifle slung over his shoulder.

My first reaction was to pull my sidearm and shoot. Instead, after pushing my boat away, I contrived a trap by dragging Dimitry to the rim of the shell mound.

The croc, twelve feet long, ruddered in pursuit, only a few dozen yards away.

"Climb," I told the man. "Climb as high as you can and make it fast." We had stumbled to the base of a gumbo limbo tree. With my hands I made a stirrup and boosted him up. "No matter what happens, don't tell your people about me. You got that?"

He was unaware of the mercenary—now two men—tracking us.

"Why would I talk to a— Hey, what was that thing, an alligator? Goddamn, it's huge. You sure I'm safe up here?"

Across the water, a spotlight blazed. I ducked when it panned the foliage.

Dimitry whispered, "Oh, my God. Think they saw us? Who is it? Maybe that tall freak, Pavlo, the one who—"

I baited him again, saying, "Not one word about me, damn you," and disappeared toward the top of the mound before ducking back to the mangroves. At water's edge, I drew a Randall dive knife and watched.

Two men were in the water with flashlights. *Good.* No night vision optics. One of them searched my boat. The other switched off his headlamp, checked a GPS wrist device and waded toward the tree where I'd left Dimitri. One tracker, one wingman. Military once upon a time, perhaps, but each moved with a fentanyl boldness. Bulletproof, immune to pain. Brain-buzzed killers, safe within a withered aspect that had no conscience.

The tracker stopped upwind of me. Close enough to taint air molecules with nicotine, mothballs, vodka. He unslung his rifle and consulted the wrist device. The rifle became a compass needle. It moved laterally. It tilted vertically and found Dimitry's gumbo limbo tree.

The mercenary's raspy voice called, "Anatoli, my brother. Talk to me. How we can talk if I don't know where you are? This American, he with you? They pay bounty. What you say, brother? Big bounty, you and me, if we find him." Broken English. A playful smile in his offer.

The wingman said something in Russian. My boat had become a shield that he pushed toward his partner. When he spoke again, he pointed in a way that communicated concern.

To my left, limbs snapped. A massive weight moved toward the water.

The tracker noticed. His rifle adjusted for deviation. "Anatoli, no bullshit time. You the boss man. The Monk, what we care for him? Talk to me. Tell me where is American. You safe, I swear." After several seconds, he dropped the act. "*Pizdá* bitch, you want me shoot? I hear you. Now I come, feed your nose to Grigori if you don't—"

Dimitry hollered, "He's here. The biologist. He's got a gun, I'm not sure where. See? I'm trying to help you."

The tracker's legs went out from under him at the word *gun*. He became a moving target. Just his head above the water, rifle up and ready. His partner rushed to provide my boat for cover. Both men ducked behind it.

Some of Dimitry's bravado returned. "About time you're taking orders from me again. I'll come down but not until I can get in a boat. You, too. There's a goddamn alligator or something, I'm serious. First, I want some guarantees about that freak Pavlo before—"

One of the men, maybe both, opened fire in the direction of the gumbo limbo. Impossible to be certain because I was moving fast to distance myself from stray rounds. When I looked back, the croc had launched itself in silence. Neither mercenary noticed the torpedo-like wake.

Knife drawn, I watched...then didn't want to watch. The trap I'd set had teeth. When the frenzy subsided—it took a while—

I retrieved my boat and crossed unseen to the backside of Millionaire's Row. A tactical victory for me, but victories seldom last, nor do they scar. Memories sometimes do.

In 1945, fleeing Japanese soldiers had been dismembered by crocodiles in a South Pacific swamp. Hundreds of men. The shrieks, panicked gunfire, the minefield explosions of a reptile's death roll. What I had just heard, what I'd witnessed, was a similar horror.

I didn't look back until Dimitry wailed, "I've been shot. Hear me? Gotta get me to the mainland, Ford. Shot in the belly. You can't go off and let me die."

"Already have," I whispered.

The knife I had just used to dispatch the tracker—a kindness, perhaps—went into its sheath.

27

Millionaire's Row is a quarter mile of waterfront, rough sand and rocks, an isolated stretch serviced by a single shell road. I exited the mangroves in the last outgoing flow of tidal surge and stopped, unsure where land ended and the bay began.

A fire blazed near the Lászlos' concrete mansion. Half an acre to my left, a third-floor lantern marked Weatherby's observation post. But the tactical boats he'd described were either gone or hidden among a ridgeline of wreckage.

"Max, Max, you copy? Where are they?" My earbud noise system had failed to pair with my handheld, but I wore them, anyway.

No response.

My priority was helping Weatherby or the two elderly poodle lovers who were either dead or trapped, unable to escape. A tough call. Either way, I needed elevation to get a visual, so I plowed toward the Lászlo mansion through a lava field backdropped by flames.

A vehicle had caught fire in the adjacent carport. A flurry of activity at the edge of the property caused me to change course. In the bushes was an overturned wheelchair coated in mud. When I gave it a kick, a cloud of crabs, insects, rodents scurried away from what, at first, I thought was a bag of garbage.

It was a person. An old man, although difficult to be sure because of what scavengers had done to him. No pulse, body still warm. I gauged the angle and distance to the mansion. The wheelchair-bound do not venture out in a storm. So he had been jettisoned by a killer. Or, terrified for some reason, the old man had launched himself off the highest balcony.

I went up the mansion steps and entered through a shattered door. Inside was a space that seemed darker for crystal chandeliers. A ballroom. Lightless, the marble floor slick with marl. Walls, once a museum of artwork, barren. Furniture had been overturned, cushions slit with knives.

Pistol at low ready, I moved to the next room. There on an antique divan sat a woman, hair in disarray, eyes closed as if asleep. She wore spattered white yachting attire, an elegant lady, late seventies, yet her face was a timeless cameo of symmetry. A beauty years ago, a beauty now. Two small stuffed animals lay on her lap. Not real. Childlike comforters—a tableau that squeezed the heart.

I positioned a flashlight on a table, switched it on…hesitated because of what I saw…then knelt beside her.

"Mrs. Lászlo. I'm a friend, a neighbor," I whispered. "You're safe now. Are the men still here?"

Eyes of gray-jade opened. Startled, the woman recoiled. "Don't touch me again. I will not tolerate it—not after what you did to my husband and our sweet dog. Kill me. Or leave. I don't care, but I refuse to be afraid anymore." Her eyes squinched shut, braced for whatever abuse that might follow.

The stuffed animals were toddler-sized, imitation toys, with ribbons and yarn hair, weathered playthings from a previous generation. Her girlhood, perhaps.

Max had mentioned the Lászlos owning a prize poodle, but the dog was not in the room.

"I'm sorry this happened, ma'am. Let me help. Where are they? The men who did this."

She stiffened but this time scanned the room. "Is this really...? Please tell me I'm dreaming. Who are you?" Jade-gray eyes focused. "You're not him. You're not..."

I said, "Nope. But I'll find him. Is he still in the house?"

She seemed to awaken when I touched a finger to my lips.

"I'm...I'm not sure. For God's sake, call the police. A man—a man with horrible tattoos—he murdered my husband because Benjamin wouldn't tell them the combination. So they used a bomb. Dynamite, I guess. And then he and another man did the same thing to our—" the woman stroked the curly comforters on her lap and sobbed "—to our sweetest little girl. She didn't even try to bite him. A tall man—a monster—with some other men."

The woman sat straighter. "Do you have a gun? My husband wouldn't tell them the how to open the vault, so they tied his hands and did it—threw him off the balcony into that terrible flood. I watched a whirlpool take my sweet Benjamin away. I don't suppose it's possible that he's... No. No one could survive what they did to him. Young man, you will need a gun."

I said, "We'll search for your husband. But first, I need to check the upstairs. Where's the vault?"

Her head tilted. She pointed a finger at a marble staircase and asked, "Are you sure you're one of my neighbors? I don't recognize you. Your name is...?"

"I'm a friend of Dr. Weatherby," I told her. "The tall guy with the tattoo and how many others, Mrs. Lászlo?"

"A friend of Max's?" The woman blinked her confusion away. "Dear God, that's where at least two of them went. I heard them talking. You must warn Max. But no, you can't leave. They'll come back and kill us all."

Above us, a door slammed. Heavy footsteps clumped across an upper floor.

The woman squeezed my hand. "Maybe that's him, the monster. If you have a gun, I'll do it. Give it to me. I *want* to do it."

We left her stuffed animals on the divan. I led the elegant lady into a bathroom, gave her the flashlight and told her, "Hide in the tub and keep the door locked unless you hear my voice. I'll be back, Mrs. László."

I followed my pistol up the stairway. Tritium night sights, fore and aft, swept the landing, then a wide switchback that opened onto the second floor. Someone was up there with a flashlight. At least one man—his boots and knees came into view before he jogged up to the third level.

A piece of wooden furniture skidded. Glass shattered. Russian profanities were muffled by my earbuds. The man was foraging for leftovers. His sloppiness provided cover while I did a quick sweep of the second floor and trailed him up another flight of steps. I timed it right. Hugged a wall, waited for the flashlight to pivot and surprised him from behind. A collapsible steel ASP baton, two feet long, makes a distinctive *CLICK* when deployed. As he turned, the baton cleaved his right thigh. A second blow between shoulder and elbow put him on the floor, semiconscious in shock and pain.

I used zip-tie cuffs and frisked him. Two pistols, his passport, a cheap stiletto, a few pieces of jewelry went into my bag before I bulldozed him out onto the balcony. By then he'd recovered sufficiently to moan and protest in broken English.

Thirty-six feet down, among the ruined landscape, was Benjamin László's wheelchair, his body a cauldron of activity once again. Considering the force of the tidal surge, the angle and distance meshed.

I slammed the guy against the marble railing. "Why did you kill the old man?" I didn't expect an answer, but did when I demanded, "Is there a woman in one of your boats? Where is she? Who is she? Talk or you're going over headfirst."

When he tried to pull away, I got a close look at him. Christ— just a kid, midtwenties. Nose, tongue and ears adorned with rings. A triad of teardrops beneath his right eye; tats that bragged he'd killed at least three people. Ornamental scars, self-inflicted. They mirrored a deeper, starving disfigurement.

"My arm, my arm, it is...you have broken my arm," he groaned. "Broken is my leg, also. Why you do this? My friends come back, oh you so sorry then, son-bitch."

Wind brightened the darkness, a shower of sparks from the nearby fire. My face was revealed. The NV monocular I wore was the single glowing eye of a cyclops.

"Who...who are you?"

I raised the baton as if to hit him again. "A guy your team was supposed to kill. Tell me—is there a woman? Where is she?"

"I...I don't know. In other boat. A, uh, a policewoman they said. Alive... I swear. Hurt, yes, is possible. I do nothing. Hurt no people, not old man, not dog—no matter what old bitch woman say."

He was lying.

Lieutenant Birdy Tupplemeyer came into my mind. Was he talking about her or the FWC officer who'd already been rescued?

"What's your name?"

"Is...Donald. Donny."

I'd seen his passport. This was the second fake Donald I'd met today.

"Of course it is," I said. "Where did your people launch from?"

It took a while to explain the question. His answer was evidence that the SUV in Hannah's drive had been scouting for a base with high ground and a boat ramp. The guy claimed he didn't know who had named me and my family as targets.

"The big bosses, maybe. Miami, Moscow—they tell us shit-nothing. Me, I am just peasant. Take orders from crazy man. Yes, true. He is called—"

Pavlo is the name I heard.

"How you say, like large eagle, black, a meat bird on road. A priest. A crazy bird priest, yes. I think he will kill me, too, all of us and take everything. Help me, I show you boat. Our boat, not crazy priest's boat. His boat is large, much more large, but ours, it is close, see—"

I relaxed my grip when he raised a left arm and pointed, his fingers near my face. This side of Weatherby's ruined dock, shielded by debris, was a small tactical boat, black vulcanized tubes instead of fiberglass. Only one man aboard, the deck overloaded with metal boxes to protect their swag on the wet trip back to Gumbo Limbo.

On the young mercenary's thumb, a diamondesque flash caught my attention. I used a wrist come-along to lever his hand back and yanked off an ornate gold ring. A huge gem was set flush in a square signet mount. Illuminated by a pocket LED, the stone was a dazzling Gulf Stream blue.

"The Kashmir Sapphire," I said, hoping for a reaction.

I got it. The guy—"Donald"—tried to grab the ring from me, saying, "Is mine! You know worth? I know worth. You help, we split, but is mine."

After staring down at where Benjamin László had come to rest, I stepped back. "You killed the old man. Took this off his finger and threw him over while his wife watched. Turn around."

"No...please." His left hand came up as a shield. "It was accident. Was crazy priest, not me."

I said, "A lot of accidents happen during hurricanes. There's a nice lady downstairs who's heard enough screams for one night. So do it—turn, face the railing. Now."

He refused. It didn't matter.

I used the baton.

28

I went down the steps and tapped on the bathroom door. Mrs. László refused to cry when I squeezed the ring into her hand, saying, "This belongs to you, ma'am."

"Benjamin. He's gone, isn't he? You don't have to lie." Her eyes swept the marble staircase. "Are they still in our home? How many?"

I said, "Just one—but he was gone by the time I got upstairs. Follow me. Watch your footing. It's slick." Using the pocket LED, I led her through the ballroom.

"But how could that man have left without...? I didn't see him come down the steps."

"Hard to say, Mrs. László. Maybe a rope ladder or he climbed down somehow. I cleared the other two floors. They cleaned out your walk-in vault, I'm afraid. Come on. You're safe for now."

She stopped, placed a hand on a Steinway baby grand. "But you can't be sure of that. What if the man you heard...what if he comes back?"

I knew what she was asking. I muted the light and looked into her face. "He won't."

"Are you saying—"

"That would be my guess," I replied and watched some of the tension go out of her. "Here, take the flashlight. I recovered some other stuff that belongs to you."

On the piano, a spectacular diamond tennis bracelet and a couple of necklaces formed a glittering pile. She used the light to illuminate her husband's ring. "It is beautiful, isn't it? The Kashmir Tsar Sapphire—quite a famous stone. Did you notice the etchings on the side?" She turned it in her fingers. "Harps. Grecian lyra. I used to play the harp—a hundred years ago."

I smiled but, internally, noted the link—a meaningless irony— to a pal who was last reported sailing toward a constellation of the same name.

Still fondling the ring, she selected the tennis bracelet and took a seat on the divan. Good manners forbade an emotional outburst, but she did say, "This is very thoughtful of you. I'm Rebecca. Becca to my friends. May I ask your name?"

I said, "Stay here. I'll be back as soon as can. Or I'll send someone. Dr. Weatherby—Max, he could be in trouble. Until then, take this." I placed a spare VHF radio on the couch. "To talk, just push the button and—"

"I know how to use a radio, young man. I've sailed catboats since I was a girl. Don't patronize me. I know Max is in trouble because that's where those men went. I told you that, didn't I? At least two of them." Her thoughts moved to what had happened upstairs. "My dear stubborn Benjamin—a poor boy from Hungary; worked the carnivals as a pickpocket. Very tough, street-savvy, which made us rich. My teacher in many ways. A man like him didn't deserve what they did. He's dead, isn't he?"

I cleared my throat. "I'm afraid there's not much hope."

She let that settle. "Thank you. It's okay now that I'm sure. I've been through a whole family of funerals. Death is…it doesn't seem important anymore. All just noise in the past. The man you…the one who took my husband's ring, did he have a tattoo?" Her hand moved to her breasts, more of a protective reflex than to illustrate. "A horrid bird with talons."

"Not that I saw, Missus…uhh, Rebecca. Just three teardrops under his right eye. Do you remember him? The guy I just described?"

Yes, she remembered. "A much younger man, late teens I'd guess. I hope he burns in hell. He shot at our poodle, the last I will ever own. My sweet Maggie, the sensitive one. A beautiful champagne-colored standard. Scared her so badly she jumped off the porch during the worst of the flood. Nothing—not Benjamin or Maggie—could survive that."

I said, "I hope you're wrong," while the woman touched her cheek.

"Three little tattoos," she said, "and he laughed when he did it. Shot at sweet Maggie. I don't think he hit her, but maybe… Then left me alone with the tall one—the monster—so he could…" The woman shuddered, looked up. "Do you have an extra gun? I don't want to be left alone again. I know how to shoot. We did sporting clays and targets. I'm…I'm quite good, actually."

I'd already considered leaving the confiscated pistol. But the lady was in shock. On overload from an assault that would have pushed the most stable of people to the brink of sanity. Yet Rebecca Lászlo projected a bedrock solidity that suggested she could be trusted.

Nope…couldn't risk it. Not here amid so much loss and ruin, a woman recently widowed, already near the end of her years.

I said, "I won't be long, Rebecca. And you've got the radio."

Unexpectedly, she stood and hugged me in a motherly way. Voice soft, she patted my right hip and said, "When you come back, don't be afraid to entrust me with your name. The police will never hear it from me. I swear…Dr. Ford."

I stepped away from eyes of jade, her face a cameo that had not aged. "Why pretend you didn't know?"

"To protect us all." She stared at the shattered door, sitting again. "Benjamin has...he had contacts at the British Embassy in Cape Town. Diamonds, you see. Certain government agencies can be very vindictive."

I couldn't pursue what this implied.

When I turned to leave, she slipped something beneath a cushion—her husband's ring and the diamond bracelet, perhaps.

Outside, from the porch, I located the beached tactical boat and studied the lone mercenary. He was fumbling through a stack of metal boxes. Drunk, perhaps. Clumsy, uncoordinated. Wind had dropped to fifteen-twenty, the bay a washing machine that banged the rubber boat's stern up and down.

Weatherby, on the radio, told me, "Don't overreact, Ford. I have a slight bullet wound, but it's not bad. Trapezius muscle, left shoulder. All hunky-dory now. Do you see that larger boat coming in?"

"Negative. But there's another one beached about fifty meters east of your place. One man aboard. Max, your weapon—whatever it is—I don't know your range...capabilities, I guess. Should I take care of him?"

"I already have—for now, anyway," was the Brit's evasive reply. "Look to the north. Perhaps too far for a visual. Wait, you're still wearing NODs? I'll show you."

I turned toward his house. A shaft of infrared light exited a third-floor window. My monocular converted the crimson beam to heat-lightning blue. The beam pierced two miles of mist and sparked reflective tape on a vessel that had yet to appear.

Weatherby said, "That's one of their transport boats. It comes and goes. I can't do anything because I'm not sure who might be aboard. Copy? I need a visual."

I touched the mic key. "How many people are we dealing

with?" Through the Lászlos' shattered door, I saw Rebecca put the radio to her ear. She was monitoring the conversation.

"This is a bigger operation than I expected," the Brit said. "Perhaps you feel the same. At least two larger transports, I'd say nine meters long, plus two or three smaller mule boats on the beach. A couple of their people we don't have to worry about— at least for several hours."

"Incapacitated. As in no longer dangerous?"

"For now. I can make it permanent."

"Come on, Max. I need some details. Your weapon, what's the range? Is it portable?"

"Eyes and ears," he warned. "Light and sound. Not thermal. At the Lászlos' place, I tracked you to their third floor. You engaged another person. Did he jump or did you—"

With the mic key, I garbled what he was about to say and told him, "Mrs. Lászlo is fine. Unfortunately, her husband is… still missing. Her favorite poodle, too. I gave her a radio until we get help. She's a…she's a strong one."

The Brit understood. "Ahhh. A lovely lady, Rebecca. One of the great beauties of her time. I'm sure she'll come through this with all the grace that— Ford." His voice became more urgent. "Switch to secondary channel. Something's happening out there. Look to your right."

I did and switched channels. Barely visible were two men, perhaps more, a few hundred yards down the shoreline.

"Got 'em," I said.

Weatherby came back. "There must be a couple of teams on the island. Getting interesting, what? Now both transports are coming our way. I count two, repeat, two boats, a total of five armed people aboard. Suggest we discuss this—privately. QSL?"

Weatherby wanted me to join him on the third floor. Radio silence. But I couldn't leave Mrs. Lászlo unprotected. On the beach was a third mercenary so close he could be up the steps inside her home within seconds. A few hundred yards away, the other two men could be there in minutes.

I said, "We need a diversion, and I've got an idea. I'll be there as soon as I can."

29

I crossed through wreckage coated with petroleum slime. Power was off on the mainland. There were no mushroom city halos, no boundless pockmarks of overpopulation.

In the midsized mule boat—a rubber Zodiac—the lone mercenary continued to fumble with boxes. His shoulders were bear-sized beneath a floppy boonie hat. I approached from behind. Wind covered the suction cup noise of my boots. When he paused to light a cigarette, the flame of his lighter dazzled—diamonds, gems and jewelry spilled from a sack he'd been holding.

His profanities had a childish ring of helplessness, not anger. He slammed the bag, flicked the lighter again and somehow managed to burn his nose.

The distraction allowed me to approach faster through the slime. I holstered my pistol and deployed the collapsible baton. Only a few yards away, my feet skated out from under me. I landed on a pile of tin roofing that clattered like an alarm bell.

I rolled, pulled and came up ready to shoot.

No need. The man sat smoking, oblivious to the noise. Pistol drawn, I retrieved the baton and walked closer.

Still, no reaction. Jewelry lay strewn on a deck loaded with storage boxes. The boxes crammed full, some with lids, others covered with tarps. On the console, within the man's reach, was a machine pistol—Uzi-sized. A litter of spent brass was no proof the weapon was empty but might explain how Weatherby had been wounded.

I raised the baton when I was within striking distance. He had hunched low and was searching for the gems he'd spilled. Strange, the experimental way his hands slapped the deck.

I took a chance. "Don't move."

He didn't hear me.

In a louder voice, I warned him again.

No reaction, so I poked him in the back. The response was bizarre. He yelped, scrambled overboard and sprinted a crazy circle until he collided with an overturned golf cart. A second attempt tripped him into a logjam of trash.

When I got to the man, he was on his knees as if in prayer, pleading in Russian—not pleading with me, but to anyone who might attack from an ungaugeable silence.

He didn't react when my pocket LED flashed on. I painted his face with the light and understood. Blood dripped from both ears, and his eyes were no longer eyes. They were exploded grapes, two milky membranes of gray.

In the world's oceans, killer whales did the same to the swim bladders of fish.

I looked toward the physician/inventor's home and whispered, "Holy shit, Max."

The mercenary began bawling, a tearless surrender, when I zip-tied his wrists and frisked him. An envelope full of purloined diamonds went into my bag. In his cargo pocket was a Baofeng radio so cheap that military encryption was unlikely. I switched it on. A low battery warning flashed. The guy had probably gone hoarse calling for help before saving the radio for later. Memory recall provided only two base mobile frequencies, both unfamiliar to me. Neither was within the marine channel spectrum.

I keyed the microphone and growled with a nonsensical accent, "CQ-CQ-CQ," which is the universal Q code for calling any station.

The response was not immediate. I had dragged the man above the high tide line before someone who had to be nearby responded in Russian.

Radios can be tracked with a handheld RDF antenna—or a sophisticated weapons system. The radio, power off, went into my pocket. There was no internal debate about the morality of leaving as little evidence as possible.

I lifted the man, saying, "Get up." It was a pointless command to a person with ruptured eardrums. I freed his hands and urged him toward the water with a friendly nudge. He stumbled several steps, then splashed into deeper water, face-first, where the current swept him toward distant mangroves. Whatever happened after that was for the authorities to decide.

As I'd told the young merc with the teardrop tats, there are all sorts of accidents during a hurricane. Flying projectiles can blind or kill with the force of a chrome-headed steel baton.

To my left was Weatherby's house. In silhouette, the man stared down from the third-floor window. I had taken the Zodiac's ignition key and the mini-rifle that was not an Uzi. I waved the rifle.

My radio squelched and the Brit replied, "Now you know what my device can do. But the range is limited. Switch channels, keep it brief."

The mercenaries had scanners. No doubt about it now.

On channel six-eight, he said, "One vessel has stopped, but the second, at current speed, will be here in twelve minutes or less. I have to engage soon, or they'll open fire again. My walls aren't bulletproof and neither are you. Suggestions?"

I said, "Hold on, I'm headed your way. Wait—the men down the shoreline, what's their status? I lost track. You see them?"

A light was still visible through the Lászlos' shattered doorway.

"There's no time," Weatherby said. "There are only two of them. Five in the transports, four heavily armed. But I can't be sure they're all bad guys."

Something in his voice, not cold but pragmatic, made me start toward the mansion. "Max, I left Mrs. Lászlo alone. Where did those guys on the beach go? I have an idea. Just give me a few minutes and—"

A double-tap of gunfire echoed as if caroming off a marble floor. Then four more shots, rapid-fire. The Lászlos' doorway flared with a much brighter flashlight. Mercenaries were inside, searching. I unslung the weapon I'd stolen. It was a Century Draco, an AK-47 clone that could not be traced to me. The thirty-round mag had been emptied by half. I flipped the selection switch to single-burst.

"Max, how many are there? They're in her house, goddamn it. Is there anything you can do?"

"Not without…think about Rebecca. Ford, the transports will be here in less than ten minutes, I'm sorry, I'll have no choice. It's probably too late for her, anyway. Six shots, weren't there?"

I said, "And I'm the dope who left her alone without a gun. I'll be there when I get there. Stand by."

The porch of the mansion was slick with debris. At the door, I crouched and listened. Instead of killers banging around within, the only sounds were wind and percussive waves beachside. I stepped through shattered glass, rifle in sync with my eyes, finger on the trigger…until I saw Mrs. Lászlo. She was on the divan, white yachting blouse bloodstained, and aiming a pistol at me.

I lowered my weapon. She lowered hers and put a trembling

hand to her lips. "Thank God, Dr. Ford. You came back. Are they dead?"

Nothing I saw made sense.

"Rebecca, where are they?"

"Still here, I think. I can't bring myself to look. So weak all of a sudden. I don't believe in fainting, but I might if they're not...if they're still alive."

I switched on the LED and crabbed sideways to the couch. The marble floor was a blood trail of activity. On the stairway a man sprawled wide-eyed, face up. He had tried to escape up the steps, but a back or chest wound had stopped him.

The woman motioned with the pistol. "The other one crawled over there somewhere. Maybe the next room. Such terrible groans at first, then nothing, so he might have escaped. Or he could be... Would you mind checking?"

Her second attacker had nearly made it to the guest bath-room. Curled on his side, shirt bloody, arms extended. Shot in the belly and the jaw it looked like. His sidearm, a Glock, had been flung across the room. I left it for police to find. The same when I searched the man near the stairs.

"They're both dead, Mrs. László. Don't worry, you had no choice." I knelt and found the first-aid kit in my bag. "Were you shot? How badly are you hurt?"

Even dazed, a thin smile formed. "Oh, don't kid yourself, I had a choice. Damn right I had a choice. They thought I was harmless. And I speak Russian. How could I not, married to a Hungarian Gypsy? They were going to kill me—or worse. I heard them talking. Rude, disgusting things. So, first chance I got—they'd looked away—I shot them with your gun."

My fingers found the full-sized Sig Sauer on my right hip, then moved to the empty small-of-the-back holster. She'd taken my backup pistol during what I'd believed to be a motherly hug.

The woman said, "The look of surprise on their faces, then they tried to run. What worried me most was I couldn't find your gun's safety. I pulled the trigger, anyway, and, well… Are you angry?"

I held out my palm. "There is no safety. Do you mind?" She handed me the little Sig-365. Chamber cleared, the mag showed four rounds had been fired. "Pickpocket; sleight of hand. Clever," I said. "I had no idea it was missing. Let's get a look at your shoulder. Were you hit anywhere else?" I was replacing leather gloves with surgical gloves. "Not mad, ma'am. Relieved. You're a tough one, Becca."

"And better than you realize." Her inflection suggested a double meaning—not tawdry. Something sly. "There are other reasons to hug a man. I detest modesty. It's so time-consuming compared to dealing with a braggart." She touched the top button of her blouse. "I'd prefer not to take this off."

"Just the sleeve," I said and used scissors.

A strip of flesh had been cleaved away from her lower left arm. Not serious but a lot of blood; a seeping black venous flow. I opened a quick-clot compression bandage. Stuffed it into the wound and did a couple of wraps. "Hold this. I'm not a physician. We need Max to have a look. Think you can manage?"

She needed boots. I helped with the laces.

"Turn off your flashlight," I said when we were outside. She had been searching the yard.

"Benjamin taught me so much. I can't bear to think of him out here all alone. You'll look for him. Please?"

Offshore, a vessel was bucking toward us a mile or so away but cautiously. I wondered why. No lights visible through my night optics monoc. The vessel stopped. It turned, and waves sparked in synch with a firecracker burst of gunfire. Several rounds smacked the wooden siding of Weatherby's house.

On the third floor, a shutter emitted a wedge of light. Then a string of infrared beads zapped the water with a silent percussion that rattled my spine.

Mrs. Lászlo felt it, too. "My God, what was that?" She winced and touched her ears.

"Stay low, keep moving," I urged. Didn't stop until we were shielded by a wall of debris. The mercenary's cheap Baofeng transceiver came out and I called, "CQ-CQ-CQ."

The response, in Russian, was immediate.

"What did he say, Rebecca? You said you understand the language."

"You're in touch with them by radio?" She was taken aback, perhaps concerned I was a traitor. "He wants you to identify yourself. Like he expects a code word or something. Why would they answer you, an American?"

I said, "Tell them to stop firing, we'll make a deal. In Russian. Can you do that?"

"Well...I can try. What kind of deal?"

"Anything. Just convince them to stop firing. Tell them—" I looked toward Weatherby's place. The third-floor light was off, as was the sonic laser. "Tell them your neighbor has a million dollars in art and bullion. Say he has a boat; that he's about to sneak off and leave you alone. Like you're pissed. Twenty minutes, tell them, you'll guide them in if they'll just leave you alone."

"Certainly. But wait. If they don't see a boat leave, they'll know I'm lying and—"

"There is a boat and I'll be in it," I interrupted. "What you need to understand is you're risking most of what they stole from your house. I'll dump what I can on the beach, but the rest of it..."

She dismissed the subject with a head shake. "Give me the radio. Don't worry, it's all insured."

Her indifference was startling.

I don't know what Mrs. Lászlo told the Russians. But it worked.

30

By radio, Pavlo told his lead boat to open fire. Then, in a rush, he ordered Yenin, "Turn, turn, get the hell away from that British bastard's house. Let those peasants be the bait."

"Bait?"

"Don't ask questions." He reached in front of Yenin and slapped the throttle forward. "Now…turn again. Try to keep some trees between us."

They banged through quartering seas for another hundred meters, mangroves to the left, before stopping.

"That was some scary shit back there," Pavlo said. "What the hell kind of weapon…? Goddamn! In that shithole, Crimea, Israeli advisors—"

"What?"

The wind was loud and their ears were still buzzing.

"Israeli spies," Pavlo hollered. "They had some kind of laser device. Iron Beam, they called it. Bastards could set a tank on fire or scramble a man's brains. We're gonna have to disable the thing or kill Weatherby, then get ashore and load up."

Yenin wiggled his jaw experimentally. "Made my teeth hurt. They still hurt. And that beam of light—looked like a hose pissing little bubbles. It wasn't even aimed at us. Our guys on the beach, think they're dead?"

"Screw them. All I care about is what's in the mule boats," Pavlo said. "And a painting the Brit has—supposedly worth millions. Or wait...think about what the oligarchs would pay for a weapon with that kind of technology." He went silent before deciding, *Nope. That would put me in the gun sights of too many men like Sasha.*

The mercs in the lead transport—three shooters and a driver— had emptied a magazine or two into the physician's house. On the console, a handheld military radio rattled with a man's voice that didn't sound Russian.

Pavlo pressed the mic key. "Security check. Reply with confirmation."

The password was *Donald Orlando,* the idea of that useless American who had either died in the storm or was hiding. Either way, no loss.

Instead of a password, a woman responded in excellent Russian, "Your people have already blown up our safe and killed my husband. I want to make a deal. If you're the man who assaulted me, you know exactly who I am. Are you the tall one with the beard?"

From a distance, Pavlo could see only a wedge of the László mansion. "Tall, yes. You sound very lonely. Are you lonely? Tell me about this deal." He was picturing the crippled man's wife who was old but fit with a Renaissance face; a face that glowed like paintings in a museum. Still young since the days of the czar.

The woman said, "Stop shooting, leave me alone and you can have anything you want. You're going to be robbed. You hear me? Robbed. I know how and when. I won't share the details if you keep shooting."

Anything you want? Was the woman offering herself? Earlier, she'd scratched so violently Pavlo had had to abandon his fun in order to rejoin Yenin on the transport vessel.

No. Pavlo guessed she intended to kill him. Or try to kill him. *Interesting.* He also suspected the Brit was nearby, feeding her information. If so, this was an opportunity to lure the billionaire away from that damn brain-jarring laser.

"Liar," Pavlo said into the radio. "My men wouldn't rob me. Here's the only deal. The Brit comes out alone. Just him, no weapons. He has a painting I want. He knows the painting. Ask him. And something else—your husband's ring, a famous stone. The Kashmir Sapphire. We didn't find it in the safe."

In English, the woman said, "It is you."

Pavlo responded, "Then I'm right. You are lonely. Speak Russian. It's the language of poets, my angel." Before she could respond, he thought of a better way—use her as cover; make the rich lady hand the painting and the sapphire over to him personally. Make the exchange, then drag her into the boat.

A British gentleman wouldn't fry the brain of his female neighbor.

Pavlo restated his offer.

Mrs. Lászlo, a tough lady. She had brokered deals before. "Now, you listen to me. The man who's going to steal your boat and everything you stole from us isn't Russian. And he isn't Dr. Weatherby. He lives here. On the island. That's all I'm going to say. Stop shooting. That's the deal. When I'm convinced, I'll radio and tell you when and where to find the thief. No more talk."

Pavlo pressed the mic key. "Wait. The doctor—Weatherby—has to guarantee us safe passage if I agree to—"

The woman was gone.

"That sour old cabbage needs sweetening," Pavlo said to Yenin. He clipped the radio to his belt. "A thief who's not Russian. Who is she talking about, you think? Hey—our other boats. Are they still on the beach? That bitch might be telling the truth."

Yenin had the binocs. "I think I see her. Two people...yes, they left the big white house—the old jeweler's place—almost to the British guy's house, sneaking around in the wreckage. Should I—" He reached for his rifle.

"Not yet. Get the binoculars...not those, the big ones in the wooden case."

Oversized military binoculars with fifty-millimeter lenses so heavy they had to be braced on a railing. Pavlo said, "That's her in the white clothes. But who's the guy? Big guy, wide shoulders. He's helping her...like maybe she's hurt. Damn it, I hope she doesn't die before I— Unless she's with Weatherby. That could work."

He tilted the glasses and found the Brit's house, third floor. A light moved across a narrow crack in the retractable shutter. A man's visage there, the outline of a face.

"Yenin, she's with someone else. A guy we don't know about. And definitely not that twit, Dimitry. Too big, and he wouldn't have the nerve. Yeah...there's a third man on the island. *Shit*."

The binocs pivoted to the inner rim of the bay two miles away. No lights showing at the marina near where, yesterday, they'd left the stolen boat and the FWC woman who was surely dead by now.

A thought came into his head. "The marine biologist, possibly? He's on Sasha's list. That would be excellent luck. A large bonus from Sasha. Good. I hope the biologist does try to rob us."

Pavlo didn't need to check his notes to remember the name, *Dr. Marion Ford.*

31

On the beach, a hundred yards from her home, Rebecca László said to me, "What...my God... Is that an animal on the ground? No...it's a man."

I said, "Keep moving," and left it at that.

Beneath Max Weatherby's pirate ship piling house, one of the Brit's attackers crawled zombie-like, one arm an outstretched antenna. Even in darkness the lady had seen movement.

"Think he was injured during the storm? I don't suppose we should offer to help."

I replied, "Might be wise to wait until they stop trying to kill us. You did a fine job using that radio, ma'am. How're you feeling?"

"For pity sake's, stop calling me 'ma'am.' You make me feel ancient. At least allow me the illusion of not being a liability."

"Far from it," I said, and got a hand around her waist.

She seemed to be in pretty good shape despite the grazing flesh wound. I helped her up the steps.

The Brit met us at the first-floor landing. The right side of his neck was bandaged with gauze. A tall man, as expected, dressed for hiking, not a gunfight, East Indian antecedents in his facial structure. "I'll take Becca from here. Ford, we don't have much time to figure out which transport to target. What's the plan?"

I hadn't risked specifics on VHF.

I said, "I'm going to try to get them to chase me."

"On foot? That would be rather—"

"Steal the boat they beached near your dock. I know the water, they don't. If I can run them aground or... I don't know, play it by ear, I guess, until I figure out if they have any hostages aboard. First, tell me about your weapon. Sonic and laser, you said. Is the damage permanent?"

He was checking Mrs. Lászlo's vitals. "Depends on the power setting. It can vaporize collagen inside the human eye and cause the brain to vibrate. Temporary deafness at the lowest frequency, but fine-tuning requires a stable platform. And lots of amperage. It's essentially a focused long-range acoustic device coupled to—well, that gets complicated."

"Is the thing small enough to carry?"

"Doable but not ideal. It needs a pretty hefty power supply." The Brit stood and spoke to Mrs. Lászlo. "You're going to be just fine, dear, but I'd like to get an IV in you for good measure. We're all probably dehydrated, and you've lost a lot of blood. Becca, can you make it inside? I've got a couch and some other things all set. First floor, no more steps. Isn't that lovely?"

Weatherby returned with a small bag. We were alone. He said, "Okay, let's say you're right. We've got fourteen, fifteen minutes before they start shooting again. So, assume the worst and you should use what's in here for protection."

The bag contained industrial earmuffs, mirrored glasses and quad-lensed NOD goggles. Panoramic, I was told. Thermal imaging fused with infrared and low-light night vision. The unit mounted into the same headband I'd been wearing as did a small box that clipped on the side. I pressed a button and focused. Offshore, both transport vessels had stopped, ready to ambush anyone who attempted to flee Dinkin's Bay.

So far so good. They had believed Mrs. László's story about me, the thief. The lead transport was a quarter mile off according to the stadia metric rangefinder. Aboard were four men highlighted in orange like video game targets. Beyond was the second transport, the heat of its engine a plume of red. A button at the bottom of the unit anchored their location on an inboard geo map.

"You invented these, Max? I've never bought a stock in my life but, after meeting you, I'm tempted."

His mind was on something else. "If they're willing to trade for artwork, I might have another idea. I know what they want from me. I've known all along. If Rebecca is up for it, I might ask her to— I didn't know she spoke Russian."

"Your art collection," I said. "She's already made contact about that. Convinced them to stop shooting and you won't blow them out of the water. We have a deal—not that I trust the guy. How many signed Rauschenbergs do you have?"

"Several. Some of his smaller works, easily transported. One in particular sold for— Wait here a tick."

It was no coincidence, I felt certain, that a briefcase-sized aluminum case was within easy reach.

"This contains a little-known piece: *Bicycle at Twin Palms*. I bought it just before Rauschenberg's combine, *Buffalo II*, sold for eighty million at Christie's a few years back." He placed the case at my feet. "Take it. It could be useful. Fully waterproof, and there's a tracking chip inside—if satellites come back on station. See what it says?"

R. M. Rauschenberg, in script, was engraved near the lock.

"But no artwork inside. Or it's fully insured," I said. "You're after Grigori Pavlo—the serial killer—and a Rauschenberg is a lot of bait. Not that I mind. Our deal—I'm talking about you and me—our deal is this: if there's the slightest chance they have a hostage aboard, hold your fire until I'm sure. It could be a woman, a friend of my fiancée."

"Understood, Commander." This was offered with an insider's knowing certainty. "Well done, you. You're right about my search for Pavlo. If you find that deviant, the insane monk, I'd like you to bring him to me. No… I insist you bring him to me."

I said, "Because of your niece? No guarantees, but whatever happens, we have to cover each other's butts when the feds show up. And they will. Here. Take this."

He considered the little pistol in my hand. "My lovely young niece, Hilary. Yes. I won't ask your source. A gun, though… I'd rather not use it."

"Mrs. László will," I told him. "Give it to her."

Before I left, I added, "Have her stand by the radio. She knows what to do next."

I've used night optics in many parts of the world. Nothing compared to Weatherby's quad-lensed NOD binoculars. A little graphic overlay showed GPS and compass heading. The unit provided a bright, unencumbered path to the beach and the tactical boat, a twenty-one-foot Zodiac with a two-fifty Suzuki outboard. Plenty of power but not when overloaded with hundreds of pounds of stolen goods.

Several boxes were jettisoned above the high tide mark. I stowed the aluminum case that might or might not contain artwork by a good man named Bob Rauschenberg, then shoved off without starting the engine. Staccato waves drifted the Zodiac toward the two transport vessels waiting, lights out, at the channel entrance. Aboard the closest, framed in video game orange, were three men with automatic weapons. A fourth man, at the helm, searched the area with binoculars. When those wide, fifty-millimeter light-bucket lenses swung toward me, I started the engine, buried the throttle and spun the wheel as if escaping toward the marina.

They didn't expect that.

Nautical charts show only one marked channel in and out of Dinkin's Bay. Which is accurate. Along the western mangrove wall, however, is a deep-water notch, thirty yards wide. It opens into Pine Island Sound, the island of Gumbo Limbo and the mainland a few miles beyond.

Years ago, Jeth and some other guides named the opening Fool's Cut because it's gated, both sides, by oysters and sand. Local knowledge is required. If you don't know exactly where to turn, say goodbye to your prop. Or your shattered hull.

A glance over my shoulder confirmed the lead boat had jumped onto plane to follow. But not the second vessel.

Oh, hell.

I backed the throttle. The Zodiac reared as if a parachute had deployed. Both boats, both crews, I wanted to lure them all away. *Engage, separate, isolate.* It's a strategy that links indigenous hunters, guerilla warriors and predators of the lowest form.

Maybe an escapee from Black Dolphin Prison was aware I was attempting to bait them.

A military spotlight speared the darkness. When the mercenaries realized what the Zodiac contained, a second spotlight charged toward me in pursuit.

At heavy-weather speed, I disappeared by hugging the mangrove rim. Their spotlights found Maria's grounded houseboat. A muted pop, three round bursts, hammered the walls. To make my location known, I switched the LED to strobe, fired it for a few seconds, then, lights out, steered toward Fool's Cut half a mile away.

The bay was a floating junkyard. The marina's commercial icemaker, a U-Haul trailer, logs and swamped skiffs created a slalom course that also provided cover when a column of light latched on to me.

I squatted low. Navigated by peering over the wheel. A bullet smacked the console. Shards of fiberglass—or shrapnel—stung my neck. The temptation was to turn and fire blindly. I couldn't. Aboard one of those vessels might be a woman who'd been kidnapped. On the chance it was true, I wanted to keep her alive for what I hoped would happen next.

After a series of maneuvers, a notch in the mangrove wall appeared to my right. A vague nothingness to those in pursuit. To me it was a lighted passageway. Narrow as a mineshaft. To enter directly guaranteed crashing aground.

No one without local knowledge could have known what to do next.

I did. Fifty yards south of the notch, I trimmed the engine, turned and jumped a sandbar on the Zodiac's starboard chine. Back and forth I spun the wheel. Port chine, starboard chine, each rotation angled the propeller just enough to cross the shoals at planing speed.

At the tunnel's entrance, the bottom dropped away from a few inches to fourteen feet deep. Mangroves formed an awning overhead. "An auger hole," my journal-keeping uncle, Tucker Gatrell, had called such places.

When the deck settled beneath me, I killed the engine and drifted into a cloak of overhanging limbs. While I waited, I secured the boat, gulped a bottle of water and foraged for mercenary gear. Two flashlights, another Baofeng radio and a sack of glow sticks were useful finds.

A better find was a fresh mag for the AK clone. Russian ammo, red-tagged, 7.62. Thirty rounds. A coil of rope and some other stuff were tossed into mangroves for later use. If needed. And to need them meant I would have to get lucky. Very, very lucky.

The aluminum case went over last, *R. M. Rauschenberg* engraved near the lock.

From the northeast, searchlights probed the opening. The

boats, running wing-and-wing, turned and kept coming, full speed.

Good. I hoped they were thinking, *If he can do it, we can do it.*

I tightened boot laces and leather gloves. After pocketing the Zodiac's ignition key, I grabbed my bag and slipped over the side into the bushes.

Mangroves are sometimes called "walking trees" because they can do it. Walk. Or at least appear to move in slow motion. Their tentacle-roots creep out into the shallows. They collect sand, detritus, and create islands of their own making. In mangroves, you don't stroll. You vault over rubber hurdles, you climb, duck under limbs and climb some more. It's a monkey bar process. Twenty yards can take ten minutes.

On a speck of high ground grew a buttonwood tree, the bark animated with pulsing insect life of some type.

I focused the high-tech NOD binocs.

A swarm of red velvet ants—a type of wasp, actually—had claimed the tree as a refuge during the flood. Unusual for this solitary species. Mostly females—no wings—and they were huge compared to commonplace ants. The size of bumblebees.

I kept my distance from the swarm and watched the Russian mercenaries. The second boat slowed. Foolishly, the lead boat did not. It maintained speed until the keel plowed aground in water ankle-deep. Its propeller's *WHAW-WHAW-WHAW* complaint failed to shoot a muddy rooster tail—typical of a spun hub.

The second boat reared to a stop and backed off. Aboard were a driver and a man riding shotgun. His shotgun, though, was an AR-15-type with an extended magazine. If a kidnap victim was aboard, dead or not, she was probably bound, lying somewhere on the deck.

Both boat crews took defensive positions until their spotlights, after a quick search, failed to find me or the Zodiac among a lattice of foliage. Bickering in Russian commenced. Was I armed?—a possible topic. Or had I followed the cut into open water, where the seas were a tumult of spray?

All three men on the grounded vessel got out and tried to push the skeg off the bar. Not a chance. From the trailing vessel, the guy riding shotgun waded in with a flashlight and a chain—maybe they could snatch the damn thing backward. His partner, the fifth mercenary, hidden by the console, remained seated. He shouted orders, his gestures contemptuous, profane.

Their leader, no doubt—a man who needed watching. I got a glimpse of shoulder-length hair and the hat he wore. In profile his face was a beak connected to a ZZ Top beard. When his spotlight grazed the Zodiac, I dropped to prone position near the buttonwood tree. There was a shout of discovery followed by an order that sent the mercs into a splashing retreat. From behind the grounded lead boat, they all opened fire. A wild spray of rounds, chest-level, sheared a rain of twigs around me.

After a second burst—silence. There was only wind and the lapping smack of waves against the Zodiac's hull. A full minute passed. Because I didn't return fire, they now assumed I was unarmed.

That's precisely what I wanted them to believe.

A radio amplified Mrs. László's voice in Russian. The leader stood and spoke into a handheld. I got to my knees for a better view. It was him, Grigori Pavlo, the serial killer. NBA-tall, a scarecrow of sinew, veins and hair.

I cupped a hand to my ear. From the elegant lady's guttural syntax, the name "Rauschenberg" emerged. Pavlo's response rang with the sincerity of a shyster's lie. His eagerness, however, betrayed him. The Vulture Monk was hooked.

I handcuffed the aluminum case to the tree and got moving.

32

The easy life in a First World country numbs our primate wariness. Not true of Third World gangsters. I had to be careful with the trail I left. Too obvious, they'd spread out or start shooting again. Not obvious enough, they might stumble into me when I backtracked.

Pavlo, done with Mrs. László and the radio, initiated another volley of fire. He seemed to enjoy spraying the darkness, indifferent to who or what he might kill. I heard the clack of fresh mags mounting, then orders that demanded haste. Two, possibly three, of his four underlings splashed their way toward me, into the trees.

Finding the Rauschenberg case, I hoped, would coax their leader ashore.

Not far from the buttonwood, I dropped an expensive multitool as if it were an accident. Another couple of minutes passed before I lost my ball cap—both signs of a panicked man on the run.

My pursuers were either afraid of the crazy monk or very sloppy. They crashed and grumbled and cursed their way through the swamp, two of them wearing LED headbands. I exited on the big water side, left fifteen yards of muddy footprints, then reentered the bushes. It was the narrowest part of the peninsula, only a couple hundred feet wide. A good choke point, if needed.

Ahead in a green haze lay a surreal totem. Signage from the 7-Eleven and the Mobil station had been lofted across Dinkin's Bay, high into the tree canopy from miles away. Plastic marquees, oversized, tangled in yellow streamers that fluttered like prayer flags. An image of my Buddhist pal, Tomlinson, flashed and was gone. There was no humor left in me. Just cold impatience and a deeper dread of irretrievable loss.

An upside-down catamaran was at the bottom of the pile. It was one of those two-man jobs, a single seat aft in each hull. Trampoline netting was torn but created an effective theater screen. I took a foraged flashlight, switched it on and angled it against a log. The catboat became a luminous moth above a misting flame. The Mobil sign glowed with a ruby-red boast: *Fuel Tech Synergy.*

Behind me—hard to guess how far—there was shouting, and someone whistled. This began an excited exchange in Russian. The word *Rauschenberg* produced clarity once again.

They had found the aluminum case. A handcuff key or a pick would be required. There was also a colony of pissed-off red velvet ants to deal with—another surprise. It bought me some time. And the sound of splashing boots allowed me to backtrack faster.

Bayside, I poked my head out. Their boats, a baseball throw away, appeared to be empty. Pavlo was wading toward shore. He carried a tactical light and maybe tools. But no rifle. Apparently I was unarmed and harmless in his mind.

In my mind, the Vulture Monk was demoted from sinister to just plain dumb.

We were both fools.

He climbed into the mangroves. I gave it a minute before I slid closer, using tree branches to steady myself as I walked. Water was up to my waist. Floating cans, Styrofoam, plastic bags had to be pushed aside. A few dozen yards from the opening, an alligator exploded from the prop roots and startled the hell out of me. Not huge but big enough to twist off an arm. The gator submerged. When it didn't resurface, I flushed a second gator while stumbling up the bank, the animal more startled than me.

Time to stop and rethink. Now I not only had to risk crossing open water, I was separated from Pavlo's boat by two sizable carnivores. The timing sucked. The mercenaries were busy at the buttonwood tree. Their voices rumbled from the darkness. I heard a machete chopping wood. Then yelps and agonized profanities.

The men had found the ants—or vice versa. Better known as "cow killers," folklore claimed their venom is strong enough to do just that. Kill cows. It wasn't true, but the sting has been likened to a hot branding iron coated with boric acid.

These solitary insects, colonized by a flood, were defending their turf. From all the racket, the ants seemed to be winning. Gators or not, I couldn't miss this opportunity. I unslung the Draco AK and pushed my way out to Pavlo's boat. Black floatation tubes, black console and a low transom. I didn't have to go aboard to be disappointed. There was no kidnap victim on the deck. Just bedrolls, a bucket and plastic bags as if they planned on doing some camping. I kept moving—drifted then waded twenty yards to the second vessel, which was hard aground. Same thing. No bodies inside, alive or dead.

I returned to Pavlo's boat with the vague plan of stealing it and leaving the mercenaries stranded. What if they actually had kidnapped a woman, though? If she existed, I'd have to force one of them—Pavlo, ideally—to talk. That's when two men tumbled out of the bushes into the water. Like their clothes were on fire because of the ants. They slapped and splashed and cursed, then got busy retrieving the Zodiac. The ignition key was in my pocket, so they would have to tow it across the shoals before transferring valuables I'd left aboard into Pavlo's larger transport boat.

No time to linger. I swam and belly-crawled, just my head showing, into the mangroves. I switched the NOD binocs to thermal and scanned the area. Occasional blips of body heat showed a man a quarter mile away following my false trail south. I hurried north toward the buttonwood. Grigori Pavlo was there with another guy. All five mercenaries were accounted for. So...would the crazy monk's next move be to track me down? Or would he order his men to abandon the chase, content to leave with the Zodiac and its valuable cargo?

None of the above. Beneath the buttonwood tree, Pavlo and the guy were arguing. He yelled a name—"Yenin"—and I watched him shove the guy and yank the Rauschenberg case from his hands. There seemed to be a disagreement about how and when to breach the lock and open the thing.

Yenin was insistent. Pavlo was contemptuous. He didn't want to damage a multimillion-dollar piece of art before wading back to the boat.

No surprise he won the argument. What happened next, though, was unexpected. The guy, Yenin, turned his back, and Pavlo, moving catlike, brained the man with a hammer. Not just once. A sickening series of blows. Then the tall man—longhaired in profile—knelt, dipped his hands into the mess and...

I turned away, thinking, *He's going to kill them all.*

Engage, separate, isolate. That's precisely what the Vulture Monk proceeded to do.

I trailed him to the cut, where he watched two of his men load boxes from the Zodiac onto his larger vessel. When they were finished, halfway to shore, he stood and unslung an automatic weapon. Didn't say a word; took aim, and a series of three-round bursts danced his flunkies backward and left them bleeding, face down.

Three dead, one to go.

Chilling, the way the tall man moved. Methodical. As if savoring each moment. He turned. He stretched and yawned, then, through cupped hands, called out a summons to the man he'd sent to follow my flashlight trail south.

This time there was no response.

Pavlo repeated his orders.

Silence.

My guess was, the guy had seen his comrades murdered. Now he was either hiding or moving to attack.

Pavlo came to the same conclusion. He banged a fresh magazine home and changed his approach. His tone became conciliatory. When that didn't work, he pleaded—the voice of convincing reason. A voice that could be trusted.

Serial killers are master manipulators. Survival requires it. If not, their first outrage would have ended the fiction of normalcy. Compulsions would have gone unfed. Their sickness would have starved.

Behind me, branches rustled. A branch snapped. I balled myself into the bushes, pistol ready. The wayward mercenary nearly stepped on my hand before continuing into the water, where Pavlo, unarmed it appeared, made his location known by waving a flashlight.

Incredible. I expected the flunky to hesitate. Expected him to stop, turn and run, or at least question his leader's comforting tone. But he didn't. The flashlight became a guide to his leader's bear hug of forgiveness. A touching scene. The transgressor mewed with relief—until a knife skewered up through his chin.

A monster, Rebecca László had called the man with the vulture tattoo.

I don't believe in monsters. But the joy Pavlo took from inflicting pain was monstrous; a slander to all primates, even chimpanzees, who are merciless killers.

The transgressor didn't die right away. Pavlo chided when he begged. The knife became a teasing device to prolong the misery. His boot ended the fun by pinning the man's head underwater.

Arms raised in victory, the Russian faced the trees and howled to get my attention. "Ford, you hear me? Is just us now. I have deal for you. Very good is deal. Come out, we talk. What hurt is it for you to 'least listen to truth?"

The word *truth* was pronounced *tru-ssst*, the R rolled. Otherwise, his English was remarkably good.

He scanned the darkness in a way that told me he had no clue where I was. Yet he seemed certain of my identity and that I was close enough to listen.

"Mari-Ann Ford! Such pretty name for a man. I know about you. Tell me what happen to diplomat in South Africa. Dead is fine. Alive, where is he? See, so simple these answers. Me? What do I care?" He spit his contempt for whoever wanted the information, and said it again, using the diplomat's name. "Is to me a job. I get paid, you don't have to die. No fingers must I take. We make trade, how 'bout it?"

Manic laughter trailed me north to where I'd hidden the Zodiac earlier. Along the way I dropped a couple of glow sticks in case he followed. He didn't. I activated the LED strobe, hung it on a limb and returned to my original position at the water's edge. The strobe brightened the treetops with rapid-fire halos. Pavlo almost took the bait. He started toward the cut, stopped and reconsidered. An inherent wariness turned him incrementally in my direction as if tracking the seconds that had passed and the distance I had covered.

With the flashlight, he explored, then accurately marked my view port. I scampered backward while he placed the light on his boat and made a show of disarming himself. A sidearm went onto the bow near the aluminum Rauschenberg case, which lay open.

"See? Like you now. No guns. Come out, we talk. Tell me of diplomat." He banged the case with his hand. "And where is painting? I am not goddamn fool."

The case, apparently, was empty.

I hollered back, "Step away from the boat or I'll shoot you."

Strobe bursts showed him splashing toward me, one hand on his knife. "Hah. Such a liar's joke you tell. All this time, you no shoot. No gun is reason. So how you plan to do such a magic thing?"

He stopped grinning when I exited the trees and waded toward him, not fast but steady in the slippery footing. Several paces away, I pulled the Sig P-226. "Like this," I said, and fired twice, front sight focused on the iliac crest of his pelvis.

The monk's legs buckled. He collapsed as if paralyzed. Maybe he was. I'd taken my time; had held a target-practice breath and aimed with care. I've never been an exceptional shot with handguns, however, so it was no surprise that he struggled back to his feet.

"Son-bitch, you did it!" He was wheezing, exploring his right side. I'd hit him only once.

I said, "Get your hands away from that knife or I'll put a round in your belly. Where's the woman you kidnapped?"

"Son-bitch, you lied. Say we talk, make deal."

"Dumbass, you didn't listen. Hands behind your head—do it. Now turn, face the boat." With the baton, I reached and gave him a shove. "Make like you're kissing the motor. Head down...lower."

He cursed when I took his knife, and he threatened a world of harm if I didn't let him suture his own wound or get him to a doctor.

"That's our first stop," I said. We were aboard the transport by then, me at the console, him cuffed, belly-down on the deck. The bullet had clipped the love handle area, possibly too high to have shattered a bone. "On the way you're going to tell me if you're holding a woman hostage. And where. Lie to me, mister, they won't find you. But you'll be just as dead."

33

Pavlo, the wannabe monk, started kicking at one of the metal containers when we were underway, either in pain or just to piss me off. Not that I cared, but it was a distraction. Driving a stolen, badly maintained vessel was distraction enough. The steering was sloppy, the throttle too loose, and the kill switch had been bypassed.

We were a quarter mile from Weatherby's place when the Russian's tantrum began. I hollered, "Knock it off." An instant later, the hull hit something submerged and sizable that I wouldn't have seen, anyway.

The boat lurched, veered sharply to port. Containers skidded with centrifugal impact. I was thrown into the throttle, away from the helm. The engine redlined. The bow reared. A bucket burst open, and its contents spilled aft. Among the landslide was an asymmetrical bowling ball that thumped the deck like a melon as it rolled. I got a hand on the wheel and, instinctively, reached to intercept the thing before it smashed into the transom.

What I grabbed wasn't a bowling ball. It was a human head. Mouth taped; eyes wide. Female or male, I couldn't be sure.

In that shocking instant, the wheel spun free, and I was hurled against the portside gunnel. Pavlo was on me instantly. He had stepped through his tie-wrap shackles, so his hands were in front. Nothing else explained the crushing weight on my spine while he attempted to wrestle my service weapon from its holster.

I got my knees under me, bucked him high onto my shoulders and used an elbow to break his nose. It knocked the man sideways while the boat continued to slam through a heavy circular wake. It was the equivalent of fighting in a cement mixer, but no problem. For me, public school was a decade of wrestling tournaments interrupted by the occasional need to study. I'd already won this fight. Even before I'd grapevined the Russian's legs and locked a rear naked choke, I knew it was over because my sidearm was still holstered.

But it wasn't over. Somewhere—probably from the box he'd been kicking—Pavlo had gotten a pistol. I was beneath him, on my back. His manacled hands tilted the barrel and fired two deafening rounds past my ear. I rolled him belly down, an attempt to immobilize his arms, but he kept twisting and shooting blindly.

I grabbed a rail for balance, drew my weapon and tried to stand. That's when the boat nosedived through a wave that vaulted me overboard.

Instead of surfacing, I swam through and beneath the wake. Put some distance between me and where I'd gone in before taking a peek. I'd managed to hang on to my pistol, but the impact had knocked the quad-lensed binocs askew. They hung from a retainer strap, as did my glasses. Worse, Pavlo now had my tactical bag—if he had the sense to use the protective eyes-and-ears Weatherby had provided me. I got the binocs repositioned and saw the tall man at the helm. The boat slowed, did a one-eighty. A spotlight flared on and swept toward me.

I submerged and swam a pool length closer to Ladyfinger Lakes, where my Dorado twenty-five awaited. Above water, or in darkness below, the image of a human head was acid-etched in memory—as was the reality that it might be Hannah's friend Birdy. Or possibly…Hannah.

I had to find out. Could not move on or function effectively until I knew for sure.

The spotlight found a tangle of crab trap buoys thirty yards to my left. Pavlo started shooting with what sounded like the little Draco AK—a distinctive metal-on-metal clatter deepened by muzzle brake gases. It takes luck or first-tier skills to hit a target from a boat in rough seas. The Russian had neither. His three-round bursts sprayed so wildly that one damn near hit me. Skipped past my ear with the piercing buzz of a bumblebee.

Shallow water, boots anchored in mud, gave me the advantage when I thumbed back the hammer of the 9mm Sig. Even at a distance, a thirty-foot boat is hard to miss. Two rounds amidship shattered fiberglass. When the trigger clicked to reset, I took aim at the white Suzuki outboard. Disable the motor, shoot the driver and climb aboard. That was my intent. But 9mm hollow-points are designed to impact flesh, not pierce an aluminum cowling. Twice I hit the engine out of several tries. The big four-stroke didn't even sputter. Before the searchlight could find me, I sank to the bottom, holstered the pistol and breaststroked as far as I could before surfacing face up. A low profile.

No need. The Russian was wounded, his nose broken, and my shooting accuracy had spooked him. His boat, on plane, followed the curve of Woodring's Point toward Millionaire's Row and Dr. Max Weatherby's home.

This was not a foot race. Pavlo would be there in five minutes. It would take me thirty. I had to wade several hundred yards and somehow avoid a six-hundred-pound croc that, hopefully, had been sated. I sloshed double-time and hailed the Brit on VHF without success.

The backcountry here was a soup of dead and dying creatures. Stunned fish, birds, an otter belly-up. The tree canopy was alive with squealing creatures. When my boat was in sight, I pulled my weapon and proceeded more cautiously.

The shell mound where I had abandoned the outlaw insurance exec lay to my right. A dinosaur's hump of elevation. The bodies of the two mercenaries were either gone or had been consumed.

I hacked off a walking stick, hugged the bushes and tried the radio again.

Weatherby responded, "Ford, where are you? He—the lunatic Monk—he's here. On the beach, getting ready to leave. One man. What happened to the others?"

I broadened my strides, which was as close as I could get to running. "That's him, Pavlo. All alone, so do what you need to do. Shoot him, laser him, whatever. Just don't kill that son of a bitch. Not yet. I'm on my way. Ten minutes, copy?"

The Brit's startling reply was, "I've tried. Several times. I don't know what's the bloody problem… Sonics had no effect at all. Hang on, I'll try again before—*Rebecca*—" He shouted the woman's name. "Stop there. Don't go down those steps. Becca, please."

We cross talked before his voice broke through. "A megadecibel, full intensity that… Just in case, the eye and ear protection I gave you? Put them on, Ford. Immediately. QSL?"

I said, "Damn it, that's the problem. I screwed up. Pavlo must've gotten the safety gear from my bag. Why is Mrs. Lászlo—"

"You gave him the—"

"No, he found the goddamn stuff. What about Mrs.—"

Weatherby cut in, "It's the deal she made. Ford, you're saying you left your laser protection on the boat? Then how am I supposed to—why in the hell would you—" He shouted the woman's name again. "Rebecca! Come back."

There was more cross talk. Our cross talk was interrupted by two sharp gunshots. Then a third.

"Max—hey. What just happened?" I had stopped. To the right

something large and dark, a spear-shaped head, was swimming what might have been a corpse toward a clearing not far from my twenty-five Dorado.

"Oh, my… Rebecca is—I'll be damned. Well done, her." Weatherby's voice had lost some of its urgency. "She shot Pavlo, I think. That was her plan. Deliver the Rauschenberg and… Wait, oh no—he just forced her into the boat. So maybe she's the one who was— Ford, get here as fast as you. They're pulling out…leaving. Rebecca's still aboard."

I said, "She's better off blind and deaf than what that guy will do to…" I couldn't finish the sentence. "Max, pack anything you might need. Extra flashlights, a medical bag, whatever. I'll meet you beachfront in fifteen. We're going after her."

I was at the wheel. Weatherby seated to my left said, "This makes no bloody sense. The damn satellites still aren't locking in. I've even tried Bei-Dou Chinese and the GLONASS, Russian satellite networks. This is such…in the modern world? Total bollocks. Must be that solar flare/hurricane anomaly thing."

I was beginning to believe it was true. The only electronic I had not stripped from my boat was a Simrad chart plotter, a twelve-inch colorized screen programed with nautical charts, but its blinking satellite icon indicated the GPS was not functioning.

The bay was calm compared to what lay beyond the entrance. Thirty miles of constricted water, Charlotte Harbor to Estero Bay, framed by the eastern mainland and barrier islands to the west. It was a microsegment of the ICW, the Intracoastal Waterway, a dredged, well-marked ditch that traces three thousand miles of coastline, Boston to Key West, then north to Pensacola and west to Corpus Christi, Texas. Every night for decades, it had been a dependable maritime pathway lighted by red and green or white strobes. But not here, not on this night. Tonight, the ICW was a time warp, a desert expanse of spuming four-foot waves.

I said, "Try your thermal imaging gizmo. The Russian has at least a twenty-minute head start." With a finger I indicated my high-tech binocs. "Flashers are out, but I can still spot a few markers that weren't blown down. And a lot of floating crap. That's all. Maybe you can find his outboard's heat trail."

Weatherby's "gizmo" was the size of a commercial camera with a telephoto lens. I idled dead-slow, bow into the waves, while he steadied the unit on the console. I gave him a minute.

"Anything?"

"Not from sea level. Damn, which is expected if he's more than three or four kilometers away. Wait…there's something up ahead. Something swimming. Body heat. A mammal of some type. Not that monster crocodile. Give you a bit of trouble, did it?"

"I still don't know for sure it was the croc," I said. "But probably. The thing had a collection of bodies behind your house."

"Bodies?"

I told him, "Shine the infrared."

He lofted a handheld spotlight capped with a filter. With night vision, it blasted a Hollywood beam.

"What is that…a dog, possibly?" the Brit guessed.

Interested, I idled into the waves. What could have been a dog turned out to be a couple of island-bound feral hogs. Spaniards brought the first of them to North American in the 1500s, and they've thrived in the wild ever since. In shipwreck folklore, pigs, unlike horses and humans, always know the shortest route to land.

He said, "Bloody things must be lost. Where do you think they came from?"

I noted the crow-flies track the pigs had negotiated and motioned to St. James Point, two miles across the sound. "They'll eat anything, including carrion, so I guess they're following their noses. By tomorrow, there'll be a feeding frenzy. How's your shoulder doing?" I was concerned about the gunshot wound but also knew I could bang along faster without a passenger. "This is going to be a hell of a rough ride. Long one, too, because we can't get up on plane. We're gonna have to plow for the next three, four miles, so maybe you should—"

"Not a chance," he said. "How are we going to find Pavlo? My God, it is nasty out here—not that I'm complaining."

"And it'll get worse. The guy needs medical attention, and if he didn't make you treat his—"

Weatherby interrupted, "No, just took the Rauschenberg and Rebecca and left in a hurry. Any idea where he's heading?"

"Fairly certain," I said. "Trouble is, I doubt if he knows how to get there. So he'll probably get lost or hit something or run aground. In this area, an oyster bar's the most likely place to find a missing boat. Damn, I hope Mrs. László's okay. If you had to guess—"

Weatherby replied, "Don't know. She handed him the Rauschenberg—that was the deal—then shot him. Two shots. Or tried, at least. I saw her arm come up, and that's when he grabbed her. The third shot, he might have shot her."

"A Rauschenberg print?" I asked.

"The original. Couldn't risk a print," was the response. "The lunatic would've killed Becca straightaway."

This was reason enough to throttle faster. I looked back at the Brit's house. "The truth. On the radio, I heard a woman's voice. If it was your niece, we can't go off and leave her hiding in some room. They could have another team nearby and—"

"It wasn't Hilary you heard," Weatherby responded. "Yes, she's at my house. But in an urn. A cinerary burial urn above the fireplace."

I backed the throttle a notch. "That's what this is all about, isn't it? You and Pavlo. I'm sorry, man."

"A blessing in a way. Hilary, so young, so brilliant and the kindest soul I've ever... My favorite, obviously. Like my daughter since childhood. But she was never the same after what that deviant did to her." Weatherby ducked a sheet of spray and looked over. "Almost three years it's been. I've got an inventive mind. A hurricane, I decided. Lure him here or to the St. Pete house and…well, you've already figured out the rest. Legally speaking, a body found after a storm improves my odds of avoiding detection."

We'd been plowing north. The feral hogs, I realized, had made a wiser navigational choice. I said, "Legally speaking, it's best if Pavlo just disappears. Hang on, and tighten the strap on your PFD." I swung the bow toward St. James Point.

"Disappears, of course, in an ideal world." The Brit said this as if it weren't possible.

I timed the rollers, trimmed starboard-side down and surfed the boat onto plane. After two miserable miles of a sloppy beam sea, York Island put us in the lee, but I still had to raise my voice to be heard. "On Pavlo's boat, I saw a human head. Depending on who it is—"

"A what did you say?" Weatherby got to his feet.

"A head, a human head. Decapitated. Female or male with the mouth taped. We've got to find his boat. When we do, leave it to me, Max. In my world, it's not unusual for people to disappear."

34

It was after midnight, an hour into the next day, when I pulled close to St. James Point and shifted to Neutral. "We might need these," I said to Weatherby. He watched me rig safety lines to both stern cleats, a line off the bow and a couple more amidship, the working ends of the forward lines half hitched to the console railing.

"I thought we were in a hurry."

I placed the aft portside line between us. "We are. Give this a wrap around your waist. Don't knot it, just a loose wrap. If we hit something, grab on. It might keep you from flying overboard, which would really set us back."

We each wore the inventor's high-tech binocs. His sonic laser unit was in a case beneath the leaning post.

"In a hurry, not a rush. Well done, you. But I don't see any markers ahead, and—we own a twenty-five Boston Whaler— I've always avoided this area. Too damn dangerous."

"You can run a boat?"

"Nothing compared to you. If memory serves, according to charts, this area isn't navigable unless—"

I said, "Right, unless you grew up here. It's all sandbars and oysters and some limestone rock. Not a marked channel north or south for the next twenty miles. Sort of like in the city, you use back alleys instead of the interstate. It'll be better than beating ourselves to death in open water. If Pavlo ran aground, he should be somewhere between here and Gumbo Limbo—a little fishing village, Sulphur Wells. That's about four miles, but it's a tricky four miles, so stay alert."

I double-checked the lanyard that linked the ignition key to my belt—the kill switch. If I went over the side, the engine would stop instantly. The backcountry conduits to Hannah's place required full attention, so I hailed Big Sammy on VHF while I had time, idling toward Crescent Island. The lone structure there was dark, the beach a maelstrom of wreckage that had been blown across miles of open water.

I wondered if the feral hogs had lived there.

"Negative contact. Clear, standing by," I said, and placed the mic on the console.

"The last time you spoke to your friends was when their house flooded?" Weatherby had switched his binocs to fused thermal, and was scanning the mangroves.

"An apartment," I said. "More like a stucco mobile home about a mile or so from the Causeway. Five adults, two kids. And at least one of the adults can't swim. Cadmael's his name. A good guy and his wife, Mayans from Guatemala. Those poor folks. They never seem to get a break."

"It is an unfair world, Marion." The Brit was to my left, hands on a rail, nervous, already anticipating an unexpected impact. "Don't give up hope. Animals, mammals of some form, they survived. Raccoons, possibly. Small heat signatures. See them along the shoreline? If they made it, maybe your friends are—"

I interrupted, "If we don't get on plane here, we'll have to idle a quarter mile to the next pothole. Hang on."

Throttle forward, the boat launched itself into a mangrove creek not much wider than my boat.

Weatherby squeezed the grab rail harder. To speak as we banged along, he had to time the waves. "Are you sure this isn't rather reckless? If we hit something, we're goners...but you know these waters like the back of your... Since childhood, you said?"

"Until tonight, I knew them pretty well. Sit down. No talking for a while."

Since childhood. That was true. The serpentine tunnel called Long James Cut threaded the darkness and years of memories. To the left was York Island, an abandoned homestead with coconut palms. There was an artesian well there that bubbled from the ground summer and winter. You can't grow up in rural Florida without getting a taste for sulfur water. Sulfur sweet tea, tangy with feral citrus like the trees Hannah was raising.

Or had been raising.

I increased speed from twenty-five hundred RPM to thirty knots.

How many nights had I made this run? No GPS, just visual range markers in silhouette. Power poles that linked Gumbo Limbo, an island seventeen miles long, came into view. The crossing there was risky. I trimmed the engine to a rooster tail angle, juked left to avoid chunks of submerged limestone, then resumed speed.

In memory, the next visual should have been a gothic black mangrove that marked MacKeever Keys. Not only was that tree missing, the foliage rim had been sheared flat for miles. Another troubling element was that, behind us, the distant flare of the historic lighthouse had gone dark.

"Geezus," I muttered. "This is bad...worse than I...but we'll deal with it."

Weatherby sensed my confusion. "What's wrong?"

I said, "Take a seat on the deck."

"What? On the..."

I motioned him down and handed him the VHF. "It's guess-work for the next few miles. On the deck, brace yourself and try to raise Big Sammy. Try six-eight, then twenty-two."

"That's... Coast Guard monitors channel twenty-two. I thought we didn't want them involved."

I said, "Something good has to come from this storm. I don't care. If Coast Guard responds, tell them Davidson Road near the Causeway. Two families and kids that need an evac ASAP. Their luck needs to change, man."

On the console, the chart plotter was a useless distraction. The same with the artificial confidence of night vision optics. I removed the binocs, hit a switch and allowed my eyes to adjust.

"What are you doing?" Weatherby looked up from the hand-held.

"Going back to basics," I replied. "Watch for floating junk. I've got to concentrate on landmarks."

"Land...what landmarks? My God, Ford, we might as well be at forty thousand feet in a bloody fog. I can't see anything without these." He straightened his head strap and got to his feet. "Whatever you say, I guess. Are you sure?"

"I'm never sure about anything, Max, until I get to where I'm going."

I revved the engine and took a last look over my shoulder. On York Island, a ragged palm became an aft directive that pointed us north toward Hannah's place—and hopefully, Grigori Pav-lo's hostage.

35

Sammy Martinez didn't know it was his friend Doc motoring through the mangroves on the other side of an island where a palm tree bristled up, a ragged slash visible against the midnight sky.

"Stay low. Cover the children," he ordered the others. "Maybe it's that crazy man again. If he comes back, he'll start shooting."

Seven of them, including Cadmael, had been adrift in the rubber life raft since late afternoon. No food. Worse, no water. The storm had ping-ponged them across the bay in seas so heavy that even Sammy had puked. And when the wind peaked, it had pitchpoled the raft end over end like a desert tumbleweed.

When that happened, Sammy told himself, *We're dead, screw it. I'm tired of this* mierda, *anyway.*

It was a giddy, sickening sensation, spinning airborne in a tent without windows. A relief in a way. Emotionally, it was a letting go of fear and liability. Everything human—even hope. But the rubber tubes had held. The zippered doors had kept the waves out.

After Cadmael's many ordeals, he, too, had surrendered to destiny. "To hell with the crazy man. Let him shoot. But why would anyone—even gringos—want to kill us?"

Sammy replied, *"Quiet."* The motorboat was still out there, moving slowly on the other side of the mangroves. "A foreigner, not gringos. A drunken thief who doesn't want to leave witnesses, probably. I already told you it was the man with the expensive camper truck. When that boat's gone, there's land and a palm tree only a few hundred yards away from us. We'll paddle ashore and look for coconuts."

"Coconuts are good, but we should have brought a can to catch water before the goddamn rain stopped," Cadmael replied. "I saw the crazy person. A gringo with the long pointed beard. A devil beard. Or it could be the *federales* looking for us and want to help. If not, who cares? God can't save us from every little emergency, can He? How are you feeling, Patron?"

The old man, curled on the floor, bleeding, said, "Like I got kicked in the ass by a donkey. Stop bothering God. It's selfish to pray for more than three miracles in one day. Even for a Catholic. Enough. Let me die of thirst in peace."

Sammy waited through a minute of silence. "The police, not *federales*, but why would police search for us? Unless Poncho called them. Naw… Poncho doesn't know where we are. Hell, I don't even know where we are." He paused. *"Listen."*

A few hundred yards away, on the other side of the island, the boat with a fast engine roared north. Sammy poked his head out a flap that served as a door. The palm tree was still there, a delicate thread like a wisp of smoke.

The raft, in canvas pockets, was equipped with a paddle and three flares. Early on, he'd used two of the flares in their desperate search for Cadmael. The Guatemalan had been swept beneath the Causeway bridge, where they'd found him clinging to a cement girder, half-drowned and cut to pieces by barnacles.

That was the second miracle of the day. The third was when

the storm surge turned and pushed them west, inland, instead of out into a thunderous blackness that was the Gulf of Mexico. It would have meant agony; a certain death that might have lingered for days.

Once again, though, they had been spared. All afternoon, a pendulum had teased them with hope only to torture them with a new threat. Like a few hours ago around sunset. They'd thought they were safe when the raft banged aground near a navigational tower marked "13-A." A fourth miracle, it seemed, was when a large rubber boat appeared. Instead, the foreigner with the beard had opened fire. Would have killed them all if he hadn't been a quarter mile away separated by waves and a sandbar.

Several bullets had caused the raft to leak air, and one had hit the old man's leg. The raft was slowly sinking, they were all thirsty, but the patron would die if he didn't get water soon. The same was probably true of Cadmael's wife, Itzel. She had to produce milk for her baby.

Sammy had never thought much about the quiet teenage mother. Why would he? Itzel understood a little Spanish but spoke only K'iche'. After what they'd been through, though, he was impressed. Not once had she complained or screamed out in fear. If a job needed doing, Itzel was on it before the others could move.

He nudged the young woman's foot and spoke slowly in Spanish. "How does a nice green coconut sound? Maybe build a fire, too. Hand me that paddle and the flare kit."

She complied without comment, then returned to treating the old man's wound with one hand, her baby in the other arm.

Paddling the sinking raft was like paddling a saucer. Frustrating until water was shallow enough to get out and wade. Clipped to Sammy's PFD was a mini strobe light that he'd used sparingly inside the tent. It was disorienting, and they'd all vomited enough for one day. The palm tree guided the big man through the mangroves to a path that led up a shell mound to a structure of some type.

He activated the strobe. It was the foundation of an old house, collapsed tin roofing and homemade concrete. At the base of the concrete steps was a stem of rusted pipe. Caked around the pipe was a heap of white marl that stunk of sulfur.

Salt, Sammy guessed.

It should have been easy to find coconuts. It wasn't. The palm towered above a tangle of windfall. Heat, darkness, the slick footing complicated the search. Every few steps, clumps of prickly pear cactus had to be hacked away with a stick. Ten minutes of this was too much. Exhausted, Sammy cleared a place on the steps and plopped down. Until then, he was unaware that his duct tape stitches had ripped open. The gash above his belly button was bleeding again.

Dizzy. Nauseous. His tongue felt swollen, grainy with sand.

Years ago, he had experienced the same symptoms during a desert crossing from Nuevo Laredo into Texas.

Don't pass out, he told himself. *If you pass out, you'll die like the others. Think about the children.*

Sammy resumed his search among the litter using the strobe. The mound wasn't large but high enough to have weathered many floods. Finally—a single ripe coconut lay just out of reach in a basin of huge whelk shells.

He dropped to his knees, pulled limbs away. A blast of white light showed movement near his hand. An animal of some type. Dark iguana eyes and scales.

Ouch. He felt an acid sting and yanked his arm back. On his thumb were several black teardrops of blood. The damn thing, whatever it was, had bitten him.

Sammy stumbled away and collapsed next to the rusty pipe that bubbled with the stink of sulfur. Mud was sometimes good for pain, so he plunged his hand into the white marl there. The result was surprising. The sudden pressure seemed to burp the pipe clear, and it became a bubbling fountain.

Madre de Dios!

He rinsed the mud away. He leaned, he sniffed. He put his lips to the pipe and swallowed what he expected to be salty, but was sweet and cool.

Before Sammy collapsed again, exhausted, he managed to summon Cadmael by croaking, "Water... I found water. All the water we can drink."

36

When the old homestead on York Island was behind us, mangroves crowded in. Serpentine tunnels that opened or closed without warning. On night runs in thin water, air temp and odors vary with each sharp turn.

Weatherby was still nervous. I didn't blame him.

"Wish you would use the NODs, Ford. How in blazes can you see?"

I said, "We're okay. My eyes are still adjusting. It's only been ten, fifteen minutes, and it can take hours according to the experts."

"Experts? I *am* a bloody expert, and your sources are wrong. Slow down, man."

"If we drop off plane here," I told him, "we'll have to idle for the next mile or so. Think of Mrs. Lászlo."

Gradually, subtleties of gray and black gathered definition. Islands became a flatland maze interrupted by markers familiar since boyhood—high shell mounds a thousand years old. Buddies and I had camped on most of them. Uninhabited outposts, valleys and peaks, some forty feet high, constructed of whelks and conchs that resonated like bone beneath modern footwear. Ahead, to the right, was an unnamed mound north of Galt Island, another pre-Colombian antiquity.

"I know where we are now," I said. "Once we make this turn, we should be in deeper water."

"It's shallow here?"

"Couple of feet at most."

The Brit locked both fists on the grab rail.

The ancient ones were gifted architects. They'd built their temples with a signal fire view of the sea. Often, shoals were additional protection against marauders, but it seemed to us, just kids, the narrow, secret cuts through those shoals were no accident.

I banked to port and put the bow on a wall of low trees. When we were fifty yards out, the Brit stammered, "Ford... Marion, you see that island, right? Geezus, man, we're going to—"

The wall of trees parted. A peephole of gray appeared that was the westward horizon. We drilled the opening doing thirty and turned north where elevated guideposts—Demery Key, Josslyn—marked an archaic route that had once been industrious with dugout canoes.

The Brit tapped my shoulder. "I know I shouldn't doubt, but up ahead. I'm sure you see...you *do* see that, don't you?"

I thought he meant the string of fish shacks off Captiva Rocks. "Yeah, can't believe they're still standing. Incredible, that old Florida pine—"

He tapped me again, more urgent. "No, no...slow down. *Stop*, or we're going to—"

Seconds before a collision, a hulking black shape caused me to back the throttle and veer hard a'starboard.

"Sonuva—what is that thing, Max? It sure as hell shouldn't be out here." The threshold stop had created a backlash of waves.

Weatherby focused his binocs. "A car...no, a black...the damn thing looks like an undertaker's hearse. That was very, very close, Marion." He took a calming breath. "I suggest you put your eyes on."

The man had been right from the start, so I did. It was a Cadillac Escalade that had floated out to sea. The rear end bobbed like a bobblehead while the engine's weight grounded the front tires in a few feet of water.

"I suppose we should have a look in the cabin. Please tell me it's not from some funeral home. That would just be too flippin' bizarre."

We used infrared to check for occupants, alive or dead. Nothing inside.

"As a physician, I'm embarrassed to admit to feeling great relief." The Brit sat back; opened a bottle of water. "This is starting to feel like some hellish Faustian bargain. I think I need a Scotch."

"A what bargain?" I had spun us around, the bow pointed at the fishing village of Sulphur Wells and a pyramid of darkness that was the shell mound where Hannah's family had resided since 1910.

"A nightmare. A bad dream from the Middle Ages," he said. "How many people you reckon were trapped in their cars today? Or their homes and swept...dear God, I wonder what the body count will be? Looks like this area has been hit hard. But not nearly as bad as we got it."

I didn't respond. Inland, a mile away, a vehicle's backup lights flared on a narrow ribbon of road, picked up like beacons on the fused thermal goggles. There was a boat ramp a few hundred yards east of Hannah's place. The tension I'd felt all day redlined. I was finally close to confirming the woman I loved and the son I adored were safe. Or that the unthinkable had happened.

"Here we go, Max. Grab something." I throttled hard toward the ramp. "You have that laser weapon stowed under the console, right?"

"Whoa, why so fast, Ford? That was a damn close call we just had."

I pointed. "See the vehicle on the road up ahead? Looks like an RV, a truck with a camper. Why the hell is someone loading or splashing a boat at one in the morning? It could be Pavlo's people. Tell me about the laser."

"I thought I had. Not just a laser—a saser, my engineers call it. A high-frequency, focused acoustic transmitter that—well, it's complicated. All combined with laser technology. Slow down... slow down for God's sake. If we hit something at this speed—"

"Relax, we're fine. Yeah, a military-looking RV. See the size of those tires? Off-road tires." I motioned to the right. "That looks like Pavlo's boat over there. From the way it's listing, he hit an oyster bar or something just before he got to the ramp. How the hell did he make it this far?"

It was puzzling. Either the Russian had a working chart plotter, or his people had laid private marker buoys after the storm.

I said, "What kind of physical damage does your invention do? To a person, I mean. Can you set it to stun?"

"You mean like in a *Star Trek* movie? No. Well, yes...sort of. At close range on a stable platform, but not from out here. One miscalculation and—I told you this already. Hey—what the hell was that?"

"Muzzle flashes," I said. "*Oh...hell.* They see us. Get down."

Simultaneously, two, then a third round sledgehammered into the hull. I made a hard left and zigzagged north toward the dock where, until a week ago, Hannah had moored her flats skiff and a beautiful old Marlow cruiser, *Esperanza*.

"Are you hit?" Weatherby had collapsed on the deck. "Talk to me, Max." Without slowing, I tossed a bulky commercial life jacket overboard, then a second life jacket, hoping the reflective tape would draw fire.

He rolled onto his side. "Those pillocks don't care who they kill. We could've been a boatload of kids for all they… Damn, landed on my bad shoulder. Bleeding again. Are they still—"

"Yeah, firing, but they lost us, I think."

Squatting behind the wheel, I looked back. The life jackets had worked as decoy flares. Several rounds peppered the water behind us while I banked close ashore, past Hannah's place, out of sight.

Ahead was the commercial fishing co-op and a marina. The four-tier aluminum storage barn had collapsed, boats scattered across the lot, but the co-op docks looked in pretty good shape despite the muck and trash.

I slowed and shifted to Neutral. "How's your shoulder? Need something for pain?"

Weatherby was using quick-clot powder and gauze to stem the bleeding. Next, he opened the leaning post seat, placed the laser device on the console and connected it to the boat's auxiliary power plug. It was the size of a mini boom box with an electronics board and a honeycomb of lenses.

He said, "I'm fine. Drop me off here. I'll slip around and— Damn it all, I should've brought a tripod. Never mind, I'll find a place to steady the axis and— Ford, I'm going to stop that mad bastard before he destroys someone else's life. Pull up to that dock please."

I shook my head and removed the kill switch lanyard from my belt. "You're good at what you do, Dr. Weatherby. Now stand down and let me do what I'm good at. Take the wheel."

"What? No. I've waited more than two bloody years to turn that man's brain into—"

"It could still happen," I interrupted. "You said you own a boat? Take the wheel before we drift into those mangroves."

He had no choice when I opened an aft hatch and flopped a pair of black dive fins, a custom mask and a tactical belly pack onto the deck.

"Ford, what the hell—" He over-shifted from Forward into

Reverse. Gears ground. The engine revved, the stern bucked. Finally, he found Neutral. "Sorry. I'm not familiar with—"

"You'll figure it out," I said. "I want you to idle into the marina basin. See that line of sunken boats? Raft up, shut off the engine and stay down on the deck. Keep the VHF volume low. When I'm ready, you can pick me up here."

"On one of these docks? Personally, I think it's a bad idea to separate."

"No, more likely I'll be in the water." I pointed toward Hannah's property and removed the Blackwater twelve-gauge from the rod holder. "That's our backup rendezvous spot. You know how to use a shotgun?"

"A Purdey, yes, but never one like that."

"It's a pump action, double-aught buckshot. Eight rounds. If Pavlo's people come snooping, run, get the hell out of here. If you can't run, shoot the bastards, then take off."

I knew what the Brit was thinking. Before I slipped over the side, I told him, "Don't worry about the police. By the time they get here, we'll be long gone. Trust me, Max, there won't be anything here we don't want them to find."

37

I swam on my back, otter-style, until a pair of armed men appeared on Hannah's dock and used a spotlight to search for
the boat they'd failed to intercept. Acres of trash, waves and
the stink of diesel cloaked my approach.

The light skipped toward me. I submerged. Thirty strokes of
my old Rocket fins should have put me close enough to hear
their voices. Instead, in the murk, I banged headfirst into a piling and surfaced beneath the dock, the men's boots inches above
my nose.

An exchange in Russian sounded like back-and-forth questions. They'd felt the collision through the wood. The guy with
the light dropped to his knees so fast I didn't have time to sub-
merge before he blinded me. All I saw was an arm and the outline of a head. I grabbed the arm, then his neck and pulled him
under. My legs got a wrap around a piling, and I held him there
ten, fifteen seconds, until a series of pinging bullet trajectories
caused his body to spasm. He'd been hit. There was another
shot. The man, after a wild struggle, went limp in my arms.

I kicked his body away. His spotlight floated with him.

Overhead, heavy footsteps tracked the light. Hannah's dock was more than two hundred feet long. I stayed beneath it and pulled myself, piling to piling, closer to shore. In the shallows I stayed low and waited. To my right, one man...no, a different pair of men, appeared to have finished wading boxes from Pavlo's grounded vessel to the camper truck with the big tires.

If Mrs. László was still alive, that's where she would be. I couldn't investigate, though. Not yet. Strapped to my chest was the belly pack. I deployed the steel baton and listened. When heavy footsteps approached overhead, the smart thing to do was to shatter the guy's kneecap and drag him under.

There was no need. In the truck's headlights, Pavlo appeared, an automatic rifle up and ready. It was Fool's Cut all over again. He shot his two flunkies before they could run, then opened fire on the man at the end of Hannah's dock. I submerged behind a bulwark of pilings and listened. A football field separated us. A full mag wasn't required, but Pavlo savored the moment by emptying it, anyway. A bowling ball splash marked where his third victim had fallen. Underwater, I found the man and robbed him of his sidearm and an extra mag.

Kill them all; keep the artwork, the gems, everything. That had been the Vulture Monk's plan from the start.

You fool, I thought. *Now it's just us.*

I started toward shore, then changed my mind. Even if the bridge to the mainland was operational, Pavlo's off-island escape route would require a chain saw and a crew to clear the lanes. It's always that way after a bad one. Roads become liquid conduits. Anything and everything that floats ends up on an asphalt sluice. Every few hundred yards, he would have to get out and deal with another logjam if he tried to escape in his vehicle.

And he would, of course. What other option did he have? Stick around until tomorrow, wait for the cops and try to explain the bullet-riddled bodies of four fellow mercenaries?

This gave me a way to rationalize what I did next. Instead of rushing to find Mrs. László, I hid my snorkel gear and slipped through the mangroves to the edge of the road. Hannah's house lay squat, stolid in darkness atop the mound, tin roof leaden gray among a tornadic ruin of trees.

South, down the road, lights were on inside the camper, the truck's diesel a vague rumble muted by the crash of barrier island surf miles across the bay. Pavlo was still busy arranging boxes of stolen goods.

My brain argued that Hannah's house was empty. No sign of movement, no sheriff's squad car parked in the drive. And Hannah's SUV was gone, which made sense. It would be parked at Southwest Regional. Emotionally, though, I had to confirm for myself that she and our son—her cop friend, Birdy, too—were safe.

I went up the mound to the porch and was sickened by swaths of blood on the porch and more inside on the kitchen floor. This was a crime scene, so booties and surgical gloves were required. Standard gear in my unusual vocation. I spent several minutes going from room to room. The struggle had started in the spare bedroom. It had escalated to the century-old fireplace where an antique shotgun hung undisturbed over the mantel, but an axe was missing. On the side porch, a pair of hooks dangling from a rafter added to the horror of what had happened here before the storm. Or after the storm. No telling, and it didn't matter when I found a torn uniform blouse with a name tag that read, *Lt. Liberty Tupplemeyer.*

Liberty. I'd forgotten the ginger-haired woman's unusual first name.

Emotional ties and loyalties are ungovernable in the human conscience. The linear image of what had thumped across the deck of Pavlo's boat was tempered—displaced, in truth—by my relief when I verified that items required for a mother-toddler trip to North Carolina were missing.

Hannah, our son, Izaak, and her crotchety old mother, who was in Fort Myers, had been spared.

A random intersection with a killer, and Birdy had been his coincidental victim. It was a quirk of timing that, in me, ignited an awareness that I should have felt guilt, remorse or something other than relief. But I didn't.

It happens daily, hourly, minute by minute worldwide. Make a wrong turn, choose the wrong seat, smile at a stranger—all forgettable decisions that can turn disastrous, yet life flows on. My pal, Tomlinson, claims the word *coincidence* is an invention that defines our own confusion better than it describes a unique occurrence.

I don't agree. Try explaining Divine Order to the family of Lieutenant Liberty Tupplemeyer. Wherever she might be.

Wait… I knew where she was. Or part of her, anyway, had been two hours ago. If I was incapable of grief, Birdy's family, at least, deserved the courtesy of closure.

I swam toward the boat ramp, head up, and watched Pavlo duck into the camper. He was in no hurry now that he had eliminated his "teammates." The difference between psychopaths and mass killers is that psychopaths don't embrace politics as an excuse. Statistically, they are less organized and less intelligent. That serial killers are diabolical geniuses is a Hollywood device.

Thus far, the failed novitiate had tracked an unpredictable line between the two poles. I was done overestimating his abilities. In the Russian's mind, he was in the clear. No one else around to stop him at 2:00 a.m. on this evacuated island after a Cat-Five storm.

He was wrong.

I sculled toward his abandoned boat in search of Lieutenant Tupplemeyer's remains. There was also a chance Mrs. László was still aboard. She wasn't. The bucket and the severed head were gone, too. A forensic team would be needed to confirm my suspicions.

The bay was a viscous soup, body heat temperature. My fins kicked a silent wake toward the boat ramp. The camper door opened, lights on inside. The Russian got out and lobbed something onto the road. A glass plate or dish, it sounded like.

Christ...

Thinking of the two missing ladies, I cringed. Pavlo had been inside cooking dinner minutes before he'd executed four of his own men.

It was time to lure the psycho away from his vehicle. To anticipate behavior, assume the mindset of your adversary. He was an unhinged sadist who was overconfident but didn't know the area. In the Russian's brain, the fastest route of escape would be to follow the only road that edged the bay. It was a narrow ribbon of macadam that arrowed south away from Hannah's home, then carved a series of switchbacks north, then east along the mangrove fringe.

I swam parallel to the road, crouched low and duck walked backward into the lee of an invisible moon. My fins were large enough to fit over my boots. I traded snorkel gear for quad night optics. After cleaning the four lenses, my vision was transformed from poor to a precisely focused panorama, one hundred twenty degrees.

An oddity I noticed from the bushes: no whine of mosquitoes or acidic assault from sandflies—no-see-ums, tourists call them. Had the flood surge killed them all?

The surgical gloves were gone, replaced by shooting gloves, the trigger fingers bare. I touched the NOD's mode pad, and a thermal overlay showed the camper truck's combustion schematic. Within a pair of windows, Pavlo was highlighted in orange. The pinpoint heat of his brain and his beating heart were tempting amber targets. I might have gone in hard were it not for a second heat contour—a propane stove or possibly a person lying on a bed. If the Russian didn't climb into the cab and take off soon, though, I would have to attack, which meant risking a standoff with Mrs. László as his hostage.

It was better to surprise the guy. An ideal ambush spot—a choke point—was where the road made a hairpin turn north. I made my way through the shadows and used mangrove roots as a seat. My full-sized Sig Sauer nine came out for a quick inspection. Spare mags were shaken dry, springs taut, ready to feed an additional twenty-one rounds each if needed.

Next, I checked the pistol I'd stolen. A Glock 17, a proven weapon with a superbly crisp trigger and seventeen rounds of nine in the mag. I didn't expect it to have a threaded barrel, but it did.

Perfect. In my belly pack was a sound suppressor made by Thompson Machine, Crawfordville, Florida. A few drops of salt water inside the can were actually to my advantage—temporarily, anyway.

I threaded the can onto the Glock, dry-fired several times to test the reset. Then I shucked a round into the battery, checked my watch and waited.

Three minutes, I told Pavlo. *You have three minutes to get in that truck or you'll be dead in five.*

The camper and the cab of the big diesel truck were to my left within easy sprinting distance. But it was better to let the Russian come to me. Wait until he was in the cab alone. He would slow for the turn, probably stoned, no longer on full alert, and that's when I'd take him. Put several rounds through the windshield. If that didn't force the man to jump and run, there was another hairpin turn to the right, both lanes clogged with trees.

I would catch him there.

Either way, if authorities found the Glock, it would be under Hannah's dock where I'd dumped it, or near the body of one of the Russian's own men.

Keep it simple—a maxim that acknowledges that nothing ever goes exactly as planned. And adversaries—even those of questionable intelligence—are unpredictable.

Two minutes into my wait, the camper door opened. The door closed. Pavlo got into the truck, which was already running, and slammed the thing into gear. I got to my feet and hugged the tree line, waiting for headlights to sweep past me.

It didn't happen.

Instead, my adversary made what seemed to be the stupidest decision possible. Rather than turn south toward freedom, he revved the engine and sped north past Hannah's house toward the fish co-op and marina. Brake lights flared and the camper bounced down a muddy dead-end lane toward the citrus grove behind Hannah's house.

What the hell was going on in the guy's head?

The fiction of the brilliant psycho dissolved. Off-road tires or not, there was nothing back there but trees, pasture, shell mound ridges and swamp he probably couldn't hike through, let alone drive a truck through.

A light went on in my head. Something else back there were unmarked graves—at least one, possibly two, all the work of Hannah's mom and her crusty bingo partners, a quiet coalition that did not tolerate abusive men.

There was a third grave known only to Hannah and me. Until recently, I'd believed that secret to be more binding than wedding vows. Now, though, that isolated space, a hole deeper than it was wide, presented a more utilitarian option.

Done right, Pavlo would never be found.

I hailed Weatherby on VHF. "We've got him cornered, Max. I'll meet you at our secondary location." A moment later, I amended, "Wait...maybe I'm wrong. Could be he has a different exit plan. I don't know, I might see a chopper inbound, possibly. Check the eastern skyline."

The Brit acknowledged with three clicks of the mic key.

38

Weatherby came up the mound, slipping and sliding in the mud, carrying the Blackwater shotgun and a waterproof bag. I noticed he was favoring his injured shoulder. "You're right," he said. "It's a helicopter. We need to finish this business and get back to the island. Agreed? Pretend like whatever we do here never happened."

"It never did," I said, and relieved him of the shotgun's weight. "Keep that in mind."

Without special optics, we wouldn't have noticed the helo sliding toward us from several miles away, low on the horizon. No obligatory one-second strobes, white, red and green. But a funnel of infrared glazed the tree canopy like a drifting curtain of rain.

The Brit placed his bag on a gardening table and started toward the porch's back door.

"Don't go in there," I said.

He stopped. "Not thinking clearly, I guess. This old wing

of mine is starting to stiffen up. But you're right. The clock's ticking."

"The house is a crime scene, Max. You should stay here, take a break. Don't touch anything. I won't be long."

"Crime scene…? Oh, no, I am sorry, Marion. Your fiancée and son… I hope they're not… Anything I can…?"

"Not Hannah. A friend of hers was murdered here, I think. A deputy sheriff."

"The woman you mentioned? It was him, of course."

"Yeah. Pavlo. I didn't find a body but a lot of blood. Could be she got a call out for help before he—" The last two words, *beheaded her*, were better left unsaid. "Max, I'm not convinced that's a law enforcement chopper."

Weatherby understood the implications. "Mercenaries. Backup. Or an extraction. I'd be surprised police would scramble a helo before first light. Ford, a few minutes ago, I heard gunfire… His men, where are they, the ones who shot at us?"

"Gone."

"As in they got away?"

"As in dead. I had nothing to do with it."

"No…naturally. Understood."

"I mean it. Pavlo shot them all, and I suspect he still has Mrs. László. That chopper… I don't like it. Even if it is law enforcement, we've got to get moving. Come on. There's a path to the citrus grove—or used to be."

The Brit warned, "If we do this, you're going to need eye and ear protection. Or you'll have to do exactly as I say."

I led him past the tool shed where there was an antique John Deere with a grappler bucket, then over a fence and up a ledge of shells to a mound that provided a view of the acreage below.

The camper truck was there, headlights off, but the camper windows were aglow.

"Set up here," I said. "Can you use a tree or something to

steady that…whatever it is? What's your range? Are we close enough?"

"This will do nicely, my friend. Optics off, please."

"What?"

Weatherby tapped his NOD binocs. "Infrared. If we can see the helo, the pilot might see the reflection off our goggles. The fewer targets, the better. Just give me a sec to scan the truck's windows, then we'll go covert until we're sure where Rebecca is. After that—I'll tell you what to do when it's time."

I took a last look at the chopper. A medium-sized aircraft, blacked out, riding the tree line contour, dipping and lifting as if riding waves, an altitude of two hundred feet max, maybe eight miles out.

"That guy's flying Nap-of-the-earth low. So he's either one hell of a pilot or he's got terrain tracking radar," I said after toggling the power off. "Now I'm thinking it is law enforcement. Private aircraft don't have that sort of equipment. Let's think about this for a sec. If it's the police, why not guide them in, let them deal with Pavlo while we get the hell out of here? God knows there's evidence enough to put him away for a lifetime."

In the darkness, the physician/inventor's head tilted in an odd way. "Is this a test?"

"That's up to you. You don't want to be a part of what happens next. I have a reason to be here and, well…tidy up later. You don't, and the cops aren't going to like that one bit."

"No worries. Worth the price of admission," he replied. "I know more about these people than I've admitted. Pavlo, as despicable as he is, is just an asset. A moneymaker—blackmail, extortion, the sickest sort of films. I know. There's video of what he did to my niece, and they've been blackmailing me ever since I—"

"*You?* Max, we don't have time for this. Not now. Check the camper, find Mrs. László. I'm going down there. Use the radio. I'll leave the shotgun."

He had the mini sonic device out, plus a battery pack, and was steadying it on the trunk of a tree. "This organization is... There's an oligarch, he's behind it all. East Coast, former KGB. He was also a MiG pilot with just about every flight certification there is."

That stopped me. Without optics the helo, less than three miles out, had vanished.

I said, "You think that's him?"

Sasha Olegovich, Lauderdale Coast, was the name I'd filed away.

Weatherby replied, "If it is, my friend, after tonight, he'll be out of the country by tomorrow or next day. Mark my words. And they're not going to let either one of us just walk away. Those people are better financed than most small countries."

He put his eye to a lens; touched the sonic laser's electronic keypad. "Okay, okay, I've got a target. Get your legs under you. There's only one person in the camper. Make sure it's not Rebecca...then run."

The camper truck was Kevlar and diesel. Tricked out with security cameras and a multisensory imaging pod atop the cab. I stayed low and crawled to the passenger window.

Empty. The engine was off, so lights inside the camper were powered by the hum of an auxiliary generator. Portside there was panel access. I popped the latch, found the unit mounted within and clipped the ground lead wire.

Lights blinked out. I waited at the door, pistol drawn, expecting the Russian to investigate. Inside, someone stumbled in the sudden darkness. There was the sound of running water—a shower, possibly. Soft tiptoe footsteps scurried to the rear of the camper.

That wasn't Pavlo's style.

I tested the door handle. The handle flipped up, but the door didn't open. That told me it had been dead bolted from the inside, not locked with a key from the outside.

The cap of an ASP baton is spiked with ceramic pins designed for shattering windows. These windows, though, were storm-grade acrylic or polycarbonate, so I tapped politely and whispered, "Mrs. László. Are you okay?"

It was a risky move. There was no response, so now I was committed.

Years ago, at an executive driver security course, we learned that even big-ticket RVs come with cheap pot-metal locks. Easily picked with a rake and a tension bar to avoid damage. A faster way was to lever the dead bolt free, which I did, using the baton. One sharp blow. The door swung wide.

Pistol at high ready, I peeked into a space that had a meat locker chill, prepared to shoot, or duck and run.

Instead, a woman's voice said from the shower closet, "If you come in here, I'll finish the job. I swear to God I will. And this time I won't use my teeth."

I holstered the pistol, swept the area with my LED and cringed at the nightmare that had befallen Mrs. Rebecca László. On the floor, among abduction paraphernalia, were totems of Pavlo's excesses. Trophy clothing and worse; evidence that would have to be left undisturbed rather than cloud the forensics. Among the mess was proof of Liberty Tupplemeyer's fate.

I said, "Mrs. László, it's me. Marion Ford. Come out. Where is he?"

The shower closet door opened an inch. "Dr. Ford. Oh...oh, thank God. Are you sure he's not coming back?"

"Nope, not sure, so hurry. Are you hurt?"

"Do you have a gun?" she demanded. "If he comes back, you have to promise to shoot him. Or I will—and this time I won't miss."

Her calm, under the circumstances, suggested that her injuries were manageable—her physical injuries, anyway.

The shower door opened wider. When I saw the condition

she was in, I put my flashlight on the floor and turned away as a courtesy. Her facial contours had changed.

"Grab a blanket or something," I said. "Shoes. You'll need shoes and pants and a shirt. Don't worry about your other stuff now."

She replied, "I have to take everything. I don't want anyone to know what happened here. Understand, Dr. Ford? *Ever.* I've already used a towel on my handprints and tried to shower myself clean. Whiskey, vodka, anything alcoholic. I need that most of all or I'm afraid I'll vomit again."

I understood. On the floor were kneeling cushions that told a story. Nearby, in a blood-black pool, lay what might have been the featherless neck of a European vulture.

"You can put the knife down," I added. "If the guy hasn't bled to death by now, he will. How long ago did this...how long since he left you here alone?"

She wasn't sure, but it had been before Weatherby and I had spotted the camper.

I said, "Get dressed. We need to get you to a safe place."

While waiting, I found the truck's hidden ignition key and put in my pocket.

39

The lady and I went through the citrus grove toward Hannah's house while I updated Weatherby on VHF, my words more cautious now to shield the woman from involvement.

"Max. We're done here. The subject—the guy?—he's probably headed for the east pasture, a big open area where there's a stack of boxes. A possible LZ. Check it. Where's the chopper?"

"About two miles out. Yes, on a definite rendezvous course with…and I see the boxes. What do you mean, 'let him go'?"

I said, "The subject. Disengage. Your patient is with me and needs attention right away. To hell with everything else. We'll meet you at the house."

The helicopter's *WHAP-WHAP-WHAP* chased us up the mound, roared low, then banked hard toward the pasture. Weatherby had to wait to respond. "Sorry, negative. I'm not ready to walk away just yet. Not without sending a quick good-bye to…to the subject. I see him…yeah, range and distance… I'll squelch three times. After that, you'll have thirty seconds. QSL?"

Yes, message received. We were near the tool shed behind the old house when it happened. A static warning gave me time to tell Mrs. László, "He's gonna use that sonic laser again. Close your eyes, look at the ground, open your mouth and cover your ears."

I did the same, prepared for an acoustic assault that I couldn't have seen anyway without optics. There was a spinal micro-jolt, felt not heard, that wasn't nearly as intense as what we'd experienced earlier. An instant later we heard a spray of gunfire. Several purposeful bursts that shredded the tree canopy above our heads with the hiss of tearing silk.

I muttered, "Goddamn you, Weatherby."

The woman got to her feet. "MI6," she said. "But you didn't hear it from me. Dr. Max has a wealth of connections. He's friends with the royal family, you know. Instead of damning him, trust the man to do his job."

This might have been bravado catalyzed by shock, but it was said without the incoherence of a person with a serious head injury. Reassuring.

"Sorry. You're right," I said, and steered the woman to a workbench next to the antique tractor and helped her up. The LED became an effective lamp. From my belly pack I took out first-aid items—a chemical icepack, Betadine cleanser and antiseptic. No vodka, but I had four ounces of hydrogen peroxide.

"Clean your mouth with this," I said.

She grabbed the vial from my hand, rinsed, gagged and spit until it was empty. "That sick animal," she said softly. "I need liquor, gin, anything I can swallow until the taste of… That taste is—" Her eyes focused on me. "Please don't tell anyone what happened back there. You *know* what happened. I can tell because you haven't asked."

I said, "You used a knife to defend yourself. What's to tell? Gin, I doubt, but rum maybe. I'll slip into the house and see what I can find."

"A knife," she agreed and dabbed at her lips with an alcohol swab. "My pickpocket skills weren't much help until he'd freed my hands. I hope the bastard does bleed to death."

Weatherby triple squelched to announce his arrival.

I said, "Pavlo did this to her. Is he——"

"Afraid not. Crippled, disoriented, possibly. There was no time for a proper job, and I only managed a fifty percent charge from your boat's auxiliary power. The helo locked onto my IR and I had to—well, you heard the shooting. Now I'm afraid the helo will swing back around and——"

"We can't let that happen," I said. "How accurate was the gunfire? Did a weapons system lock in, too?"

"Probably not, but I imagine he was using LiDAR to navigate at tree level. But we can't use night optics until the helo clears this area."

"What about thermal imaging?"

Weatherby had turned his attention to Mrs. Lászlo, saying, "Well, my dear, you've had a quite a day. If Marion will excuse us, I want to check your pupils and a few other things. We need to get that neck of yours stabilized and then we'll go for a nice boat ride." He turned to me. "As fast as possible."

I said, "If that chopper has thermal—if it swings back—you won't have time to get her stabilized. I'll try to keep them busy for a while."

Mrs. Lászlo heard me shuck a round into the Blackwater twelve-gauge and, her voice soft, said something about a present, as if she owed me something.

"Just be ready when I pull the boat around," I said and hurried away.

Outside, gen four optics guided me down the mound. Maximum sensitivity. No need for telltale infrared. I went past the camper, over a fence and into a clearing where cattle had once grazed. On the fence, a bloody handprint marked the Russian's recent passage. And his destination was marked by the helicopter's spaceship-bright lights, still on after landing a few minutes earlier.

I unslung the shotgun and jogged to within fifty yards of the diesel roar, just outside the worst of the whirlybird debris. An empty oil drum provided a place to kneel and observe. In the cockpit, only the pilot was visible. He might not need a wingman to spray bullets at an infrared target, but where was Pavlo?

The chopper's portside door opened. The pilot got out and began loading a half-dozen boxes stacked there. Among them, I had no doubt, were stolen gems and the Rauschenberg. The pilot, a wide-bodied man, wasn't nimble. This suggested age and previous injuries. It had to be the oligarch and former MiG pilot. The man wasn't a physical threat, certainly not if I took him by surprise.

One by one, options came to mind. One by one, they were dismissed. I own a small amphib, a handsome blue-and-white Maule that, I hoped, was still safely hangared inland. A multimillion-dollar chopper, however, was way beyond my abilities. And there was no way to make the damn thing disappear—not by tomorrow when law enforcement arrived.

So…why not rob the robber, let the oligarch fly away and track him down later?

That's what I decided to do. I started to approach the man from behind when, to my left, Pavlo came hobbling out of the darkness, bent at the waist in pain. Deaf maybe, possibly blind. I dropped to one knee and tracked him with twelve-gauge ghost sights. The oligarch/pilot had just loaded the last metal box. He turned, saw his visitor…yelled something in Russian—a command—and, in a rush, climbed into the cockpit.

Pavlo, after a panicky glance over his shoulder, kept coming.

He wasn't blind. In the tall grass behind him was movement. Animals of some type. More than a few. I flicked on combined infrared and night vision. Warm-blooded coyotes, tongues lolling, heads low in pack formation, were on the man's trail. He knew it and galloped Quasimodo-like to the chopper. He got his feet on the skid and a hand on the starboard door.

I watched the man's mouth open in rage or fear—his words muffled when the rotor blades accelerated to lift-off RPMs.

The helo buoyed upward…tilted in a curtain of windfall. Pavlo banged at the fuselage with his fist. The pilot, instead of helping, focused on the controls. Too late, I ducked out of sight, but his electronics had already targeted me.

A window slid open…an Uzi-sized weapon came out…and my oil drum shield boomed with a rapid-fire burst of rounds. I crouched lower, waited for the tail rotor to swing my way, then shouldered the twelve-gauge. Three times I squeezed and shucked. Double-aught buckshot starred the Plexiglas capsule.

The oligarch didn't expect a shooting response. The chopper tilted stern high, gained speed, then banked to port twenty feet off the ground. This gave me a clear view of Pavlo. He clung to the skid with both arms. The fuselage spun—a crack-the-whip gyration that flung what might have been a GoPro camera off the Russian's head. Seconds later, the man's strength gave out, and he dropped into a swampy, shallow pond several hundred yards away.

I waited until the chopper was a mile east, bound for what I suspected was Lauderdale—or the Bahamas—before using the VHF.

"Max, you copy? How's your patient?" As I spoke, I pocketed the spent twelve-gauge casings.

He replied, "She's okay but worried about you. We heard more gunshots. Did you find, uhh, the you know? Over."

"All clear for now," I said. "Wasn't able to recover your property. Sorry. There's some cleaning up to do, but I can have the boat out front in fifteen minutes if you need to roll now. Thirty would be better. Your call. How is the patient?"

"In charge—two words," he said. "Stable for now, I think, and insists upon home care only. Which I can handle with the proper kit—but only temporarily. Is ten minutes doable? The sooner the better. Or is the aircraft still a problem?"

His urgency suggested that Mrs. László was in bad shape. She needed to get back to the island where he had medical supplies, and then to a hospital.

"Ten it is," I told him. "I'll call again when I'm five out from the dock."

I signed off and did a fast search of the area. A blinking low battery light led me to a mini camera attached to a headband—evidence that went into my bag. The fading hum of rotor blades sharpened the rhythms of wind and a man's distant bellowing howls.

Pavlo had survived the fall.

I checked my watch and ran to another fence, then down a cactus-crusted mound. It leveled into a swampy area, once a canal system built for trade by Florida's indigenous people. Centuries ago, there would have been cooking fires, canoes, long-houses large enough to hold hundreds of people. Now, though, all that remained were the bones—human and architectural—of a civilization that had been swept away.

The Russian was there in water up to his chest, crippled, exhausted. I could have used the stolen Glock to finish the job from forty yards away. Bracketing shots, walk the rounds in until they found the target.

I didn't. No need. Pack animals had blood-scented the Vulture Monk. A dozen or more yapping, water-shy coyotes. They trotted, lunged, snapped at Pavlo's struggling hands, then dodged away, tails beneath their legs. Gang tactics that signaled coward-ice but were not. It was instinctual. Survival behavior.

As I watched, the pack whimpered and scattered to make room for a pair of oversized alphas that came bouncing out of the bushes.

Coywolves, I thought. A canid hybrid, a mix of coyote, eastern wolves and feral dogs. Or were they red wolves? The species had once thrived in Florida only to go extinct in the 1970s.

Whatever the animals were, the lead male was not water-shy. He crashed into the pond, grabbed Pavlo's arm and dragged him toward shore with a series of powerful backward lunges.

Pavlo had gone limp, silent, face down in the water.

I checked my watch again. When I looked up, I realized the displaced coyotes were now trotting toward me. I didn't run, didn't back away. I retreated sideways, shotgun ready, until they started to circle. A single shot into the ground put an end to that.

When it seemed okay to turn and run, I gave it an extra minute to be certain.

Coywolves might be more determined.

One was. Weatherby and I had gentled Mrs. László into the boat when a wolfish silhouette mounted the dock and trotted heavy-pawed toward us.

Too late, I warned, "Behind you, Max. Move. Get in."

Weatherby froze for an instant, surprised by the big-bodied canid. He waved his arms, but the animal kept coming, not fast, not growling, stoic as if curious, and banged its head into the man's outstretched hands.

"Good dog, nice dog," the Brit whispered, not sure what would happen next.

What happened next is, I noticed that the coywolf didn't have pointed ears. I noticed a familiar blockheaded demeanor. The dog, a retriever, acknowledged me with dark, knowing eyes that would have been yellow if it hadn't been three hours before dawn.

I reached for him. "Pete. Pete! It's me." This was said with a degree of emotion to which we were both strangers.

My dog allowed me the familiarity of a brief tongue slap. He pulled away, hiked a leg to piss, then galloped down the dock toward the charcoal shape of another large alpha—probably not male—and didn't look back.

Mrs. László, lying on cushions aft, covered with a blanket, didn't open her eyes. "Pete? Who's Pete? Is someone else getting on the boat?"

Weatherby was looking at his hands, using a light. "Jesus Christ, where'd all this blood come from?" he wondered. "Your dog's mouth, I guess. Normally, I'd say we shouldn't go off and leave him, but I'm afraid we're in a bit of a hurry."

I said, "It's not my dog's blood. He'll be fine."

"How do you know?"

"Because I saw him drag—" for the lady's sake, I amended "—because he likes staying at Hannah's place. By tomorrow, probably, there'll be a boy here to look after him. They were... they *are* buddies."

On the way back to Dinkin's Bay, we ran the Mailboat Channel, a mile northwest of McIntyre Creek. To port, I noticed a fire on uninhabited York Island where, as a kid, I'd drunk sulfur-scented water from an artesian well.

"That's a campfire," the Brit said. "Who in their right mind would go camping after a hurricane?"

I said, "Let's take a quick look. If someone's stranded, I'll come back and get them later."

Weatherby agreed but reluctantly. Neither he nor Rebecca László could risk meeting eyewitnesses. His head tilted and searched the sky, still worried about the helicopter and the trigger-happy oligarch who might have doubled back.

Stay covert, no infrared, the Brit almost warned again, but dropped the subject. Even for a man like me, it was dangerous navigating the shallows without night optics.

40

Speaking K'iche' Mayan, Cadmael said to his wife, Itzel, "I hear a boat coming. *Listen*. Do you think we should put out the fire? What if it is that crazy devil man again?"

The woman, late teens, five feet tall, had taken charge from the instant they'd stepped onto a shell mound in what seemed to be the middle of a jungle that reminded her of much larger stone ruins—pyramids—in the jungles of Guatemala.

It was a feeling. A scent. A density in the air.

Seated on a log, Itzel nursed their infant son while tending to a grill she had fashioned over hot orange coals.

"Ask Samuel about the boat," she said. "Samuel speaks English. Maybe he can talk to the boat people. Clean another large seashell. I'll need more water for tea."

"What if the crazy man starts shooting again?"

"Then we will be dead. But at least we will have a hot breakfast first." She raised her voice above the noise of wind and the approaching hum of an outboard motor. "Oye! Samuel!"

The big man had been snoring for more than an hour. He

stirred. He groaned. He got to his feet and staggered from the shelter Itzel had made using the deflated raft and palm fronds. The toddler girl child was inside, curled up asleep.

"Something smells good," Sammy said. "Or was I dreaming?"

He rubbed his eyes. It wasn't a dream. The young mother had gone foraging rather than sleep. Old whelk tools had become boiling pots, dippers and serving bowls. Blades of prickly pear cactus had been scraped clean of thorns and were roasting over coals. The purple-colored fruit had been braised, peeled and sliced into a gel that included overripe sea grapes and shredded coconut.

"*Nopales,*" Sammy smiled, meaning the cactus pads. They were a favorite food back in Mexico. Excellent with beans and salsa. "What is that roasting on a stick? Meat? Where did you find meat, little mother?"

Itzel spoke, her husband translated. "She found it in the hole where the animal bit your finger. A very large iguana. See? You will have your revenge by eating its tail."

"You killed that mean *pendejo*?"

"Not me. My wife is the hunter in our family."

Itzel said to Cadmael, "Tell him about the boat people. I need to clean his wound again. It is already infected. The same with the patron's leg. My nose is never wrong about such things. They will die if I can't get medicine soon. So let us hope it is not the crazy devil man coming back. If not, we must ask those people for a ride."

By then, Big Sammy had heard the outboard motor. He used a walking stick, made his way down the mound to the water's edge. Out there in the darkness not far away, a gray shape steered toward shore. He hid in the mangroves and waited. In his hands, the walking stick became a club.

The boat was close enough to smell exhaust fumes when a man's voice called in English, "Hello, sir. You, standing in the trees. Do you need help?"

Sammy backed deeper into the bushes. How was it possible that he'd been seen?

The man switched to Spanish. "We're not the police. I saw your fire, so if you need help, say something or we'll be on our way."

That voice, Spanish with a gringo accent, was familiar. Very familiar. But impossible. Was this, too, a feverish dream?

"Who are you, amigo?"

"Doesn't matter. Do you want me to stop or not?"

Grinning, Big Sammy stepped out and threw his arms wide. "Hey...hey, Poncho. Is that you? Turn on a light. Prove it. Yes... hell yes, Doc. We need help."

Ford, the biologist, said to a passenger in the boat, "I know that man. Sammy Martinez, he's the friend I told you about."

"No lights until you're on shore," a voice with a British accent warned.

The biologist got out wearing a strange gadget on his forehead, gave Sammy a bear hug and was surprised to see the tidy makeshift camp, food cooking over a fire in shell pots that might have been used the same way hundreds of years ago.

He wasn't surprised to see water bubbling from the artesian well.

"Incredible. The luckiest possible place to wash ashore. I was worried about you, my friend," Ford said. "And you all made it. Any injuries?"

Sammy replied, "No. Uhh, yes." He indicated the old man, who had finally drifted off to sleep. "The patron was shot in the leg."

"*Shot?* By who?"

"And I have this small cut on my belly." Sammy lifted his shirt. "Is nothing. But there are five of us and two babies. Is there room on your boat?"

From Ford's reaction, there was not. And the biologist seemed more troubled after inspecting the big man's wound. He said,

"I've got to get you and the old man to a friend of mine who's a doctor—or a hospital. At the very least, take the babies and the women and come back for you in an hour or so. Or—listen to me—the Coast Guard could send a helicopter. A medical emergency, they're not going to care what your green card says. They could have you at the ER by sunrise."

"A helicopter?" Sammy liked the sound of that.

The young mother said something to Cadmael in K'iche'. Cadmael translated in Spanish. "She wants to know if you have medicines on your boat. We have experienced many miracles this day. It is bad luck, my wife says, for our families to separate now."

The biologist had an argument going on in his head. Sammy sensed this. Maybe something to do with the unidentified passenger with the British accent. But Ford said, "You need a doctor. Come on, pal, get your stuff. We'll make room. Kids first, then the patron. I want to hear how the hell you ended up here—and who shot at you."

Sammy argued, "Poncho, I'll tell you everything. Go, take your friend wherever you're going. We will be fine here for another few hours." He motioned to the fire. "Look, a feast awaits us. But I...I lost the little radio. I'm sorry. I'll pay you back."

"Not until you tell me who shot the old man."

Ford, when he heard about the foreigner with the beard and the fancy camper, was relieved but didn't explain why. "Doubt if you have to worry about him anymore. Yeah, you should be okay here for a while. Take this." He removed a belly pack that contained first-aid supplies, a radio, a fancy little flashlight that had a couple of complicated buttons.

"When I come back, I'll radio first, then signal with my spotlight, so you'll know it's me. Acknowledge with the strobe but don't use the infrared. And the radio, don't say much and don't use names, okay?"

Sammy was used to being secretive. He was clicking buttons

on the complicated LED. "A red light? I don't see a red light, Poncho. I see only white."

"Exactly. You can't see it, so white light only. Understood? Definitely—listen to me—don't use the infrared. Clean your cut and that gunshot wound with this, and here's some antibacterial salve. In fact, take the whole bag. I won't be gone long."

Itzel waited for the stranger to leave and was the last to eat. She'd fed the toddler and the patron after doctoring his wound, then sat by the fire and used a clam shell as a knife and spoon.

"This *tolok* meat is more tender in the mountains. It needs salt," she said to her husband, referring to the roast iguana. "I would have cooked oysters, too, but the water here is—" her expression showed disgust "—we would all have the brown-butt sickness. If I could have found some wild *ajís*, maybe. Chili peppers keep the intestines clean. One day, perhaps, I will have a garden again and be able to cook a decent meal for my family."

Cadmael knew this was another not-so-subtle hint that his wife longed to return to Guatemala, the high country where the Rio Chioj flowed south, clear and cold, toward the village of Chichicastenango. More than ever before, he agreed. Today had been the most terrifying day of his life. That feeling of being swept into a black hole, nearly drowning, of nearly losing his infant son. And then to be shot at by a madman. It was better to be poor and safe in a mountain village than to be rich in a dangerous land of storms and noise and cities.

Patiently, he replied to Itzel, "When we have enough money, we will go home. I *want* to go home. But the modern world isn't all bad. Soon we will find a nice apartment. Our own bed with air conditioning and TV." Sammy had demonstrated how to use the powerful little LED the biologist had left with them. "There are many conveniences. On a night this dark, would you rather have a candle or this?"

He pressed a button. A white light, dazzlingly bright, illuminated the cavern of trees.

Itzel shaded her eyes. "You are blinding me. I prefer a cooking fire and candles. Enough."

Cadmael touched another button. The light went out, although a tiny red bead continued to pulse. He handed the light to his wife.

"Keep this until the biologist returns. Or until Sammy needs it. Learn to enjoy what Gringolandia has to teach us so we can teach our children later."

Itzel had slipped off to a private spot to squat at the water's edge when a helicopter thundered past, flying low, black against a boiling black sky. From the distance, Sammy called to her, "Shine the light. Press the button!"

There was no need. It was as if the pilot already knew their location. The helicopter slowed. It turned and sailed toward the young mother, nose down like a dog tracking a scent.

Itzel fumbled for the button but, aside from the flashing red bead, the light it produced was visible only to the man at the controls, a former MiG pilot who had doubled back for a strafing run on what he believed to be a biologist—and an American spy—with a shotgun.

41

Weatherby's crow's nest deck, fifty feet above the beach, provided a vista of thunderous clouds that pulsed and flickered as they spun northeast. The island was a gray anomaly, lightless. On the horizon, barely perceptible, a contrail streak suggested activity. An aircraft of some type was out there.

I went down the steps to the main floor. Max was on the porch, where there was a TiCAM thermal imaging target locator on a tripod.

"A helicopter?" I asked. Into a bag I began loading supplies to take to Sammy and his people.

"Afraid so. Looking for us, most likely," the Brit said. "I told you they wouldn't just let us walk away."

"*They?* Don't overrate those people. They're not smart, just kill-happy and sloppy."

"Better than underestimating him and the Brotherhood. The oligarch. Sasha Olegovich. He needs to be dealt with, Ford. You're aware of that, I presume."

"Probably a subject we shouldn't discuss," I answered. "Targeting me, yeah, I understand. But my family, friends of my family. That's not the way this business is supposed to work."

Weatherby countered, "Suppose they could argue that diplomat members of the Brotherhood aren't supposed to defect. Or disappear. I'm not asking, so please don't tell me. I'm sure they'd like to know, and they won't give up until they do."

Center room was a fireplace, stone, double-wide. On the mantel was a cremation urn, handcrafted and mounted on a brass elephant of East Indian colonial design.

"They targeted your family, too, Max." I lowered my professional shield by adding, "The three-letter operatives are lightning rods. We put everyone close to us at risk. Selfish as hell, and it's about time I admitted that to myself." On the counter was an emergency medical STAT kit. "Mind if I take a few things out of here? My friends need first aid and a hospital."

"Help yourself." Weatherby was looking at the fireplace. "Dear Hilary finally has her revenge. Three years it has taken me. Two after she died. Grigori Pavlo, that loathsome...aberration. A novitiate monk—how obscene. I'd like to think he suffered far more than my niece. But that's unlikely."

"He could still be suffering, Max. It wasn't pretty what I saw. If he lives through the night, I guarantee he won't last until sunset. Are you sure it's the same chopper?"

The man put his eye to the target locator scope. "Guess it could be a different one. No running lights, though, so I doubt it. Olegovich is doing a quick search at best. He can't risk being intercepted. Or ID'd. His twelve-hour window is about to close, so his next move—tomorrow, most likely—will be to leave the country. Contrive a postdated alibi. Here. Take a look."

The chopper was a couple miles northwest, engine heat bright as a comet's tail. After a few seconds it arrowed east, back on its original course toward Lauderdale.

I said, "What the hell...? We just came from that area. York Island. So, what's the attraction?" I thought for moment. "Oh...

hell. I left a flashlight with my pal Sammy. An LED with in-frared. But I told him only use the white strobe if he needed to signal someone. I've got to get out there and check."

Weatherby said, "Maybe he did signal. It's possible he con-tacted Coast Guard on sixteen and I'm wrong about it being Olegovich. Try your friend on the radio."

Sammy didn't respond on VHF.

Mrs. László was in the guest bedroom, door closed, with ice-packs, a neck brace and another IV drip.

I asked Weatherby, "How is she? We could pack her up, too, and have them all on the mainland by first light."

"Normally, I would insist," he said. "Head injuries are al-ways iffy, and the situation can deteriorate fast within the first twenty-four hours. But another boat ride in rough water is—well, better, I think, to have her medevacked in the morning. She'll argue, of course. Refuses to talk about what happened tonight. And refuses to leave until she's found her husband. Let her sleep for now and I'll keep a close eye." The man was silent for a thoughtful moment. "Ford...what did happen back there?"

Rather than respond, I pointed to the far edge of the Lászlos' property. "I found her husband's body out there. Don't let her see him. Not with a head injury—she took a hell of a punch to the face. You sure it's wise to let her sleep?"

The physician/inventor, with a stern look, assured me that he kept up on medical protocols.

I went toward the door. He followed, saying, "Once I rig another antenna, friends in the UK should confirm my plane, and a medical team will be waiting for Rebecca and me at Fort Myers Executive. Noonish tomorrow, I'm hoping. You're wel-come to tag along."

That stopped me. "Plane? Going where?"

"London first, then straight to Cambridge Neurological, I hope. A Gulfstream G4. Plenty of room. The twelve-hour window is closing on us, too. It would be unwise for a man in my position to stick around and answer unpleasant questions."

I turned. "You planned on leaving the day after the storm from the start. Didn't you?"

"Not the particulars but, yes."

"By medevac, as in private? You have a helicopter, too?"

Weatherby replied, "Friends. Associates who have deep pockets and a long list of assets. I'm going to pose a question that might sound like an offer. Here, in the States, certain agencies might not allow you to work within, let's say certain boundaries. Territorial boundaries. I have contacts with an organization I think would value a man—a freelancer—with your skill set. Your restraint. Professionalism. That's rare. Then add in your maritime expertise. Would there be any security issues if they run deep background?"

Skill set. The term had not been used accidentally.

I said, "You already have or you wouldn't ask. I didn't hear an offer in there. Who've you been talking to?"

"But you understand the offer," Weatherby responded.

"Not sure. Does this have something to do with getting your Rauschenberg back?"

He said, "If Olegovich leaves the country, that's as good a gambit as any for getting a foot in the door. Have you ever flown in a G4? For a biologist of note, unlimited research opportunities anywhere in the tropics, my friend. Think about it. Maybe we'll have that Scotch one day and discuss."

42

What I thought about on my way to evacuate Sammy's group was, why had a helicopter buzzed York Island? Attracted by their cooking fire, hopefully. If it had been the gun-happy oligarch, my sloppy decision to loan Sammy a multi-wave LED might have played a role.

It was 5:00 a.m. It's in the wee hours of the morning that I lie awake and punish myself with a litany of what my friend Tomlinson calls "wince trauma." Small, stupid things I've said or done that, even years later, make me cringe. There is no statute of limitations. I have accumulated more than my share.

I hadn't slept since…when? Nobody sleeps the night before a hurricane. And after the rare bad one, drifting off is damn near impossible. I'd been up for more than thirty-six hours, which sparked a reminder: pay attention, take all the little safety precautions. The boat's kill switch was clipped to my belt. I wore PFD auto-inflate suspenders, something that should've been a habit when running alone day or night but wasn't. A redundancy of lights, handhelds, mosquito netting, gloves, a box of favorite MREs—cheese tortellini, sweet and sour chicken for Sammy's people—and an extra pair of heavy boots in case I hit something and had to get out and push.

A few hundred yards off York Island, I flicked on running lights and used the radio.

"You copy, Sammy?"

This time he responded but reluctantly. "Doc, Doc, yeah. Are you alone? You *sure* you're alone? *Mierda*, man, this has been a crazy night." He was whispering; sounded nervous.

"What happened? I don't see your fire. Wait, I'll hit the spotlight. Do you see me?"

"Poncho, Poncho, no lights. We need to get out of here. Is that helicopter still around? We gotta move fast, man. Yeah... yeah, I hear your motor now. We're headed your way."

"Coming in," I told him. "There's a boarding ladder off the stern. Wait until I get the power poles down. I'll get out and help."

The patron wasn't in terrible shape but not good. We created a bed against the transom where the ride would be softest. Sammy sat next to me while Cadmael got the kids covered. His wife, who seemed to know what she was doing, got busy redressing the old man's leg. A bullet had gone through his thigh. She appeared to be bleeding, too. Fresh blood on her left hand and wrist.

In Spanish I asked, "Itzel, are you hurt?"

A shake of the head, no eye contact, was the response. I sensed a simmering anger that was directed at me for some reason.

Sammy spoke in English while he searched the sky. "Itzel doesn't talk much, but she is tough, that one. There was a helicopter. Did you see it?"

"What happened?"

"Man, it came right at us. At first, I thought you'd sent help, so I told her to shine the light. The light you loaned us? Right away they start shooting like the people knew we were here. So we ran. Itzel fell, fell hard, and a stick went through her hand. Like, you know, clear through. She pulled it out. Didn't make a sound. That's why we put out the fire, man. That flashlight, Doc, I'm sorry. I was afraid to pick it up after that. Itzel is superstitious. She thinks the thing can be seen only by devils."

I said, "She blames me?"

"Your modern toys, everything. Don't worry about it, Poncho. She's just an ignorant girl from the mountains."

I gentled the boat onto a gradual hobbyhorse plane and steered toward Dinkin's Bay. Witnesses or not, my friends needed a doctor and a place to clean up and sleep. We'd have to risk it.

"She's right. I was an idiot to give you that light," I said.

Sammy took this as criticism.

"Hey, man—I didn't lose your light on purpose. I'll pay for it. Or go back and find the thing. How much? Or I can work it off. But here—" he placed the VHF loaner on the console "—at least I didn't lose this. Now we're almost even."

My stomach knotted. I'd nearly gotten these good people killed.

I said, "Your campfire wasn't the problem. It was me. That flashlight, I should've explained why it was dangerous. The pilot was trying to shoot me, not you. I've screwed up too many times today. Sorry, pal."

"Shoot you why? No, Poncho. All day long, crazy people— evil spirits, who knows?—have been trying to kill us. Itzel says it's a sign. Like an omen. We've got to leave this bad place. Hey, where we going?"

A mile to the north where the Causeway's mainland span had collapsed was a kaleidoscope of flashing blue strobes. I'd spun the bow toward the only activity for miles.

"You need medical attention. I didn't think they'd scramble emergency services so soon. Don't worry about that green card crap. Not after what you've been through."

"The cops?"

"It's the quickest way. They won't start sending evac choppers to the island until morning. I'll find a place to beach and cut you loose."

"We can't do that. I mean we *won't do it*, man."

Cadmael got to his feet and stood at my shoulder. "No police," he said in Spanish. "Please, we just want to go home."

"That's where I'm headed," I told him. "Punta Rassa. Your apartment isn't far from there. First the hospital, then you can come back and secure your personal property. Start cleaning up your apartment. I'll help but not today."

"This is not our home. Guatemala is our home," Cadmael countered. "I promised my wife. No police. Please? We just want to get to a bus station where there are roads."

Sammy spoke into my ear. "Doc, listen. He's got no personal property. None of us do. It's gone, all gone, man, clothes, papers, everything we owned was... Nothing left but mud. Me, I'm gonna spend two more weeks here, work my ass off for cash, then take my family back to Mexico before Florida kills us all. Cadmael and his wife, they're scared. They want to leave right away."

I said, "After this, no one's leaving right away," then thought about the Brit and Mrs. Lászlo. "Look... I'm not the only one involved with what happened tonight. I'll do what I can. Okay? But I've got to speak with a couple of friends first."

Sammy lowered his voice. "That helicopter, don't know why a crazy man would want to shoot you. And I ain't asking. But I promise you this, Poncho. We won't say shit to the police if that's what you're worried about."

I changed my mind and turned toward the mouth of Dinkin's Bay, where lantern light tinted a third-floor window. "My doctor friend lives there. He owns a plane and might be willing to help you guys out. We'll see. Give me five minutes with him alone."

On the porch, I confided to Weatherby, "You can trust Sammy."

He asked, "What about the others? Rebecca is concerned because of what happened to her. The police will want answers. And they'll want to know what happened to her attackers. She's been through enough hell for one day."

I said, "Sammy has his own reasons not to get involved with law enforcement. They all do. I'll talk to Mrs. Lászlo. Is she asleep?"

The elegant lady was dozy but awake when I entered the guest bedroom. A night-light provided a mushroom of visibility.

"Oh…you, Dr. Ford. Don't look at me. I know…I know I'm a mess. But thanks for all you've done. I am in your debt."

It was the second time she'd said that.

I explained about Sammy.

"If you trust him, that's good enough for me," she said. Eyes of gray-jade noted my filthy khakis and boots. "You'll need a good wash and scrub when this is done."

"I'm better off just throwing these clothes away."

"Don't you dare," she said with an edge. "Not without checking the pockets first. Benjamin used to do that." She grimaced, closed her left eye in pain. "You found him, didn't you? My Benjamin."

I nodded.

"Near here? I hate to think of him outside all alone."

"I'll mark the spot and make sure he's in a safe place."

"I at least want to say goodbye. When you say 'safe,' you mean his body. The thought of animals finding him… I couldn't bear that. Vultures. I have a horror of vultures, particularly after—"

I told her, "I'll take care of it. Mr. Lászlo—your late husband—he's outside, but too far to walk. Nothing we can do for him now." I motioned to an opening in the automated shutters. "You can say goodbye from here without getting out of bed. I'll leave you alone for a few minutes."

Eyes closed, she whispered and made the sign of the cross. Then, once again, touched her head and winced.

"Are you okay, Rebecca?"

"A thrumming headache, but never mind that. I'm concerned about you. There are cuts on your face…and a nasty little slice on your forehead. Ask Max for some medical-grade alcohol." Before I could break away, the woman extended her hand and found mine. "It's a terrible imposition, I know, us counting on you to cover for us. But under the circumstances, I think it's wiser for me to be on the other side of Atlantic. Ben would understand. I'll send for him later."

"The farther away, the better," I agreed. "Don't worry. As far as I know, you and Max weren't here. Gunshots, I might have heard a few. Maybe a bunch of drunken mercenaries got into a turf battle. I wouldn't be surprised. Doubt if the cops will be, either."

Mrs. László's jaw flexed—another stabbing pain that she did a nice job of hiding.

"Do you really think it'll go that smoothly?"

"Not a chance." I smiled. "But they're going to have a hell of a time piecing together evidence or finding eyewitnesses. When you get to the UK, you'll need to have a physician notify authorities that you're safe. You know, a medical emergency. Maybe an attorney if someone presses for details."

Weatherby followed me out the door.

"Ford, you're not leaving, are you? I could use some help stringing that antenna. Once I get my HF kit up and running, we'll have full contact with the outside world. I can make a balun, hang it off the balcony. Then all we need is wire and some insulators. Grounding tackle is already in place."

I said, "Are you sure that's a good thing so soon after the storm?"

"Encrypted," the Brit explained. "My associates will get nervous if I don't make contact soon. And it's possible they've heard something about your friend, Tomlinson. I think I mentioned I have some unusual Masonic acquaintances."

"You put the word out? Thanks."

"Of course. About that antenna—"

"Sure, happy to help. First, though, let's talk about another friend—Cadmael—from Central America. His wife and an infant son. They lost everything in the storm, and they want to go back to Guatemala." At the bottom of the steps, I stopped and let that settle. "It would have to be without any paperwork or red tape involved. Think you can help them out?"

Weatherby replied, "That might take a few weeks to arrange. I'd have to make some calls."

"No. Now. They need to leave with you in the morning."

"I don't understand the urgency. What about the others— Sammy, is it?—him and his family? There isn't room. And Guatemala isn't exactly on the flight path to Heathrow."

"Sammy doesn't want to leave," I said. "Not really. He's been here for years. Once they adjust to life in the States, they don't go back—and, if they do, they don't stay long. It's different with Cadmael. He and his wife, their baby, if they don't leave now, they never will. I've seen it happen too many times in my life."

"You're serious about this."

I said, "I almost got them killed tonight. The least I can do is help them get home safely. They won't get another chance, Max. The old man needs attention now. Tomorrow, I'll make sure he gets to the mainland, then a hospital. But Cadmael and his family need to leave right away."

Weatherby said, "Would this be part of our deal?"

"No. I'm asking a favor. That doesn't mean we can't discuss a deal."

"Fair enough," he said. "The British Consulate in Miami has TDY housing. A quick call can get that sorted. We could drop your friends there and make arrangements for Guatemala later. Possibly—no guarantees. They would at least be out of harm's way and safe under diplomatic immunity."

While the physician/inventor tended to the old man's leg and

Itzel's badly damaged hand, I fashioned an upside-down coffin from a derelict canoe and kept my promise to Mrs. Lászlo.

"Your husband's safe now," I told her, meaning *safe from carrion feeders*.

It was cold comfort, but the only comfort I could provide.

43

At dawn, on the way back to what was left of the marina, I felt a sluggish reluctance to view the damage. To confirm what had been lost was to lay bare a lie that was human and inevitable. Denial. So I dawdled at slow idle in an oppressive gray light that matched my mood. Told myself the mess could wait. It was wiser to boat across the bay to Hannah's place and find my dog—assuming he was still my dog.

I would have done just that—fled toward the past, not the future—but I saw a lone stick figure waving to me from the marina's boat ramp. From a distance, the scarecrow mannerisms provided a moment of hopeful confusion.

My God... Was it Tomlinson? How was this possible? My brain jury-rigged a wistful scenario. On Saturday or Sunday, my pal had turned inland. He'd weathered the storm in some hurricane hidey-hole. Somehow, he'd made it back to Dinkin's Bay and had waded ashore.

Too eager, I bounced onto plane only to damn near lose my

skeg to debris in the channel off Commodore Creek. The boat jolted; the engine died, and I drifted shoreward.

A familiar voice hollered, "Doc, is that you? Man, yeah, I was hoping you hadn't bugged out. We need some help."

It was a friend, a fishing guide, Paul Boudreaux, not Tomlinson. He was a solid guy, rational, a longtime islander who had never let his prosthetic metal leg slow him down.

Instead of disappointment, my mood brightened. Paul was a stalwart of the past but also a present reality. Better yet, my engine fired first try.

I hollered back, "Anything. What do you need?"

"Your boat, but not right away." He was waving me toward a piece of seawall dockage that had survived. "We're going through neighborhoods, looking for folks who need to be evacuated. There are already three—an elderly couple and a diabetic." He looked toward my lab. "I don't suppose your base station radio survived?"

"Lost my antennas, but I have a couple of handhelds. I'm surprised anyone else stayed on the island. How many you think? Has law enforcement showed up yet?"

No, it was just me, Paul and his son, Alec, who knew his way around boats and electronics, and already had some first responder training. My mindset switched from loss to what could be saved before the professional cavalry arrived.

"Geezus, this sludge makes it damn near impossible to walk," Paul said when I was ashore. The mud was ankle-deep, water sometimes up to our calves. "The first thing we need is transportation of some type. Any ideas? Alec is back at the house monitoring VHF."

"You have much damage?"

"You kidding, everyone did. Ground-floor houses, forget it. Same with my truck and boat."

Outside the parking lot, vehicles from miles around littered the mangroves like abandoned Christmas ornaments. My eyes moved from my old blue GMC to the expensive gray Raptor that had floated into a mosquito ditch. Then I noticed a cluster of canoes that looked undamaged near the bike rack.

"Improvise," I said. "Do what locals did before there were roads."

We salvaged two aluminum Grummans, loaded a bicycle and tools into each, and waded down Tarpon Bay Road, sometimes paddling, but more often using the canoes as mud sleds. Every few hundred yards, when I believed the destruction couldn't get any worse, it got worse.

I made mental notes. Bailey's General Store, established 1899, was in ruin. Same with most of the buildings along the main drag. Across the street, the post office was still shuttered, but the front door had somehow been wedged open.

"Federal postal inspectors aren't going to like that one bit," Paul, the dutiful citizen, said. "I'll take pictures, then wire the place shut. Keep animals out at least."

I wondered if unseen mercenaries were responsible, and if they were still around. But why hit a post office? My fingers found the holster at the small my back. Paul crossed the parking lot taking long, careful steps as if on cross-country skis, then stopped abruptly.

"Whoa Nellie, this is not good," he called. "You got to see this, Doc. Use one of those paddles as a walking stick. This crap is slick as hell."

I joined him a few yards from the entrance, where there was a mud trail that led inside the building. Huge footprints with five webbed claws, a serpentine swath left by a reptilian tail.

"There's a freakin' gator in there," Paul said. "Or tried to get in. Look—" he placed his hand next to a track for comparison "—damn claws are ten inches wide. How big you think it is?"

I said, "Too big to get much closer. Snap some photos. Police need to know before the postal inspectors go stumbling in there. I'll use a flashlight and peek inside."

A detritus stain above the door showed the storm's high-water mark. Nine feet deep. The building had flooded. Inside, in a shadowed corner, the LED illuminated a pair of coal-yellow eyes separated by a snout that was at least a foot wide. The animal hissed and lunged.

I backed away. "Ten-twelve-footer. And it's aggressive. Let's secure the door and get moving."

We stayed in touch with his son, Alec, by handheld. He'd already made contact with St. Pete Coast Guard, which had promised the arrival of a helicopter soon. Nothing would be coming in by road for days with a Causeway bridge gone. That was in my mind when, a few minutes later, Weatherby's private helo breached the Dinkin's Bay tree line and turned east toward Fort Myers Executive with Cadmael and his family aboard.

This was the second small victory of the morning. Before sunrise, mainland side, I had waved goodbye to Sammy and the others before paramedics had carted them off to the hospital.

Small victories, indeed, in a world that been laid waste. I made more mental notes as we continued to mud-sled toward the Gulf of Mexico.

Trees down, houses, destination hotels dissected, scaffolding scattered like discarded body parts. Boudoir secrets, honeymoon mattresses had been disrobed, flung outside bare for all to see. The road was a rat's nest of wires that had been exhumed. The wires tracked decades of abandoned technology—telephones, satellite TV, HBO cables, fiber optic bundles, a vein work of insulated scars buried, out of sight and out of mind until now. Solar panels, snagged in the low limbs of trees, creaked with temporal indifference.

We turned beachside onto Gulf Drive. The stretch resembled the bombed-out coastline of Beirut. Casa Ybel and the Island Inn had imploded—a century of class and history in rubble. Families who had vacationed there for generations were now rootless, forever displaced from their past. West Wind Hotel, the best pool bar on the island, had been gutted, doors blown off, each room a shell that emitted piercing rhythmic shrieks—battery-driven smoke alarms.

We had been sumped into an environmental gyre, a regurgitated excess that hinted at irreversible ruin. *Entropy* was the term Tomlinson had used. He'd claimed it was an invisible force that governed chaos and the death of the universe. I doubt all tidy apocalyptic theories. Yet something inexorable, a global dynamic, had cleaved ashore and marked its territory before moving on.

"I hope no one tried to ride out the storm in those condos," I said. Then looked toward the Gulf of Mexico, a boiling convexity of green. "If they did…well, their bodies are out there somewhere."

Paul remained positive. "Maybe not. Alec heard rumors on VHF, but nothing confirmed. Hell of a mess, huh? This will take years. But we'll come back. We always do."

I'd been reluctant to broach the subject, but finally asked, "What about the lighthouse? It went dark last night. Did the storm knock the lighthouse down, too?"

He frowned, shook his head. "Not sure. But I'll bet five bucks it's still standing. You kidding? Seems like only the modern stuff got blown to hell."

Ahead, a lone figure used a stick to poke at a pile of trash. It was an old woman in a peacock-green satin robe.

"Are you okay, ma'am?" we asked.

Startled, she looked up, bewildered, eyes glassy. "I'm looking for our insurance papers. Once I find them, my husband and I will be just fine. He's back at the house, too crippled to walk."

They were the first survivors we had medevacked out. A pair of orange helos appeared off Lighthouse Point. I made radio contact and provided the couple's home address. The crewman's surprising response was, "We don't have GPS street map capabilities. If you have a visual on us, can you direct us in? Are you north or south?"

Neither. We were five miles west. Maybe Weatherby had been right about the effect of hurricanes and solar flares on satellite transmissions.

That's the way it went. Alec or me, point by point, vectoring the helicopter closer, saying, *Turn starboard by X degrees…now turn port X degrees.*

At treetop level, the chopper hovered with admirable precision. A combat swimmer, legs out, was cabled down to the road, where he unsnapped his Triton full-body harness. They loaded the woman, then her husband, into a rescue basket, and soared away.

Others in the neighborhood staggered toward us, a sparse zombie-like procession. More choppers arrived. The process was repeated.

As Paul observed an hour later, "I actually feel good about paying taxes after working with pros like that."

The U.S. Coast Guard, he meant.

I was exhausted. Back at what was left of my lab, Crunch & Des was okay but in a pissy mood—so what else was new? A can of Fancy Feast salmon offered reparations. There would be no power for weeks, maybe a month, and the damn generator still wouldn't start. The rain cistern on the aft porch, however, provided a cold-water shower. I soaped and sudsed, but the storm's aberrant mud clung to my skin like axle grease.

Next, I fulfilled a dreaded duty that required surgical gloves. When Pavlo's GoPro camera was cabled to my laptop, I clicked on *Image Capture*, then clicked *View All Images Saved on This Device.*

A stack of video thumbnails cascaded down the left side of the computer screen. Dozens of them time-stamped with dates. The zoom bar brought a waterfall of faces into focus, mostly females. Among them was a blonde FWC officer. And the late Lieutenant Birdy Tupplemeyer.

I dragged and dropped en masse onto my laptop, then did

the same with a pair of memory stick back–ups, including the encoded IronKey.

There was no need to impose by actually viewing the horrors Pavlo's victims had endured. Nor was I tempted. But to confirm the data had transferred, I had to open an anonymous file on each backup, then look away after a repellent few seconds.

This was proof enough. I'd done my job, damn it.

When finished, the computer offered the option of deleting all images from the GoPro.

Nope. When investigators arrived, I wanted them to find a camera loaded with evidence within arm's length of Grigori Pavlo's dead body.

I didn't need to shower again, but I did. A psychological response—or a ceremony of disengagement.

The GoPro went into my tactical bag. The damning memory sticks went into the waterproof safe beneath my bed in case backup evidence was needed.

Clean clothes, clean weapons, fresh boots and gloves, I crossed the parking lot and forced myself to finally triage the damage done to our little community. Docks gone, roofs destroyed, windows shattered and the mechanic's shed was still smoldering. But the foundation of the office and Mack's house had survived, as had the seawall and rows of pilings. The tribal footprint still existed. A massive loss, yet, perhaps not terminal.

A painted plywood sign had landed in the limbs of the now wind bare poinciana tree.

It read:

Dinkin's Bay Marina
Bait, Fresh Fish, Tackle
Beer, Souvenirs!
Fishing Guides Available
Open Daily

Using a hand drill, I reattached the sign to the office wall and readied my boat. Once across the bay, I wanted to gather my dog and do a quick in-and-out before the cops arrived and started finding mercenary bodies. Among them would be the perpetrator, Grigori Pavlo. The crazed monk had been shot. He'd been mutilated—theoretically by his own men—and left face down in a pond inhabited by reptiles and surrounded by a pack of coyotes.

The feds had access to the same state department intel I'd been provided. They would piece the puzzle together—once they'd viewed the contents on the GoPro.

The Vulture Monk had gone on a killing/robbery spree and was now dead.

Case closed.

All I had to do was plant the camera, then lay low, stay out of the way until Hannah returned in a day or two. How to explain my role in a crime scene that was her house, and her friend's bloody clothing, would require tact.

And honesty, I promised myself.

It was three hours before noon when I exited Dinkin's Bay and boated toward the island of Gumbo Limbo.

44

A few hours before noon, still on Gumbo Limbo, Grigori Pavlo awoke in the camper, the door wide open and two empty blood transfusion bags on the floor.

What the hell...?

It took some effort to connect it all. He was naked. His pelvic bullet wound and mutilated groin were bandaged, the bandages orange-tinted with disinfectant. Battlefield sutures, syringes, a pack of fentanyl patches and bloody gauze lay on the counter. In the sink was an empty vial of intramuscular dopamine.

Nothing confusing about this. When very stoned, cut, or shot or self-mutilated, Pavlo, the army corpsman, had treated himself for traumatic injuries before.

How long had he been unconscious?

There were no burner phones around. No weapons, no GoPro camera, either. His vison was tunneled—like peering out from a cave. Barefooted, he limped down the camper steps into the aftermath of a flood and checked the truck's dashboard clock.

It was morning the day after the storm. He'd been unconscious—not sober, anyway—for several hours.

Yesterday's events began filtering back. He had killed his whole team, left their bodies where they lay, trusting Sasha to fly the two of them out of the country with a fortune in art and gems.

The oligarch—that tricky old bastard—had left him for dead, and as the lone suspect when American cops arrived.

Were the cops out there now?

He had to hurry.

In the camper, the Russian dressed, still concerned about his vision. The bathroom mirror brought back more details. He'd fallen from Sasha's custom chopper into a pond where a gang of animals had attacked him. While he was drowning, unable to breathe, one of the animals had dragged him to shore.

Rescued by what? A dog?

Rescued, hell. The mirror said otherwise. His face, his scalp, were a lacerated mess of bite wounds. Above his beard and broken nose, a bloody socket, empty, stared back.

His left eye was gone.

Jesus Christ.

Pavlo had seen worse in the Crimea. Hell, he had done far worse to a hundred victims. But this was *his* face, *his* eye, and, goddamn it, he was in pain. Searing pain that throbbed.

A passage from the Book of John chided the failed novitiate: *Who eateth my flesh and drinketh my blood shall have eternal life.*

The irony ignited a chemical rage. Goddamn dogs. A wolf pack like in Belarus. Devil creatures. They were worse than humans, priests, even nuns. This caused Pavlo to confirm what the old László woman had done to him.

He spread his legs, peeked beneath the gauze. He whimpered and glared at the ceiling. He howled.

Piece by piece, his body was being consumed by beasts, eaten away by shithole peasants and mortals.

And the searing burn of these wounds! The empty eye socket was a toothache in his brain. This pain was nauseating, not purifying.

The failed monk vomited. Then, with a fist, demanded action from a fentanyl patch applied to his inner thigh. Another patch was used to cover exposed bone that had been an eyebrow. He returned to the truck and did a frenzied search. The ignition key was gone, but beneath the seat was Andy Dimitry's fancy Glock-nine. Fake pearl grips and a full mag, hollow-points. But the slide and mag were a muddy mess because the floor of the cab had flooded.

Pavlo limped toward the bay, thinking, *I will kill them all.*

Damn right he would. Anything, anyone who got in his way. This included cops who would be in the area soon if they weren't here already. Roads would be heavily patrolled. So... maybe it was good he couldn't find the truck key.

A boat was a better choice. That's what he needed. A boat. Steal a boat and take hostages if available. A woman, children, perhaps. They would be his ticket out of here.

The Vulture Monk smiled, thinking about that. The fentanyl was kicking in. Skin cold, clammy. Breathing shallow. He had to remind his lungs, *Breathe...breathe...breathe.* Pain had been nibbling at his brain, eating whole chunks of consciousness. But that would soon fade, replaced by the cold euphoria of the drug.

Uh-oh. The pain, Pavlo realized, would return by nightfall. Why? Because he'd gone off and left the box of fentanyl in the camper. *Idiot!* At the pasture gate where the road curved along the bay, he stopped and tried to think clearly. Should he stop or keep going? Either way, he had to find a fast boat and get the hell out of here.

To his right was the marina. Some activity there. The grinding sounds of heavy equipment. Chain saws. To his left was the old house on the hill where he'd tried to have some fun with a little ginger-haired female cop.

That hadn't gone as planned. Then it did go as planned when the bitch pulled a gun, but not in time to dodge the axe he'd taken from the fireplace.

Worldwide, cops hated cop killers. Could be there were opiates somewhere in the old house, but he didn't want to get caught revisiting that scene. And judging from the noise, there were more than a few men—construction types—at the marina.

What to do?

Pain...he couldn't tolerate more pain. Pavlo started to backtrack through a miserable hundred meters of brush and mud and broken limbs. The camper truck came into view. He paused, hands on knees, breathing labored. A wild howling sound pierced the air.

I'm hallucinating, he thought, and believed it was true when a pack of wolves fanned out from behind the camper. Ten or more, all small, skinny, sodden except for the lead pair. A tall, curly-haired she-wolf trotted like a fancy show horse. The pack was led by a muscular, block-headed alpha male. It sniffed the air, grunted and galloped closer, golden eyes ablaze.

Hallucination or not, Pavlo stumbled backward, pulled the Glock and got off four fast rounds. There was a yipping scream; the quick visual of a wolf tumbling before the fifth round misfired. Military training kicked in. With a slap, he reseated the mag, shucked a clean round, but the trigger froze.

He raised the pistol to throw it but didn't. The pack had scattered except for two wounded animals that continued to howl as they belly-crawled away.

"Damn brutes," he hollered in Russian while he backed toward the road. No choice now but to risk stealing a boat from the busy marina. That plan evaporated when three trucks towing heavy equipment, then a cop car, cruised past.

Pavlo ducked, limped into the trees, up the mound toward the house, unsure what to do next. There were no vehicles in the drive. In the carport, though, was an old green tractor he had noticed earlier. *John Deere* in yellow letters; an end-loader bucket with steel teeth for digging.

The Russian stopped. His head cleared. After seeing the key in the ignition, he grinned at a new and wiser plan.

No one would stop a man driving a tractor. Not after a hurricane. The roads would be full of trucks and heavy equipment. The trip would take a while at tractor speeds, but so what? It was the perfect cover for a killer on the run.

Pavlo congratulated himself, thinking, *The police might even escort me off the island.*

His ancestor, Rasputin, the czar's Dark Angel, would have been proud.

But first, there were things to do. With one click of the ignition key, he confirmed the battery wasn't dead. Gearshift in neutral, the tractor fired on the second try. The fuel gauge read three quarters full. Engine off, the carport became a source of supplies. A five-gallon can of diesel, a shovel, a hammer, a tow chain went into the bucket loader.

All great cover if there were police checkpoints.

What else did he need?

Painkillers—aspirin at least. Water. Liquor. A cell phone if he could find one. He went up the steps, into the house and searched. In the bedroom where there were old women's clothes, the family Bible was open on a reading stand. A silk ribbon marked a passage in Proverbs that he labored to translate from English into Russian:

A just King builds up the land, but he who exacts gifts for profit tears it down.

Pavlo continued to rummage and found something unexpected under the mattress—a baggie of weed, two sweet doobies already rolled.

He lit one and was searching through the refrigerator when—goddamn it—a van with an Uber sticker pulled into the driveway.

Pavlo scurried toward the back porch but was trapped. He put his good eye to the kitchen window and watched. The driver, in a hurry, exited and helped an elderly woman out the sliding door, her gray wig askew, wearing jeans and white rubber boots. Only one small pink suitcase. No other passengers aboard. The driver returned to his seat, waved and tooted the horn before pulling onto the road.

Pavlo took a last drag on the doobie and released a slow breath, relieved.

By then, the old woman was through the screen door on the front porch, muttering and cursing and talking to herself.

The Vulture Monk's assessment: *Senile. Harmless. Too old and wrinkled for any real fun.*

On the other hand, he couldn't allow her to witness his escape on the tractor. It was also likely the old crone had a phone.

In a kitchen drawer was a white-handled knife, the kind fishermen used. He tested the blade—sharp as a razor—and waited, listening to the lady babble about an imaginary king.

"Your Highness—Carlos?—I'm home," her trembling voice called. "Without my prude-minded daughter for a change. So, let's get to it, Chief, while we're still young." Then after a shuffling silence, complained, "What the blazes...blood all over. What dirty joker killt a chicken on my goddamn porch?"

The front door opened. Pavlo hugged the wall. Shuffling footsteps crossed the floor toward the kitchen, then stopped in the living room. He heard the clank of what might have been fireplace tools.

"Come out, you lowlife bastard," the woman called. Not trembling now. With an edge. "Killin' my chickens is one thing. But stealing my stash is something folks around these parts don't abide. You thieving cur... I can *smell the smoke, you hippie dumbass.* Show yourself."

The Russian stepped out, expecting to see the woman armed with a poker iron. Wrong. She was shouldering an antique shotgun, sighting down the barrel, aimed belly-high.

He lofted the knife, and walked toward her thinking the doddering old fool would collapse in fear.

Instead, she hollered, "Better men have tried, but…by God, you're a tall one. Ugly, too. Stop right there, you spawn." She paused to straighten her ridiculous gray wig. "Now march your ass outside so I don't have to clean what's left of your brains off my walls."

Pavlo thought this was funny. A skinny antique woman with an antique gun that probably didn't work. Or wasn't loaded.

"Yes, ma'am." The Vulture Monk grinned. "After you."

He stepped aside with a gallant wave and, with the knife behind his back, followed the old woman out the door.

45

From Hannah's dock, the only oddity I noticed was that her mother's old workhorse tractor, a John Deere, was missing from the carport shed. Everything else was as expected. No vehicles in the drive, no movement on the porch, no workers in the yard, which was a tangle of fallen trees.

A tractor thief? Possibly. More likely, though, a neighbor had borrowed the thing to get their cleanup started. Fishermen on the island of Gumbo Limbo were a communal bunch. Some were already digging out. There was activity around the bend at the commercial co-op and marina where the storage barn had collapsed. I heard the backup warning beeps of heavy equipment, and someone was using a chain saw.

Instead of going ashore, I drifted and observed for a while. It would have been unwise to stumble into a fresh police investigation.

Wind had dropped below twenty, a blustery, balmy day compared to what we'd just been through. Water was the color of jaundiced clay. Starting at Hannah's dock, I scanned the surface.

No bodies there. My search area broadened. I began to relax. The four dead mercenaries were either hidden among acres of floating debris, or they'd been swept toward the Gulf of Mexico.

An FP&L truck idled past, then another. This suggested the road to the mainland was finally open. Law enforcement would soon follow.

There was a lot to do, not much time. I had to find Pavlo's body and plant the GoPro camera. But from a distance. I couldn't leave inquiring footprints for authorities to find later in the day. Or later in the week, most likely. The feds would be called in. What the Russian brotherhood had instigated was a terrorist assault for profit.

Pavlo's videos would prove it.

Retrieving Pete, my feral retriever, was also a priority.

I docked the boat, crossed onto the mangrove path and did another scan. No bodies trapped in the prop roots, either. Good.

Keep moving. In and out fast.

That was the plan.

Atop the mound, Loretta's house—aside from a flapping panel of plywood—had weathered the blow just fine, as it had a century of previous storms. The eccentric stroke victim and pot smuggler would be happy about that, at least. For a moment, I considered trying to clean up the blood trail Pavlo had left. Spare the old woman the shock of what awaited when she returned home in a day or two.

Nope. Couldn't do that. Birdy Tupplemeyer's family deserved the truth. So did Hannah. I wasn't going to start our reunion— and hopefully our marriage—with another lie.

Tidal surge had made it only partway up the mound so there was no petroleum sludge, nor footprints to worry about. At the side porch, a look confirmed the place was still a crime scene, undisturbed since last viewed.

At the door to the back porch, though, I wasn't so sure. The door was ajar. On the steps was an anomaly.

A cigarette butt. Strange. None of Hannah's friends or family smoked.

I squatted and investigated with gloved hands.

It wasn't a cigarette. It was the stub of a joint, still fresh.

An unsettling thought came into my head—her mother, Loretta, did smoke dope occasionally. Had she already returned from the mainland?

I knocked, I hollered her name, then searched inside.

The living room door was open. On the floor near the fireplace was a small, outdated suitcase, pink, that hadn't been there last night.

Loretta's carry-on.

The bathroom and bedroom closets were empty. I did an about-face and knelt by something I hadn't noticed in the drive near the rear deck. It was a knife. A commercial fillet knife, white-handled with a smear of blood on the blade.

Now I was scared. Because of me, Hannah's best friend was dead. Had her mother been attacked here, too? Why? By who? A crazed tractor thief? Unlikely on an agrarian island populated by fishermen.

A numbing possibility came to mind—Grigori Pavlo had somehow survived. If true, he was in bad shape, which made sense. If he'd taken the tractor, it was to transport something too heavy for an injured man to carry. Or to bury yet another victim. Someone dead…or someone—I admitted with a chill—who was still alive.

The eyes of a terrified old woman, staring up from a grave, would appeal to the Vulture Monk's aberrant brain.

Out the door I went in a rush. In the carport was more disturbing evidence. Sand had yet to absorb a pool of fresh blood. Nearby, also bloodstained, lay the sort of wig Loretta had worn since her brain surgeries.

Oh…shit.

My full-sized Sig drawn, I slalomed down the mound toward the citrus grove. The camper was where I'd left it. Heavy knobbed John Deere tires had cut deep tracks in the mud toward the pasture a few hundred yards away. What had been a chopper's LZ in darkness was now a noisy burial site, the tractor visible, still running, but no one at the controls I could see.

The fence line provided some cover. It also required a circular route that might allow me to take the Russian by surprise. But where was he? At the property line, pasture ended and elevated into a dense woodland of pine and scrub. There was also the pond where I'd gone off and left the man for dead. Had he finished with Loretta and escaped toward the road on the other side of the pond? Or was he somewhere in those pines?

I jogged, crouched, studied the tree line and jogged some more until a furred, inanimate shape to my left caused me to pause.

In a clearing too far, too risky to inspect, lay a dog. Or a coyote. Dead.

I gave a low whistle, anyway.

"Pete? *Pete.*"

Overhead, a lone vulture circled.

"*Pete…come.*"

The animal didn't stir even when the carrion bird spiraled down.

I turned, didn't look back, didn't stop until I'd knelt behind the same oil drum that had protected me earlier that morning. This provided a side view of the tractor, close enough to hear the engine's diesel clatter. The grappler bucket, on steel arms, angled upward like the tail of a scorpion. Framing a hole recently dug, a hillock of muck told me that if Hannah's mother was in the hole, the Russian hadn't finished covering her body.

My God…was it possible she was still alive?

I got up, pistol leveled, and scrambled to the rear of the tractor. Before making myself an easy target, I searched the trees again—and there he was, Pavlo, the Russian escapee. He came stumbling out of the shadows at a half run. Something in his hand, an axe or a hammer. Glanced over his shoulder several times as if being pursued.

My snap assessment: he'd tried to hijack a car, and now the car's owner—or the police—were after him.

Potential witnesses. Geezus.

For Loretta, the clock was ticking, so I stood, used the tractor as a brace and fired four bracketing rounds at the man from half a football field away.

The Russian jolted to a stop, surprised, not because he'd been hit. He spun around, stumbled and galloped a serpentine path back into the bushes.

I started after him, then prioritized. Peered into the hole where water seeped. No corpse there, no human appendages. The hole wasn't deep, so I dropped my tactical bag and slid down into the seepage, thinking the woman might be only partially buried. With my hands, I probed and clawed deeper and deeper, and finally gave up.

It was pointless. Loretta could not have survived more than a few minutes buried beneath several feet of muck.

I climbed out. No sign of Pavlo, nor any pissed-off witnesses thus far. After collecting my spent brass, I crossed the pasture into the trees in modified stalking mode. Four fast steps, pause… listen. Sniff the air. Several fast steps up an incline to a patch of prickly pear cactus. Someone had stumbled through the patch recently, indifferent to the spines. A swath of broken cactus blades led downhill again, where I stopped, ears alert.

Bushes rustled.

Moving slowly, I stepped toward the sound, and there he was—Pavlo, framed by an oval of foliage, fifteen yards away.

The Vulture Monk was pulling cactus spines from his legs, his face a bloody mess, and mumbling in Russian.

Maybe he'd taken a spill among the prickly pears.

It didn't matter. The man I had dismissed as a walking pathogen was precisely that. There was no need for drama. Just an anonymous extermination.

I thumbed the Sig's hammer back. Balanced Pavlo's head atop the front sight, a blade of green Tritium. Trees in the background blurred. When I took a calming breath, though, the man went stiff and spun around, startled by what I assumed was the *CLICK* of my pistol's hammer.

That wasn't it. He threw out his hands and turned his back to me, saying, "Please...no. I am man of God. You read Bible. I know you read Bible."

Babbling, pleading for his life in broken English.

My depth-of-field vision sharpened. An unexpected person moved into the framework of trees. I dropped my tactical bag and rushed out, saying, "Don't. Stop. Stop right there."

Too late. Hannah's mother pulled the triggers—both of them— and was sighting down the barrel of a shotgun as I approached. One deadly eye still open.

46

Loretta Smith, frail, eighty-some years old, remained frozen for several seconds, crouched, aiming at what was left of the Russian's head. Then seemed to shake herself and awaken, alert, immediately outraged by my arrival.

The antique shotgun pivoted toward my feet.

"What the blazes you doin' here, fish doctor? Now I suppose you're gonna go squealing to the po-leese. Can't let you do that."

She levered the weapon open, ejected spent shells, then fished in the pocket of her baggy slacks for more ammunition.

A haze of black-powder smoke still hung in the air.

I grabbed my bag and moved closer.

"Calm down, Loretta. I need to get you out of here."

"Hah! Off my own land?" Now she was searching her other pocket for shells. "That foreigner killt some of my chickens and stole my stash. Then tried to kill me—damn right he did. With a knife. My best fillet knife! Would of aimed for his pecker if he hadn't pulled that stunt." As proof, she flexed a bloody hand. "I don't know where your kin come from but, on this island, me and the king don't abide thieves or assassins."

King of the ancient Calusa—the woman's imaginary lover. Loretta's mind worked like that. Her dazed tone signaled a transition from reality to fantasy.

Typical.

I was close enough to kneel and pick up her spent twelve-gauge casings. Birdshot; crimped paper hulls, light dram loads. They were better for downing quail than a giant of a man.

"How many times did you shoot this guy? Had to be more than once. Talk, Loretta—I'm trying to help you."

"That's a laugh. Help me how? Bury that fool?"

Her wounded hand was trembling. Without a wig, the woman appeared tinier, fragile, aged by the accumulated scars of a hard life. And still angry about those scars.

I stepped closer to Pavlo's body. He was dead. Unmistakably dead. The GoPro camera came out of my bag and landed near the man's bloody forehead when I tossed it.

Loretta didn't notice.

"We're not going to bury him," I said.

"The hell we're not. I already got the damn hole dug. If I listen to you, they'll lock me up in Raiford and make me piss into a jar."

"Not if we clean up evidence," I said, "then get you to the mainland. Come on."

She stepped away, the shotgun in the crook of her arm. "Just leave this joker here?"

"The faster the better," I said. "He murdered at least eight people last night, and the feds—the police—need to be able to find his body. You don't want to be involved when they come asking questions. Damn right they'll arrest you, Loretta. You can say goodbye to your bingo friends."

"Oh...hell's bells," she said. "Well...maybe you ain't as dumb as you look."

We went down the hill through the trees to the pasture, me saying, "Mind if I see that shotgun?"

I snapped the weapon open, both chambers empty. On the barrel, stamped in script: *Damascus Steel; Acme Company.* Scratched into a silver trigger plate, beneath twin hammers, were the initials *E.J.W.* I'd seen the old side-by-side over the fireplace but, out of respect for its age, hadn't put my hands on it.

I said, "I'm surprised this thing still works. Light-load bird shot—how many times did you shoot the guy?"

One round at the house, the woman explained, after she'd been stabbed, but the second barrel had misfired. The man had either played possum or regained consciousness and ran off while she was on the tractor, digging his grave.

I said, "We've got to get rid of this weapon. Loretta, who was—" I squinted at the trigger plate. "These initials—who was E.J.W.?"

Tight-lipped, she responded, "My great-granddaddy. That's why I ain't getting rid of it. Plus, Hannah don't want you to know."

"Know what?"

"No more questions. There's lots that girl don't want you to know, Mr. Fish Doctor." This was added cryptically with the flavor of a threat. "Now give me back my property."

I did. We didn't have time to argue.

Hannah's mother drove the tractor to the house while I walked toward the corpse of what I'd believed to be a dog. A lone vulture, black-cowled, kited skyward with a reptilian hiss. It had been feeding on a coyote—a big one—that had been shot at least once.

So where was Pete?

I whistled, I called. I kept moving.

In a muddy stretch between the open grave and the trees, footprints had to be smeared—all but Pavlo's. Heavy grass at the pasture's edge provided safe passage up the shell mound to the carport and the sandy black stain that was Pavlo's blood. It took a while to find two ejected twelve-gauge casings, one shell fired, one a misfire with a dented primer. These, along with the bloodstained wig, went into a Ziploc, then my tactical bag. The antique shotgun was dismantled into three parts—stock, forearm and barrel, all easily concealed in a tarp.

Loretta appeared in the porch doorway, a fresh wig on her head, the pink carry-on suitcase at her feet. She had already bandaged her stab wound.

"It weren't chickens that foreign bastard killt in there," the woman said. She sounded shaken, her rheumy eyes a peeled-grape blue in the morning light. "If you know something about what really happened, don't tell me. I mean it. 'Cause I don't want to have to be the one to tell my Hannah."

She had seen Birdy Tupplemeyer's bloody blouse. Now the woman was eager to leave.

Aboard my boat, idling away from the dock, she pressed, "You sure you ain't gonna turn me in to the po-leese? Don't make me sorry I didn't shoot you when I had the chance. My God…I couldn't bear goin' to prison again."

Again? This was a secret my fiancée had not shared.

I ignored that by replying, "You don't have to worry, ma'am. Last thing I want to do is cause your family problems. You're safe now."

"Why? After all the meanness I've shown you?" she demanded. "If it's money you're after, you're barking up the wrong tree."

The former pot smuggler, a single mother who'd never married, had gone broke long ago. Over the years she'd depended on the generosity of men—some abusive—to provide for her daughter.

"Because Hannah loves you," I said. "And you're my son's grandmother."

"No, I ain't," Loretta snapped, "and thank your lucky stars.

We got bad blood in our family, mister. Look at the initials on that old shotgun again if you don't believe me."

She sat and fumed and got angrier seeing acres of trash floating on what had once been the pristine bay her people had fished for a hundred years.

I knew what was in the woman's mind. I knew the mean truth she wanted to share. It had little to do with the shotgun or the initials it bore.

Regarding that mystery, I had already sketched a theory.

Gazing back at the ridge of shell mounds and her family home, the woman's tone became accusatory. "This used to be a damn fine place to live. These islands. Florida. Water clean and clear. Fish and birds so thick that—" she stabbed me with a glare "—until folks like you started showing up. Now look at the junkyard you people have made of our land."

I countered, "Years back, did you know a man named Tucker Gatrell? Had a ranch near Chokoloskee. Cow hunter and ran crab traps."

Loretta made fluttering sound of contempt. "*Him?* A fast-talking con man is what that joker was. Ol' Tuck ran a hell of a lot more than just crab traps. Thief and a liar. Probably a killer, too, but, by God, I'll say this—that man had his charms. And the prettiest blue eyes. Why would you care?"

"He was my uncle. Thought I'd told you that before," I said, which was true. "Point is, I've got some bad blood in my family, too."

"So?" The woman, at least, was interested now.

I said, "Don't we all? Tuck used to tell stories about an outlaw lived south of his place. Bloody Ed Watson, they called him. The initials E.J.W.—" I clicked the boat into Neutral before looking into her eyes and asking, "Loretta, what was your great-grandfather's middle name?"

That fluttering noise again. "What nonsense you talking?"

"Edgar Watson," I said. "Down there in the Ten Thousand

Islands. Killed dozens, some believe, including one of your distant relatives—if I'm right."

I was right. It was in her reaction.

The woman stiffened, hands in her lap, prissy as if in a church
pew. "None of your business. That's Smith business. Mr. Watson
murdered a few folks, sure, but not who you're saying—didn't
kill the first of our women kin named Hannah. Was one of his
drunken gang did that. But the old bastard did manage to get
one of our cousins in a family way, and that shotgun was passed
down along with a family curse and a lot of nasty rumors."

She huffed and looked away at a waterscape of uprooted con-
sumption. "There—you satisfied? The women in our family.
Cursed. Every generation. Now, God help us, we gotta deal
with this mess."

Her voice softened. "We all got secrets, Marion."

It was the first time she'd called me by my name. I placed a
gentle hand on her shoulder. "Do me a favor, Loretta. Explain
that to your daughter. I don't believe in curses."

The woman shook her head, looked up at me, eyes lucid.
"We'll see—when Hannah shares another secret she found out
a few weeks back. And she will, good Christian that she is. Ain't
for me to say."

This time there was no meanness in what had previously been
a threat. Just concern.

I started to respond to the inference. No matter who had
seeded Hannah's child, I was the father—didn't care—and nothing, marriage or not, would change my affection for little Izaak.
Before I could finish, though, the old woman pointed aft and
warned, "Put that damn kicker into gear. We got a big damn
coyote following us."

I turned. I looked. I whistled and gave a hand signal.

It wasn't a coyote that climbed aboard my boat.

A second dog followed—a muddy, burr-infested standard-
sized poodle that Mrs. Lászlo had called Maggie.

47

Fifteen days after the hurricane, and a week before our scheduled wedding day, Hannah, on the phone, gave me a post-storm update. Sharing local news avoided the discomfort of an intimate topic we were obligated to discuss.

The collapsed Causeway had been patched and, in a few days, would be open to traffic—an architectural marvel that no one expected. Something else no one expected was for government officials to do what, thus far, was the best job in decades of dealing with a catastrophe.

And it was a catastrophe. Fishing guides, marinas, hotels, restaurants, schools along thirty coastal miles were out of business. Some would recover, many would not. When the eye of a hurricane passes, it is only the beginning of an assault that, economically and emotionally, continues to scar for years.

Although the historic lighthouse had been snuffed, and the surge had snapped one of its four massive supports, the structure still stood. A pirate-like peg leg would soon be welded in place. It was on the island's priority list.

That made me smile until Hannah moved on to personal matters, her voice clear on the phone from four hundred miles away.

"I probably shouldn't ask, but you've been gone for..." She withdrew what might have sounded like criticism. Instead said, "I hear music in the background. Tropical. Where are you, Doc?"

I was in Mexico, Cancun International, the private aircraft lounge north of Terminal One. At my feet, disguised in festive wrapping paper, was an aluminum case engraved with the name *R. M. Rauschenberg.* The Yucatán Peninsula, Campeche to Quintana Roo, is a transnational smuggling pipeline. Beachfront mansions there, some owned by Brotherhood members, are untouchable—unless a visitor has diplomatic backing and strong ties to the working class K'iche' Mayan community.

"Out of the country," I replied. "I'll tell you more when I get home. How's your mother doing?"

This was a safer topic.

"Loretta? Oh, she's... What I can't figure out is why Mama seems to like you all of a sudden. Well...could at least abide the idea of us getting married. Says with some training you might make a not-so-bad husband."

Hannah laughed. It was the first laughter I'd heard since sharing the truth about the fate of her best friend, Birdy Tupplemeyer.

Not all of the truth. It was up to investigators to reveal details. *If* they revealed details. That would take months in the aftermath of a storm that had left thousands homeless and killed many, including an unknown number in the village of Vinales, Pinar Del Rio, Cuba.

Thus far, no word yet regarding my baseball friends there. As Tomlinson had said, few of his Cuban Comrades were licensed to use ham radios—and most of those qualified were regularly jammed.

I explained, "Loretta and I got to know each other better

while you were in Carolina. Turns out we have more in common than she realized. Net fishermen and ranchers like my uncle
Tuck, back before Disney World, everybody knew everybody.
We've all got skeletons in the closet, so stop worrying about your
family genetics. Can you put the boy on the phone?"

"Marion, of course, when he wakes up." She took a breath
as if summoning courage. "I know what you claimed was the
reason we should break it off. But I need the truth before seeing you tomorrow. Are you sure it doesn't have something to
do with not being Izaak's real father? It's only natural that—"

"I am his real father," I interrupted.

She talked over me, saying, "Honey, I truly didn't know…
well, not for sure, anyway, until I spit into that stupid tube for
the genealogy thing and—"

Again I interrupted, "DNA is bull… I mean, it's something
we share with chimps and people—strangers, who knows?—
from the past, good and bad. Not that I've been a good father,
but this time, by God—" I hesitated because of my language
"—things will be different. Thought I'd made that clear before I
left. And after what happened to Birdy, we both agreed that—"

"I know, I know, I've worried about that for months," she
said. "You and your damn secret life. But we can't put Izaak at
risk again. Or Mama, either. She's gotten old, Doc. Her imagination spends more time with that Calusa king than on her soap
operas. Last couple of years…well, let's face it, Loretta, poor old
thing, can't take care of herself anymore."

Don't bet your life on it, was the tempting response.

Through omission, though, I stuck to an agreed-upon story.
The same story I would tell the feds if needed. Loretta, after returning home, spooked by blood on the porch, had summoned
me by radio for a boat ride to the mainland.

Days after that boat ride, when police forensics was done,
the porch, the floors and walls had been scrubbed clean thanks
to my pal Big Sammy and his crew. But Hannah, traumatized

by the fate of her friend, had yet to spend the night in the old house on the mound.

That would change tomorrow when I returned.

Not for the first time, I asked, "Are you sure you want me there? I mean, of course I want to see you and Izaak. But the place is so small, and Loretta would—"

"Mama, she's staying in town."

"What?" This was a surprise.

"Izaak, too. I can trust Uncle Arlis and Luke to look after him for one night, so it'll just be us."

"Just, uhh—for the night?"

Captain Hannah Smith, who had an outlaw ancestor, often affected an icy exterior to cloak a secret bawdy side within. This was signaled by a huskiness when she responded, "Yep, just us, Dr. Ford, and maybe a glass of wine. You okay with that?"

I got up, gathered my bag, the Rauschenberg case, and carried them to a window that overlooked the tarmac. Private jets neatly berthed in morning light. Cessnas, a cobalt Cirrus Vision, and the Gulfstream G4 that had picked me up in the Glades more than a week ago.

"Yeah," I said. "I mean, *yes*, definitely okay. Question is, are you?"

Outside, diplomat parking only, a Range Rover, black windows, had pulled in.

Hannah said, "Remember, the other day, three weeks ago, you, me and your dog on the dock? What I said about you two having something in common?"

"Umm…wait, I do. No petting. Something like that. It was pretty funny."

"Not just petting, as you know darn well. Pete's changed since that poodle showed up, so maybe it's time to… But, you're right. My brain's *not* sure what's right and what's wrong. The rest of me, though, thinks, who cares? Why not have some fun for a change?"

The rear door of the Range Rover opened.

"Gotta go," I said.

"Tomorrow night," Hannah pressed. "We'll make dinner, watch the sunset."

"Sounds good. I'll be there," I said. Then amended, "Unless something comes up."

Soft laughter implied the obvious retort, but that faded. "Hold on, Marion. I don't want to be in that house alone. Not yet, not overnight. Understand? Please, don't disappear on me again."

I went toward the exit. "Relax. I'll call you from Miami. Promise. Oh—and I've got a present for you."

This put some sunlight in her voice. "Really? Doc, I've got everything I could possibly... But thank you. What is it?"

It was the diamond tennis bracelet Mrs. László had slipped into my pocket while stealing my hidden Sig Sauer pistol. I'd found the bracelet and her late husband's ring during a last-minute check of my muddy clothes just before dumping them in the trash.

The Kashmir Tsar Sapphire—among the rarest of gems. It was packed with the Rauschenberg, a present from me to the elegant lady—if and when she awoke from a coma.

Physicians at Cambridge Neurological had become less optimistic during the last week. Either way, the sapphire was an heirloom that belonged to the László family or to history, not me.

Hydraulic doors opened and I stepped out onto the tarmac, saying to Hannah, "You'll find out tomorrow night."

48

My contact from the British Consulate, Hotel Zone, Cancun, via London was waiting for me at the boarding ladder. Linen slacks, crisp collared shirt, aviator sunglasses and a briefcase that I assumed contained a weapon or two and a passport embossed in gold: *King's Messenger/Courrier Diplomatique.*

It was his, not mine. Although a similar document wasn't an impossibility—or so Max Weatherby had intimated in one of our encrypted conversations.

At the top of the steps, I said in a confidential voice, "Ian, are they already aboard?"

Ian. That was the name my contact was using.

He ushered me in and indicated a privacy curtain three rows back. "Aft cabin, sir, along with a steward if they need something. Thus far, they seem quite happy. A bit nervous about flying, perhaps, which is to be expected."

"Can I say hello?"

"Afraid not, sir. Agency protocol. As much for their protection as yours." Three times he tapped on the cockpit door—a signal to the pilots it was time to go. "Standard regs, unfortunately. You're aware that—"

"I am," I said. "No phone calls, no outside communication with anyone and no discussing our destination until we're—"

Ian held up a warning finger. A pushback tug had moved the aircraft into position, ready for takeoff. Before I took a seat portside—it would provide a better view of the blue hole cenotes off Belize—I presented Ian, an MI6 agent, with a small insulated Biogel container and the festively wrapped Rauschenberg case.

He touched the container.

"A DNA swab?"

I replied, "Not exactly. DNA plus a fingerprint. A digital sample."

"Digital." He repeated the word slowly and pulled his hand away.

"I'll need a receipt for that. A generic receipt when we're feet wet."

Ian was buckling himself in starboard side. "Certainly. After our informal debrief. Preliminary. No worries, sir." His attention moved to the Biogel container. "I gather things went quite well during your stay here."

I replied, "That's for you and your analysts to decide."

Engines revved; accelerated. The plane ascended during a standard left turn that shrunk Cancun into a caricature of cruise ship tourism. Rainforest jade transitioned to Van Gogh pastels off Cozumel, then traced forty miles of beachfront hotels and estates. Inland on the road's jungle side was the inevitable tenement fringe, tin-roofed strands that housed anonymous maids, cooks, day laborers.

Ahead was Tulum, Mayan ruins there, not far from where Sasha, the oligarch and former MiG pilot, owned an expansive hacienda.

Ian was leafing through some notes. After eyeing a bulkhead monitor that tracked our flight path, he turned to me. "Some of the most beautiful water in the world down there. Yet I heard—two days ago, I think it was—a wealthy tourist, a *Ruso* they said on the news, went for a late-night swim. He'd been hosting a party. An expat sort of affair. Didn't show up in the morning and they're still looking. I wonder what the chances are he'll be found?"

Ruso was Spanish for Russian. Our "informal debrief" had begun.

"Couldn't say," I responded. "Don't follow the news. A party is a… Well, alcohol and swimming alone at night is a dangerous combination. Probably happens more than people realize. Local cops, though, I'm sure they deal with that sort of thing all the time. Surprised it even made the news."

"Quite right," the agent agreed. "Bad for local tourism. Doubt if it will make the news again."

I nodded my approval.

"Anything to add?" he asked.

Below in popsicle shades of turquoise was the Bay of Ascensión. Uninhabited. Mangroves. Dark rock rectangles, precision cuts, visible beneath neon water where locals had quarried limestone to build pre-Colombian pyramids.

Ten centuries later, a pal and I had caught bonefish, tarpon and permit there on fly rods.

I checked the bulkhead monitor. "Guatemala City, an hour flight. Then what?"

Ian said, "Our embassy is only a few blocks from the terminal. A driver will be waiting. Papers are already prepared."

"But no red tape. No passports will be—"

"Exactly," he said. "Those will be provided."

"What about compensation?"

"Their fee?"

I said, "My friends don't expect to be paid, but that's the deal I made with your people. Four hundred thousand quetzals—what, about fifty grand, US? That's a lot of money here. You'll have to explain it to my friends in some way. And it can't involve me."

That, too, had been arranged.

Ian continued, "They'll be made to feel welcome but without fuss. Their legal documents, a brief interview, easy-peasy, then a local limo service will take them wherever they want to go. No need for you to disembark. I'll shepherd them around the embassy, and you'll return alone."

That wasn't good enough. "Not a limo service. An official vehicle with a security pro aboard. Those people provided a key name—a maid, four levels removed from a primary contact—so I don't think they're in any danger but... One more thing. My friends can't be used in this sort of operation again. Ever. Agreed?"

Ian straightened, a habit possibly schooled at Sandhurst Officer Training. "Not for me to decide, sir. But, considering your... connections with Home Office, it shouldn't be an issue."

We landed, Guatemala City, a mountain range of patient geology to the west. Volcáns de Fuego and Tolimán were forested lava cones that towered ten thousand feet above remote Pacific beaches forty miles away.

Pilots shut down all but auxiliary power. A step trolley was positioned aft.

"Mind if I take a peek?"

Ian had his briefcase open, in his hand a manila envelope labeled *Inter-Departmental Mail*. "Help yourself, sir. Then I'm afraid we must finish up here. I'm in a bit of a rush if you don't mind."

Through a crack in the privacy curtains, Cadmael was fitting his infant son into a belly pack while a uniformed steward handled a stroller and a pair of cheap suitcases. Itzel, the young wife, was the last to descend the steps.

I returned to my original seat, lifted the window shade, and there she was, looking up at me, unsurprised. Stony-faced, she nodded a dismissive awareness. Some residual anger apparent, it seemed. That's all. Then followed her family across the tarmac west, mountains in the background that were home.

Ian, before he left, presented me with the manila envelope. "A couple of things in there for you," he said. "I was directed to suggest you review them before deciding on your next destination."

"My next...? What do you mean?" I popped the security band—two smaller envelopes inside. "Miami's my destination," I said. "Officially, anyway, but the landing strip in the Everglades. The pilots haven't been briefed?"

Dade-Collier Training and Transition Airport was the misleading name.

Ian chose his words carefully. "It was suggested you read Dr. Weatherby's note first. And download a thumb drive that contains a recording. You can listen to that later. I am authorized to report that the wreckage of a sailboat owned by someone known to you was found five days ago off the Mosquito Coast of Honduras."

I'd been standing. Now I sat. *"Honduras?"* I whispered the word. That was four hundred jungled miles southeast. *No Más* had been spun off course like a moth in a wind tunnel. "Did they...did they find a body?"

"Just the vessel's EPIRB. Wasn't recovered, but one of our aircraft tracked the thing to wherever it washed ashore. Someone—someone very high up—must have pulled important strings, sir. We have a base in Belize as you know."

Ian indicated the envelope. "It's all in there. If you're still undecided, open the thumb drive. There's a full Morse code intercept sent from what our sources believe to be a clandestine radio transceiver in Pinar del Río, Cuba."

I removed two smaller envelopes while triangulating a navigational puzzle. Cuba, Belize, the western rim of Honduras. Jungle coast freckled with eco-tourism outposts, all isolated by thousands of hectors of rainforest and open ocean horizons.

My pal's spore had been scattered like ashes.

But Weatherby's typed note offered encouragement in the

form of lat-long coordinates, and a partial transcript of the Morse code intercept. It was a C-W transmission from a pirate operator who'd been in contact with *No Más* three days *after* the storm had hit Cuba. A mayday call from a skipper who'd been seriously injured and was adrift.

In pen, Weatherby had added, "Let's have that drink when you get back. Celebrate our new arrangement—until the next monsoon comes along. I hope your friend survived."

The weight and feel of the second envelope suggested it contained credentials of some sort. A passport, possibly. The MI6 agent was exiting when he noticed the envelope's heavy bond paper, the ornate waxen seal. A lion and a griffin—two heraldic beasts—beneath a crown of gold.

"The Royal Cypher," he said, more impressed than his tone communicated. "First I've seen since the coronation. Good luck to you, sir. My compliments on a job well done and—" a knowing smile provided emphasis "—on your unusual skill set. I trust we'll meet again."

We shook hands.

The aft door closed. I sat and thought about Hannah, alone in her old house on the mound. I wrestled with my conscience and dissected Max's claim that a pirate ham operator had been in contact with *No Más* days after the storm had hit Cuba.

My nagging, destructive inner voice argued that I was in the region already and I'd be gone only an extra day or two. A week at most. Plenty of time to give Hannah a heads-up and reschedule.

Which registered as bullshit until my rational, usually trustworthy side reminded me that, when torn between two options, the most difficult choice is almost always the right choice.

Why the hell was that so often true?

Decision made.

With the pilot's permission, before we took off for Roatán, Honduras, I ended a lengthy phone call to Hannah, saying,

"He might still be alive, darling. I have to do it. I have to try to find Tomlinson."

My ex-fiancée, no tears in her voice, said before hanging up, "Doc, you're always welcome to come see your son. But don't ever 'darling' me again."

★ ★ ★ ★ ★